Prelude

He had fled from Canada months ago, headed as far south as he could possibly travel. All that he longed for was an escape from the thoughts and memories that threatened his sanity and turned his dreams savage; nightmares that always ended in the same way. He relived that night in continuous slow motion; blood drenching his body, the tremendous waves of horror that rose up within him as he witnessed his comrades fighting and falling by his side. Entire families had been destroyed and torn apart in the passing of those few gory minutes and those few that escaped death had scattered like ashes in the drifting wind.

He had willed the wolf to take over afterwards, longing to conceal his human misery within the deep, dark confines of the huge black beast. Although some human thought processes still existed, they resurfaced only occasionally in the animal's brain. If nothing else, the notion of any further bloodshed sickened him and he would fight from his position hidden deep inside to assure that no more of it came by the beast's violent nature. It became a struggle to challenge its power and one that the wolf fought against aggressively. It yearned for control and Shane had relinquished full power to it and it had seized the opportunity and became strengthened by its new position of dominance.

He wasn't aware of where the wolf was headed and he didn't care. Instincts kept the animal close to the wood line which insured their safety; its profile broken up by the trees and thick underbrush. Black fur blended well within the dark shadows of the forest, assisting it with staying discreetly hidden in new areas where it traveled. The change in the climate had become evident, from scarcely any humidity to the now hot, heaviness of the air that seemed to close in around him; smothering him. The wolf panted heavily as its body attempted to cool itself while its eyes scanned the horizon in search of the water that it had scented.

Chapter 1

Thirst drove the wolf across the wide open field to the protection of a stand of aged, whitened sycamores close to the edge of the lake. From the safety it surveyed its surroundings, its brain processing the landscape, searching for any sign of danger. The suffocating hot breeze blew gently in its face bringing with it the scent of much needed water and along with it, something much less desirable; a human.

Immediately becoming aware of the wolf's quickening breath, Shane fought to resurface. It was a necessity for him to regain some small piece of control over the creature to prevent ill-fated circumstances for the individual whose luckless timing had thrown them into the wolf's path. Shane's attempt was met with resistance and a deep throated snarl but with persistence, the wolf finally gave in and allowed him a small fraction of its power.

In retaliation, the wolf challenged him, irritated at the disruption in its control. *It has been a long time since you have attempted to silence me,* it snarled. Shane refused to acknowledge the defiance and instead concentrated on the matter that had pulled him from the deep, secure shadows of the animal's brain back to a position of influence. The wolf wasn't completely powerless even though it had yielded to its human's higher influence; it strained against his hold to draw in another long, deep breath as if savoring the scent. Its ears pitched forward and its lips drew back over its teeth in a sinister smile. *It is a human female.*

Shane paused, allowing his own human senses to digest what the wolf had recognized. He could smell the sweet scent of her; felt his body begin to ache. It had been a long time since he had held a woman close and the wolf knew the battle that would rage inside of him because of it. Wanting to back away and leave this place before circumstances veered out of control, the wolf's thirst was the motivation that persuaded him to remain.

From across the small lake, the wolf's eyes settled on the figure that rested upon the far bank. Sitting on the dry, hardened and cracked ground, her knees were pulled up against her chest with her arms wrapped tightly around them. Her face was hidden, her forehead leaning against her pulled up knees. She didn't see the wolf's approach or feel its eyes upon her as it lowered its muzzle to drink, quenching its thirst.

Shane's mind was struggling as he fought to keep control of the beast. The scent of the female was wreaking havoc on his judgment and he didn't know if he would be strong enough to maintain control. The wolf lifted its wet, dripping nose and stared across the water towards the girl, quickly assessing her size and gauging the potential fight. From the looks of her, there would not be much resistance; she was oblivious to the dangerous threat that he represented.

Realizing the threat the girl faced if he couldn't get it and keep it together; there would be no dominating the wolf if he couldn't keep his own thoughts focused. Gut instinct told him to run away but his loneliness pleaded with him to stay, begging him to experience her soft skin, to revel in the distinctive scent of her as he forced his body against hers.

Although weakened from allowing the wolf prolonged control, Shane used all of the strength to crush it down in an attempt to show it that he was still in charge. It fought him only for a moment and then was still, sulking. This allowed Shane the time that he needed to figure out his next move. He had come across humans many times before but had managed to stay in the shadows and pass without detection. This time was different. Before him was a woman in the middle of nowhere, obliviously unaware of his presence.

It would be easy and uncomplicated to shift into human form, satisfy his cravings and disappear into the protective shadows of the forest with no witnesses, no trace of another human being left behind to be detected. His mind whirled with deliberation of doing just that. He yearned for human contact and his desires screamed at him to take advantage of the opportunity that was laid out before him. But Shane's conscious would not allow it. He had never forced himself on any female and he was not going to start now.

The tepid breeze stirred the woman's dark hair and appearing suddenly awakened by the gentle movement, she raised her head and as if it were her absolute intention, her eyes fell directly into his gaze. There was immediate eye contact and for a moment he witnessed the fear flash across her delicate features but as quickly as it had come, it disappeared and was replaced with something else…..perhaps confusion?

Shane's senses awakened as the woman's eyes bore into his and her distinctive scent drifted across the lake to invade his nostrils. As if time stood still, they stared across the water at one another, neither allowing their gaze to falter. The emerald green eyes of the human female seemed to search his very soul and he sensed something else there as well; something he couldn't identify. Shane was surprised that she displayed no fear of him and the wolf raised its nose to the air to search for the unmistakable scent of alarm or panic, but no hint of it lingered there.

    The lake water rippled slightly in the heated afternoon breeze as I sat on the bank of the lake. It tossed my hair messily about my face, whipping it into my eyes. This place had always been my tranquility, my place to retreat to when my mind seemed overwhelmed with life. After losing my parents unexpectedly a couple of years before, I found myself winding up here often, feeling closer to them on the banks of this lake than anywhere else. Spending many summers here at the lake cabin as a family, the memories played out in my mind like they had happened only yesterday.
    I pulled my knees up and wrapped my arms around them tightly, leaning my forehead against them. Closing my eyes, I sighed deeply. Feeling alone and sorry for myself, a single stray tear slid from my eye and dropped onto my bare leg leaving a wet trail as it slid down the inside of my thigh. Lifting my head and opening my eyes, I was suddenly startled by what I glimpsed across the water's surface. My heart began to beat harder in my chest as it lifted its head and stared back across the lake towards me without an inkling of fear in its eyes. Reaching behind my back, I let my fingertips move over the handle of the pistol tucked snuggly into the back of my shorts. The smooth surface calmed and reassured me.

    Shane knew that wolves were not native to this particular part of the country. He had never picked up on their scent while traveling so he was certain that a wolf was not a normal sight to her. With that knowledge, along with his menacingly large size, he was confident that she should be very afraid and he found that he was now the one confused. Breaking away from her gaze, he checked his surroundings. Maybe there was a reason she wasn't afraid, a reason that perhaps he hadn't noticed before since he had been distracted. But he found nothing unusual; no sign or scent of danger lingered here. His eyes returned to her and in the short time that he had looked away, she had stood - but her eyes had never left him.

Slimly built with dark, chestnut colored hair that hung slightly past her shoulders, her features were delicate. A small, slightly upturned nose above a soft, full set of pink lips and the green eyes that studied him were framed with long, dark lashes. As his eyes raked down her body, Shane took in her perfectly curved proportions and he once again felt the wolf demanding action. He softly growled his refusal.

The wolf had remained in the deep shadows of his mind but did not fail to seize the opportunity to pressure him. *Just take her*, it snarled. Shane growled again but in response took a deep breath inhaling the woman's scent. The sweet smell of her intoxicated him and there was something vaguely familiar about it. As if mesmerized, he turned and walked along the bank, closing the distance between them. Inside, a conflict was raging; if the woman decided to run he wasn't sure what might happen and if he got closer, what did he expect to do? Would he be able to refrain from doing anything? His mind was spinning as he advanced; his large paws making deep imprints at the water's edge as he crept slowly closer.

Minutes seem to pass at a snail's pace as I stared across the lake at the animal. It was huge, black and at first glance I had thought it may have been a black bear but my fleeting notion was quickly replaced by the reality of what it actually was. There were no wolves around here and never had been to my knowledge but the animal that stood on the far bank certainly met all of the criteria. I shifted nervously as it began to pick its way along the edge of the water cautiously in my direction. My options were limited as I watched it move closer and I debated about running. Common sense persevered loudly, screaming that it would be plain stupidity so instead I stood there and watched it press on. All that I could do was follow it with my eyes as it drew nearer and hope that my small caliber pistol could take it down if I needed it to.

Helplessly, I gaped as it came toward me and stopped only a few feet away. I noticed then the unusual color of its eyes as it studied me; a bright blue that contrasted sharply set within the black fur of its face. It cocked its head and looked away as if it was distracted and then growled.

Although he could now sense her unease, the woman stood her ground as he inched nearer. His wolf sensed it too and rose to the surface again, demanding submission. Within only a few feet of her he stopped, their eyes still locked. Feeling her nervousness he had imagined that she would run, but instead she stood tensed and straight, feet planted slightly apart, eyes never faltering. The wolf inside was agitated now and paced within the prison of Shane's mind. The woman refused to lower her gaze in submission and although Shane attempted to quiet it, it snarled its disapproval fiercely. He replied with a low warning growl before a quick movement swiftly brought his attention back to the woman in front of him…. and the pistol that was now pointed directly between his eyes.

For a moment Shane was bewildered by her sudden turnabout but he soon realized that she had taken his growl as a threat. Uncertain, nervous confidence seeped from her pores as she fingered the pistol's trigger, waiting. She held it in both hands steadily, her thumb on the hammer while her index finger rested on the trigger. What she failed to realize was that the gun could not kill him- hurt like hell maybe, but not kill him. Briefly staring at the weapon in her hands, he drew in another deep breath. At this closer proximity she smelled even sweeter; her nervous sweat riddled with pheromones, flowery shampoo and laundry detergent. He could also smell the unique scent of her femininity; along with it something else faintly familiar that wafted through the air. What was it that his senses continued to associate with her?

The wolf sighed, dropped his gaze from her and sat down on its haunches. With the pistol pointed at his head, he didn't want to make her any more anxious than she already was. Although it couldn't kill him, a bullet could certainly put him out of commission for a while and he didn't want to take that chance. Abruptly lying down, he stretched his head out onto his paws and raised his eyes back to hers before rolling over on his side. This was as submissive as he could get.

My brow was creased with puzzlement at what had just occurred and slowly I shook my head trying to clear my vision; disbelieving what had just happened. Allowing my hand to fall limply to my side, the pistol dangled loosely in my fingertips. For a moment all that I could do was just stare down at the animal with uncertainty. The blue eyes looked up at me as if waiting.

This was a wild animal, unpredictable and large enough to annihilate me if it so decided. I was tense and honestly frightened by its strange behavior but I also found myself overcome with curiosity. After giving it much thought, I eased warily toward it and crouched down low to appear less threatening. Its eyes never left me and feeling overcome by my own inquisitive nature; I slowly reached my hand out and touched it. The dark fur was soft beneath my fingers.

Shane didn't move a muscle, even when he saw the pistol on the ground beside her and the impending danger gone. Instead only his eyes moved as he watched her ease out a hesitant hand towards him. Touching him, the electricity moved through his body and he succumbed to the pleasure of her contact. It was the first touch of a human hand upon his body for longer than he could remember. Her eyes softened as she moved her hand along his neck and down his side, fingers nearly hidden in the thick, black fur. She stroked him softly and for the first time, spoke. They were only simple words but the strange tone of a human voice was a special melody to his ears.

"Where did *you* come from?" she asked as she continued to massage her fingers through his fur. Shane knew it wasn't a question that she expected an answer for. At this moment he only wanted to savor every languorous second of the feel of her hands on him. Her touch began to empower him, spread feelings through his mind and body that he hadn't felt in a very long time. Having longed for a simple touch, he had also missed the voice of someone talking to him and he yearned now for a conversation that he knew they could never have.

He continued to allow her fingers to stroke him, across his face and neck and then move down the length of his body; her hand nearly disappearing within the sea of thick black fur. He breathed in the scent of her, closed his eyes and for once let his body and mind relax. The wolf had given in and hadn't tried to fight him any longer but instead had retreated quietly into the shadows of his mind. Maybe it too had longed for the contact of another.

He didn't know how long he had lain there, stretched out on the ground next to her when he suddenly realized how carelessly he had compromised his own safety. How long before she told someone about what had happened and how long before he became the hunted instead of the hunter. He had to keep moving. Abruptly getting to his feet, he shook himself, dislodging bits of dirt and grass from his fur.

Sitting on her knees, she looked small as his eyes met hers and he took a couple of steps towards her. She shrank away as he leaned forward, placing his face near hers for only a moment, inhaling deeply. Quickly he turned and loped across the field to the wood line where once well hidden, he stopped and looked back across the distance. She stared after him for a few minutes and then stood and began to make her way through the field in the opposite direction. When finally out of sight, he set out after her; determined to see where she had come from and where she was going. There was something about her…something that called to him. Her gentle, kind touch had quieted the demons that lurked just below the surface.

Chapter 2

My mind was racing as I hurriedly made my way back to the cabin. It had been a strange and unbelievable encounter and I still didn't understand it nor quite believe it. Crossing the yard, I climbed the steps to the deck while openly admitting to myself that I hadn't been very smart about the entire incident. Opening the door and stepping inside to coolness, I thought about how that huge animal could have mauled me or killed me and no one would even know. I was alone here and I silently acknowledged that I needed to be more careful.

Randy had been gone for three months now and I was still struggling to get over the sting of that relationship. I had tried like hell to find the good in him. Generally a kind-hearted guy, I soon realized that his self destructive behavior and way of life was not one that I cared to be included in any longer. He had tried to contact me several times during the first month's separation but as the loneliness crept in, I'd been tempted to cave in more times than I could count. Knowing it was the right thing to do, I had remained strong and when I didn't return his calls he had finely stopped trying.

It was nearly 5:00 by the time I reached the cabin and I was reminded that I hadn't eaten all day by the deep gurgles of my empty stomach. I had been to town earlier and ran a few errands and then had stopped by Edna and Dan's for a short visit before heading home. Being lifelong friends of my parents, after the accident they had automatically stepped in and became my rock solid foundation. I owed them so much. Thanks to Dan, my freezer had been stocked with a newly butchered beef and the thought of a T-bone steak on the grill made my stomach rumble with anticipation.

I checked the answering machine and my cell phone to see if anyone had tried to call, but there were no messages. Grabbing the charcoal and lighter fluid I stepped out on the deck to start the grill. After loading the pit with enough charcoal to grill the steak, I doused it in lighter fluid. Once that set and soaked in, I would return to light it...probably just about enough time to jump in the shower.

The cabin was modestly built but had all of the necessary appliances to make it a cozy home. Everything was here that I needed and I rarely had to leave except to buy groceries or something of that sort. My parents had made it clear that the cabin and the acreage were to be mine in the event that something happened to them. Little had we known that the time for us to part would be so soon...

They knew that I loved the lake property and that I felt more at home here than I ever did in the lavish house in town where I grew up. They were always a little surprised at how well I had adapted to and enjoyed country life. With Edna and Dan's help, I had decided to sell the house in town and was able to lay back a substantial amount of money which Dan continued to help me invest. My bills were minimal and the money would last me forever as long as I spent it modestly.

After they died and the funeral was over, I had retreated here to hide within my sorrow. I mourned for months and became a recluse, rarely leaving the property. It had been Randy that helped pull me out of my grief and I would be forever grateful to him for that but the fact still remained that he was on a one way road to nowhere and I didn't want to ride along.

I gathered up some clean clothes and went into the bathroom. After removing my sweaty shirt and shorts, I turned on the shower and stepped in. The cool water felt good on my heated skin and I stood for a few moments enjoying the refreshment. I lathered the shampoo into my dark hair and felt the thick suds run down my naked body before I rinsed. It didn't take too long and I was soon clothed in a clean, light sundress with a towel wrapped securely around my head, ready to light the grill. My stomach insisted once again that I hurry things along. Maybe I would grill two so I could eat one tomorrow for lunch or it was also possible that I was hungry enough to devour two in one sitting!

Finding a couple of potatoes in the pantry, I scrubbed and wrapped them in foil. They would be a nice addition to the grilled steak. Meandering out to the deck to light the charcoal, its hot blaze forced me to momentarily back away. Soon enough the flames died down to a nice steady burn. Once the charcoal turned white, I would be safe to proceed without the horrible taste of lighter fluid to accompany my dinner.

I went back inside and grabbed a cold beer from the fridge and slid it in the cooler cup that I kept in the drawer by the fridge. On hot evenings, it had become my custom to drink a cold beer if I cooked outside. Unscrewing the cap, I raised it to my lips and savored the ice cold liquid as it ran over my tongue and down my throat. Carrying the beer in my hand, I made my way back outside and sat down in a lawn chair to await the charcoal's readiness.

Sitting there relaxed and cool after my shower, my mind immediately roamed back to the strange experience this afternoon. As much as I tried to rationalize it, it didn't make any sense that the animal had reacted as it had. It was crazy for me to believe that it had understood the seriousness of its predicament with my pistol pointed towards it, strangely seeming to realize that I was in control.

The entire incident was unreal; weird even. I remembered the feel of its soft, thick fur between my fingers as I had rubbed my hand along its side, losing sight of them within the thickness. The animal was huge, much larger than any dog that I had ever been close to. Had it been a fluke that I had witnessed its existence? Had I just been in the right place at the right time?

The gnawing pain in my stomach brought me back to the task at hand and I stood and glanced at the charcoal. Its white appearance and soft smoldering was a certain indication that it was ready and after another long gulp of beer, I sat it on the patio table and went inside to get the foil wrapped potatoes. They would take quite a bit longer to cook than the steaks as I tended to like my steaks a bit on the rare side. Once I settled them on the grill, I shut down the vents to keep the heat inside and closed the lid. In a few minutes I would add the steaks and everything should be ready approximately at the same time.

Chapter 3

    Shane watched the woman's comings and goings in and out of the cabin as she prepared her meal and even though he was hidden from her sight, he could smell that she had freshly showered as the flowery scent of soap wafted into his nostrils. Her long dark hair was pulled up messily in a clip at the back of her head and still appeared to be damp. A couple of strands had come loose to frame her face but they quickly fell away as she raised the bottle to her lips.
    Why had he followed her here? He had nothing to gain by watching her from the shadows and he was only tormenting his already tortured body and mind considering that he couldn't deny the affect that she had on him. Something lured him to her. Maybe it was because he had longed for human touch and she had given it to him, willing and unafraid or maybe it was something more.
    He sniffed the air, searching for any human scent other than hers, but there was no trace of another person in the surrounding area. The wolf had quieted the longer that he remained in control and tonight would be the opportune time to shift into his human form again. It had been a long time since he had stood upright and walked on two feet instead of four.
    After he left Canada he had lost the will to fight the wolf for control. There hadn't been a need until now but he must change soon to safeguard the dominance he had recently reasserted. It would have to be soon or he would lose the advantage. Once the shift took place, he knew it would be a struggle to stop from coming back here. His craving for human contact was strong and he was barely able to suppress his desires, even now.
    He watched her enter the cabin again and then return with a plate of raw meat. Opening the lid of the grill, she placed the seasoned meat above the hot coals. Immediately the aroma of the searing steaks filled his nostrils causing his stomach to roll and churn in response. It had been days since he had last eaten and the opportunity of an easy meal had awakened his sleeping hunger. She returned to her seat and picked up the bottle and tilted it to her lips again. He studied the movement of her throat as she swallowed before returning his gaze once again to the steaming grill; staring at it hungrily. Smoke had begun to emerge from under the lid dispersing the mouthwatering fragrance that now enveloped him in a heavy cloud of enticement. For the first

time in the past few hours his wolf stirred within, anxious about the possibility of filling its stomach.

It wasn't very long before she stood and walked back to the grill. Using a long fork, she flipped each steak over on its opposite side to seal in the juices that dripped and sizzled into the coals. Returning to the table, she picked up the bottle and emptied it and then disappeared from his view again.

The opportunity presenting itself, Shane left the safety of the shadows and moved toward the steps that led up to the deck where the tasty meal continued to tease him. When he was nearly to the grill, the door of the cabin swung open and the woman stepped out, another bottle of beer in one hand and a plate in the other. Alarmed, the full bottle fell from her hand and shattered on the deck sending shards of glass in all directions.

"Shit!" I blurted out as I scrambled to hold onto the doddering plate and move away from the mess that I had created. The bottle had exploded on contact and glass had scattered all over the deck. Startled by the wolf's unexpected appearance, I only vaguely perceived the small sharp pain in my shin. After a quick look downward, I noticed the trickle of blood where a piece of glass had impaled my skin.

Staring warily at the animal, I walked slowly over to remove the steaks from the grill. As starved as I felt, I wasn't about to allow my dinner to burn up even with the mess at hand. The animal stood a few feet away at the top of the steps and I gazed at it with wonder. Where had it come from? Feeling a bit shocked that it had followed me home; I picked up the plate and headed toward the door. "You scared the hell out of me." I said while its piercing blue eyes regarded me curiously.

The wolf turned to begin the descent back down the steps; his meal opportunity now gone, when the cabin door flung open again and the woman emerged with a broom and dustpan. She looked at him and smiled kindly before beginning to clean up the broken remains of the bottle. "Are you hungry?" she asked warmly, again making direct eye contact with him. He stared back into her emerald eyes with intent while inside he groaned to tell her how hungry he really was...and for everything that he hungered for.

In a few moments she returned with two plates, a steaming steak on each one. One plate had the potato unwrapped while the other potato remained covered. She sat them down on the patio table and ventured back inside, returning shortly with another bottle of beer and a bowl filled with water. Sitting the bowl on the deck floor close to the table she then took a chair and scooted up to the table. Taking the fork in one hand and the knife in the other she cut one steak into bite sized pieces and once finished, cut the potato into quarters. She then took the plate and set it by the bowl of water, looked at him and smiled.

Shane didn't hesitate once she turned to him; it was his queue. The aroma of the meat had roused his human hunger as well as that of his wolf. He moved toward the plate slowly and picked up one of the cut pieces gently in his teeth. Trying to chew it slowly to enjoy the delectable taste as it moved across his palette, his hunger refused him the privilege of enjoyment. He didn't look up at the woman again until his tongue was licking all remaining crumbs and juices from the empty plate. When he finally did, she was staring silently at him and had not even started to eat her own dinner.

"I see you were very hungry." she spoke softly, reaching her hand toward him. He shied away from her touch, but sensed her disappointment as she allowed her hand to fall. Lowering his massive black head to the water bowl he began to drink and didn't stop until it was empty. She had taken that opportunity to start eating her own dinner but stopped abruptly to retrieve more ice cold water and refill it.

With his belly now full, some of Shane's cravings and hungers had been satisfied. His only fear was that other desires might push forward even stronger than before. The wolf was quiet for now and seemed content but how long did he have? Lying down with his head on his paws he closed his eyes. His body felt heavy and tired and strangely enough he felt safe enough to relax.

As I finished eating my steak and potato and sipped what was left of the beer, I eyed the large animal curiously. It was obvious that even as intimidating as he was, he meant me no harm. He settled in contentment near the now empty plate. Clearly having been hungry, I felt a small sense of relief pulse through me to know that I would not be next on his menu. The entire situation was extraordinary and I couldn't seem to get past the incredible strangeness of the entire afternoon. The animal's actions at the lake had been bizarre and afterwards he had followed me home without me having any idea he was lurking around.

Not thinking, I scooted my chair back to get up and take the plates inside and just that quickly, the animal went from relaxed to on his feet and near the steps to flee. "It's alright." I apologized as I picked up his empty plate and stacked it on mine. Sitting the empty beer bottle on top, I vanished inside again and came back empty handed. Still standing at the top of the steps, he watched my every move.

I was overwhelmed with interest about this odd behavior and I couldn't stop myself from moving towards it. Walking slowly past it, I sat down on the top deck step as if not paying any mind to it at all when in reality, I was nervous as hell about what might happen. I could see it shift restlessly on its feet out of the corner of my eye before it moved closer and sat down a couple of feet behind me. The beast sighed and I felt the weight of its head come to rest on my left shoulder, its hot breath against my neck. Tensing for a brief moment unsure of its purpose, I then guardedly lifted my arm and encircled its great head, stroking its neck. When nothing happened, I leaned my cheek against its massive head.

Shane's mind debated on the best course of action. He wanted nothing more than to lie on the deck of that cabin until morning, to feel safe just for one night. Her touch was the remedy for his loneliness; she had the power to save him from the hell he had been running from for such a long time.

They sat like that for a while, her stroking his neck and him breathing in her scent, searing the imprint of it into his brain until his body relaxed and demanded sleep. Stretching out on the wooden planks on his side, he closed his eyes. Never had he felt the safety and security as he now did in her presence. Suddenly, he felt her movement and when he opened his eyes, she had lain down beside him and he was staring directly into her deep green eyes. Her dark hair had come down from the clip of earlier and spread about her face. Her hand rubbed down his side, submerging itself in the thick black fur; a constant motion that relaxed his entire body.

"I have been alone here for a while," she whispered "and for whatever reason that you're here I am glad to have the company." Her eyes were misted and he sensed sadness. Finding himself wanting to cry out that he too had been lonely, he fought the urge to respond in any way as it would be a mistake. He more than understood her loneliness and had been alone for months; had left his life and family behind not knowing who survived and who had died. There had been no contact with any others of his kind since he had left and it was a rarity that he would come upon the scent of any during his travel. When he had, he retreated quickly before being detected. A rogue wolf was dangerous and unpredictable and many packs would just as soon kill him as allow him to wander.

He felt immense contentment in the feel of her touch and his mind drifted into much needed sleep. The sounds of the late evening awoke him much later and when he opened his eyes, the light of day had given way to darkness. How long had he slept? The woman still lay beside him, her hand resting on his side but she too had succumbed to sleep.

Shane took this opportunity to study her delicate features. The night did not affect his vision and he could make out her profile easily. Her dark lashes now lay heavily against her cheeks, closed in deep slumber. Chestnut hair pooled around her head with the exception of a few stray strands that had swept across her forehead. She was a beautiful human. With no trouble, he could distinguish the outline of her body beneath the light sundress that she wore and with the hem pulled up slightly on one side, it revealed a well defined, tanned leg. Allowing his eyes to travel farther up, his body stirred with the thought of what was hidden beneath the dress. With that on his mind, he suddenly rose to his feet and struggled with the thought of whether he should stay or retreat into the night.

He wanted to stay close to her, feel her skin next to his all night but he knew that it couldn't happen; there would be no controlling the desires of his body and mind. What was happening to him? He shook his head as if trying to pitch all thought from his brain. Never had he allowed himself to be in a situation like this or get close to a human during these past few months. Having gone out of his way to avoid any type of contact or conflict with her kind, he had so far done a good job….until now.

Realizing he couldn't stay any longer, he couldn't leave her asleep where she lay either. Stepping forward, he nuzzled against her neck and was immediately alerted to his mistake. His body responded to the scent of her and the warmth of her skin against his sensitive muzzle. The desires that he had been able to push back suddenly roared in his ears as his blood became heated and pulsed through his veins. The wolf inside awakened and he could feel it grinning and sneering at him; pushing past his frail attempts to remain at the surface.

Once again, his conscience and his primal instincts battled for control of the situation. He moved to stand above her, legs on each side of her sleeping body. Oblivious to the inner raging of the beast that stood above her, she roused but didn't wake. He lowered his head down to her again and breathed in the light and airy perfume of her scent. Her soft breath against his face sent small electrical shocks throughout his body and it demanded that he take her. *Take her.* The wolf encouraged him, pushing him to his limit and attempting to shove him over the edge where there would be no return. Struggling against it, and against the betrayal of his body, the war raged within.

The woman stirred again and shifted beneath him, her soft form brushing against his leg. The slight movement interrupted the struggle and he took advantage and moved down the steps and into the shadows. Stopping at the edge of the woods, with great effort he attempted to calm his breathing and regain control. Inside, the wolf laughed. *You are weak,* it snarled defiantly. Shane silently agreed, raised his muzzle to the night sky and filled the silence with a long, soulful howl.

Suddenly jolted awake by an unfamiliar sound that penetrated my slumber, I bolted upright and took in the pitch black night sky sprinkled with millions of stars. How long had I been laying out here? Remembering why, I automatically scanned the darkness for any sign of the wolf. I couldn't see beyond the shadows that the dusk to dawn light created but a strange empty feeling invaded me and I realized that it was gone. Standing, I stretched for a moment before moving toward the cabin door. Stiff and a bit sore from lying on the hard deck planking, I imagined the comfort of my bed and how nice it would feel.

Once inside, I flipped on the light and locked and bolted the door behind me and then turned toward the bedroom. After changing into my nightgown, I turned the lights off in the kitchen and then went and crawled into my cozy, comfy bed. Exhausted, my mind only wandered momentarily before I again dozed into a dreamless slumber.

Chapter 4

Shane wasted no time getting away from the cabin and hastily followed the trail back to the lake. Running until his lungs burned and his legs ached he had succeeded in driving the thoughts out of his mind. At the edge of the lake he decided it was time to shift. It had been long enough that the wolf would not make it easy for him and although it would be a painful fight it was something he had to do.

Initiating the change, the wolf fought hard, his body twisting and contorting; the pain excruciating and almost unbearable. His bones shifted and popped while muscles felt as if they were tearing away from the bones. The wolf snarled and snapped violently as it fought against the transformation which resulted in agonizing pain for Shane. It took nearly a half an hour to complete the full transformation but in the end, he won.

He lay silently on the bank of the lake; the sweat glistening on his naked flesh, his breath came in long, hard gasps. Waiting for his body to relax and his breathing to return to normal he felt the wolf inside quiet and become still, acknowledging defeat. It took several minutes before he calmed and his breath to become even again. The change never had been this complicated and painful but now, since he had asserted his dominance over it once more, it should become easier.

He attempted to stand but it had been so long since he stood on two feet that it was like learning to walk again. His balance was off center and he crashed hard to the ground on his shoulder, wincing at the pain as the rocks gouged into his skin. Without hesitation he struggled to his feet again and was soon standing confidently and slowly meandering around, testing his legs. It all came back quickly to him then and before long he had walked halfway around the lake.

A dock protruded out into the still, dark water only a few yards away and Shane decided that he felt secure enough to take a late night swim to loosen his human limbs. Making his way out onto the platform he scanned the night, searching for movement among the shadows and his eyes settled in the direction of the cabin. Just the thoughts of the night's occurrences reawakened his senses and he felt heat move through his lower body. "Damn." The sound of his own voice seemed strange to his ears. Then, without hesitation he dove into the blackened waters.

The coolness washed over his unclothed form as he swam with ease, breaking the mirrored surface of the water. This type of exercise would do him good to help get the feeling and usefulness back in his arms and legs. He moved effortlessly as the water washed away the sweat and heat from his skin, refreshing him and calming his mind. Making a final dive, he submerged his face and head before climbing back upon the dock. Stretching out on his back and gazing up at the dark night sky littered with stars, he allowed his mind to begin to work through his present situation.

Clothes. He would definitely need clothes, but where could he get them? With no money, no transportation or identification his options were limited. There had been no time to think things through in his haste to vacate the Canadian pack land and certainly no time to load a suitcase or grab his wallet. It wasn't as if he could walk into town naked and buy clothes even if he had the money, but he smiled to himself as he imagined the responses that he would more than likely receive.

It wasn't that he didn't *have* money, just none that he could get his hands on in his current circumstances. His mother's family was quite wealthy and as an only child he had never wanted or needed for anything. It was only as he grew into adulthood that he found fulfillment and a sense of satisfaction in working hard. By doing so, he had built a construction business from the ground up which had resulted in his own success and affluence. It was now just a matter of finding someone to send him what he needed...if anyone had survived.

In his attempt to wonder through his list of possibilities, Caleb drifted across his thoughts. Always a loyal, human friend to his pack, he would be more than capable of getting him what he needed if he could find a way to contact him. Canada was a long way from this place so it could be weeks before he might receive anything. Considering the circumstances that he had put himself into with the woman, it would best if he moved on anyway.

Well, that was it then. Caleb was his only solution. Devising the plan in his mind, he would wait until the woman left, break into the house and use the phone. He would give Caleb the location to leave the money and supplies, and then he would be able to leave the cabin undetected and she would never have an inkling that anyone had been there.

Feeling confident with his intention and that he had a strategy in place, he got up and moved down the bank toward the edge of the woods. The grass and dirt felt strangely odd beneath his bare feet as he made his way toward the security of the woods. He couldn't stay out in the middle of plain view but he didn't want to allow the wolf back so quickly. The longer he stayed a man, the more power he would reclaim. Finding a comfortable spot slightly back inside the dark confines of the forest, he stretched out in the leaves. In a few moments he had drifted to sleep.

 Shane awoke as soon as the sun began to lighten the early morning sky. The birds were just beginning to sing even though it was still relatively dark. Getting to his feet he stretched and absentmindedly brushed the dirt and debris from his naked flesh. He had never been uncomfortable with his nakedness and had very little reason to be. At six foot, four inches, his frame was nothing but pure muscle that rippled beneath tanned flesh. From the broad width of his shoulders to the distinctive power in his calves he was an astounding image of human maleness.

 His black hair was a bit longer than he normally cared to let it grow, but given his current situation, a haircut had been of least importance. An extra growth of beard gave a rugged appearance to his handsome features. Blue eyes stood out markedly from under dark lashes and brows and set into the sun darkened face, they were even more striking.

 Deciding it would be best to convert back to wolf form in order to stay hidden in the shadows of the woods, he prayed that the next change wouldn't be as vicious as the last. Inside, the wolf awakened, stretched and yawned. It was ready. He allowed it to come fully to the surface before he began to shift, letting it have its way and easing into the transition. Learning over time that it made things much easier to allow the wolf its freedom upon occasion, he gave into it freely. It was less likely to fight so hard when he needed to control it.

 Within minutes, the black wolf stood where Shane had last been. It lowered its head and front legs and stretching its body like a cat, caused the final few joints to pop into place. Shane let it have free range this morning; he felt its hunger and knew that it had hunting on its mind. Nose in the air it started a slow trot through the woods.

 It had been a couple of days since I had seen the wolf and I assumed that it had decided to move on. It didn't belong in this area, I was sure of that but where it did belong or came from, I didn't know.

Busying myself with housework and laundry, I decided that this evening I would make a trip into town and pick up a couple of things. But for now, the day had already warmed considerably and the lake was on my mind for an early afternoon swim.

I dug my suit out of the drawer and quickly changed, then pulled a pair of cut off jeans over the bottoms. Grabbing a towel and sunglasses, I slipped my feet into a pair of tennis shoes. The 4-wheeler was locked in the shed and after locating the correct keys on the key hook I proceeded out the cabin door.

It wasn't a far drive along the wooded path so within a few short minutes, I had arrived. The lake was a beautiful sight and the memories with my family suddenly flooded back, bringing with them raw emotion. With vision clouding by the onslaught of unexpected tears, I couldn't help but question God's plan yet again, as I always did when the sadness welled up inside. Life was unpredictable and I had learned about devastating loss within the span of a few short hours. It was a bitter lesson.

We had spent many a summer weekend here together and I did my best to keep it up to what I my parent's expectations would have been. Wiping the tears away with the back of my hand, I drove the ATV around to the dock, and climbed off. Grabbing my towel, I walked out onto the deck, laying it down near the middle so that it didn't blow off into the water. Bending down to remove my shorts I noticed something strange at the water's edge just a few feet down the bank.

I plodded toward what I'd had seen and upon further investigation found that it was a distinguishable footprint in the mud; a large, fresh human set of of footprints. My eyes jerked upward and I nervously scanned the surrounding area. "What the hell?" I mumbled to myself.

My mind reeled with the possibilities and then I suddenly remembered….maybe it was the neighbor. I had told them any time they wanted to swim or fish to come over and not bother with asking. They were always welcome, anytime, but to my knowledge they never had went swimming, only fishing. Who fishes with their shoes off? I decided that it was more than likely them but I would make a phone call later just to be sure. Convincing myself that everything was fine, I walked back out on the dock and kicked off my shoes and shorts.

Shane had purposefully steered clear of the woman and the cabin for the past two days. Even letting the wolf have full control, it had stayed in the area but had never ventured that direction. Upon hearing the ATV start, he could easily distinguish the direction it was headed. Curiosity got the best of him and he loped off toward the sound. Biding his time, it was his intent to make use of her absence from the cabin to put his plan in motion. Maybe this was his lucky day.

Keeping to the shadows of the woods, he noticed her studying something at the edge of the lake. Wondering briefly what it had been, he gave it no more thought once she moved back to the deck. Seeing that she planned on swimming and clad only in a bikini top and shorts it was unknown to her that she was in a precarious situation. Watching as she removed the shorts, revealing more skin than the skimpy bikini covered, he found himself struggling to maintain some sense of control.

He nervously took note of the bikini's lack of concealment as he hungrily devoured her body with his eyes. Her curves were in all of the right places, ample breasts and a flat, trim stomach, long, slender legs well defined by lines of muscle. This was the time he should be making his phone call but he found it difficult to drag his eyes away. With immense reluctance he turned and dashed rigorously through the woods toward the cabin.

Once there, he was thankful that the transition back to human was quick. Luckily, she had not locked the door so he was able to step directly inside. The cabin was cool and it felt refreshing on his naked skin while for a few fleeting moments he allowed his eyes to scan the room, taking in the simple, homey appeal. Closing his lids, he inhaled the familiar scent of the woman that lingered there and then opened them and begin searching for the phone. Once he located it, he picked up the receiver and began to dial. It felt awkward and unfamiliar in his hand as he listened to the ringing on the other end. A voice that he recognized spoke from the receiver. "Hello?"

"Caleb? It's Shane. I don't have much time but I need some help," he sputtered hastily, moving nervously from one foot to the other.

There was a slight hesitation, "Shane? Shane, I thought you were dead! My God man, where are you?"

"That's just it Caleb, I need you to send me some things. Money for one, and clothes as well," he paused, "can you do that for me?"

"Yes, yes of course, tell me where you are, and it will be on its way……today." Caleb stated matter of fact. Shane always felt that he could depend on this man; still yet, he wasn't comfortable giving up his location considering everything that had happened.

"I don't have much time so this is going to be quick," he replied. He began to rattle off a list of things that he needed Caleb to send and then indicated a drop off point. It would involve some traveling on his part, but that suited him fine as he felt a pressing need to get away from here. Once he felt certain that Caleb had all of the details he brought the conversation to a rapid close.

"You know you can always count on me Shane. I hope we can meet up when you come back home." he said.

Shane was a little confused but didn't reply right away. Why did Caleb think he was coming back home? He didn't have a home to go back to. "Sure Caleb, I will look you up."

"Can I tell them when they can expect you then?" Caleb asked.

"What? Who do you mean?" His attention was quickly drawn away at the sound of the 4-wheeler making its way back toward the cabin. "Caleb, I have to go....we'll talk soon. Thanks for everything." He blurted before slamming down the receiver. Exiting the cabin quickly, he moved stealthily down the steps and into the woods. Barely making it behind the shed before the ATV pulled up in the yard, he quickly shifted but remained hidden there until the woman pulled up and turned it off. Sliding off the seat, her wet hair fell across her face and she reached up unconsciously, tucking it behind her ear. She didn't notice him there as she gathered her towel and jogged across the yard toward the cabin. Even with the door closed behind her, his keen hearing was able to pick up the sounds of the phone dialing and her side of the conversation.

Damn, Shane thought to himself. How could he have been so stupid? How could he have not thought she would question human footprints at the lake? Once she found out it wasn't the neighbor's, she would be uneasy and nervous. It may be difficult to gain her trust when he returned.

He was immediately perplexed at the automatic assumption that he would be coming back here. What the hell? Was that his ultimate plan, to return as a man and win her over? He had never felt the draw to someone that he did to this human female....could there be more to it than the loneliness that he had first thought? Sorely confused about the entire situation and now, the conversation with Caleb haunted him. Who was Caleb planning to tell that he was returning?

This was as good of time to leave as any and he would deal with all of it when he returned. He bolted from his hiding place and ran as fast as could for as long as he could, crashing through underbrush, hurdling ravines and ditches. Twigs and branches dug into his skin as he vaulted into them head on. Wild animals scattered before him but he paid them no attention as his mind was a million other places. When he finally stopped, his lungs on fire, he dropped to the ground and closed his eyes.

Several weeks had passed since my last encounter with the wolf and the Ozarks fall was in now in full force. The green in the landscape had disappeared other than that of a few random cedars that speckled the edges of the woods and stubbornly refused to give into the demands of any season. Colorful leaves littered the ground and soon they would all turn brown and the long cold winter would set in.

I was thankful that the heat of summer was gone, but I was a little less thankful that Randy had once again come back into my life. Since the wolf's departure though, I had found a strange loneliness had crept in and I succumbed to Randy's companionship as if I was trying to fill some kind of new, unfamiliar void. He would never live with me here at the cabin again but I did allow him to come out for dinner and maybe a movie with the firm stipulation that he was required to leave afterwards. He swore that things would be different and that he had changed. It was nice to have the company but I wanted nothing more intimate and Randy seemed to accept that and didn't push the matter. Seemingly content with our friendship I often wondered how long it would be before he started to demand more.

Hundreds of miles away and a few weeks before, Shane had located the items that Caleb had sent and he now was equipped with a cell phone, identification and money. Along with those items, Caleb had included a handwritten note.

Shane,
I hope you find everything here that you need. If you need more or anything else at all, give me a call. We didn't get to finish our conversation before. There are three left here in the Canada area that I know of. I have been in contact with them and let them know that you made it out. There might be more but with everyone trying to stay under the radar it could be impossible to find out.
When you get a chance, call me so I know you found this.
Caleb

Chapter 5

During the past few weeks he had purchased a truck, stocked his wardrobe and was now on the drive back to the woman that had set up residence in his head. Never drifting far from his mind these few weeks, she was the driving force that pulled him back in that direction. He had missed her like he had never missed anyone before and he was anxious to make contact with her again; see her face, hear her voice and perhaps feel her touch. He had spoken to several realtors in that area about potential property and had an appointment this afternoon to look at one that he found that interested him. It was a small cabin just a few miles from where the woman lived and it didn't matter what the price...he would pay it.

Driving through the familiar landscape again, he rolled down the window and took a deep breath. Why did this place feel like home? He was anxious as the rolling truck came to a stop alongside her property line and the smell of the lake permeated his senses. Inhaling deeply again he wondered if it might be possible to catch the vague scent of her on the cool fall air. Finally convincing himself to move on after a few minutes, Shane met the realtor at the property location and she took him on a tour of the cabin and the surrounding acreage.

There had never been a lack of female attention in Shane's life. It seemed that wherever he turned, there was a female more than eager to satisfy his hungers. The realtor was no exception. When he stepped out of the truck, he could immediately identify the affect that he had on her. Not only was her face suddenly flushed with heat, the smell of her arousal filled his nostrils. Being an attractive woman he should have been excited by the possibility since it had been so long; but his mind and desires resided elsewhere. He would however, use the effect that he had on her to his own advantage.

After their quick tour, Shane realized that this would be the perfect place for him to settle. There was sufficient room for his wolf to run on the vast acreage without detection or danger. The cabin would need work but it was nothing he couldn't handle. After living in the wilderness for so long the little cabin seemed like heaven.

Andrea Sutter shuttered involuntarily when Shane Matthews stepped out of his pick up. *Oh my God,* she muttered softly to herself. Behind her darkened sunglasses, her eyes traveled from the top of his head to his cowboy boots. He wore a plain white t-shirt that stretched tightly across his chest and was tucked neatly in his snug fitting Levis. The white shirt against his dark skin only added to the magnificence and the black hair that slightly touched his collar seemed absolute, wild perfection. As she walked toward him she nearly stumbled but he reached out and gently grabbed her arm to steady her. When he touched her, Andrea's face flushed and she felt the dizzying warmth travel down her body. *Man o' man*, was all she could think. And then he smiled, a dazzling, brilliant smile and removed his sunglasses to reveal the most beautiful blue eyes she had ever seen. *Holy. Crap.*

"I'm Andrea Sutter from Circle Realtors", she managed to stutter.

"Shane Matthews." He said and once again took her by the hand. He could feel the heat in her skin and he grinned to himself.

They made a bit of small talk about where he was from and what exactly he was looking for. All the while that the realtor spoke, Shane witnessed how she fought to keep her eyes from traveling all over his body. He had always had this affect on women but he wasn't interested in this one. After what seemed like a million questions, she finally asked if he was married. Smiling his perfectly white, toothy smile, he understood that question was only for her benefit.

"No, I'm not married but on a professional note, I'm interested in this property as an investment only. He lied."I don't plan to stay in the area." He added, hoping to throw her off. She nodded and continued her discussion of the property's highlights.

After what seemed like the longest hour of his life, she finally ended her selling strategy and point blank asked him if he was interested in pursuing a contract for the property. Telling her what he was willing to pay for it, he also slipped in that he would pay cash if she could get a contract going in the next couple of days. Andrea seemed surprised but smiled and nodded. She presented him with a business card with her office, home and cell phone numbers.

"Do you have a pen?" He asked her after he took the business card from her slightly trembling hand. Nodding she retrieved one from her purse and handed it to him. He turned over her card and wrote his cell phone number on the back of it and then pushed it towards her. Confusion crossed her perfectly painted features for a moment.

"*You* call me when you have the contract." Shane stated with unmistakable authority all the while flashing that charming smile. "If I don't hear from you in two days the deal is off the table and I will look elsewhere."

Andrea immediately stuffed the card into her purse and nodded. "Thank you for your time Mr. Matthews. I will begin the process as soon as I return to the office this afternoon." Smiling, she reached for his hand once again, which he accepted graciously. "It has been a pleasure." She purred.

The corners of Shane's mouth turned up to form a forced smile. "Yes, thank you Ms. Sutter. We will talk again soon, yes?"

She nodded, retreated to her car and climbed in. The engine started and he watched as her car disappeared down the long driveway. He leaned against his black Chevrolet pickup and surveyed what he hoped would be his new home. Was it too soon to pay a visit to his new neighbor? He thought not and besides that, he couldn't wait any longer.

The smell of fall was thick in the air and I decided that it was passed over due to repaint some of the interior of the cabin. I had just completed the bathroom and was now working on repainting the kitchen. It was a mess but something that had to be done and it had not been repainted since my parents had passed. It was time for a little bit of change.

I heard the sound of a vehicle coming up the driveway before I could ever see it. It could be Randy but he had been very good about calling and not just showing up; which I greatly approved of. When the vehicle rounded the corner I immediately realized that it was a black pick up and I had no idea who it could be. Retrieving the pistol from my purse, I quickly pushed it into the back of my jeans.

Watching cautiously out the kitchen window, the truck pulled up beside my SUV and stopped; the engine shut off. I couldn't tell anything about the driver until he stepped out and then my jaw hit the ground. *Wow, who is THIS guy?* I thought to myself as I absentmindedly smoothed my mussed hair. Tall, dark and handsome were only a few of the words that popped into my mind. He seemed to glide across the yard toward me and I couldn't tear my eyes away from the broad shoulders and the t-shirt stretched tightly across the muscular chest. I stepped out onto the deck as he made his way to the steps but before taking the first step, he paused and looked up.

Her dark hair was pulled back in a ponytail and she wore and old gray t-shirt and jeans that were tucked into a pair of boots. Holding a paintbrush in one hand, the other rested on her hip. A bit of red paint smudged her cheek as well as streaked her jeans here and there. She was a beautiful sight and Shane smiled. "Hi." He said cheerfully. "I hope that I'm not interrupting."He drank the sight of her in eagerly and he fought the urge to pull her into his arms.

Shane took a deep breath, inhaling the scent of the woman that he had longed to see for so long and his smile broadened. But as quickly as it appeared, it vanished as he picked up the revealing scent of another human; a male. Jealousy rose like bile in his throat and he desperately tried to calmly force it back down. He continued up the steps toward her and just like before she stood her ground, unflinching. He was certain that behind her back was her gunmetal colored confidence and she was fingering the handle; ready to use it if threatened. Without any further delay he extended his hand to her. "I'm Shane Matthews."

Smiling weakly and a little preoccupied with the notable appearance of my guest, I glanced over at the paintbrush in my hand then back at him. "It's alright." It was obvious that he had made a wrong turn; this man was beautiful and didn't belong around here. If so, I would have surely seen him or knew that he existed.

For a moment I hesitated when he held out his hand towards me but then I extended mine in return. When he took it in his, a spark of current fired between us and I jerked my hand away, embarrassed. "I'm so sorry," I stuttered, "I shocked you!"

He smiled, and then removed his sunglasses. My eyes settled on his for a moment and something familiar flashed through my mind while staring into the dazzling blue eyes of the man before me. Had I met this man before? No….it wasn't possible. I certainly would have remembered this gorgeous man. No, it was his eyes; something hauntingly familiar about those blue eyes.
"I'm Elisa…..Brewer." I paused, "Are you lost?"

The man shook his head, his lip curled up on one side as if he had discovered something interesting. "No, I'm not lost." He replied, "I'm out meeting some of my neighbors."
"Meeting neighbors, huh? You bought property around here?" I asked, hoping that I wasn't too forward.

"I'm about 5 miles down the road there." Shane pointed the direction of the property and then returned his attention back to the woman. Elisa…he had never known her name.

"The Hawkmeyer place." I said, nodding. "It's been for sale for a while but I heard they were asking too much for it." I added bluntly. "For the shape that the house is in anyway."

He flashed a brilliant smile just as he had done to the realtor but strangely, this woman didn't melt into a puddle at his feet. "If the contract goes through, I got a really good deal. Andrea Sutter, do you know her?" he asked.

Now it was my turn to chuckle. "Yep, I know her." I left it at that. Andrea was one of the loosest women around. Apparently she had already been putting her moves on Mr. Gorgeous, but then again, who wouldn't? Yet for some reason, it caused a peculiar twang of jealousy in the pit of my stomach and I turned my thoughts quickly in a different direction, "Anyway, would you like glass of tea?" I really needed to get back to painting but I just wasn't quite ready to let this hot new neighbor go on his way just yet.

The smile on his face widened. "Yes, I would like that." He replied.

While she was inside, Shane tried to pick up more information on the scent of the unknown male that had been here. It was difficult to detect it over the smell of the fresh paint and now Elisa's intoxicating scent in the mix. Looking down at the deck floor, his memory was launched back to the night when she had shared her food with him and where she had lain beside him until darkness had enveloped their sleeping forms. Sighing heavily, he felt the same old feelings that had come to be second nature. The want….the desire… the need.

I couldn't get over the strangely familiar feelings that this guy provoked. There was no way that I had ever seen him before. He had a face…and a body that a woman would just not be able to forget…even in random passing. He oozed masculinity from every one of his pores and I suddenly felt my face flush at the direction of my thoughts. Shaking it off, I continued to fix the tea.

Returning outside, I sat one glass down in front of him. "I didn't ask you if you liked sugar in yours or not, would you like some?"

"No, no sugar…thanks." His deep, friendly voice answered. I found myself staring into those blue eyes for a little longer than was appropriate and I quickly proceeded to ask him a few questions about the property and his plans.

    Shane could barely answer her questions for the excitement that was building inside him. He could feel the attraction between them; see the flush on her cheeks. There was an unexplainable tingling shock whenever they touched along with the strong pull that he felt towards her. While he had been away, she was all that he had thought of and he couldn't wait to get back to her. Sure, he had an effect on most women but this was different; *he* felt it. It might take a while to figure out for certain but he was nearly positive that she was…..his mate.
    The sound of the phone ringing inside drew their attention and she politely dismissed herself. He could hardly sit still as he wanted nothing more than to grab her tightly and press his lips against hers. Tapping his foot on the deck in nervousness he waited for her to return. He could hear her soft voice as she spoke to whoever it was on the phone and then the louder sound of the receiver being placed back in the cradle. When she returned, she seemed distracted. "Is everything okay?" he asked, genuinely concerned about the change in her behavior.
    I smiled and nodded in return. "Yeah, just have a friend coming over tonight for dinner and I haven't even started it." I answered. "I've been busy with painting and totally lost track of time. I told him to pick up a pizza on his way out."
    The twinge of jealousy surfaced in Shane again when he caught the *him* in her reply. He picked up his glass and took a long drink hoping to camouflage his noticeable disapproval. The grip of his hand on the glass was exceedingly tight and it shattered beneath the pressure sending glass and tea all over him and his clothes. He jumped up suddenly, surprised by his own actions.
    Leaping out of my chair I quickly ran over to him. "Oh shit, are you okay?" I couldn't help but notice the piece of the glass had had pierced his cheek and the immediate line of blood that was now forming along the gash. "You're bleeding, let me get you something." I uttered nervously and hurried inside. Grabbing the closest thing that I could, I returned quickly with a kitchen towel.
    Shane knew that the glass hadn't been defective; it was his own rage that had broken it and now he was entirely wet and bleeding. "I'm

fine, really it's nothing." Sitting back down he allowed her to hold the towel to his face. She grabbed his hand and placed it on the towel to hold it against the wound while she continued to pick up the glass from his clothes. The nearness of her and smell of her heightened his already peaked senses and he shifted uncomfortably in his chair. "I should get out of here if you have company on their way." He said, almost too coldly. She stopped and looked up at him, and he thought he saw a flash of anger through her eyes before they softened.

"I can't let you go all wet and covered in glass." I said simply, "and bleeding." I pulled his hand away along with the towel to examine the cut. It was still bleeding a good deal and the towel was quickly becoming soaked by blood. It dripped down on the white t-shirt that he was wearing leaving dark splotches on the snow white fabric. I shook my head with worry. "Stand up." I demanded.

He did as I asked and I took a small hand held broom and began to dust off his clothes in the attempt to get any small pieces of glass off that remained there. I felt a bit uncomfortable as I swept down the length of his legs with the soft bristles.

Shane too felt a bit nervous as she ran the broom across his legs and wondered if she had noticed the slight bulge at his crotch. He needed to get out of here, and quick. "I have a change of clothes in my truck." He said promptly as she continued the merciless assault with the broom. It might just be easier to change clothes than to go through all of this. A bead of sweat began to form across his brow.

She looked up and nodded. He hadn't noticed before how petite that she seemed as she stood beside him. Being a good foot or more taller than she, he nearly dwarfed her with his size. The strong desire to reach out and stroke her hair and feel it against his hands overwhelmed him, but he dared not. Not yet. "I'll go get the clothes if you don't mind," he said.

"Sure." I replied. "Then I want to put some peroxide and a bandage on that cut." I couldn't help but stare as he walked down the steps and to his truck. He was nice to watch walking away...or walking toward me….. or really just moving around in general. I grinned to myself at the thoughts in my mind but they were quickly replaced with concern and guilt for having caused him injury. If that had been his eye he could have been blinded!

Returning with a duffle bag, I led him inside to show him where the bathroom was. It was a little strange that he didn't hesitate or wait for me to show him the way, but instead he moved ahead as if he already knew. What was even weirder was that I didn't feel uncomfortable with this intimidating tall stranger alone in the house. I realized at that moment that I had felt various peculiar feelings since his arrival; more than I had ever felt before. There was no denying that I was affected by his good looks and his powerfully built physique but there was something else about him; something that I couldn't quite put my finger on. As my thoughts wondered, the bathroom door came open and he stepped out. He had traded his white shirt for a black one and his dark jeans for a lighter pair. *Wow, he was so hot.* I felt my face flush.

"Thanks for letting me change. It may have gotten a bit prickly on the ride." He teasingly grinned.

I smiled back, but couldn't quite look him the eye; somewhat afraid that he would be able to read where my mind had been. "I'm just sorry it happened. I don't think I've ever seen a glass just blow up like that." Pulling out a chair from the table I motioned for him to sit down. "I'll get the peroxide." With that, I quickly disappeared into the bathroom and came back carrying it along with a cotton ball and a large band-aid. He sat patiently while I saturated the cotton ball with peroxide and started to put it to his face. It was then that he moved his hand from his thigh where it had rested and grasped my forearm gently. A charge of electricity shot through me where his skin touched mine and I jerked my eyes toward his.

I almost chuckled as I saw the concern in his blue eyes. This substantially large man seemed uneasy that the stuff might actually burn! "Would you like to do it?" I asked after noting his hesitation. He shook his head with refusal, but his hand remained on my arm.

I was now very distracted with Mr. Gorgeous' hand on my arm. It was warm and beginning to send small chills up the rest of my body. My legs were starting to feel like jelly and butterflies were swarming in my stomach, moving downward bringing heat and wetness with them. *Shit!* I just met this guy, how could I feel so attracted to him? My hand trembled slightly as I applied the moist cotton ball to his face. Gently cleaning the blood away I was pleasantly surprised at how good that it looked. "It isn't as bad as what I first thought." I mumbled as I looked down and noticed the big grin that spread across his face as he removed his hand from my arm.

Shane felt it. He felt it in her skin, smelled in radiating from her body, saw it on her face. She wanted him, he was sure of it but it was too soon to act on it. "I think that I'm good. I'll get out of here so you can enjoy your company." Even coming from his own mouth, he felt the jealousy rise up. What was he going to do about this? He stood abruptly, picked up his clothes and duffle bag and exited the cabin. Elisa followed closely as he made his way to the steps before he turned unexpectedly to face her.

I shuddered as he reached down and took my hand once again, holding it gently in his own. "It was a pleasure to meet you Elisa." He paused momentarily as his eyes seemed to search mine. "When I get settled I would like it if you might come and enjoy a meal with me one evening." He said before letting my hand fall from his own. Smiling shyly I somehow managed to stutter. "I would like that very much……"

Admiring him as he moved across the yard, I watched as he got into his truck, tossed a quick wave in my direction and disappeared down the driveway. Strangely overwhelmed with disappointment, I was in no mood for Randy's visit. I quickly went inside and picked up the phone; intent on cancelling our evening together. When he answered, I explained that I had been painting all day and really wanted to finish up this evening. He told me he understood, but I could hear something else in his voice. I found myself not really caring since my mind was preoccupied with thoughts of Mr. Gorgeous new neighbor. How in the world did he affect me like that? I had only just met him and was already swooning, light in the head and love sick. Geez. What am I….sixteen?

Shane didn't know where he would stay that night. He didn't feel like driving back to town and he was fairly certain that Andrea had made the deal. Soon the Hawkmeyer place, as Elisa had called it, would be his. With his mind was still raging over the male visitor that she was expecting, he dwelled on it until it festered in his mind. He decided to park his truck at his soon to be home and let the wolf do some wandering. It had been a while and this might be the best way to get a good look at Elisa's male visitor.

Changing quickly into the wolf, he left his newly acquired boots and clothes locked in his truck. He hid the keys so that if anyone came around his items would be safe inside. Traveling the distance between their homes was effortless and he was soon at the edge of the woods behind her cabin. Not catching the scent of anyone besides Elisa, he soon heard the rumble of a vehicle coming down her driveway. He could see her inside, still painting and dressed in the same clothes as when he had visited. Hearing the vehicle as well he watched her move to the window to look out. When the headlights rounded the corner he saw the look on her face. It wasn't one of joy.

    Anger flared up inside as I watched Randy's truck pull into the driveway and park underneath the overhanging tree limbs on the opposite side of the drive. The headlights shut off and the engine stopped and he stepped out. For some reason, I strongly detested the fact that he hadn't listened to me and I was in no mood for his company. I could tell he was drunk as he came across the yard, stumbling and cursing as he made his way to the steps. With any luck he would fall back down them and I would just leave him there to drown in his own puke.

    The wolf watched from the shadows and Shane felt hostility build towards this human with every step he took. He could smell the sweat and the liquor that seemed to ooze from his skin and something else that he couldn't quite identify that put his mind in defense mode. Elisa had turned the outside light on and had come out onto the deck, waiting to greet the man that could barely mount the steps. When he finally made it, he leaned against the railing and studied Elisa through hazy eyes.

    "What are you doing here Randy?" I asked, not attempting to mask the anger in my voice. "I told you that I had things to finish tonight."

    He was a tall man with sandy blond hair that was covered with a baseball cap but curled up slightly around the edges. Wearing a white t-shirt with some sort of advertisement on it, it hung sloppily on the outside of his jeans and his work boots were covered with dry concrete, a sign of his profession. He chuckled uneasily at Elisa. "I just wanted to see you tonight is all." He slurred.

    "You're drunk Randy. You won't even remember seeing me."I angrily replied. This episode was just one of the many reasons that our relationship hadn't worked out. When he drank, he drank a lot.

    In a swift movement he advanced toward me and grabbed me around the waist, pulling me against his body.

    "I just want to be close to you tonight….like we used to be close." He stammered. His breath mixed with beer was a nauseating smell and I pulled back, trying to put some space between us.

In the shadows the wolf growled, his lips pulled back over long sharp deadly fangs. His own anger was rising to levels which he may not be able to control once set into motion. Elisa was meant to be his and another male had no right to touch her.

I struggled against Randy's hold but he would not release his grasp on me. If anything, he pulled me tighter against his body, pinning me there. I planted both hands against his chest in an attempt to push him away but he held firmly and refused to let go. "Don't fight me...I want you Elisa. You know in your heart that you want me too.... you've always wanted me." He faltered over the words, the alcohol influencing his ability to speak.

I shook my head, "You're wrong." I said, my voice cracking as I became defensive. "I used to want you...until...." My words were abruptly stopped as he forced his lips onto mine. I felt my own lip split as the pressure of his mouth crushed against it. His hand move down my side and to the button on my jeans and I felt panic suddenly rising. Never had he tried to pull something like this! I struggled, trying to free myself from his grasp as he jerked the zipper down but my arms were pinned against my own body by his and by the steel grip of the one around my waist.

The wolf had moved silently from the shadows and made its way up the deck steps. Standing behind the male human now, his head was lowered and eyes blazed with rage. Witnessing Elisa's continued efforts to push him away; they were futile. Randy continued to hold her against him with one hand while the other trailed down her side to the button on her jeans. Shane heard the button snap and the sound of the zipper as it was quickly lowered; all the while Elisa struggled against his advances.

The line had been crossed. The wolf emitted a loud, low guttural growl that echoed through the stillness of the night. Randy stopped his attack abruptly and stood quietly for a moment, staring into her face. Elisa backed away at this point; her eyes wild with fear and the surprise of Randy's aggression.

Through the pounding of my own heart I heard something strange from behind us. Randy heard it too and hesitated, pulling away from me slightly and giving me the opportunity to slip from his clutches.

I saw it then, standing boldly behind him and a chill crept up my spine. "What the hell was that?" Randy questioned, his eyes bearing down on mine. Once again, the low rumble repeated and Randy turned to face the source.

Shane's eyes locked on the human's and for only a moment his conscious fought his instincts. He stepped forward and the human retreated two steps backwards. This scenario continued until Randy was pressed against the deck railing on the far side with nowhere else to go. Shane could smell the fear resonating from every inch of him and the strong stench of urine as the front of his jeans darkened. Shane growled again, his lips curled back to expose the long, sharp teeth the he intended to tear him to shreds with.

I came back to my senses and realized that the wolf was defending me. Where it had come from I wasn't sure and didn't care. Feeling suddenly calmer and reassured by its presence, my breathing evened out and I moved towards it without hesitation. I stopped between Randy and the wolf and turned to face my offender as he cowered close to the rail.

"When did you get a dog?" Randy stuttered, his body trembling. He suddenly seemed to have sobered up in the course of the past few seconds.

"I didn't." I replied softly as I stared at the big black beast in our midst. I watched helplessly as the wolf stepped slowly towards Randy. It snarled aggressively, the dusk to dawn light glinting off its exposed fangs making them appear to glow in the darkness. Fear rose up in me at what the wolf's intentions were and I couldn't stand by and watch it kill him. He needed to go home, not die.

This few moments gave Shane enough time to quiet his rage and let his conscious take over. He had no problem killing this man and had killed men for much less. Stepping nearer to the human male he began to snarl and snap getting closer and closer to his body.

Randy could feel the hot breath of the animal through his jeans and he wondered how soon it would be before it reared up and ripped out his throat. He was backed against the railing as far as it allowed and he felt like prey about to be devoured. The wolf shook its head violently, sending droplets of saliva over Randy's skin but never breaking their eye contact.

The useless waste of air began to tremble uncontrollably and looked to Elisa for help. Satisfied that he had the human convinced he meant business, Shane slowly backed away, allowing Elisa to move forward.

Breathing a sigh of relief as it skulked backward away from Randy, I immediately stepped toward him. "I think it's time you leave Randy." I said. I almost felt sad for him and the fact that he had been scared enough to piss himself.

Still trembling, his eyes wild, Randy nodded and moved toward the steps but his path was blocked by the large black beast. Shane could hear the rapid beat of his heart and smell the fear resonating from him and knew he was terrified. Stepping to the side, he allowed the idiot to pass by. When he was halfway to his truck, Elisa yelled out to him.

"Randy!" I shouted, making him turn around quickly. I could see the dread on his face, afraid that the beast was following him across the yard. But it hadn't. It still stood on the deck watching his retreat with defiance. Randy's eyes flicked back to mine and I could see the panic. "Don't come back here again." I told him. He stared at me for only a moment before turning his back and climbing into his truck. Starting the engine, he disappeared down the driveway hastily; gravel slinging out behind him. Turning my attention then to my companion who I hadn't seen for months, I looked at it questioningly, speaking to it like an old friend. "Where you have been?" I asked as I extended my hand.

The wolf raised its head and met her touch; he had waited a long time for her affection. She continued to speak as if she thought he might respond, "I'm glad you came back." Her hand stroked his wide head and fondled his ears tenderly. She gazed into his eyes as if she was waiting for his reply, but then smiled and gave him a soft pat.

Stepping closer, he brushed the length of his body against her legs. He had definitely missed her as well and he didn't plan on leaving again, not for any reason. Her fingers traced down his head, neck and along his broad back sending shivers from one end of his spine to the other and in response, he rubbed his head against her leg, marking her with his scent. Affection was only a small part of what he felt for her.

I was a little surprised at the friendliness the wolf returned as I rubbed my hand along the thick fur of its back. Genuinely happy to see it; oddly enough it acted as if it had missed me as well. After the amount of time that had passed I had just assumed it had moved on and I would never see it again, our strange encounter forever etched in my memory. But, here it was again like my guardian angel showing up from wherever it had disappeared to, to save me.

Chapter 6

    The next couple of days passed without incident and Shane got the phone call that he had expected from Andrea. Her flirty, purring voice gave him the good news and told him that all he had to do was to come into town that morning and sign the papers and the deal was done. The cabin and property would legally his and he could begin renovations on the outside before the dead of winter set in. He could work on the inside during the colder months and by spring he was hoping to have everything accomplished that he had planned.

    It was about a thirty mile round trip to go into the town so to be neighborly, he thought he would drive over to Elisa's and see if she would like to accompany him or if she needed anything. He admitted to himself that it was only an excuse and he actually had a hidden agenda. It had been two days since he had last laid human eyes on her and it had already been far too long. He secretly hoped that she would choose to go with him so that Andrea's advances might fall quickly by the wayside. Not only that, he craved her company.

    For October, the weather had turned off nicely. This central part of the country generally had a good spring and fall, or so he had read but it had turned into a proven fact. It was cool in the evenings and required a light jacket but warm enough in the day to wear a t-shirt and be comfortable. He was definitely enjoying it. Fall in Ontario was short lived, the high temperatures 60 degrees at the most; so far the Missouri weather appealed to him.

    Climbing into his truck he started it and glanced down at the time. It was only 9:00 a.m. and his appointment with Andrea wasn't until 11:00. By the time he gathered up Elisa and drove in it would be close enough to their meeting time; she might even agree to have lunch with him. Realizing that it was more likely than not that she would decline since they had only met a couple of days ago, he still felt compelled to ask. He knew that he could be intimidating but she hadn't seemed frightened by him.

    Easing the truck down the long, rough driveway to the gravel road he turned to head toward Elisa's property. It was about 5 miles by the road but not nearly as far by the way the crow flies; or maybe he should say by the way the wolf runs. He chuckled to himself. In a few minutes he was turning into her drive and soon pulled up beside her SUV. Striding across the yard, he headed up the steps to the door. No motion could be detected inside and peering through the window he could see that the cabin was still dark and the shades drawn. He glanced out toward the shed where she kept the ATV but the door was closed, the lock still in place. Opening the screen door, he grasped the door knob but it too was locked. Could she still be in bed at this hour? Concern etched his handsome features.

    I was roused from sleep by the sound of footsteps on the wooden planks of the deck. Bolting upright in bed, my ears strained to hear. As quietly as possible, I slipped off the edge of the bed and tiptoed into the kitchen to peer out; the curtain providing my concealment. I pulled it back slightly, just enough to make a small crack and look out and I was startled to see Shane's back moving away from the door and toward the steps. What was he doing here so early in the morning?
    Overwhelmed by not only curiosity but also by the pressing distress that he was going to get away, I hurriedly grasped the doorknob and jerked open the door. I stood there like an idiot, staring at his grinning handsome face before I suddenly realized what I must look like.

    Turning to cross the deck to be on his way, the cabin door came open and Elisa stepped out. He swung around and had to chuckle quietly to himself at the sight of her. Her hair stuck out on one side of her head and she looked as if she was having trouble focusing on him. She was clad in only a pair of skimpy cotton shorts and a t-shirt that molded to her body along with a pair of short white ankle socks. His eyes traveled down her body and stopped at her breasts which were responding to the coolness of the early morning air and before he could avert his eyes, his body began to respond. Possibly having noticed where his gaze had ended up or perhaps she was indeed cold; she quickly crossed her arms over her chest.
    Shane cleared his throat, "Good morning," he said smiling awkwardly, attempting to keep his eyes on hers. "I didn't mean to wake you."
    I found myself returning his smile, but slightly uncomfortably. "Good morning, and you didn't. I was awake, just hadn't crawled out of my warm bed yet." I lied.

Shane's mind wandered over that scenario for a moment. A warm bed, a warm body next to him...he would have definitely had a problem leaving a bed like that on any morning.

"What...uh.....are you doing here?" I managed to stutter as I consciously attempted to run my fingers through my sleep ratted hair. In my haste to stop his departure, I hadn't given my appearance much thought.

"I'm headed into town in a little while....wondered if you'd like to come with me; maybe show me around a bit. I need to pick up a few things and go to the realtor's office to finish up some paperwork on the property." He replied, hoping that she would accept his invitation.

Pursing my lips together, I contemplated his offer. I didn't really *know* this man. But yet, somewhere deep within me I felt a strong urge to comply with his wishes. I almost felt that if I declined that he might walk away forever and I shivered at the thought. "Would you mind if we had a cup of coffee first?"

Shane smiled with relief and nodded. "Coffee sounds great. Just have to get there by 11:00."

"Good." I replied in return. "Let's go inside where it is a bit warmer. It won't take long to brew but it will give me a little time to do something with myself!" I laughed nervously. Here I am again, inviting this strange man inside my home with little thought of what could happen to me. It wasn't as if I could fight him off....but would I want to?

The sound of her laughter was melodic to his ears and he laughed as he followed her inside. "Well, if your damn neighbor didn't show up at the crack of dawn!" he responded. They both laughed again as she motioned for him to sit down. He removed his jacket and placed it on the back of the chair before seating himself while she moved about the kitchen getting the coffee ready. With her back to him he enjoyed the opportunity to watch her while hidden from her view. He admired her shapely tanned legs, small firm ass, and trim waistline. Even with her hair in disarray he felt his attraction for her growing stronger.

I could feel his eyes on me as I put a new filter and coffee in the Bunn. Embarrassed by the heat in my face that he somehow always managed to provoke, I felt suddenly self conscious in my too short shorts and no bra. Hurriedly, I finished my task so I could get out of the prying line his vision.

She suddenly turned toward him, disrupting his thoughts. "I'll be right back. Help yourself to the coffee when it's finished brewing." She pointed toward the cabinet near the sink, "Cups are in there."

He dipped his head in appreciation, "Thanks."

She was gone long enough that he did indeed help himself to the coffee. It had been quite a while since he had sat and enjoyed a cup of morning brew in a home, at a table, in a real stoneware cup.

Looking in the mirror I stared horrified at my reflection. Oh my sweet Jesus! I looked like ….like shit! Quickly I splashed some cold water on my bloodless face and picked up the hairbrush in an attempt to tame the freaked out hair on the side of my head. I can't believe that he saw me like this! I smoothed some eyeshadow over my lids and brushed my cheeks with a bit of rouge just to try to perk up my pale complexion. Pulling the sides of my hair up into a clip I then evaluated myself; much better.

When she returned she had dressed in jeans and boots and a dark blue long sleeve shirt that fit snuggly against her frame. The v-neck of the shirt revealed a bit of cleavage but not so much that it left nothing to his imagination. A small gold chain encircled her neck and lay delicately against her skin. She had pulled the front and sides of her dark hair back away from her face but the back had been left long to trail past her shoulders. Having added a small bit of color to her face, she now looked refreshed and awake. He met her eyes and she smiled.

"Better?" he asked jokingly, the laughter dancing in his eyes. They followed her to the coffee pot where she took down a cup and filled it to the rim with the hot brew.

"Much better…don't you think?" I asked as I turned back toward the table grinning. I knew that I *had* to look much better with no contest. Boldly, I pulled out the chair closet to him and sat down, taking a sip from my cup and then looking up into his eyes.

"I have learned that you never tell a lady the truth when she asks about things of that nature." Shane answered, somewhat joking but he had learned that here was a lot of truth behind the words.

I laughed out loud at his remark, knowing that he was indeed right. "You're a smart man Shane…I like you already!"

They exchanged a bit of small talk before Shane noticed the clock on her stove. He needed to get rolling if he intended to keep his appointment with Andrea. "Are you going with me then?" he inquired. "I need to get on the road."

I nodded, feeling more at ease. "Yep. I'll fill a couple of go-cups so we can have coffee for the drive." I stood up and walked over to the cabinet and retrieved a couple of cups. Shane had already pulled his jacket back on so I handed his cup directly to him before moving past to grab my own jacket from its hook behind the door. I accidently brushed up against him and felt the slight electricity where our bodies touched. He must have felt it too and as I apologized again for shocking him, he just looked at me through those bright blue eyes and grinned. Shaking it off, I pulled on my favorite tan jacket, turned off the coffee pot, grabbed my cup and purse and followed Mr. Gorgeous neighbor man out the door. This could possibly turn into a very interesting day.

Shane, without delay moved swiftly to the passenger side of the truck and opened the door, waiting for me to climb inside. I smiled and softly replied, "Thank you." Nodding, he shut the door.
The truck was warm inside as the fall sun shone through the glass, heating the interior. It was filled with the enlivening smell of my chauffer, even before he settled into the driver's seat. There was a distinctive smell that he emitted, a strong exciting scent that caused my heartbeat to slightly increase. I glanced over at him as he reached down and started the truck, hoping that he couldn't detect my thoughts.

"And we're off." he said as he put the truck in reverse and backed out. I enjoyed the relaxed conversation as we traveled the gravel roads to reach the state maintained black top highway that would take us into town. He asked about my family and if I had any siblings and I explained that my parents had both passed away from a car accident a few years before and that I was an only child.

As I answered his questions, I took the opportunity to let my eyes wander across to the man behind the wheel. I hoped like hell that through my sunglasses he couldn't see my eyes roaming freely and admiringly over his body. One muscular, dark arm was extended to the steering wheel while the other rested on the console between us, his long fingers tapping absentmindedly on the edge of it. He wore a black jacket over a black button up shirt and dark jeans that stretched across powerful thighs. He was rugged in his appearance with the shadow of a beard just beginning to show on his jaw line.

Squinting, I could only barely make out the fine line where the glass had busted and sliced his cheek. The thought crossed my mind that there should be a definite scar as it had only been a few days but I dismissed it and continued to concentrate on his features. I shuttered involuntarily as my eyes roved over him….he was indeed….gorgeous.

    Shane was taking pleasure in watching her try to hide her obvious response to being so near to him in the small enclosed area of the truck's cab. He knew that she could feel something between them but she didn't realize the extent of what was happening…not yet. His senses too were greatly under the influence of her scent and her close proximity. He tried to keep his mind moving in other directions to dissuade his body's reaction to the situation, but he could nearly feel the static in the air between them.

    Their conversation during the ride was relaxed and natural and he felt very much at ease in her company. She told him a wealth of knowledge about her life that he mentally stashed back to recall later. In turn, he shared some of the facts of his own life; of course leaving out a few incriminating details. Sharing that he had been born in the northern United States and later moved to Canada with his family, he had then grown there into adulthood. Hearing great things about the Ozarks region, he had decided that he needed a change and had packed up his truck and headed south until he found this area and felt it suited him.

    I listened intently to him speak; his deep voice was soothing to my ears. When he brought up having lived in Canada I couldn't stop myself from asking about the wildlife there. He told me about the big game animals such as moose and elk that populated that area. He then went on to talk about the large predators that were hunted.

    "So….were there a lot of wolves in Canada then?" I implored.

    Shane glanced over in her direction before he responded. Odd question but he thought he already knew were the discussion was headed. His eyes went back to the road ahead and he nodded. "Yeah. There were plenty of wolves up north," he paused, "Why do you ask?"

    I wasn't sure if I should reveal the secret of my mysterious companion but I felt compelled to tell him. "Well," I said, "You probably won't believe this story that I'm about to tell you."

    "Try me." He answered, stealing a glance in her direction before returning his eyes to the road.

    "I've seen a wolf on my property," I uttered. "At least I think that is what it is."

Shane was silent for a few moments and then smirked, "Really? Why do you think it's a wolf? Maybe it's just someone's dog."

I shook my head. "No. It wasn't a dog." I answered, "The thing was huge and black." I extended my arms in a wide gesture to add emphasis to just how large it was.

Shane baited her, "If it was far away, you would have a pretty difficult time being able to tell just how large something was at a distance."

Again, I shook my head. "No. I've been close………I've touched it." I said.

His eyebrows rose with mock question, "A wild animal let you just touch it? I don't see that happening, not a wolf. Not how the wolves were where I came from."

He seemed awfully quick to dismiss what I know that I saw and it rubbed me the wrong way. Suddenly I wished that I had just kept my mouth closed. Sighing I answered smartly "Yeah, well, I know what I saw." I turned my gaze to look out the passenger side window.

Shane couldn't help but grin and he knew that he shouldn't just lure her into more conversation about it when she was in fact stating the truth. "I didn't say that I didn't *believe* you Elisa. I think that you've seen something but whether it is a wolf or not is to be determined." He reached his hand over and patted her leg, reassuringly, but instead of removing it he left it there.

Where his hand touched me, I instantly felt the heat permeating through my jeans and I turned my head to look at him. The warmth spread quickly upward and settled between my thighs. *Damn, what was the affect that this guy had on me?*

He hesitantly removed his hand and laid his arm back across the console. Smelling her arousal from his touch, his senses instantly skyrocketed. Feeling his own groin respond he took a deep breath, letting it out slowly in an attempt to calm his body. Luckily they had just driven past city limits and would be in downtown in only a few minutes.

We reached the realtor's office with very little additional conversation and when Shane pulled up to the curb and got out of the truck, I stayed inside. He came to the passenger side and opened the door looking strangely assuming that I would be getting out. I stared back at him questioningly, but remained in my seat. "You want me to come in with you?"

Shane nodded. "Well yes. I don't want you to sit out here for who knows how long."

"This is your personal business. I don't feel that I should be aware of your financial affairs." I answered.

He shook his head, grinning. "Elisa, I don't mind. I have nothing to hide from you…come now." Holding his hand out towards me, he continued. "I want you to."

Still feeling confused about why he insisted that I needed to be involved, I tentatively reached for his outstretched hand. Upon placing my hand in his, his smiled widened. I had never had something as easy as a simple touch have such an effect on me. Returning his smile, I did so with uncertain, nervous laughter. Once out of the truck I tried to remove my hand from his but he didn't allow it, tightening his gentle but firm grip. He used his free hand to retrieve a small case from behind the passenger side seat and then swung the truck door closed behind me. Pushing his sunglasses to the top of his head, he revealed the startling blue eyes that I found so vaguely familiar. Why did this all feel so *right*? For a moment he just stared at me before turning and leading the way towards the realtor office's door.

When Andrea saw Shane open the door to the office, she swiftly stood up from her desk, straightening her skin-tight pencil skirt. Running her fingers through her bleach blonde hair she came around to the front of her desk and in the sweetest voice she could muster she greeted him as he came through the door. "Mr. Matthews, it is so good to see you again," she crooned. Her demeanor changed rapidly when she saw Elisa. "Why Elisa, it has been a long time," she grimaced through the phony painted smile, "I see you have met my Mr. Matthews."

I forced my own indifferent smile back in her direction. "Hello Andrea, how have you been?" I asked as callously as possible not caring about the answer, which I didn't receive anyway.

Shane responded to Andrea's welcoming charm. "Hello Ms. Sutter. Good to see you again as well." He paused."But I wasn't aware that I was anyone's Mr. Matthews… just yet." He flashed his famous smile at her which directly caused Andrea's face to flush.

She returned the smile with a dazzling, flirty grin of her own. "Maybe we'll have to see what we can do about that."

I thought that I might just throw up in my own mouth. We had gone to high school together and she and I had quite a bit of history. It wasn't a history that I cared to recall. Always after the hottest guys in school she had been labeled as one of the loosest girls around and it wasn't uncommon to find her name written on a bathroom wall right next to the words "for a good time call". It didn't appear that she had veered too far off course.

"Shall we get started on your paperwork?" Andrea asked with forced sweetness in her voice as she looked from Shane and then back to me. "You can sit out here," she pointed at the line of chairs along the wall as she stared directly at me."This won't take too awfully long, honey."

I felt the undeniable urge to rip the woman's face off but I wouldn't dare make a scene in front of Shane. I hadn't expected to sit in on his meeting with Andrea anyway so to be civil, I nodded and smiled politely before moving toward the chairs. As I turned away, Shane reached out and gently grabbed my arm, stopping me.

"I want you to come in with me." He said, a flicker of amusement crossing his fine features. Behind him I could see Andrea's displeasure and the sneer that darkened her freshly made up face. I suddenly realized at that moment that even Shane knew what was going on and he wanted me to be a willing pawn in his game.

"If that is what you want." I replied, laughing inside at Andrea's silent but readable response to the situation. Shane was turned so he couldn't see her face but I could, and I knew she was pissed. Plastering on the phony smile, her voice was again like sugar.

"Well then, let's get this going so we don't hold you up Mr. Matthews." She said.

Shane and I followed her into the office and sat down in the chairs opposite her desk while Andrea walked around the other side and seated herself in the plush office chair. I tried to remain aloof and let my thoughts wander so that I didn't appear interested in their conversation or the paperwork. It was going well until Shane presented the case that he had brought from the truck. Carefully sitting it on the desk, he flipped open the latch to reveal a substantially large amount of cash. Not capable of hiding my surprise, my eyes widened and I looked from the case to Shane and back to the case again.

"I believe this will take care of it." He said as he pushed the container towards Andrea whose face openly revealed her pleasure."It's all there but you won't offend me by counting it."

Andrea's smile broadened, "I don't see a need to count it Mr. Matthews," she purred, "I believe that I can trust you." Her eyes reflected her satisfaction as she gazed across the desk at Shane. Reaching into her side drawer she recovered a set of keys and casually handed them across the desk toward him. When he reached his hand out to take them, she deliberately let her fingers trail across the palm of his hand all the while holding his gaze. "I hope you find your new home to be satisfactory." She paused, "and I hope we can do business again someday."

Shane stood and extended his empty hand to her which she took appreciatively in a business-like handshake. "Thank you Ms. Sutter."

Andrea held his hand longer than was necessary, "The pleasure was all mine.....Mr. Matthews."

I just sat there, staring at the case and wondering what kind of business this man was in exactly. Finally closing my gaping mouth and pulling myself back to the moment, I stood up and heard the last bit of their conversation. I couldn't believe the gall of the woman! Even with me sitting right next to him she had continued her flirtatious advances. I couldn't keep from boring a hole through her with my eyes and as if she realized it, she turned to look at me. "Take care Elisa." Her voice had turned cool and it almost sounded as if she was issuing a warning.

I brazenly met her stare and replied, "Sure, you too." Turning then, I walked toward the office door but before I could reach out and open it, Shane's hand was on the doorknob and the other on my lower back, as if escorting me through the opening. Behind us I was certain the that Andrea's face exposed her disgust as she watched us leave the building but I didn't turn back to witness it.

Once again, Shane opened the passenger side door of the truck and allowed me to climb in before he shut it securely behind me. He walked around the front and in a moment he was shutting the door and reaching down to start the truck. Looking over at me I regarded him with a questioning gaze. "Why did you really want me to come with you?" I inquired.

He smiled a devilishly handsome smile in my direction, flashing those perfect white teeth and chuckled. "I needed saving."

I couldn't help but smile back. The man was charming and beautiful and made my heart dance. Laughter had come back into my life in the very short time that I had known him. "I don't think I was much of a deterrent!" I pointed out, giggling.

We laughed together then, taking turns commenting on Andrea's desperate attempts to impress him as we pulled away from the curb. I couldn't remember the last time that I had laughed until my stomach ached and tears rolled from my eyes. It was a wonderful feeling. "Okay! Okay! I have to catch my breath or I'm going to die!" I managed to spew out between gasps for air.

Shane wasn't sure how he was even driving in the right lane of the street, laughing so hard that he could barely see clearly. "I know! I'm going to wreck if we don't stop!" He muttered, struggling to breathe.

Finally the laughter slowed and our breathing returned to normal. We looked at each other, which caused one more additional outburst of laughter that died down more quickly than the previous time. Shane inhaled and exhaled deeply trying to clear his head of the hilarity that was right on the brink of spilling over again. It felt good to laugh.

Chapter 7

"Do you mind helping me with something?" Shane asked, in a more serious tone.

"Sure, if I can," I answered.

"Where's the nearest furniture store?"

"Um…..I know that there's one on 5th street just past the railroad overpass," I thought for a moment, "and maybe another across town." I pointed as we neared the bridge, "Make a right on the next street."

He turned as I instructed and we were soon pulling into the lot of Patton's Furniture store. Not waiting for Shane to open the door for me this time I was out of the truck and waiting for him before he even got out. We walked toward the door in unison, his large frame only inches from me. I realized then that he wasn't too considerate about personal space but strangely enough, I didn't really mind. There was something uncomplicated and easy about being near him. When we reached the door it was the same scenario as before. He reached for the door with one hand and placed his other against my lower back, almost as if herding me.

The store was beautifully set up with every kind of furniture that a person could imagine. Stunning dining room sets and cozy living room furnishings stood in one area of the store while the other side housed exotic four poster beds with matching accessories and anything a person could imagine for a home.

He ushered me toward the side with the bedroom furniture first. I watched intently as his eyes browsed across the inventory and settled on a dark mahogany set in the far corner. He gently grabbed my hand and pulled me through the sea of dining room sets towards it, flanked by a salesman looking for a potential sale. It was a beautiful set with the four posts that stood high on the corners. Engraving trailed along the entirety of the headboard along its edges in long horizontal patterns. The mahogany wood had a deep sheen to it, as did all of the pieces in the set and a king size pillow top mattress completed the ensemble.

"Do you see anything you like?" The salesman's voice came from behind us. He was an older gentleman with graying hair and a friendly face.

Shane nodded, "Can you give us just bit?" he asked politely.

"Sure!" the salesman replied, "My name is Hank and if you have any questions just give me a holler." He said, pointing toward the center of the store, "I'll be right over there," he said with a welcoming smile.

"Thanks Hank," Shane said, "I'll sure do that."

Hank turned and made his way across the store to where another customer had started browsing among the kitchen appliances. Shane looked to me then, "What do you think of this?" he asked, his eyes locked onto mine.

I shrugged and said, "It's beautiful, but it doesn't matter what I think."

Shane reached out his hand and placed it on my shoulder. "You like it then?" he asked.

"Well yes, it's beautiful but…." He cut me off before I could finish.

"That's it then." Shane said, motioning for Hank from across the showroom who had obviously been watching. He hustled back across to where we stood.

"Well Hank, I believe that I will take this bedroom collection," he said to the salesman. "Is the mattress included in the price?"

"It's a great set but sadly no, the mattress is only for viewing. It must be purchased separately," he replied courteously.

With that, Shane turned and crawled up in the middle of the bed. He stretched out on his back, he turned on each side and then on his stomach. It seemed like minutes ticked by slowly while he tried out the feel of the mattress in all types of sleeping positions. I turned to look at the salesman who at the same time turned toward me. I shrugged, slightly turning red and smiled; Hank smiled back. "I've seen this before." He said quietly; nodding, "Aren't you going to see if you like it?" he asked.

I felt the heat creep into my face. "Oh, no," I stuttered, "we aren't together." I looked back toward Shane. He had turned on his back and was staring at me from his place on the bed and I couldn't be sure but I thought I saw disappointment. Climbing off the bed he walked back to where I stood beside Hank.

"I'll take the mattress too." He said.

Hank seemed ecstatic with his choice. "I'll get the paperwork together." He exclaimed excitedly. But Shane stopped him. "I'm not near finished yet, Hank." He said.

I listened with amazement as Shane told the salesman that he wanted the bed delivered today along with a refrigerator and stove that he would pick out momentarily. He would also be back at a later date to pick out some other items that he would want delivered as well once he had finished some of the renovations. Hank continued nodding in agreement; smiling happily as the dollar signs added up in his mind. After Shane was finished, he scurried away and left us to more shopping.

"Wow." I said, staring up at the man standing beside me. "Did you rob a bank or something?"

Again he beamed that brilliant smile of his and chuckled but avoided my question altogether. "Come now, help me pick out a stove and refrigerator." He said, grabbing my hand and leading me to the area of the store where appliances lined the wall. After a few minutes, he had chosen a stainless steel side by side fridge and a matching stove. After giving my approval, which oddly seemed to carry a lot of weight, Hank returned in a flash from out of nowhere and took down the information, all the while exceedingly enthusiastic with Shane's choices.

"Oh, one more thing for today," Shane paused, searching across the store, "I need a recliner."

The salesman was quick to point them out and led the way to where there was a vast array of colors and styles of recliners. It wasn't long before Shane had picked out a large, comfortable black leather lounging recliner which Hank quickly added to his list.

"I think that will be all for today. If we can get the paperwork completed now I will give you directions for the delivery." Shane said.

Hank happily led the way to the center of the store where several desks were set up within a large circular area. He asked us to be seated near his desk while he drew up the paperwork, indicating that it would only take a few moments. While we waited, we made small talk about the items that Shane had decided on and he seemed rather satisfied with his choices. Agreeing with him but particularly taken with how beautiful the bedroom set was, I found myself greatly impressed with his elegant choice.

Hank returned quickly and sat down across from us at his desk. Smiling, he appeared very pleased with himself at the substantial sale he was about to close on. He pushed the paperwork across the desk towards Shane who gingerly picked it up and after a quick look, nodded in approval. Stealing a sideways glance at the total on the bottom of the page I felt myself suddenly teetering on the edge of the chair. No wonder ol' Hank was so excited! It was more than what my SUV had cost when I bought it!

Shane leaned forward and pulled out his wallet, removing a check from its folds. "I suppose a check will do?" he asked.

"Sure will! As good as cash!" Hank responded.

Shane removed an ink pen from a cup by Hank's computer and begin writing out the check.

"You don't have to fill that out fella," the salesman said, "all you have to do is sign it and we'll run it through the machine over there," he pointed toward the check writer near the cash register. Shane acknowledged his response, signed the check and handed it over the desk toward the salesman.

"Let me get the directions from you and we will get this delivered within the next week." Hank replied, reaching for the check.

Attempting to pull it from his outstretched hand, he found that Shane's fingers held tightly to the other end. Hank's eyes rose in question.

"I need these items delivered today... as I mentioned before." Shane said as respectfully as he could muster, still holding the end of the check.

"It's already 2:30 sir, I don't think that we can get to it today." He stuttered, remembering that Shane had indeed mentioned the delivery to him before. Hesitantly, he released his hold on the check.

I could see Shane's back muscles tense and a nerve twitch in his jaw. When he spoke, there was a calm authority in his voice. "I apologize Hank, if I failed to make myself clear." He started, "However, I am spending a considerable amount of money here today in your store that I could very well have spent elsewhere."

I sat silently next to him and looked down at the floor, slightly embarrassed. It was easy to see that Shane was used to getting his way and he felt no guilt for pointing out what he intended to have.

"I understand Sir." Hank replied, comprehending Shane's meaning quite clearly. "Let me see what I can do." He moved from the desk and towards the back of the store with haste.

A few uncomfortable moments went by and I wasn't sure if I should say anything. I felt a bit uneasy at this turn of events and even felt pity for poor Hank. Looking over at Shane I could see the frustration on his face. He turned in my direction and his features softened a little.

"I'm sorry." He said softly."I'm used to things going my way."

How should I reply to that? If I said what I thought he might get upset, but being me, I spoke anyway. "You don't say." I teased, trying to lighten his mood. "But wouldn't tomorrow morning be just as good?"

He looked away for a moment and when he turned back he was smiling again. He shook his head in agreement. "You're right. Tomorrow morning would be acceptable."

My lip quirked upward in a doubtful smirk to which he responded to by reaching over and patting my leg. "I will fix it," he said.

At about that time, Hank reappeared with a look of disappointment on his previously contented face. "I'm very sorry Sir, but there is no way that we can load the truck and make an out of town delivery this evening," he paused, "I will understand if you decide to purchase your pieces elsewhere." His eyes fell away in distress.

Shane looked at the salesman momentarily and then responded, "You know Hank, tomorrow morning would be fine for the delivery." With his hand still on my leg that for some reason he had not yet removed, I felt the reassuring squeeze of his fingers.

Immediately the salesman's eyes lightened and the happiness returned to his face. "I'm so glad Sir, they can be there at 8:00 a.m. tomorrow morning!" He exclaimed as he took the check that Shane held back out to him. Standing, he then shook Hank's hand and quickly jotted down the directions to his cabin.

"Tomorrow then?" Shane reiterated.

"Absolutely Mr. Matthews, 8:00 a.m." Hank responded quickly. "I greatly appreciate your business!"

Shane smiled widely. "Thank you Hank, it has been a pleasure."

Standing up to follow him back across the showroom, Shane stopped, letting me come up even to his side. We made our way back across the parking lot and he proved to be the gentleman once again by opening the door. "You don't have to do this every time." I said, looking up to meet his eyes.

His shoulders moved up in a shrug, "It's the right thing to do."

Once in the truck, my curiosity peaked again. "I have to admit that I am quite interested in your line of work." I looked at him boldly but grinning, expecting some kind of answer.

He smiled, "You are, are you?" His fingers moved to the ignition and he inserted the key, firing the truck's engine and again failing to expand on my unsuccessful attempt. It was plainly obvious to me that he didn't want to talk about the fact that he was wealthy or how he got to be that way. I debated on pursuing the issue but decided I had enjoyed the time spent in his company today and if I continued to probe into matters that weren't my business, this could be the first and the last day that I might get to enjoy it.

So far, this had been a wonderful day. Shane insisted on taking me to dinner and allowed me to pick the restaurant. Enjoying our comfortable chitchat throughout the meal, I could feel myself growing more and more relaxed in his company, even with the mystery of who he really was hanging over my head. As we made our way back to the truck I unintentionally walked so close to him that my arm swayed against his and made contact with his bare skin. Suddenly consumed with the feeling of wanting to touch him, I couldn't stop my hand from trailing down to his and intertwining our fingers together. It felt good to feel my hand in his, my fingers nestled within his warm touch.

He stopped walking and looked down at me, a shadow of surprise on his face; desire in his eyes that had been initiated by my touch alone. He lowered his face towards me and I prepared myself for the feel of his lips against mine but instead, they brushed my forehead gently before he stepped back, pulling his hand slowly from mine.

Shane's heart rate seemed to triple with her contact and every sense that he had intensified as he felt her skin against his. Not speaking, he just looked down into the emerald eyes that stared back. She didn't understand what her touch did to him or that it wouldn't take much to send him spinning out of control. Slowly he leaned down and placed his lips against her forehead as that was all that he dared to do before he broke their contact altogether. "I've got one more stop to make before we leave town." His voice slightly wavered from the feeling that he was fighting. "Do you have room for some groceries at your place until my fridge comes tomorrow?"

I nodded, although slightly disappointed at his retreat. "Sure, I can make room." I hoped that he couldn't detect it in my voice.

"Just don't want to have to make another trip in here tomorrow to go to the grocery store." He said.

"Totally understand, it's not a short drive." I mumbled.

I gave him directions to the market that I generally shopped at and within a few minutes we were inside and filling a shopping cart. He piled steaks, steaks and more steaks in the pushcart along with a little chicken, a little bit of pork, fresh vegetables and an assortment of side dishes. Eggs, milk, bread, flour, sugar and a few other staples were added but no junk food. No sweets, no chips, nothing that wasn't nutritious. Nearly three hundred dollars later, we were loading the groceries in the backseat of Shane's four door pickup.

"I guess you should be set for food for a while." I joked after we had finished loading and were on the road toward home.

He snickered."I would sure hope so."

We rode in silence for a few miles before I spoke again. After witnessing all of the purchases he had made that day, I couldn't let it go. "You know, I've noticed today that you must be loaded."

Shane's laughter was thunderous in the inside of the truck. "Loaded, huh?" he continued to chuckle, "I have money if that's what you mean."

"That's exactly what I mean!" I chortled. "Not to be nosy or rude but you paid however many thousands of dollars for some property today, in cash I might add, a sizeable amount at the furniture store and almost $300 in groceries!"

"I'm very frugal," he merely replied, stealing a glance my direction. So that was the answer I was going to get then. Three times I questioned and three times I received a roundabout reply. I supposed that might be his polite way of telling me to mind my own business.

As we drove, the sky began to dim bringing a close to the day and by the time we pulled into my driveway, it was practically dark. I ran up the steps and unlocked the door and flipped on the outside light before I returned to the truck to help Shane pack in his groceries. After about three trips each, we finally got them all inside and with bags scattered on the counter and table, I started to go through each one of them to pull out the cold items. Shane helped me search through the bags, sorting out the groceries that would need refrigerated and grouping together things that didn't.

"Do you want the meat in the freezer or just refrigerator?" I asked as I piled it in one spot on the counter.

"Freezer is fine....if you have room," he answered.

I nodded and gathered up a few packs and headed into another room, returning in a few moments to gather another armload. It wasn't too long and we had everything that needed to stay cold stashed in my freezer and fridge. We then sorted the other items into the least amount of bags that we could.

"Can I leave these here until tomorrow too or will they be in your way?" he inquired.

"Won't be in my way," I said. For a few seconds we just stood in the kitchen and for the first time that day, shared an awkward moment, neither one of us seeming to want to end the day. "Would you care for a beer?" I asked, attempting to prolong his company.

"That does sound good Elisa, if you have an extra." He said as he tried to suppress the anxiety that was starting to work on him. He probably should go home but he didn't look forward to sleeping on the cold floor of his cabin since he still had no furniture.

I opened the fridge and fought past all of the groceries to retrieve two bottles. I turned and handed one to him and then twisted the cap off of my own. Watching as he then removed his and raised it to his lips, gulping the cold fluid.

"Let's go and sit in the living room where it's a little more comfortable," I said, "unless you need to go."

He shook his head and followed her into the next room, his eyes roaming around taking in the cozy quaintness of the little cabin. It was simply decorated but felt homey and comfortable. She sat down on the couch and placed her beer on the coffee table and then motioned for him to sit. He looked at her for a moment, his mind wondering if this was really a good idea. Searching for another place to possibly sit, there was only one more chair and it was clear across the room. It might be a little obvious if he sat that far away. Reluctantly, he finally settled his body on the opposite end.

I picked up the remote and flipped the television on and then picked the beer up and took a long drink. Turning towards him, my eyes found his. "Thanks for asking me to go with you today, Shane," I said, "I enjoyed your company.....and helping you spend your money."

"I enjoyed your company as well. Thanks for putting up with me all day." He laughed as he took a drink and then sat it on the table. Being alone with her here had already started to have an effect on him and he quickly averted his gaze to the television. The news or something was on and he pretended to be interested in it. When he finally looked back over at her, she was staring at him. A flicker of desire suddenly passed through her eyes and he could sense the rapid change in her.

This was not good....if he went to her now, feeling as he did, he didn't know if he would have the power to stop himself once he touched her. His own flesh was betraying him and his wolf suddenly rose to the surface, pushing him with its own primal desires. *Damn!* He stood up unexpectedly, rising to his full height and his hands coming to rest on his hips. Dropping his head, he looked down at the floor as if in exasperation. "Listen, I really should get going. I need to get some things taken care of before the furniture comes tomorrow," he lied as he looked back to her, noting the disappointment on her face.

"Oh……ok," I muttered as I rose from the couch. His actions were contradictory and it was confusing the hell out of me. One minute he was insistent on holding my hand and the next minute it was if he couldn't get away from me fast enough.

"I'll come after my stuff tomorrow after I get the fridge hooked up and it has time to cool off….if that's ok?" he asked, waiting for her answer before he turned away to the door.

"Sure, any time would be great," I muttered.

He then spun on his heel and moved toward the kitchen and to the door. I followed closely behind him but then he stopped and turned around. "Hey, can I get your phone number?"

"Oh yeah, that's probably a good idea," I responded, "I'll write it down." I went to the drawer underneath the telephone and soon produced a pad of paper and an ink pen. Jotting down my number quickly, I tore the paper from the pad and handed it to him.

"Now tell me yours."

He recited his number and I promptly wrote it down and then safely stashed it back in the drawer.

"I will give you a call tomorrow before I come," he said. Stepping forward, he leaned down to deliver a swift kiss upon my cheek. "Good night Elisa….sweet dreams." He turned and opened the door, and stepped out on the deck. I pursued him as far as the doorframe and stopped, "Good night," I answered softly in return.

When he got to the edge of the steps he turned abruptly again. "Hey, just so you don't think I'm a drug lord or something…. I owned a construction business in Canada."There was a bit of humor in his voice as he continued, "And, my mother's family is *loaded,* as you would say."

Grinning back at him, I didn't see a need for any words. I watched as he moved through the shadows of the yard to the truck without throwing as much as a glance behind him. When he opened the truck door, I closed and locked the cabin door and extinguished the light. Hearing his truck start, I watched with discontent for a few moments as the taillights disappeared down the driveway. Hmmm…. Well, there's that. Feeling the loss of his company in the empty cabin after the full day we had shared caused me to feel disheartened at how it had ended.

I glanced at the clock noticing that it was still rather early for bed, but I padded into the bathroom and washed my face and brushed my teeth any way. Going into the bedroom I found my sleep clothes thrown haphazardly on the unmade bed where I had changed in a rush when my unannounced guest had arrived earlier. Once changed, I grabbed my pillow and made my way back to the living room couch. I snuggled under the afghan and flipped through the channels until I found a movie of interest. Exhaling a long, lengthy sigh I allowed my mind to wander back through the events of the day. After spending the entire day with Shane and learning a few things about him, there was plenty to occupy my mind.

I began thinking about the affection he had shown me and my unusual but willing response to it. There had been an uneasy feeling the first time he had refused to let my hand slide from his grasp. One moment I wanted to pull away and just as quickly I found that I rather liked the feel of my hand wrapped up in his. The intelligent side of my brain screamed that this was just crazy and I had only just met him…. *slow down* it said. The emotional side argued that I had enjoyed every second of every minute of his company and I should just go with the flow. Closing my eyes while the two sides debated what was best for me, I dozed off.

Shane dug the keys for the cabin out of his front pocket and walked up to the door. Although it was dark he had no problem pushing the key into the lock and forcing the door open. From memory, he lifted his eyes up the wall to the right of the door and located the light switch. The room was illuminated at once and his eyes scanned the interior of his new home. Empty. He walked to each room, flipping on the light as if he was searching for something, anything. But there were only vacant rooms and barren walls that greeted him.

One abandoned chair had been left behind, old and decrepit and lacking sturdiness in appearance. Shane moved to it and sat down, leaning forward to cradle his head in his hands. He sat there for nearly a half an hour fighting the powerful urge to drive back to Elisa's. At this moment, his loneliness seemed more controlling than any other emotion that he was feeling and he attributed it to the full day he had spent in her company. This pity party was going to get him nowhere.

The chair creaked loudly with the relief of pressure as he stood. He began to move about the house here and there stopping, looking and studying; his brows knitted together in concentration. Running to his truck he retrieved a small scrap of paper and a pen and returned to begin taking notes on his plans for renovation.

I woke up early the next morning from my place on the couch where I had fallen asleep. When I decided to get up I found that I had slept crooked and now had a painful catch in my neck. I rubbed it but it seemed to do nothing. Maneuvering into the kitchen I managed to start the coffee pot and then headed into the bathroom thinking that a hot shower might do the trick.

Shane never slept that night.

Chapter 8

    I still hadn't heard anything from Shane about retrieving his groceries and it was already noon. A slow rain had been falling all morning and I felt laziness had set in for the day. It was difficult to concentrate on anything as Shane drifted in and out of my thoughts. I started a load of laundry, made my bed from the day before and tidied up around the house. After much deliberation I decided to call him. It wasn't as if I was going to get anything accomplished until I heard the sound of his voice.

    He answered after six rings.

    "Hey Shane, its Elisa."

    "Good morning," he replied, his voice deep and groggy as if he hadn't been awake for too long.

    "Um, sorry if I woke you…but I was wondering about your things here," I stated, "Not that they're in my way," I quickly added. They weren't in my way at all but I needed to see his handsome face as soon as possible.

    There was a long pause before he spoke. "How much trouble would it be for you to bring them to me?" he asked, "Would it be a hassle?"

    "No, not at all, I can do that. Are you ready for them now?" I asked excitedly.

    Again, he was slow to respond and I couldn't help but wonder if he had been sleeping. "Yeah….sure," he said softly, "you can bring them anytime if you really don't mind."

    "I don't mind, see you in a bit," I replied.

    "Thanks Elisa," was his only response before he ended the call.

    After what seemed like fifty trips to my SUV, I finally had all of his provisions loaded and was on my way up the long, bumpy drive to the cabin. Pulling in and parking next to his pick up, it was then that I noticed the large heap of boards and broken lumber in the middle of the front yard. What the hell? I got out of the vehicle and stood for a moment, gazing at the destruction. Making my way to the front door I could hear the sound of banging and thumping coming from inside and I knocked softly before pushing the door open and stepping inside.

    Noting the new black recliner pushed safely into the corner of the room, he came out of an area to the left. Shirtless, the sweat glistened on his skin even though the temperature in the house was cool. Looking up, he smiled even though his eyes deceived his exhaustion. Carrying a piece of lumber in each hand, his muscles contracted to accommodate the weight. My eyes traveled across the width of his chest and down his powerfully built abdomen.

"Hi," he said, smiling wearily.

I blushed as I tried to drag my eyes back up to his face, certain that he'd seen me checking him out. "Hi," I replied awkwardly.

"Let me throw this outside and I'll help you unload," he said smoothly as he walked past me, slightly brushing my arm with his own. Following him, I watched as he cast the lumber into the pile and proceeded to my car. He opened the door and gathered up a couple of bags and turned but I met him with outstretched arms. Hesitantly, he handed them over before turning to pick up a couple more. With my arms full I still managed to push the door open and hold it for him until he was inside. We each carried in several loads and littered the kitchen counter with bags.

"This looks familiar," I joked.

He laughed wearily, "It does, doesn't it?"

"What exactly have you been doing?" I finally asked as he started to stack the groceries in the new refrigerator as I stood behind him and handed them to him one by one.

"I'll show you," he responded, taking my hand and leading me into the room he had come out of when I first arrived. I was surprised when I stepped inside. What had at one time been two rooms had overnight, been extended into one large bedroom. He had totally ripped out one entire wall in the span of only a few hours. The new mahogany bedroom set sat safely in one area away from the devastation but the other room bore that brunt of the disorder.

"Wow!" I said, astonished."You weren't kidding when you said renovations!"

He chuckled. "Nope, and last night was as good a time as any to work on it. I have lumber coming tomorrow to finish it out along with more tools."

I shook my head in disbelief, "You worked on this all last night?"

"No rest for the wicked." He grinned and began to explain his plans. I watched the muscles working in his exposed back as he stepped forward, pointing to different areas, indicating his intentions. He was magnificent and I felt my face redden slightly.

I nodded and averted my eyes from his gaze, "It will be beautiful when you get it finished." I wasn't really even sure what he had just told me. His half nakedness had caused a significant distraction and I had only caught bits and pieces of his plans.

We returned to the kitchen and put the rest of the groceries away, making small talk as we worked. Looking around the room I suddenly realized that he had nothing. No coffee pot, microwave, hand towels, soap or any of the other regular things; not even a skillet or pan to cook the food that he had purchased. Shane leaned casually against the kitchen counter as he continued to speak, his voice sounding tired; his body worn out and dusty.

"Hey," I interrupted," I'm going to run home and get you a few towels so you can at least have a shower," I said, moving towards the door.

"You think I need a shower, huh?" he smirked, looking down at the speckled bits of dirt stuck along his forearms.

I softly snickered in response. "You could use one." I paused, "unless you want to come over to the house later and clean up and I'll make some dinner…..I'm sure you probably haven't eaten."

"That sounds great," he answered, "if I wouldn't be imposing." He hesitated, "I've got plenty of food here."

I laughed out loud, "Yeah, you do; but nothing to cook it in!"

Shane smiled wearily at the concerned woman standing in his kitchen. She had no idea that if hungry enough he would devour a raw steak straight out of the package without hesitation, but he agreed that he would see her later. Before turning to leave, Elisa stole one more, quick look and let her eyes wander rapidly over his bared skin before acknowledging with a nod. Watching her cross the yard and get into her SUV, he chuckled; amused at her obvious notice of his naked frame and the interest he saw sparked in her eyes.

Shane worked on things around the cabin until early evening. Then, gathering some fresh clothes, he headed down the driveway. He was looking forward to a nice hot shower to wash the grime away and his stomach had begun to rumble a couple of hours ago indicating that it was ready to be fed. When Elisa opened the door and he stepped in from outside, his nose was filled with the wonderful aroma of Italian spices along with her own unique sweet scent. "Whatever that is smells great," he said, "my stomach has been tormenting me for the past few hours."

I grinned innocently, "If you'd like to clean up first, there are towels in the linen closet to the right of the toilet," I motioned in the direction of the bathroom.

"I sure would, thanks," he replied. With his duffle bag in hand he moved off in the way she had indicated.

The hot water was a welcome relief to his aching, weary muscles at it coursed over his body. He stood for a few moments just letting it soothe his skin before finding a newly unwrapped bar of soap and lathering up. Opening the bottle of shampoo, he sniffed and decided against using it; it was a little too feminine for his taste. He closed the lid and picked up the bar of soap instead, using it to foam through his hair.

Closing his eyes against the spray of the shower head, he let the hot water rinse down his scalp taking with it all of the suds from his hair, down his body to the drain. Turning the water off and retrieving the towel from the hook beside the shower he began to dry the moisture from his skin. It felt good to be clean but it also relaxed him to the point that all he wanted was to crawl into a comfortable bed. Recovering his comb from the duffel bag, he ran it briefly through his hair and then finished dressing. Instead of pulling on his boots, he opened the door with them in one hand and with the duffel bag thrown over his shoulder he padded back into the kitchen in sock feet.

I had set the table and placed the large cheesy casserole in the middle of it. A hefty bowl of salad and a plate of garlic bread accompanied the meal. "Dinner is ready if you want to eat now," I said.

"It smells and looks delicious," He replied as he pulled out a chair and settled his tall frame in it.

"What do you want to drink?" I asked, "I have tea, soda...or water?" I noted the fresh, clean scent of him and his refreshed appearance. The shower had done him good.

He thought for a moment, "Do you have wine?"

My eyebrows raised and I nodded. "That I do," I replied, "White or red?"

"Red would be perfect," he answered.

I busied myself pulling down a couple of wine glasses from the cabinet and then recovered a bottle of chilled wine from the refrigerator. Turning, I placed the glasses on the table, popped the cork and began to fill our glasses. Once his was filled, he immediately picked it up and took a small sip, "This is really good."

"I've only ran across a couple of wines that I really like, I'm generally a beer drinker." I answered back as I sat down in the chair across from him. After spooning salad into my bowl, I cut into the casserole. The cheeses strung across as I placed the piece on my plate and then stood up and walked to the fridge. "I have either Italian or ranch dressing for the salad," I told him.

"Italian, please," he replied. When I turned back around he was just sitting there; waiting.

"Are you going to eat?" I asked before suddenly realizing how rude I was being to my guest. "I'm sorry Shane. I'm not used to having other people here very often...please...help yourself." My face heated up again. It seemed to be a normal occurrence when he was around. His laughter was a warm pleasant sound in my ears. He then began to fill his

Shane consumed an entire plate of casserole and then went back for seconds along with an additional bowl of salad. I made a mental note that he had quite the healthy appetite just for future reference. We finished the bottle of wine and then opened a second and by this time we were laughing and joking with one another as if we had been friends for years, the wine loosening our tongues.

Absentmindedly, I reached across the table and pretended to lightly punch him after one particular jab at my cooking. After dinner was over, I was pleasantly surprised when he assisted with gathering the dishes and putting them in the dishwasher.

We moved our glasses and the second wine bottle to the living room where he sunk immediately into the comfort of the couch. "Man, I am stuffed!" he said, rubbing his stomach. "That was delicious, thank you."

"No problem." I answered and sat down at the other end of the couch. Raising the glass to my lips, I finished the cool red liquid. He did the same and sat his empty glass on the coffee table. Picking up the bottle and filling them both again before slipping off my shoes, I pulled my feet up underneath me on the sofa, the full glass of wine in my hand.

Slumping down in the softness he leaned his head back against the cushions, letting his lids close. "Hey, I've been thinking about something," he said without opening his eyes, "Looks like I need a few things there at home that I hadn't thought about. How do you feel about doing some errands for me in a day or two?"

I looked over at his relaxed form and couldn't resist running my eyes over him now that he wasn't paying any attention. One arm rested on the arm of the sofa while the other was perched on his strong thigh. "Sure, I don't have anything planned," I revealed.

With his eyes still closed he continued, "You probably know what I need ....if I supply the cash, would you go get some things to set me up?" he asked.

My eyebrows raised in question. "You mean like, just go buy a bunch of stuff for your house without you even seeing it?"

He nodded drowsily, "I'll make you a list of some of the things that I know that I need, but for the most part you have a good idea." He grinned sarcastically, knowing she already knew he didn't have much of anything.

I laughed genuinely and casually slapped him lightly on the arm. "What if I buy things that you hate?"

He raised his head and looked over at me, "I can't imagine that you could buy anything that I would hate." He leaned forward and picked up the wine glass and took another drink, "Seriously though, would you mind?"

"Well no, I wouldn't mind to go shopping with your money!" I joked, "What girl could say no to that??"

He laughed as he let his head fall back against the cushion and let his eyes close again, the wineglass still gripped in his hand. He was tired and the effects of the alcohol were winding him down even further. Without warning a yawn surfaced and he raised his hand to mask it. "That's it then," he paused, "I will get a list together tomorrow."

Reaching over, I picked up the remote and flipped on the television. Turning the volume low, I surfed through the channels until I found a movie and then taking another drink of wine, looked over at my new acquaintance. His lids were still closed and he didn't seem to be bothered by the soft sounds of the television. The half full wine glass leaned perilously in his hand and I realized then that he had drifted off. Giggling softly, I reached over and removed it from his grasp and sat it quietly on the coffee table.

After finishing my own wine I picked up his glass and poured it into my empty one and in just a few minutes had drained it as well. Taking the empty glasses I padded into the kitchen and quietly sat them in the sink. There was only a very little bit of wine left in the bottle so I raised it to my lips and let it flow down my throat as well. Taking a deep breath, I peered out the kitchen window. For a moment, I thought that I saw something at the edge of the woods but it was dark and I couldn't be sure. Could it be the wolf? It had been a long time since I had last seen it and I couldn't help but wonder each time if it would be the last.

Making my way to the door, I gently dragged it open and stepped out into the cool darkness. The cold, wetness of the wooden deck seeped through my socks quickly turning my feet into ice cubes as I shifted from one foot to the other. The chilly evening air caused me to shiver and I wrapped my arms around my body attempting to hold in the warmth. The rain had stopped and a three quarter moon along with several stars now beautifully lit up the clear night sky. I looked over toward the area where I had thought I'd seen something, but there was nothing. Standing for a few moments more, I turned back and stepping inside, closed the door quietly behind me.

Going back to the living room I smiled as I looked at the sleeping man on my couch. It was difficult to stare at him without a landslide of unfamiliar feelings crowding in my mind that I couldn't find a reasonable explanation for. Was I lonely? Yes, but loneliness provoked different types of feelings... not this kind.

Trying to ease by him, he reached out and tenderly grabbed my hand as I attempted to pass by. Startled, I looked down into the blue eyes staring back at me. "Where did you go?" he inquired, his voice soft and low.

"Just walked out on the deck for a minute. It's a beautiful night," I whispered. I dared not mention that I had thought I saw the wolf since our earlier conversation about it had been full of obvious skepticism. "I thought you were sleeping."

"I was," he answered as he pulled me down beside him, my leg pressed snuggly against his. "I woke up when you moved.... sit with me."

Feeling the heat rise in my cheeks as the warmth of the electrical charge moved between our touching bodies, I wasn't sure what he was expecting. Forcing me to be this close to him might not be a good thing...or would it? Even more stunning was the fact that he moved his arm around me and pulled me even closer against the side of his body. It felt warm and secure to be so close to him and after arguing with my inner conscious I finally sighed and allowed myself to give in. I snuggled into his grasp and laid my head against his shoulder.

Shane leaned his head back against the couch and sighed. This felt good. Her warmness permeated through his clothes and heated his skin and he could feel the soothing motion of her breathing against his body. Her scent filled his nostrils and roused his senses. This woman was his, he knew it. He had found his mate and he knew that she realized that there was something too, but didn't comprehend why she felt the way she did. The fact that she experienced it gave him extreme joy and contentment.

They sat in comfortable silence watching the movie on TV. Neither Elisa nor Shane cared about what was happening on the screen or the plot that was being played out. Each one lost in their own thoughts about the emotions and feelings that the other's simple touch incited within them.

Chapter 9

I was pulled out of my peaceful slumber by a strange buzzing noise and the sudden movement of my warm, cozy pillow. As my eyes popped open I saw Shane scrambling to unzip his duffel bag, jerking out his cell phone. Desperately he tried to quiet it by punching numerous buttons before pushing it toward his ear. It was daylight and I realized that we had spent the entire night on the couch together.

"Hello?" Shane's voice echoed in the silence of the room. The television was set on a timer and had shut itself off sometime during the course of the night.

I yawned, stretched and slowly got to my feet and glanced at the clock; 7:23 a.m. Shane looked in my direction for a moment and then said, "Jeremy?" A wide smile spanned his face and he moved toward the cabin door and stepped out on the deck closing it behind him, clearly indicating he wanted privacy.

"Shane…. its Jeremy," he heard the familiar voice on the other end of the line and his heart gave a quick jump….he hadn't been sure if Jeremy had survived. Quickly moving to the door, he stepped outside onto the deck.

Jeremy had been his best friend, both of them betas with the same status in the pack. They had formed a fast friendship and had been inseparable for years. When everything had gone down, the pack had scattered and Shane had been certain that Jeremy hadn't left alive.

"Jeremy," he paused, relief in his voice."I didn't think you'd made it out."

"I didn't think you did either, man," the voice replied, "When I got hold of Caleb he told me that he had talked to you…he told me you were coming back."

Shane shook his head. "No, I never said that," he paused, "I'm unsure as to why he assumed that."

There was a long paused before he spoke again. "Well regardless, it's good to hear your voice," Jeremy chuckled uneasily. "There aren't many of us that made it Shane…..I've been trying to locate whoever I can."

"Who else?" Shane inquired, concerned.

Miranda, David and Anna. That's it," he said, "They found each other soon after the…..well…. you know…" he hesitated, "and stayed together with the thought that they'd be safer that way."

"No one else?" Shane asked.

"No…no one." The reply came.

Their conversation continued for a few moments with Shane and Jeremy both revealing where their escape routes had taken them and where they had ended up. Shane explained the purchase of the property and his plans for it.

"Could you use a guy like me around with the overhaul?" Jeremy questioned.

Shane hadn't given having a roommate much thought but he would do just about anything to help his friend out. "I would love to have you here Jeremy. I've got a lot to do on the place yet and could use the extra hands." He paused, "But there's more Jeremy….I've found my mate," he finished.

Shane held the phone away from his ear as Jeremy whooped and hollered ecstatically. When the commotion finally died down, he put the phone back to his ear.

"I'm so happy for you man!" he said excitedly, "tell me about her!"

Shane shook his head, "It can wait until you get here…. She doesn't know." He replied.

"Oh," Jeremy retorted, quickly changing the subject. He gave Shane the details of when he would arrive; they said their goodbyes and each hung up with a more positive outlook on the traumatic occurrence of the past that they shared.

I could hear Shane's muffled voice but couldn't tell what was being said, not that it was any of my business. I moved into the kitchen and got the coffeepot started. By the time his conversation had finished, and he returned, I was sitting at the table with my first cup. I could tell by the look on his face that the discussion had been something serious. Retrieving a mug from the cupboard I filled it and sat it down on the table in front of where he stood. "Is everything all right?"

He nodded and sat down, accepting the hot mug of coffee; his feet cold and wet from the morning dew. "Everything is great," he beamed; his dazzling smile a welcome sight. "That was a friend of mine," he began, "from Canada. He's coming for a visit in a couple of weeks."

"That's great!" I said, noticing his obvious excitement. "Has it been a while?"

Shane smiled broadly. "Yeah….months. We grew up together and are like brothers. He's the closest thing to family that I have. I can hardly wait to see him."

I was genuinely happy for the future reunion with his friend but my mind was preoccupied with the thoughts of the previous evening. As I sipped my coffee I stole a glance in his direction which was met with his sky blue stare. He grinned playfully. "Are you skittish now?" he asked trying to determine exactly where my mind was this morning. "Since we spent the night together?"

"Well no…..well, maybe a little." I said and then more to the point, "But since you brought it up, what exactly is going on here Shane?"

His eyebrows raised in amusement. "Whatever do you mean?" he asked in a teasing tone as a smile spread across his face.

I cocked an eyebrow in his direction, finding nothing amusing in his reply. "Seriously… what is this that is going on here?" I noticed his face turning more solemn as he realized that I was not one to beat around the bush. He reached across the table and cupped my face fondly in his warm fingers.

"What do you want to go on here?" he asked, his eyes searching mine.

Blushing at his forward touch, he smiled softly as he continued to wait for my answer. "You seem like a great guy….but I've known you for like, three days." I paused, "I don't let strange men come in and sleep with me on my couch…….normally," I swiftly added.

His laugh was thunderous in the early morning quiet of the kitchen, "I didn't think that you *normally* did Elisa." But after his laughter subsided; his face took on a more serious tone, "Maybe three days is enough," he said.

"Enough?" I asked.

"Enough time for you to know me," he answered. "It's strange, but I feel that I've known you for much longer." He paused again, "There's some reason that I was brought here…to this area. Maybe you're it."

My eyes narrowed, "Do you believe in that? Fate, I mean?"

"Yes, I believe it. Don't you?"

Not sure how to respond, I shrugged. "I'm not sure."

I gave him a sideways glance before returning to the coffeepot to fill my cup. He got up and followed me, placing his hand on my shoulder. "Listen, I hope that I haven't upset you or made you uncomfortable," he began, "I know that things are moving way too fast and you don't feel like you know me well enough." He turned me to face him. "But please believe me when I tell you that I feel the same way." He dropped his hand from my shoulder and let it slide down the length of my arm to my hand, enclosing it in his. "And I only know one thing for certain," he delayed, "I fully intend to pursue this."

With that, he leaned forward and pressed his lips against mine. For a moment I couldn't respond due to the unexpected shock, but then my body wilted. The next thing that I heard was the crash of my coffee cup as it fell from my hand, disintegrating as it hit the floor and splashing coffee over the entire kitchen.

I jerked away and jumped back. Hot coffee had doused us both and when I looked back at him, he was laughing!

"You think it's funny?" I growled. He grabbed a towel and began mopping at the mess before he responded. I was sure he could see the irritation plainly written across my face.

"I'm sorry Elisa," he said trying to maintain a straight face. "It's not funny." My eyes flashed as I glanced at him before grabbing another towel to help swab the floor and push the glass together in a pile. "I've got this," I said, but he didn't stop or acknowledge that he heard me; he just kept wiping until the last of it was cleaned up.

Shane decided at that point that she might just be a handful when she was angry. When the floor was finally cleared of the mess he had caused, he picked up his boots and sat down in the kitchen chair and began to pull them on. He cleared his throat. "So, now that you know my intentions, do you still feel like doing my errands?" he grinned broadly, flashing that charming smile in my direction that made my insides melt.

Although I felt a bit nervous at his forwardness, I bobbed my head in agreement. "I guess so, if you want me to."

"I do." He replied, standing up. "You don't have to do it today if you don't want but it would be great if you could in the next couple of days....I didn't think about all the stuff I needed before." He grabbed his duffel bag and headed toward the door. "I'd better get home; my lumber will be showing up before long." Promptly, he turned and walked back across the kitchen towards me, leaning forward and placing his warm, soft lips against my cheek. I slightly trembled in response to his touch but he pretended not to notice. "Will I see you later?"

"I'll do it today, if that's what you want." I answered as he backed away. He nodded and smiled, indicating that I had pleased him with my response and he pivoted on his heel and turned toward the door.

I watched his broad back as he moved away from the cabin across the yard. Raising my fingertips to my lips, I recalled the feel of his mouth on mine. He had made his intentions quite clear so now I at least knew where our newfound friendship was headed; if I allowed it. I beamed inwardly at the warm butterflies fluttering around in my stomach and the new emotions that blazed within. I couldn't remember a feeling quite like this one. Smiling to myself, I turned and padded toward the bathroom to take a shower and then take care of Shane's tasks.

Chapter 10

By the time I got there, the lumber had been delivered and Shane had a list of items written down for me to pick up. Looking briefly at it, I tried to suffocate my laughter with my jacket sleeve. Snatching the ink pen from his hand, I began to walk into every room, standing for a few moments before jotting down additional items on his list. He followed me from room to room attempting to peek over my shoulder at what I had written. It wasn't until I was finished that I handed the list back to him with a smirk.

Shane's eyes swept the items with skepticism but soon realized that he indeed needed all of the things that I had added; things that he had failed to even consider. "You're good," he said, handing it back to me. He walked into the bedroom and returned shortly with a credit card and his truck keys. "Here," he announced as he handed the items over to me, "Spend whatever you feel that you need to."

I shook my head in response, "I can drive my own vehicle."

"Nope. Mine's full of fuel and you're doing me a favor. Please, I insist," he requested, "Take mine." Faintly, I recalled how he had previously mentioned that he was used to getting his way. "Oh.. and how you're in town, stop back by Patton's and pick out a washer and dryer and see when they can deliver it if you don't mind," he paused, "Just put it on the card." Dangling the keys in front of me, he smiled playfully.

I snatched them from his outstretched hand along with the list and promptly added laundry detergent and fabric softener, "Got it," I replied, turning and heading for his truck. I figured that it was useless to argue.

"Wait!" he shouted at me after I had turned to walk away. Spinning around, my face crashed into his firm chest. He put a hand on each of my shoulders to steady me from the jolt, my face turning beet red. "Be careful," he said softly, brushing his lips against my forehead, "And thanks for taking care of this for me."

I responded by letting my hand settle on his extended forearm in an affectionate gesture. "I really don't mind." His hands moved down my arms before he broke his contact, letting my hand fall to my side. The corners of my mouth turned up in an uncertain, small smile before I turned and headed to his truck.

As he watched his truck disappear down the drive Shane's mind drifted. He had been right to tell her he was planning on turning their relationship into something more; but would she want him once she found out what lay in wait beneath the surface? It was too soon to unveil the beast the hovered under his skin but the closer that he got to her the more he realized he wouldn't be able to keep it from her. With that notion, the wolf stretched anxiously. It had been a few days since it had been released and it whined persistently as it urged him to let it run. Suddenly compelled to oblige, he removed his shirt followed by his boots and jeans. The late October air was cool against his bare skin as he stood unclothed in the doorway of his new home. He quickly shifted and trotted off toward the woods.

    At the beginning of my shopping adventure I honestly enjoyed spending someone else's money to buy the things that I wanted. But, as the day waned on, my excitement faded and I was ready to get finished and to get back to….well, back to the strikingly good looking man that I had left earlier that morning. It was a little unexpected how often that I found my mind wandering back to his dark hair, blue eyes and muscular form. The touch of his hands were always warm and gentle, the feelings he incited were new and thrilling. Even as uncanny as it seemed, I felt strangely comfortable in his presence and I couldn't wait to get back.

    It was already past dark when Shane heard the low rumble of his truck and saw the headlights. As the lights veered across the front of his little cottage, he opened the door and stepped out, waiting for her to park before moving across the lawn to greet her.
    "What a long day!" I said as I jumped out of the truck, "I thought it would be great spending all of your money but it was exhausting!" Laughing, I opened the back door of the pickup. The dome light illuminated what appeared to be a hundred or more bags covering the seat and the floorboard. Well, maybe not a hundred…
    He smiled widely as he assessed the damage. "Damn!" he stated mockingly, "did you leave anything in the stores?"
    "Not too much actually." I replied grinning; reaching in to grab the first load. Following my lead he gathered up as much as he could carry in his arms and accompanied me to the house only a few steps behind. Sitting everything down in the middle of the living room floor, we returned several more times before emptying the truck. Once the last bunch of full bags had been added to the increasing pile in the floor, I immediately dropped to my knees and started pulling items out of them.

Shane joined in, kneeling beside me on the floor and lent a hand sorting through the clutter but then hesitated."We don't have to do this now," he said as he looked over at me as I busily continued rooting through the bags.

I glanced up momentarily, "Yes we do! I can't leave a mess like this!" I continued rifling through the articles in the sacks. "Oh, and Patton's said they would deliver the washer and dryer tomorrow unless it's a problem. If it is, you are to call them and they'll change the day."

Gathering up several of the items, I got to my feet and headed to the bathroom, returning empty handed. Shane was examining the comforter and sheets that I had chosen for the bed. It was soft suede material in neutral colors of browns, greens and dark reds with matching valances and curtains. The sheet set that I had picked to go with it was a rich dark, smoky green. He looked up nodding his approval in my direction.

"You like it then?" I asked anxiously, hoping that my choice had pleased him.

"I do." He replied, "I'm going to put these on now. I haven't slept in my new bed yet but I believe I will tonight!"

"Shouldn't they be washed first?"

"Nope," he paused, "I'm sleeping in that bed tonight!" he chuckled as he got up and gathered up the comforter and sheets in the wide span of his arms and disappeared into the bedroom.

Watching until he vanished from my sight, I then continued my relentless attack on the bags. Everything was pulled out when I decided to take the pillows that I had gotten into the bedroom; might as well make the bed completely how he was at it. When my eyes took in the display before me, I leaned against the doorframe immersed in laughter.

Shane had hung up the curtains and was now attempting to stretch the fitted sheet across the mattress. Apparently he had experienced trouble keeping the corners on as he was now stretched across it from one side to the other. Lying on the closest side, he was desperately trying to stretch the other corner of the sheet toward the opposite side. Turning quickly when he heard my laughter, he lost his grip on the sheet and it recoiled back across the mattress. Groaning loudly in frustration, he dropped his face against the mattress.

"Do you need help?" I managed to ask through my tears of laughter. There was no way to try to mask the humor from my voice, even if I'd wanted to.

"Sure couldn't hurt," he replied. In a matter of a few minutes, together we had the bed made complete with comforter and pillows. Standing back, he looked at it longingly."I can't wait to get into that later."

His words triggered the image of his warm naked skin sliding across the sheets and I shuddered. "Guess you've got a date later," I muttered towards the comforter, looking down and patting it; a smile dancing mischievously across my face. Oh to be so lucky.

Shane grinned and turned to follow me back out of the room but paused and turned back to the bed. "I'll be back in a little while, my love," he said tenderly. I was in the living room by this time and nearly doubled over laughing at his silliness.

Within an hour I had cleared away the last remaining items from my shopping spree except for the microwave and coffee pot. I left those in the boxes with the assumption that Shane would figure out where they needed to go. Letting out a long sigh of relief at finally being finished, I promptly sat down in the floor and leaned against the wall in exhaustion. "A dining table and chairs would be great around here," I scoffed.

"Yeah, yeah. I'll get to it eventually." He said. "Maybe if my errand lady had thought about that……." He let his voice taper off as he leaned against the doorframe into the kitchen.

I giggled as I reached into the pocket of my jeans and produced a very long piece of paper. "By the way, here's your receipt."

Moving to stand before me as I sat on the floor, he appeared huge as he snatched it from my hand and stared down at it. His eyebrows raised in surprise. "Really?"

"Really." I answered in a monotone voice, and then quickly changed the subject. "Did you get any work done today? I didn't notice a dent in your lumber pile."

"Yeah, a little." He lied. In fact, the wolf had kept him out most of the afternoon and into the evening so he hadn't even continued with his project. "I'll work on it in more depth tomorrow….. Hey, I do have a chair in the other room there." He said, motioning toward the living room.

"Really? A chair?" I answered sarcastically from my seat on the floor.

"Or a bed…." His voice trailed off as he looked down at me. Immediately, my eyes jerked upward and met his blue stare, "I do have one of those now," he said, grinning.

What exactly did he mean by that? Quickly I veered away from his comment, "What time is it anyway?"

"9:43," he replied.

I stretched my legs out in front of me for a moment and started to get up. Thrusting his hand downwards toward me, I took it and he pulled me easily to my feet. "Thanks. I need to get home I guess and let you get back to it."

"It's too late now. I'm not going to do any more tonight. Did you eat how you were out?" he inquired.

"No, I didn't. I'll grab a bowl of cereal or something to fill the void when I get to the house."

"Cereal? That's nutritious," he said teasingly.

"Twelve essential vitamins and minerals!" I retorted, "In fact, cereal is very good for you."

He nodded, concurring that I was indeed right but for some reason, I had a sneaking suspicion that he craved something much more filling. "Well, I thought I'd whip something up if you're going to hang around….but I guess I won't," he looked at me with an innocent pout. There was something very appealing to me about that particular look set into his gorgeous face and I almost felt guilty by refusing to stay. He was a charmer, this one…..

"Another time maybe," I laughed, "I'll take a rain check." Heading toward the door he was only a couple of footsteps behind me when he reached out suddenly and grasped hold of my hand, gently turning me around to face him. His eyes seemed to bore into my very soul and I met his look with a brilliant blaze of green. *Oh crap.* Would I be able to withstand what I imagined was coming without wilting to the floor?

Shane pulled me close against his body and then encircled me within his strong arms. There was no resistance to his embrace as he drew my body firmly against his. I trembled with anticipation as he lowered his lips to mine and swept a tender kiss across them. Feeling the welcoming softness of his mouth, I found myself responding readily to his touch as if I no longer had control. His tongue swept across my lower lip lightly, lingering for a moment before pressing past into my warm, anxiously awaiting mouth.

My legs began to weaken in his gentle but steady hold. The taste of his mouth awakened senses within me and I responded eagerly, pushing my lips against his. My fingers caressed his arms and moved across his broad back. Feeling the demands of his body through my clothes I was swiftly aroused by the notion; becoming heated to my very core. Why did this man have such an effect on me? The kiss turned more passionate, his hands moved down to my sides, bringing my lower body secured tightly against him.

The beast forcefully fought its way to the surface commanding its hunger to be satisfied. *Take her* it insisted, stretching upward against Shane's skin. In response, Shane deepened the kiss and began moving his hands over Elisa's body, touching and caressing. Bothered by the clothes that separated them, he slipped his hands underneath her shirt, searching for the warmth of bare skin. She gasped at the sensation as his hands came in contact with her exposed skin. *Take her now*, the wolf whispered. *She belongs to us.*

This was too much, too soon. I retreated suddenly; pulling back from his embrace attempting to lessen our contact. He withdrew his hands but remained close, his hot breath against my face, his eyes searching mine. "I'm sorry Elisa," he muttered, his voice husky and his breathing ragged, but he didn't release his hold. "I can't help myself….I want….."His voice trailed off before the explanation was given.
My eyes never left his face, "Me too," I murmured softly, my own breath uneven, "But this should scare the hell out of me."
Leaning his forehead against mine he sighed heavily, "You're right. It should."
"I just don't know how I can feel ….like this, when I barely know you," I said, searching for some kind of answer in his eyes.
Shane couldn't reveal the reason; not yet. What he would divulge would more than likely drive her away and he wasn't prepared to risk it. He needed to first strengthen their relationship before he took that step, "I know," he said simply, "I feel it too."
The wolf cringed into the shadows again but he could sense its frustration and disappointment; its lips pulled back over its teeth in a defensive snarl.
"It would be best if I went on home," I admitted as I hesitantly pulled away from the warmth of his arms. He allowed me to slip easily from his grasp but his hands lingered as if he was fighting the urge to hang on tightly. T
"You're probably right…. but it isn't what I want, he confessed.

I nodded and opened the door, stepping out into the cool night air.

The bed was instantaneous gratification as he crawled in between the soft sheets and let the coolness of them settle across his naked body. Instantly relaxed by the suppleness of the mattress, his muscles released some of their pent up tension. Groaning in satisfaction, he stretched his limbs out in all directions across the expanse.

His mind traveled instantly back to the events of the evening and his body began to respond by its own nature accordingly. It was evident that he was having difficulty controlling himself around Elisa and with every encounter that they shared, things proved to be advancing to a dangerous level. He hoped that he would have the strength to thwart the menace that lurked beneath the surface. Mentally deciding that it was time to let her come to him instead of chasing after her, sleep finally claimed him.

Chapter 11

It had been three days since the episode at Shane's. At first, I thought it might be best to just let things cool down a little bit since the response to his closeness were so out of my realm of my character. He hadn't called or came by so I tried to stay busy with my normal chores around the cabin to occupy my mind. It was almost November and today was unusually warm for this time of year so I decided that an outing was in order. It had been a while since I had been down to the lake and a nice fall day of fishing sounded right up my alley. There was nothing like fishing to clear a person's mind.

I pulled my chestnut hair back into a low ponytail and slipped on my favorite ball cap. After tucking the pistol in the back of my jeans, I pulled a sweatshirt hoody on over my t-shirt and went out to retrieve my fishing pole and tackle box.

After filling a cooler with ice and a few cold beers, I grabbed my bag chair before heading out to start the 4 wheeler. The racks on the front and back of it and the bungee straps would hold everything in place. Once it was all cinched down, I started it up and headed down the path toward the lake.

I caught three fish in the first five casts but they weren't large enough to keep. The fourth one was a keeper and I decided that fresh fish may be on my dinner menu. Sitting relaxed in the chair with my legs stretched comfortably out in front of me, I effortlessly cast my line into the deep waters. The lake was calm and my lure made a distinct splash that broke the mirror image of the water. Reeling slowly, waiting for the tug on my line I picked up my second beer and took a drink, letting it trickle down my throat slowly.

It was indeed a beautiful fall day. Scanning the tree line admiring the colorful leaves, my eyes settled on a dark shape just inside the shadows. I strained my eyes in an attempt to make out what it was. Was it the wolf finally coming for a visit? The longer I stared at it, the more I decided it was only a cedar tree that looked odd in the edge of the darkened woods. I missed the companionship of that animal; the silently acknowledged respect that we seemed to share. But, it was wild and may have found its way to wherever it was headed. I felt a sense of sadness to think that I may never see it again.

Spending a couple of hours there and without catching any additional large fish I decided to let the one go free; no sense in dirtying a knife for one fish. Slowly, I loaded all of the items back on the ATV and headed toward home. I began to mull over whether I may have upset neighbor Shane and now he was either purposefully avoiding me or it was that he was working on his cabin. I debated about driving over on the 4-wheeler, but should I? Was it too forward? Maybe he didn't want to see me ....could be why he seemed to be steering clear of my presence.

    The longer I thought about it the more aggravated that I became. After what had happened the other night and now nothing... what does he think, he can just lead me on? I left the fishing pole and chair at the cabin and continued down the driveway to the road in a huff. I had gotten myself all worked up about what could possibly be happening and it was time to find out what was going on in that man's brain.

    When I arrived at Shane's, there was a strange red Ford extended cab pickup parked next to his truck. My eyes quickly took note that the lumber pile had grown with the odds and ends of fresh boards piled in the stack. There was a strike against me – he had been working on the cabin. I supposed then that maybe he had been busy.

    I shut off the ATV and walked up to the door. Only the screen door created the barrier between me and the inside where I could clearly hear the pounding of a hammer. I stood at the door and peered in. A man's naked back greeted my eyes and as if sensing my presence, he turned and stared through the screen at me. It wasn't Shane; startled, I took a step backwards.

    Who was *this* guy? He had a handsome, clean-shaven face topped with hair about the color of my own; dark gray eyes that seem to assess my appearance....almost too eagerly. Built almost identical to Shane with the same broad chest and muscular arms, he was possibly not quite as tall. Immediately, I felt uncomfortable as his eyes lingered on me, judging me.

    As if he had been spoken to, Shane came around the corner of the room; his eyes trained on me. Relief flooded through my body when he came into my line of vision.

    Shane had smelled the sweet scent of her as soon as he noticed that Jeremy's hammer had stopped its battery of the lumber. He smiled to himself with a touch of arrogance that she had finally come around. Venturing around the corner, he found Jeremy staring full on at her through the doorframe while at the same time, he sensed his friend's over anxiousness. Elisa smiled shyly and appeared a bit relieved to see him. Stepping between Jeremy and the door, he pushed it open. "Come in Elisa," he said grinning, "What are you up to today?"

Stepping through the open doorway, I had totally forgotten that I was angry or upset and really couldn't remember what I had been up to. "I, uh....thought I would...um, see what you were doing." I stumbled through the words like an idiot. Shane looked at me with amusement dancing in his blue eyes.

"This is Jeremy," he said, motioning toward the stranger, "My friend from Canada that's only a *week* early."

As I looked over hesitantly, the man met my gaze with a dazzling smile and attentive eyes before stepping forward. He grasped my hand with both of his own in a gesture that seemed a bit overfriendly. "It's very nice to meet you, Elisa," he said in a low, throaty voice.

Shane felt a pang of jealousy deep down in the pit of his stomach as he noticed how Jeremy's nostrils flared slightly taking in Elisa's scent, analyzing her. Witnessing her flushed reaction to Jeremy's lingering touch, an unexplainable anger flashed within him for a moment.

"It is nice to meet you too Jeremy," I replied. Instant heat radiated between our hands and I quickly removed mine from his grasp; turning my eyes back to Shane. Jeremy didn't seem to take note of my rapid retreat but instead moved to stand closer. I could detect his inquisitive eyes grazing over my body.

Shane pushed his way between us and took me by the hand, leading me into the bedroom and away from Jeremy's penetrating stare. "Here's what I've been doing," he said as he gestured toward the newly framed partition.

Jeremy interrupted from behind, "Don't let him convince you that he did that all by himself," he said, a playful grin enhancing his expression. I turned and smiled timidly at him as he leaned casually against the bedroom door frame.

Shane sneered catching Jeremy's eyes with his intense gaze which he acknowledged and then winked, "I hope to talk to you a little more later," Jeremy said, "I'd better get back to work." He looked back at Elisa before he turned and left the room smiling ear to ear.

Shane was suddenly on edge with Jeremy's presence in the cabin. It had everything to do with the way he was leering at Elisa along with his overly friendly behavior. While he could sense her unease over the way Jeremy had initially approached her, he was aware that Jeremy's inquisitiveness was something altogether different.

Elisa shifted nervously bringing Shane's attention directly back to her. He needed to alleviate her troubled feelings but at the same time, he felt defensive. Jeremy's obvious interest produced a twang of jealousy that was only insignificant at the moment but could escalate if provoked. Shane knew that he wasn't a threat but he already felt distrustful.

I broke the silence in a hushed whisper, "Your friend…..he's intense," I said softly.

Shane knew that she was unaware that Jeremy would be able to hear anything that she said no matter how quietly she spoke. He didn't try to mask his own voice for that reason. "He isn't usually that forward," he replied, plenty loud enough for the neighbors to hear…if he had any, "but he knows a beautiful woman when he sees one."

Reaching over, he moved his fingertips across my upper arm letting them trail down the length to my hand. Jeremy chuckled from the living room and then resumed hammering.

"I'll take that as a compliment," I said as I allowed his hand to take hold of mine, his warm touch seeping into my skin.

"So what have you been doing the last few days?" he questioned as his thumb gently caressed the palm of my hand, lessening some of the tension that I had felt earlier.

"Not too much," I answered, distracted by his touch, "Did a little bit of fishing this afternoon but other than that….."

A silly grin graced his face, "Missed me, didn't you?"

I blushed under his direct gaze, "I thought I'd better come and see if you were still here." I teased as I intertwined our fingers together. Stepping closer, his body brushed against mine as he swept a light kiss across my lips. I leaned into him in an attempt to coax him into more but he withdrew quickly before becoming too involved. I gazed up at him questioningly as he cocked his head sideways toward the bedroom door, indicating his company in the other room.

"How about you find your way over later and I'll fire up the grill? There might not be too many more days left like this one." I said invitingly.

Nodding once again toward the other room he raised an eyebrow in question.

"He's welcome to come." I answered his silent query and laughed when he rolled his eyes in response. "But maybe he should drive himself." I openly flirted.

As he smiled broadly he pulled me a bit closer. "That sounds good…..all of it." We walked hand in hand moving from the bedroom back into the living room where Jeremy had continued to work. Again he came to a standstill when we entered the room as he turned his gaze upon me.

"Care to come for dinner later Jeremy?" I asked as my eyes met his for a brief moment and then I purposefully averted them.

Again, he smiled radiantly. "I would enjoy a good home cooked meal." He said, "It's been a long time," he paused, "and maybe we'll get a chance to talk." He added as he glanced over at Shane accusingly.

"About 5:30 then?" I inquired, looking back and forth between the two.

"Perfect." Jeremy quickly answered.

"I'll walk you out." Shane said as he followed her to the door throwing a glower over his shoulder towards Jeremy who didn't even notice as he watched Elisa walk away. Shane was fuming. There would a discussion as soon as he went back inside. Best friend or not, there would be no disrespect when it came to her and his ogling was unacceptable.

"So, 5:30 then?" he confirmed as she climbed on the 4-wheeler.

I nodded, adjusting the bill of my cap. "Yep."

"I can tell that Jeremy makes you nervous." He said. "He'll be fine later…you're just…..new." he joked. "He's just being friendly."

I laughed softly. "Friendly?.......Extremely."

Shane couldn't stop his laughter "Like I said, you're an attractive woman and he is just acknowledging that."

"I'd better go and get some things started," I paused, "I'll see you in a bit."

"Okay." He said and backed away as I started the ATV and headed down the driveway.

Shane immediately headed back to the cabin and swung the door open wide when he entered. Jeremy turned to see the annoyance reflected on his friend's face. "Alright Jeremy….what the hell?" he inquired, the anger evident in his voice.

Jeremy shrugged. "Hey man, just checking out your woman…..oh but wait," he said sarcastically, "You haven't made her your woman yet, have you?"

Shane growled lowly. "Just what are you getting at Jeremy?"

"I'm just messin' with you Shane," he paused, "but she is quite an attractive woman." He smiled; his gray eyes meeting Shane's fiery blue stare.

"She's off limits."

"No shit…damn…loosen up a little bit. You got all uptight the moment she walked in here." Jeremy stated blandly.

"Well I looked over at you and you had your tongue hanging out!" Shane proclaimed.

Jeremy laughed loudly. "It wasn't quite that bad."

"Damn near it."

"She just smelled so good……and those deep green eyes," he paused, "and that little body…….." He provoked. He knew he was getting under Shane's skin; which was his sole purpose. Throughout their lives he had always enjoyed that ability.

"Alright,…enough asshole!" Shane snarled and lightly punched him in the arm.

" Okay, okay, I'm just messing with you." Jeremy shook his head grinning sheepishly. "You know me better than that." Suddenly his face turned a little more serious. "But, I will offer you some advice."He paused, "You need to claim her. Put your mark on her. My wolf would love to get a hold of her." He ribbed.

Shane contemplated Jeremy's words and knew that even though he had said it jokingly, he spoke the truth. There was something that the wolf respected if it could smell another male on a female. If not, the primal instincts of the wolf far surpassed that of its human to contain or control it.

Shane nodded. "Maybe you should just stay here tonight…."

Jeremy appeared upset. "Ah, man…….Don't make me miss out on a home cooked meal." He replied. "I can't remember when the last time was that I had one." He paused before adding, "I'll be on my best behavior."

After a few moments of thought, Shane consented. "Alright. But if you get out of line, we're leaving." Jeremy dipped his head in approval while Shane moved off into the bathroom to take a shower, leaving him to his own thoughts.

Chapter 12

I heard the rumble of Shane's truck and stepped inside away from the grill to prepare the table. Having set three places I was now waiting for the steaks to get done so actually, they were right on time. As they exited the truck and came across the yard, I found myself lost in the sight of the two as they moved fluidly toward me. Both were superior in build to any of the men I had ever seen and markedly handsome in their features. I suddenly felt the heat rise into my face. *Damn*! Deciding that they must just grow them big and handsome in Canada, I had already made the decision that if things didn't work out here, I was packing to move.

"You're right on time," I said as they came up the steps to the deck. Shane carried a twelve pack of beer in one hand while his other arm move to encircle my waist pulling me close for a quick peck on the cheek. Jeremy smiled as he caught my eye but quickly averted his gaze from Shane's show of affection.

"You can put that in the fridge if you want," I said and watched as Shane retreated into the cabin leaving me alone with Jeremy. My eyes met his briefly and I gave an awkward smile.

"I can tell you're nervous around me," he confessed as he gazed at me, "I'm sorry that I make you feel that way."

"It's okay," I responded hesitantly, "Maybe we should just start over, okay?"

Relieved, he smiled widely and extended his hand toward me, "I'm Jeremy."

I took his hand firmly in my own and grinned. "Nice to meet you Jeremy... Elisa," he held my hand a bit too long and then instantly withdrew as Shane returned from inside; clearing his throat nervously.

"Something smells great," Shane said as he walked toward us. "T-bones?" he inquired.

I nodded, "Yep. How do you like yours cooked?" At the same exact time, Shane and Jeremy both stated, "Rare." And then they looked at one another and laughed together, a friendly boisterous laugh that somehow put me a little more at ease.

The smell of the meat on the grill brought back a memory to Shane as he inhaled the aroma and reminisced about a time when she had shared this exact dinner with his wolf. Recalling also how later, she had lain side by side on the deck with him, her hand caressing through the thick fur along his side as she had stared into his eyes .That memory brought him extreme pleasure because she had accepted him then, for what he was. She just didn't know that it was him. Would she one day accept him knowing that he was the wolf that she had once befriended? The sobering thought brought about a sudden seriousness as his eyes swept across her face. She didn't notice and was instead caught up in a friendly exchange with Jeremy; her eyes concentrated on his face. Shane once again felt his wolf shift restlessly.

 I enjoyed the meal and the company without incident while listening intently to the memories the two had shared. I agreed that they were indeed like brothers and I couldn't help but laugh as they spoke about their past predicaments. I tried to imagine what kind of chaos the two of them had wreaked together. Soon, I realized as the evening progressed, that I had taken Jeremy all wrong from the beginning.

 My eyes wandered across his face as he spoke and I found reassurance in the fact that he was Shane's friend and a now a part of my newfound relationship; whatever it was. I listened to their tales of growing up in Canada and once in a while a name would come up in conversation which would result in a look passing between them before they moved on. At first I found it odd that they didn't go into detail about the people that they mentioned but I could only assume it was because they realized I had no idea who they referred to.

 With the 12 pack of beer nearly gone that Shane had brought with him, I produced another. After a couple hours of drinking, we were all laughing and joking with one another and I felt relief that the evening had turned out so well. Even though I had initially been uncertain about Jeremy in the beginning, my nervousness simply vanished in the course of the night.

 I searched and found a bottle of unopened whiskey in the cupboard and we decided to play cards, the loser being required to take a shot if they held a losing hand. After several rounds, I quickly found myself to be the loser more often than not. Feeling the effects of the alcohol in my system, I gazed over at my opponents; their images a bit hazy in my vision.

 Shane had noticed it as well, "I think maybe we should call it a night," he said as he reached over and ran his hand down my arm. "You won," he said jokingly.

 I laughed loudly, slurring slightly when I spoke, "If I won, why do I feel so drunk??"

They laughed at me and Jeremy remarked, "Well, maybe you didn't win at cards but you sure won in emptying that!" he said motioning toward the nearly empty bottle on the table near where I sat.

Shane's troubled eyes looked over me, "Are you okay?"

I nodded slowly, "Oh yeah, I'm fine," I muttered as I pushed the chair back from the table. Starting to stand my legs failed me and I saw the floor coming rapidly upward. I would have fallen if it hadn't been for Jeremy's quick reflexes. Briskly reaching over, he grabbed my arm roughly, saving me from a hard fall that would have no doubt resulted in bruises. Laughing hysterically, I couldn't even speak as I gripped his arm.

Jeremy looked across the table at Shane who quirked and eyebrow, "I don't think she's fine."

"Yeah, me neither," Shane replied, "I'll help her get into bed and then we can go."

Jeremy looked at him in puzzlement, "Uh, I'm not sure we should leave her. What if she pukes in her sleep and chokes to death?" He looked over at Elisa; she sat with her head leaned against one hand, eyes closed and oblivious to the conversation about her.

Shane's brow creased into a frown; he hadn't thought of that. Maybe he could just help her get into bed and maybe sleep on the couch so he could hear her during the night.

"You want to take my truck home then?"

"No," he replied, "I think I'll run…….It's been a while."

Vaguely hearing the conversation, Elisa interrupted, "Run? "

Shane could see her confused face as she tried to comprehend.

"Now?" Not hearing and answer quickly enough, she gave into the unconscious nagging and dozed off again.

Jeremy's glance towards him was one of concern that Shane shrugged off, "She won't remember in the morning," he whispered as he tilted his head toward her. "I might be home later. It just depends on what happens here."

Jeremy smiled but Shane detected a hint of something else flash across his face.

"Alright then buddy," he said. "I'll see ya when you get home. I'm going to leave my stuff in your truck." Jeremy mentioned as he headed out the door.

Shane nodded and turned back toward Elisa.

"Elisa?" he said softly, stroking his fingertips across her forearm. She stirred and opened her eyes for a short time before her lids closed again, "Elisa, don't you want to go to bed?" he asked.

"Yes," she said slowly and once again attempted to stand. Shane moved hastily to her side and leant support that she gladly accepted. In one fluid motion, he bent down and scooped her up; cradling her in his arms as he effortlessly carried her towards the bedroom. His movement was smooth and gentle as he laid her on the bed, positioning her head comfortably on the pillow.

Reaching behind, he even went as far as to pull her hair loose from the ponytail allowing it to spill darkly across the paleness of the pillow case. Moving down, he pulled her boots off one by one and set them neatly to the side. Shane stared at her for a moment as he studied her deep breathing before turning to go back into the other room.

"Shane?" she uttered, her voice soft with sleep. He turned to meet her blurry gaze, "Stay with me?"

His eyes searched hers although he knew that she couldn't see him very well. "I'm not leaving," he paused, "I'm going to stay on the couch for a while until I'm sure you're alright."

Shaking her head sluggishly she added, "No…..stay in here with me," she slurred.

He stood silent for a moment in the effort to mull over his next move before he returned to the bedside. Settling on the edge of the bed he attentively stroked her hair away from her face while she lay there silently, evidently enjoying the soothing feel of his hands. He thought she had dozed again but when he stood, she took hold of his hand, urging him to stay. "Lay with me?"

She wasn't in any shape to take their relationship to the next level nor was that his plan but her pleas consumed him and all that he could think about was lying next to her warm body; his arms wrapped around her.

God help me, Shane sighed heavily in the darkness of the room trying to free some of his building tension. He knew that this situation might not be in Elisa's best interest or his own but standing up, he removed his boots anyway and allowed them to fall heavily to the floor.

Stretching his rigid body on the bed next to hers, she immediately moved closer to him; snuggling against the length of his side, her hand coming to rest on his chest. In the dimness, his eyes shifted nervously as he struggled to remain motionless.

Already his body had involuntarily begun to react to her touch and he forced his mind to veer off in a thousand directions in an attempt to flee from the situation. But each time he allowed himself to acknowledge her warm breath against his neck he came crashing back to reality. He shifted on the bed, turning to face her; his lips only a few inches from hers.

Sensing his movements and the sudden loss of the heat of his body against hers she nestled closer until she was pressed firmly against the front of him. Stiffening as their bodies compressed, he wondered if she was too drunk to notice his arousal. Her hand explored the plane of his chest and then journeyed downward across his stomach. Shane inhaled sharply and then found his lips upon hers, his tongue tracing the fullness of her lower lip. She answered his kiss passionately, shoving forward against his mouth until he overtook hers completely with his own.

My hazy mind was racing like crazy. God knows I hadn't planned it this way but here I was a drunken floozy throwing myself at my neighbor........a man that I really didn't know very well and that I had only just met a few days before. I told myself to stop the madness, but I didn't have the will. It was if my body had a mind of its own and it knew what it was after.

His hands moved over me tenderly investigating every curve while his mouth continued its own exploration. I matched his inquisition with my own hands; prompting him to pull his shirt free and remove it. Pursuing mine, within seconds he was lifting it off over my head and pulling me tight against him; skin to skin. The feeling of his naked flesh pressed into mine was overwhelming and I ground my hips tightly against his. My entire body was tingling with the electrical current that seemed to originate from every point where our skin mingled together.

The wolf began to emerge from deep down, pushing and manipulating his mind. *Take her!* And then Jeremy's words loudly echoed...*my wolf would love to get a hold of her*. Shane realized that until he put his mark on her she was fair game. Intensifying the kiss, his arms encircled her and unfastened the clasp on her bra and pulled it away. Crushing her against him, the sensation of her bare breasts against his chest encouraged him.

"I want you, Shane," she murmured groggily against his mouth. He pushed her away, rolling her over on her back roughly and straddling her, hovering above at arm's length. His blue eyes began to take on an ethereal glow as he felt his teeth begin to lengthen from his gums. The wolf was at the edge and ready to assert his dominance over the female while Shane struggled to maintain some control over it. It demanded that he take her, it insisted that it was time but Shane's own mind fought it. It wasn't the *right* time.

Elisa panted heavily from beneath him as she arched her body upward. As much as the wolf wanted this and as much as Shane wanted it; he couldn't do it. Not tonight and not this way. He pulled away slightly, causing her brow to furrow in confusion, "I can't," he said with frustration.

"But I want you…." I begged, my voice trailing off, "I need you." I whispered, rising up from the bed to trail soft kisses down his neck. He stopped me by placing a hand on my shoulder and gently pushing me back down on the bed.

"I want you too." He answered, "But you're drunk and I want you to remember."

"I will remember," I said pleadingly, "I promise."

The scent of her arousal filled his nostrils and urged him to fulfill her promise. "I don't think you will." He responded, his voice husky as he stared down into her imploring gaze. Could he dare give her what she wanted and still control himself at the same time? Her hands pulled his face back to hers and she kissed him fervently, urging his responsiveness. Groaning against her mouth, his hand traveled to her breast, encircling and kneading it in his warm hand. His mouth left hers and moved down her neck and across her chest. Suckling from one breast, he teased the nipple with his teeth and then moved to the other. Her hands tangled in his black hair as her body twitched underneath the searing heat of his mouth.

His fingers found the button on her jeans and in a few short moments he had removed them along with her underwear. Quietly he stood at the end of the bed and let his eyes drink in the sight of her naked body against the quilt. He fought the response of his own again, telling himself that this was not about him tonight; his time would come later.

Placing his large, warm hands at the top of her thighs he let them move slowly down the length of her smooth legs, across her thighs, knees and shins and then back up again. His mouth followed the same path as his hands as he worked his way down one thigh and then back up the other. Lingering over her, his wolf shoved forward once more and Shane felt the prickling through his body as it struggled for power. His eyes smoldered a bluish haze underneath the dark lashes while fangs began to extend from his upper and lower jaws. In the midst of his present conflict he heard the lone, low howl of a wolf in the distance and his eyes automatically averted to the window.

His attention being unfocused for that short few moments gave his wolf the opportunity it had been waiting for and it surged forward relentlessly. Staring down at his hands on either side of Elisa's legs, the unimaginable had happened; they had been replaced by huge black paws.

Even though impaired by the alcohol I had consumed earlier that evening, I felt the absence of Shane's movement and through blurry eyes I searched for him toward the foot of the bed. Barely able to make out a dark shape there, I waited for my vision to clear. When it unclouded I gasped at the image that manifested before me. The eyes that met mine from the end of the bed were the same blue tinged shade as Shane's but the luminous glow that was emitted from them was anything but natural. Its front legs were planted on either side of my naked body and the tongue that lolled from its mouth dripped saliva onto my bare skin; its teeth gleamed in the dim light.

I yelped in surprise and scrambled away from it, pressing my back against the headboard and oblivious to the feel of the wood digging into my skin. The fear that coursed through my body had suddenly made me more coherent than I had been for hours. A scream caught in my throat as it leapt fully up onto the bed; its feet leaving deep impressions in the mattress from its bulky weight.

With nowhere left to go there was nothing I could do but cringe away as it slowly approached my huddled form and stretched its massive head towards me. Its breath was hot against my cheek, its eyes staring with intent. Too petrified to move, I was frightened that any small fraction of motion might provoke it so I sat motionless trying not to breath. My mind reeled as I sorted through the hazy events. Where was Shane? How did the wolf get inside the house….

Its body leaned heavily against my pulled up legs and its muzzle moved down the length of my neck. "How did you get in here?" I whispered nervously, hoping that it would recognize my voice before it decided to rip out my throat. It hesitated as it listened to my words and then I felt its hot, wet tongue lick across the top of my collarbone. Slowly, I reached my hand up and placed it against its neck; my fingers sinking into the deep fur. It tensed against my touch and I prayed that I hadn't made a fatal mistake.

Close to the surface Shane continued to revolt against the wolf's hold. He could see Elisa, could sense her fear but could not reach her. With her touch the wolf stiffened, the fur along the top of its shoulders began to bristle and Shane felt its hostility build. Backing away, a low growl emitted from deep down within its throat. With everything he had, Shane plunged upward. The beast growled and snapped, shaking its monstrous head sending Elisa tight against the headboard in fear, her arms covering her face. It fought hard against him as it toppled heavily from the edge of the bed to the floor and then was still.

Trembling, I dared not move but slowly lowered my arms and gazed cautiously over them, searching the darkness. Even though I witnessed its rage and heard the crash as it tumbled to the floor, I didn't comprehend what had just happened. I could hear its breathing from off the far side of the bed combined with the wild beating of my own heart.

Almost too horrified to look, I envisioned the animal rising up in my face as I peered over the edge so instead I sat there, silently anticipating what would happen and what had happened. This couldn't be my wolf...it had never acted so violently or aggressively. As minutes ticked by, my fear was overcome with curiosity and I shifted toward the edge of the bed, pausing to see if there would be any consequence to the movement. When nothing happened, I peered over the side.

The eyes that looked up at me weren't the eyes set deep into the dark fur of the wolf's face. The eyes that stared back into mine were Shane's. My breath caught in my throat and I pushed away from the edge startled. I couldn't interpret what I was seeing; couldn't wrap my head around the disappearance of the wolf and Shane's sudden return. Stunned, confused and bewildered all at the same time, I made a hasty retreat toward the opposite side of the bed but was stopped abruptly by Shane's strong fingers gripping my arm.

"Elisa, please," he said. His voice sounded weary and tired.

Wrenching my arm free, I jumped off and fled toward the bathroom. Catching me again at the door he pulled me with ease against him, holding me without difficulty even though I resisted.

"Please," he said softly, "Let me explain."

I stared up into his solemn face, "I don't know if you can explain in a way that I will understand." Suddenly very aware of my nakedness combined with the stress of whatever had just happened, my stomach lurched up into my throat. I needed to vomit. As if he had noticed it too, Shane released his hold on me and I bolted into the bathroom slamming the door.

After a few minutes of retching and emptying the contents of my stomach I kneeled on the floor, clutching my midsection. I still felt sick. Grabbing my robe from the back of the door, I wrapped it tightly around me and with impending dread left the bathroom to face whatever waited outside that door. Moving as if in slow motion, my fingers hesitated on the cool doorknob before turning it and stepping out; what would I find waiting for me?

I searched through the dimness until my eyes settled on his frame. Sitting on the edge of my bed clad only in jeans; his head bowed forward into his hands; an indication of the utter defeat he had experienced. Standing in the doorway, I was hesitant to move any closer although I felt compelled to go to him.

When he turned to meet her eyes they betrayed her fear and confusion and he sighed deeply. He owed her an explanation and he had no idea where he should start. With pleading eyes he held out his hand towards her hoping that she would accept it. "Please," he whispered.

I didn't know what to think or how to feel; I was in shock. Part of me wanted to rush to him and allow him to enfold me in his warm embrace but the other part was confused and frightened. My mind was spinning as it tried to sort out what I had seen and make sense of what had happened; but it wouldn't allow me an easy solution. "What just happened?" I asked; a tremor in my voice.

"Please Elisa….come," his voice was strained.

I wavered in the doorway; shifting nervously from one foot to the other before I took a cautious step toward his outstretched hand. When I was close enough, I placed my hand uncertainly in his and he pulled me gently down on the bed beside him. I remained tense and he could tell that any abrupt move on his part might send me fleeing towards the door.

"I won't hurt you," he said as he affectionately stroked my hand, "I would never hurt you."

Staring into his eyes I suddenly had a striking revelation. I finally realized the familiarity that I saw there in the deep blue color, the familiar easy feeling of being in his company……..Shaking my head slowly in disbelief I quickly withdrew my hand from his grasp and edged away. "I don't understand this Shane…." I murmured.

"I know." He said soothingly, closing the space between us and picking my hand up from my lap to hold it once again in his own. His fingers wrapped themselves within mine, his voice soft and persuasive. "Believe what your eyes are telling you."

I couldn't even speak; there were no words to express my thoughts or what I wanted to say or what I wanted to demand him to explain. I shook my head, the distrust apparent on my face.

Convinced that she was too distraught to speak, he continued. "The wolf and I," he paused for a moment studying her sober countenance, "are one and the same."

My eyes lifted to stare into his for few short seconds and then I looked away. When I turned back to face him I was certain he could see the question and apprehension reflected there, "How can that be?"

Shane was exhausted and he closed his eyes briefly before exerting the extra energy to open them again, "I'm a werewolf," he said bluntly.

My startled reaction was one of skepticism and confusion all rolled into one enormous emotion. This wasn't real……this wasn't the story he was trying to convince me of, was it? "Werewolves aren't real," I retorted.

He shook his head while his eyes never veered from my face. "I am proof that they are indeed, real."

My eyebrows creased together in a deep frown and I wasn't sure whether to be scared of this man with his obviously unstable mental condition or feel sorry for him. Mostly, I felt confused why the wolf had been here and where it had now disappeared to.

"It isn't like you see in the movies or read about. I'm not a vicious killer preying on helpless humans under the light of the full moon," he explained; his voice tired and sluggish. "It's not like that."

He seemed to wait for me to say something but I was beyond knowing what to say. "You've seen something that is…….. unnatural," he said, "But believe me when I tell you that we are the same."

"You didn't believe me when I told you about the wolf," I responded frantically, "And you're telling me now that it's you?" I began to laugh; on the edge of hysteria.

He scoffed at me but his face remained serious, "The first time we met you pointed a pistol at me," he hesitated waiting for my response but all that I could muster was a blank stare. "You fed me a T-bone steak…."

"How do you know about that? Have you been spying on me all of this time?" I questioned, my voice at the breaking point.

A flash of irritation crossed his handsome features, "Elisa…just listen to what I'm trying to tell you. Isn't what you've just seen proof enough?"

"Okay, okay…stop!" I snapped. "There has to be some reasonable explanation."

"Damn it!" he growled back at me, "Would you listen to what I'm telling you? The wolf and I share the same body, but it has its own mind. Most of the time I can control it," he paused. "Tonight I was distracted and it seized my weakness to gain power."He sighed and let his fingers softly rake across my arm, his voice calming. "I know you don't understand….I'm not trying to convince you to accept this right now, but I hope over time……..you might."

I felt bewildered, "I can't believe what you are telling me! You really want me to believe this inconceivable story?" I jerked away from him again and stood up moving silently towards the bedroom door before stopping and turning to peer at him accusingly. His weary eyes followed my every movement. "I think you should go." I uttered.

He didn't question or attempt a rebuttal but instead stood up from the edge of the bed and found his boots and shirt where he had discarded them earlier. Unhurriedly, he dressed and walked toward me; brushing against me purposefully in passing. Once he had his jacket on and was headed toward the door, he turned for the last time and spoke. I still had my back to him as I remained positioned in the bedroom doorway. "I hope that this conversation is far from over Elisa." He said faintly as he opened the door and disappeared into the darkness.

I breathed a sigh of relief… or was it relief? My mind was a jumbled mess and I was torn between the feelings that I had developed for Shane and this unexpected madness that he was attempting to convince me of. How could I believe a story generated by someone who I didn't know very well….and quite possibly not at all? Even with all of that to think about, I couldn't deny the fact that he stirred feelings within me that I had never experienced before. It was unfeasible for me to entertain the possibility of truth to his story, I didn't believe in werewolves, vampires or any of that other supernatural nonsense. But yet I was having a difficult time trying to find an acceptable explanation of where the wolf had materialized from...

Hearing the sound of his truck start, I moved to the window to watch the taillights disappear into the darkness. I checked the door and locked it and then lay down on the sofa while my mind continued to work through the craziness. It all circled around and ended back at his story; his justification. I felt sick to my stomach. My feelings had been stepped on, crushed beneath the weight of his fictitious tale, even if it hadn't been on purpose. This perfect guy had been too good to be true and now I knew why.

Part of me struggled to find a shred of truth. There were things that happened that he couldn't possibly know. The first time I encountered the wolf, the steak dinner; how would he know those things? I grasped at any straw I could conjure up just to keep my heart from breaking. The wild story was bad enough but along with it my hopefulness of something wonderful was sucked downward into a spiraling endless drain.

As Shane opened the door and stepped inside, the warmness of the room brought sleep even closer. His body and mind had persistently nagged him to lie down somewhere so they could both rest and rejuvenate themselves, but upon his return home, he was met with an interrogation that he hadn't been prepared for. As soon as Jeremy heard the door he met Shane in the living room; his gaze questionable.

Holding up his hand, he silently indicated that he had nothing to say but his friend had little intention of accepting the gesture. "Glad to see you made it home," he chuckled.

Shane's eyes locked on his for a moment in warning but then quickly softened. None of what had happened had been any fault of Jeremy's. "Yeah.....thanks," he replied as he moved into his bedroom and collapsed across the bed with Jeremy close behind.

"You alright man?" The sound of his voice revealed his concern.

"Yeah, I'm alright," he breathed in deeply, "Just an unexpected turn of events."

"What do you mean? What happened?" Jeremy asked as he leaned against the door frame.

Shane raised his head to look at him, "Let's just say that the cat is now out of the bag."

Jeremy quirked an eyebrow in question, "Really?" he paused, "How'd that go for ya?" A wide grin spread across his lips.

Shane let his head fall back against the mattress before responding, "It didn't," he said, "She thinks I'm some kind of crazy weirdo." Shane spent the next half hour bringing Jeremy up to speed on what had happened.

He told him how the wolf had overpowered him and he had exhausted himself trying to fight it and now Elisa was freaked out over what she'd seen. Presently, he had very little indication as to where they stood since she had been informed him that she wanted him to leave; he had without a fight.

"I didn't want to force her to talk about it right then; how it was fresh. I hope that with some time, she'll come around and accept me for what I am."

His friend nodded in agreement. "Probably best that you handled it that way," he said. "Shane, we've always heard that the bond between true mates can't be denied," Jeremy added, "If you know that she is yours and you're certain that you are hers; then it's only a matter of time," he added.

Shane kicked his boots off and rolled onto his side to face Jeremy while he wadded the pillow under his head. "I'm certain……." he yawned sleepily and then continued, "I've never felt drawn to someone as I am to her," he closed his eyes.

"Does she know that I'm the same as you?" Jeremy's voice broke through his fading consciousness. Shane opened his eyes and peered at Jeremy through the small slits that his lids allowed.

"The conversation didn't get that far." he answered as he once again allowed his eyes to shut. This time they remained shut and Jeremy didn't pursue the conversation further.

Chapter 13

The crisp breeze of November aided to the progression of the fall season that had been initiated the previous month. The trees were now barren with only a few brown, brittle leaves clinging haphazardly to the stark gray limbs; fluttering against their inevitable fall to the barren ground below. The air held in its grasp the anticipation of the approaching winter.

Adrift on an endless river of depression I floated farther and farther from reality. All that I truly longed to do was sleep and I spent much of my time lost within its secure folds. During those precious hours my mind could at least find some comfort and peace. When I was awake, I fought hard against the cruel truth that had stared at me ruthlessly; eye to eye. And although I felt confused, another part of me yearned to rationalize the justification that Shane had so plainly handed over to me.

Jeremy's truck traveled the gravel road and turned sharply into Elisa's driveway. On the brink of his own insanity, he couldn't take the pressure any longer. It had been nearly a month since the episode between her and Shane and they had not communicated since. With every passing day, Shane's mood had continued to darken and Jeremy had allowed him space hoping that Elisa would come by, call or make contact with him in some way, but she hadn't. Now, Shane was consumed by hopelessness and Jeremy didn't have the ability to bring him out of it. All along he had done his best to stay out of it as it wasn't his concern, but something had to be done.

He pulled up beside her SUV, got out and walked with purpose up the steps to the deck. Knocking loudly on the door, a few minutes passed before he saw the curtain sweep to the side and Elisa peer out from behind. After an additional few moments ticked by, the door opened slowly.

"What do you want?" she asked sharply from behind the safety of the door.

"Can I come in Elisa?" he questioned while dropping his gaze from hers in what appeared to be exasperation.

With suspicion on my face, I contemplated my answer but then finally nodded and pushed the door open, turning away as he entered. I had no reason to believe he meant me any harm, but his company wasn't welcome and I wasn't one to offer false pretenses.

When his eyes fell on her his jaw dropped in disbelief. She had once been a curvy, lively female but the figure in front of him wasn't the same that he remembered. Her skin was pale, her frame thin; her jeans hung loosely off of her hips. With eyes that seemed to have sunken into her face, she appeared exhausted. Jeremy looked up and saw that she had noticed his eyes wandering over her and quickly responded. "Did you quit eating?" he asked; attempting to make a joke of it.

Not finding the humor in his remark, I sat down at the kitchen table and picked up my coffee cup with indifference. "What do you want Jeremy?"

Pulling a chair out from the other side, he sat down and clasped his hands together as he placed his arms on the table. "We need to talk," he said blatantly, "This shit has gone on too long."

My gaze swept unresponsively across his face, "I'm not much in the mood for your demands....or in fact, your company."

The smile that touched his lips was almost wicked while he stared unsympathetically into my eyes. "You don't care what I have to say then?"

Truthfully, I cared....I cared a lot.

I took a sip of my coffee and sat it down in front of me, "Say what you came to say."

He nodded then, as if he could see past my cool exterior and knew what skulked underneath. "I'm not here to talk you into things one way or the other, as I really don't care." he lied convincingly, "But you and he desperately need to work whatever this is out so we can all get on with our lives."

"I have been getting on with my life," I snapped; my words immediately met by his ridiculing laughter.

"Really?" he scoffed, "Look at you! You look like you haven't eaten or slept for days! If you want to call that living then you and I have two very different ideas of what that is." He could see a flash of anger in her emerald eyes so he proceeded. She needed to get angry, needed to feel something besides self pity. "You need to get off of your ass and quit feeling sorry for yourself."

"Feeling sorry for myself?" I angrily replied, "Do you think that's what I'm doing?"

Jeremy's face turned somber, "Actually, yeah I do," he paused, "But what I also think is that you miss him," His gray eyes pierced into hers, "But you're too damn stubborn or maybe too stupid to take a chance on something because you're scared of it….." His eyes challenged her, "Look at you…you're lost in your own depression while Shane is over there drowning in his misery…. It's really very sad," he said sarcastically as he motioned the direction of Shane's cabin with a wave of his hand. His mood suddenly lightened by the heavy weight lifted off of his chest.

My anger began to diminish as I thought about Shane feeling as disheartened and upset as I did. "But I *am* scared of it," I said, "He's not right……"

"Not right?" He asked me, his eyes narrowed.

"He's *your* friend," I argued, "You should know better than anyone that he isn't stable. He told me some wild story that I think he actually believes and I'm not sure that I want to be mixed up with it,"I paused, "He's crazy, maybe even a lunatic!" I couldn't read the reaction to my words in Jeremy's face, but I had a feeling that the rest of our conversation would not be a pleasant one.

"A crazy story, huh?"His voice was strained as his eyes bore into mine. At once I felt intimidated, not only by his tone but by his unflinching scrutiny and I looked away.

"Tell me this crazy story," he demanded. I could see his hands were clenched together, the knuckles turning white and although I didn't understand his tension, I felt it all around me, squeezing me from all sides.

On edge, I proceeded hesitantly to tell him what had transpired that night leaving out some of the more private details, but followed it with Shane's unhinged explanation. He sat quietly while I spoke, evaluating my face with every word that passed across my lips until I had finished.

"Is that it then?"he asked derisively.

Scowling and a bit confused by his mocking but direct question, I answered, "Yes, that's it."

He lifted his hand and rubbed his chin thoughtfully. Nodding, he leaned back in the chair for a few seconds before he stood abruptly. "Are you ready?"

"Ready for what?" I snapped.

What was going on here? Maybe he was as crazy as Shane…..maybe I had fallen into an entire nest of crazies! Alarmed, I watched as he pulled his shirt off over his head in one swift motion exposing a thick muscular chest and then kicked off his boots.

"What are you doing?" I demanded to know; startled but at the same time, overwhelmed by curiosity. When he began to unbutton his jeans I looked away, a blush heating my cheeks. Sensing my unease, he stopped and stared at me with a spark of humor illuminating his face.

"Don't worry," he said simply, "You'll see in a just a minute where this is going….." He flashed a brilliantly white smile.

Growing readily uncomfortable, I watched in silence as he peeled away the last remaining shreds of material from his body. Averting my gaze from his nakedness, I stared down at the floor, the walls, the ceiling; anywhere other than towards him.

"What are you doing Jeremy?" I questioned nervously again.

"Look at me," he replied in a deep, low voice. When I hesitated to turn my head toward him, he screamed at me, "Look at me…now!"

Shocked by his unexpected change of tone, I twisted my head in his direction. What I saw there I would never forget, something incredible and unbelievable happening right in front of my very eyes. Never in my wildest imaginings or dreams could I have fathomed the astounding phenomenon that I couldn't tear my eyes away from, not only due from fear but also morbid curiosity. The truth that it represented would be imprinted on the brittle, yellowed pages of my mind forever and it changed every perspective that my rationale had fought for.

In a matter of mere moments, the blink of my stunned eye, the man that had stood before me contorted and changed, twisting grotesquely until he was no longer a man. In astonishment, the breath that I drew in sharply, wedged in my lungs and I was unable to force it back out again. The room began to lightly sway and then swelled into a dizzying speed and with it; dark fog crept into the edges of my vision until all was black. I was falling.

A stabbing throb of pain in my head hurtled me forward to consciousness and I struggled to open my eyes. Disorientated and dazed, I could barely make out the face that hovered above me or hear the constant drone of the deep, thick voice. *Are you ok? Are you ok?*

Suddenly, the memory of what I had seen washed over me like frothy waves and I bolted upright. It was a mistake. The pain compressed into my skull, digging and penetrating and I raised my fingers to the back of my head searching for the source. A large, warm hand materialized comfortingly against my back.

"Are you alright?" Jeremy asked again with concern evident in the deep tone.

With clearing vision I looked over at him, my face alight with disbelief. His fingers moved from my back and then lightly across my scalp.

"Quite a bump you've got there."

"I'm fine," I managed to say. Remaining seated there in the floor, I attempted to gather the scattered pieces of this shocking new puzzle.

"Not such a crazy story, now is it?" He asked softly. His condescending behavior from previously had vanished.

I sighed while my eyes sought his for answers, "I don't get this," I admitted.

Jeremy exhaled with relief, "I know you have questions. Probably millions of them," he paused, "I'll answer any that you have the best that I can."

It was an open invitation and once I got to my feet and sat down at the kitchen table, I emptied my brain of everything that I could think to ask him. Jeremy was obliging and held true to his word. Nothing that I inquired about went without a thorough explanation.

"I want you to understand that it is possible to lose control of the wolf. It depends on the personality of the person as much as the circumstances and the emotions. In Shane's case, it happens only rarely if ever, because his personality is very controlled and patient." Jeremy explained, and then chuckled, "As for me, I'm a different story."

She grinned for the first time since he had arrived and Jeremy felt he had made the right decision in coming to her. Sitting in that kitchen chair for nearly two hours, he answered her questions and explained the way of his kind to her. Starting from the beginning he told her about pack life and the close relationships that made up the strength and structure of the pack. He mentioned that he and Shane both were betas in the hierarchy of their pack and that the alpha was the highest power and the decision maker for the entire group. He explained that most werewolves were born that way but some were made.

"From a bite, right?" she questioned. She had slowly discovered a new respect for Jeremy during his visit; he was proving to be an invaluable source of information.

"No, its more complicated than that. There is a lot involved that I'm not sure about," he lied, not wanting to reveal that information to her. Feeling that Shane should be the one to discuss that aspect of their lives as it might be something that they would later share together. She seemed to accept that answer and moved on and soon the conversation dwindled. Jeremy decided that he had told her everything that he possibly could and standing up from the table, picked his jacket up from the back of the chair.

"Shane needs to see you, Elisa," he said, "I've been concerned about his state of mind for the past couple of weeks. He doesn't eat, doesn't sleep and doesn't go out of his way to have a conversation, if you know what I mean. He's denied the wolf for so long now that I'm afraid when it finally surfaces he could be lost within it." He waited a moment before finishing, "This whole situation has hit him hard, and he's worried he's lost you." He pulled the jacket on and headed toward the door.

A crushing guilt flooded over me. Shane wasn't a lunatic and in fact had tried desperately to talk to me but I would have none of it. He had been devoted to me, even sheltered within the body of the wolf he had been with me for months and I hadn't known. In retrospect I thought about the episode at the lake when the black wolf had first appeared, the dinner that I had shared with it and falling asleep beside it only to wake and find it gone….the night with Randy. Until now, in this instant, I had never realized that Shane had been with me constantly, watching from the shadows. My heart flipped within my chest. I had to make this right.

"Wait, Jeremy," I said, following him to the door, "Will you take me to him?" He smiled broadly and suddenly grabbed me, pulling me against him in a one armed hug.

"I sure will!" he said enthusiastically, "Grab your coat!"

He turned me loose and I pulled my jacket from the back of the door, shrugged my arms into it, and we left the cabin. As we drove, I couldn't help but stare over at him. His persona was arrogant and uncaring yet I had caught a glimpse past it to what was really beneath his hard exterior. When he felt my eyes on him, he turned and looked at me.

"Thanks," I muttered softly, "I appreciate the time you spent with me today…shedding some light on things."

He smiled back, "I know," he said as he reached over and patted my leg, "It's all going to work out."

Chapter 14

Pulling into the driveway the cabin came into view and I immediately saw Shane working on the new deck. He didn't turn around when he heard Jeremy's truck but instead kept busy, his head down and his back to the approaching vehicle. Even though the air was chilled, he was dressed in only a T-shirt; seemingly oblivious to the cold.

After parking, we both got out and while Jeremy proceeded toward the cabin, I walked hesitantly a few steps behind him.

"Hey there, Shane," he said in a cheerful greeting, "How's it going?"

He continued on and disappeared inside, leaving me standing there in the yard. He had done what he could do....the rest was up to us.

Never turning around, Shane responded, "Fine." and then continued with his task without even looking in Jeremy's direction. Suddenly Elisa's scent filled his nostrils and he whirled around, his eyes falling upon her. Their eyes met and an endless weight of emotions exchanged in the empty air between them. Dropping the hammer that he held, he stepped off of the new deck onto the ground and strode slowly toward her as if his eyes might be betraying him.

When he reached her, he stared down into her apologetic eyes.

"Shane...." she began, but her words were muffled as his strong arms tightly enclosed her body within them. Holding her close, he buried his face in her hair as he inhaled her fragrance. The wolf inside reacted like a puppy, wagging its tail and whimpering with excitement.

Jeremy watched the scene unfold before him from his hidden position inside the cabin. Nodding with satisfaction he smiled to himself as he turned away from the window.

I returned his embrace, pressing my face against his wide muscular chest. The feel of his arms around me was comforting and I nuzzled in close; my body relaxing against his strength. It was several minutes before he loosened his firm hold, kissing my forehead before pushing me to an arm's length away. His eyes traveled down my body and I could see the concern flicker across his face. When they came back to connect with mine, he softly spoke while his hand caressed my arm. "You've withered away to nearly nothing," the sound of his voice was filled with regret.

A faint smile crossed my lips, "I'm okay," I said as I studied his face, "You?"

My hand moved across the expanse of his chest before settling on his bare forearm which was surprisingly warm. Pulling me close again, he inclined his head toward me, letting his forehead rest against mine.

"I'm much better now," he said as he closed his eyes and sighed deeply, "I have missed you.....terribly."

"I missed you too," I began, "and I'm sorry."

He shook his head, "I understood then and I understand now.....don't be sorry," he said. "Something happened that I should have been able to stop. You couldn't wrap your head around it...It's my fault."

I placed a hand on either side of his face and looked intently into his eyes. "Jeremy showed me," she paused, "We talked for a long time and he explained a lot of things."

A hint of worry flickered in his eyes, "He showed you?" his voice slightly skeptical, "So *he* talked you into coming here then?"

"No," I defended, "He didn't have to talk me into it. You're the reason I'm here. Jeremy just helped convince me that you were worth taking a chance on."

Shane smiled, suddenly more relaxed, "He *can* be convincing," he said, "What exactly did he explain?"

"Everything, but there will be more questions. I'm not sure that I will ever completely comprehend that this entire thing is……..real."

"I know that and I'm prepared for it," he answered. "Let's go inside...its cold out here," he said as he grabbed hold of my hand and led me toward the cabin.

As we entered, the aroma of onions assaulted our noses and upon further investigation we found Jeremy in the kitchen bent over the counter, dicing the offending vegetable. When he turned, his eyes were watering severely.

"Damn things," he mumbled as he looked at us. He would never, in the span of his lifetime, admit to any one that it wasn't just the onions.

Shane proceeded over to him immediately and grasped his free hand pulling him into a one armed embrace and then patted him affectionately on the back, "Thanks man. I owe you."

Jeremy smiled as he looked first at Shane, to Elisa and then back to him again, "We're brothers," he said, "Your happiness is important to me," he paused, "Plus, in a couple of more days I was going to kill you and put us both out of your misery," he chuckled.

A broad grin spread across Shane's face as he looked down at the onion that Jeremy was dicing."So…what are you doing?" he asked.

"Well, seems that Elisa looks just about ready to starve to death and I know you haven't eaten in a few days…..so I'm making stew," he answered, a mischievous grin accompanying his reply. "Why don't you two spend a little time together and I'll call you when it's ready."

Shane smiled back and then turned, took my hand gently in his own and guided me towards his bedroom. Once inside he closed the door behind us, picked me up effortlessly and sat me down upon the thick, comfortable mattress and then proceeded to pull my boots off. Suddenly apprehensive, my questioning eyes followed his movements as he slipped his off as well and sat down on the bed beside me; turning his piercing blue eyes to mine, I could see his heartache.

"Can I just hold you for a while?" he implored, his voice faintly pleading. I nodded and in a moment he had wrapped his arms around me and pulled me down on the bed against the length of his tall frame. His body was warm and the security that I felt in that moment was unlike any other I had felt before. Jeremy's words echoed in my mind……this felt right.

Shane sighed contentedly as he nestled against her and felt his muscles begin to relax. To say that he had been on edge was mild compared to what he had been experiencing the past month. The wondering and the hoping had engulfed his mind and he could think of nothing else but her. Now she was here and it was as it should be. With his mind unwinding and his tense muscles loosened up he drifted into calm dreamless sleep next to the woman that he loved.

Shane was awakened by the smell of something delicious permeating his senses and his stomach began to grumble in response. Elisa still slumbered peacefully in his arms and he hesitated to wake her but he was famished. He softly kissed her forehead and let his hand wander the length of her side tenderly caressing her awake. When she finally stirred and opened her eyes, he smiled at her.

"I think that dinner is ready," he whispered, "Are you hungry?"

I smiled timidly, "Yes, I'm starving," I said, taking a deep breath.

Before he allowed her to rise, he snuggled closer alongside her, shifting his hand down to the small of her back and drawing her nearer. He buried his face against her neck and kissed her where he could feel the hot pulse of blood in her veins.

"You have made this the best day of my life so far," he said softly against her skin. When he pulled back her green eyes held tears but she was smiling.

"I don't know why I feel this way about you," I said, "But I can't deny it."

He hesitated and then answered, "I can tell you why," he paused, "if you really want to know."

At that moment there was a light knock on the bedroom door and Jeremy's muffled voice came through.

"Dinner's ready if you want to eat," he chuckled and then added, "or not…..whatever."

I was still waiting for Shane's response but my stomach was growling crazily in response to what my nose could smell. Shane dismissed my inquisitive look and instead grabbed my hand, pulling me up with him.

"Let's eat something," he said, "and then we can finish this conversation if you want."

Nodding, I allowed him to lead me out of the bedroom and into the kitchen where Jeremy had already filled three bowls with the scrumptious smelling stew. There was also a plate of freshly baked rolls sitting in the middle of the table.

"This looks and smells soooo good," I said hungrily.

Jeremy's laughter filled the room. "Anything would look and smell good if you hadn't eaten for a few weeks!"

I cocked a cynical eyebrow in his direction as I pulled my chair up to the table.

Shane glanced in Jeremy's direction, "Really though, it does smell great."

They ate their meal accompanied with easy going conversation. I listened intently while the two talked about the future plans of the cabin and perhaps establishing a new pack.

"Why did you two decide to leave your pack any way?" I leisurely questioned as I took another bite of stew. Glancing up, I noted the uneasy look that was exchanged across the table. Then the both of them quickly dropped their eyes as if concentrating on their bowls. For a few seconds neither spoke and then Shane looked over at me.

"I wanted a new start," he paused, "but that's a story for another time," he said as he easily dismissed the subject.

Finishing our meals in silence, it was obvious to me that neither of them wanted to talk about why they left Canada. I would accept that...for now.

When dinner was over, I helped clear the dishes away and clean up. Both of them seemed to have retreated into their own worlds since the mention of them leaving their pack. Deciding that since I had initiated some kind of strange awkwardness now might be a good time to head home. Looking at the time, I realized that we must have slept the afternoon and evening away.

"I think that I need to go home now," I said, looking back and forth between them, "Jeremy, again, dinner was delicious and I appreciate that you went to the trouble."

He smiled playfully; his sense of humor always at the surface. "It was no trouble at all. *I have to eat too* you know."

I smiled back and then Shane cut in, "I'll drive you home," he said as he grabbed his coat that was hanging on the back of one of the chairs. His mood hadn't lightened much since my inquiry and I couldn't help but wonder what exactly had taken place in Canada as I pulled on my own jacket. I started to follow Shane out but hesitated and turned to look at Jeremy. When my eyes settled on his face he was no longer smiling. Giving him an uncertain smirk, he returned it with a slight nod. I turned and left.

The ride back to home was strangely quiet and uncomfortable, as though I had exceeded my limitations for questions that day. Shane was solemn and barely spoke as we turned the curve into my driveway. He pulled up and stopped and shut the headlights off but left the motor running as if he was waiting for me to get out.

"Okay," I said sharply, "Have I made you mad or upset you?"

He snapped his head around to stare at me, "Made me mad?" he questioned, "No, of course not."

"Then what is it? You barely spoke the entire trip home and now you seem anxious to get rid of me," I said hurtfully.

His mouth crooked in a doubtful half smile, "I never want to get rid of you," he said, "I've just been thinking a lot about Canada since you brought it up and there are a lot of things that you should know," he paused, "but I'm sure that now is the time with everything else that has happened."

"Now is the perfect time Shane," I responded. "You know how I feel about all of this….what else could there be that I need to know?"

He looked away momentarily and then his blue eyes pivoted back to mine, "It wasn't that Jeremy or I wanted to leave Canada, "he started, "We were driven out."

"What do you mean……driven out?"

He sighed before continuing, "There was a traitor within our pack." Shane's voice was on edge as he spoke, "And in a nutshell we were set up to be slaughtered," he said as he looked at me. "Many of our pack died and the rest of us had no choice but to scatter in order to protect ourselves….."

"How did they……..die?" I asked softly seeing the pain reflected in his face.

"It was another pack that came in and attacked us. We were celebrating a bonding that night and we all had assembled together in our recreation building," his voice wavered as he spoke, "We were feasting and partying….having an enjoyable time together; friends and family. We were an easy target and didn't even know it." He exhaled sharply, the anger apparent in his voice as he continued.

"They came as wolves from every entry way into the building; trapping us…..some lingered in the doorways to block our escape while others attacked. They went for the females and children first…….ripping out their throats and leaving them to bleed out. Everyone that was still standing bore down on the offenders with a violent hatred like none I have ever experienced before." His voice was shaky with rage. "We all shifted; tearing and shredding whatever we came into contact with until our Alpha bellowed above the commotion that we were to all run." He paused, "Most of us remained and continued to fight……..until he was taken down; and then we ran; or those of us who could run, did."

My face held the look of horror and my hand moved up unconsciously to cover my mouth. Eyes wide with terror, I listened as he continued.

"Like I said, we all scattered…..none of us knew who had survived and who didn't. Jeremy and I both thought that each other were dead….I headed south and ended up here after a few months on the move. Jeremy was a couple of states over when he contacted me." He hesitated, "There are only three others that I know of…..still in Canada."

I could barely speak; the shock responsible for the lack of words forming on my tongue. Shaking my head I was sickened by the thought of the senseless killing of helpless, innocent children.

"That is awful……was your family…..murdered?"

"None of my immediate family was killed," he said, "My father passed away a few years back and my mother lives in Boston. I have no siblings." He paused, "except for Jeremy. He's the closest thing that I have."

"His family?" I questioned.

Shane shook his head. "No, Jeremy came to our pack young. No one really knew about his family or what happened to them. One of the elders in our pack brought him in but we never knew his whole story. I still don't." He seemed to relax as he talked about his close friend.

"Some of the other boys started picking on him and they cornered him one day with the intention of beating him senseless," he smirked, "I showed up in the midst of it and together, Jeremy and I took care of those bullies. We've been best friends ever since," he finished, smile gracing his face. "

"Why did the other pack attack yours?" I inquired, my eyes never leaving his face.

His eyes locked on mine for an instant before he spoke. "Many of my pack had associations with humans," he said, "To be more exact, several were bonded to humans."

Again he waited as if allowing that to sink in, "Many full bloods feel that it is goes against werewolf law to allow a human into the pack…..and they feel strongly enough about it to kill. At least that is what I speculate. I don't think that I'll ever know for certain."

"Bonded……….is that the same as married?"

He nodded, "In a way," he began, "But it's more than just a marriage." He studied her face and knew she didn't understand.

"Let's leave this conversation for another time, shall we?" he asked reaching toward me, appearing to have come out of his dark thoughts.

Moving closer, I allowed his hand to caress my face and then I reached up and grasped his hand in mine, "I'm sorry about your pack Shane," I said softly, "I can't imagine what you've gone through."

He smiled at my apology and bent his head towards me, his lips brushing lightly across my cheek. "I retreated into the wolf for a long time afterward," he breathed against my neck, "I had very little power over it and I didn't want to control it. I just wanted to keep running..........until I found you."

He feathered kisses down the soft line of my neck to the top of my collarbone and then back up the other side before tenderly brushing his lips against mine. My mouth yielded to his and within a few short moments he deepened the kiss, his tongue sweeping across my lower lip before probing further.

The energy began to build between us as my body started to tingle in reaction to his touch. His body was warm and firm as he pulled me against him; his lips crushing demandingly against mine. Growing impatient with our bulky coats his hands were soon underneath mine, traveling down the length of my bare back. I pulled slightly away breaking our connection and his eyes searched mine for an explanation.

I returned his look with a timid smile, "Come inside?" I whispered softly.

Chapter 15

    Shane didn't hesitate but instead exited the truck and came quickly around to her side. He scooped her up from the seat and carried her across the yard, his lips finding hers again before stopping long enough to climb the steps and carry her inside. They stumbled through the darkness into the bedroom with their arms wound tightly around each other, mouths pressed eagerly together. Shane moved his hands inside of her jacket and pushed it down her arms before removing his own and letting it fall to the floor. Moving back to her, he embraced her in his strong hold once more, letting his hands rest on the small of her back.

    Moving my hands across the expanse of his broad chest and down his muscular arms, I stood on my tip toes searching for his lips. As if realizing my predicament he hoisted me up to his level and kissed me deeply as he moved toward the bed, laying me down gently across the quilt and hovering above me on his elbows.

    Shane could see her perfectly in the darkness, her emerald eyes searching through the shadows. She couldn't see him....not like he saw her beauty illuminated through his unnatural eyes. He studied the outline of her delectable mouth, her slightly upturned nose, the curve of her neck as it disappeared beneath the neckline of her shirt. Bending down, he swept his lips along the path that his eyes had previously traveled, from the tip of her nose, across her mouth and down her neck.

    She stirred against his warm caresses fueling him to continue his exploration. He moved his hands down to the bottom of her sweater and pulled it up over her head. Raising her arms to make it less challenging for him, he grinned in the darkness as he removed it and tossed it into the pile with their jackets. Reaching under her, he unclasped her bra and threw it to the side, moving his hands tenderly over her breasts. He lowered his lips to each one before instantaneously removing his own shirt which he pitched to join the others on the floor. Crawling up to lie against her, her warm skin against his exposed body aroused his senses as he sought her soft and inviting lips.

    My body ignited with excitement when his skin came in contact with mine and I found myself quickly surrendering to his every touch and every kiss as if my body had a mind of its own. I didn't fight for control because I wanted this man in every sense of the word. Returning his kisses passionately, my hands smoothed across the searing skin of his back, pulling him closer. He progressed down my legs and removed my boots which fell with a heavy thud on the wood floor. For a moment, my mind was jarred back to the last time that we were alone like this, in this room and as his fingers worked open the button on my jeans I stiffened. He hesitated as he looked up into my eyes.

"What is it?" he asked; his voice thick with passion but soft and considerate.

"Nothing," I whispered, reaching for him in the darkness. He stopped and moved upwards, reassuring me with his tender kisses across my lips and jaw. His fingers moved back to the zipper and he dragged it slowly down. Leaving my mouth for a moment he tugged the jeans down across my hips to add them to the collection in the mounting heap.

His warm hands moved up her hips and gently pulled her underwear down the length of her legs and removed them while his eyes hungrily devoured her nakedness. A pang of guilt flickered across his face as he observed the thinness of her frame before he finished removing the rest of his own clothes.

My eyes searched the shadows before I felt the bed give under his weight next to me. I could only barely make out his form as he slid his arm around me and pulled me against the length of his exposed body. His breath was hot on my skin and I involuntarily shuttered. Moving his hand down the small of my back and over the swell of my rear, he lifted me against him tightly, the hardness of his arousal pressing into me. His mouth trailed hotly down my neck and across the concave indent between the neck and collarbone before he slid lower.

The wolf paced anxiously just beneath the surface as it sensed the anticipation growing. Shane felt its presence pushing up against his skin; the familiar prickling. *Wait,* he urged it, *we will have what we both want if you will wait.........*his silent words seem to coerce it into submission and it retreated, but not far.

Shane's hands lingered on her breasts as he gently moved his fingers over the taut nipples. While his hand massaged and caressed one, he inclined his head so that his mouth could tease and lightly nip the other. He soon moved his attention down the plane of her stomach and to the junction of her thighs. His lips left a moist trail down the inside of her thigh before settling on their destination.

He inhaled deeply, his nostrils flaring as he breathed in the scent of her. The blue of his eyes began to smolder and he felt the sharp stab of pain in his gums as the fangs demanded to be freed. *If you wait, we can both have what we want,* he pleaded with the beast again as he attempted once again to contain it. With it restrained, he continued.

My body quivered as I felt the first stroke of his tongue as it explored and tasted the moist, hot core. He was unrelenting and soon I was squirming with pleasure as he lightly bit and sucked the most sensitive part. I moved my hands into his thick black hair and encouraged him, the release already beginning to build within me. He continued his assault until he knew I couldn't take much more and he stopped, moving up to position himself between my legs. Reaching my hand upward, I grasped his hot, throbbing erection gently in my hand. While startled at first with the size, I soon became excited by the mere thought of it pushing inside.

Shane's heart beat wildly in his chest and although he was finding great ardor in feeling Elisa's hands on him he was concerned. If he prolonged this, the chances of the wolf trying to take over were considerable. It would quiet once it knew that she belonged to them and then Shane wouldn't face this predicament again. He bent down and kissed her, his lips remaining there for a moment before he tenderly laid her back against the quilt.

He swept his lips across her cheek and down her neck and returned to her breasts while his hand moved between her legs. His fingers found the wetness there and he pushed one slowly inside, building a rhythm as he continued to suck and nip at her nipples. Her breath began to come in shorter, heavier gasps and her hips pushed up against his hand. Quickly moving to center himself with her, he gently pushed the tip inside of her waiting, wet pleasure. Slowly he pulled back and eased himself in a little deeper each time; she gasped as the final slow thrust filled her. He was still for a moment, allowing her body to conform to his thickness before he moved again. It took all that he had not to turn loose on her and give her all that he had but he knew it would hurt her; so he waited. She began to move underneath him, pushing her hips up into his, urging his movement.

My body quickly adjusted to the size of him and began to demand response. The feeling of being stretched around him was arousing and he responded with his own slow movement; thrusting slowly as my body moved to meet his.

Fully sheathed, he shuddered as he relished the tightness that surrounded him. He had wanted for far too long to feel himself buried deep inside her, to feel her naked flesh against his and her body writhe beneath him. Initiating a slow rhythm that she quickly reciprocated, together they built the velocity that produced a shimmer of sweat over both of their bodies.

My breathing increased and a soft moan escaped from my lips as I launched into the climb that would give me release. Shane felt it too and his excitement mounted as he thrust harder and deeper, leaning close over me.

His mouth sought the soft skin of her neck; he could hear the pulsing of her blood in his ears as loud as thunder. As his arousal continued to mount he felt the unmistakable ache in his gums as the fangs pushed through; extending to their lengths from his jaws. Grazing the warm flesh along her neck that concealed the pulsating blood beneath, he fought the urge to sink his teeth into the yielding tissue, to mark her as his own.

Teetering on the edge for only an instant, I was soon liberated. I groaned as the first waves of pleasure began to rack through my body. Shane felt the spasms of the innermost muscles contracting around him initiating his own orgasm. He throbbed with each thrust, emptying himself within me. I was suddenly startled by the unexpected sting as his teeth abraded my skin and I tensed beneath him bringing his activity to a halt.

As quickly as they had descended, the long teeth dissolved back into his gums. Withdrawing slowly, he moved from above her to lie against her, his hand traveling up her thigh and coming to rest on her stomach. He watched through the darkness as her fingers searched her neck for the source of the sting. When they came away damp her eyes sought his face questioningly through the shadows.

"Blood?" I asked in a low, hoarse whisper; concern flashed through my clouded eyes.

Shane swallowed hard, "Just a little," he paused, "I'm sorry."

"You bit me?" I interrogated.

"Yes….. but only a scratch. I didn't mean to do it………..at all," he answered as he moved his fingers across the small wounds. Although really only scrapes they oozed just enough blood to leave its trace over his fingertips. "There's more that I need to tell you."

She rolled to face him and rested her head against his chest.

"Later," she said softly, "You can tell me later."

Shane reached for the quilt and pulled it over them and then embraced her, pulling her body close. Resting his chin on the top of her head, he closed his eyes; a feeling of contentment growing from deep within him and settling over every plane of his being. His wolf was quiet for the first time in months.

Chapter 16

I was awakened in the early morning hours as I felt Shane's hand moving over the length of my body. He lay behind me; his body pressing against mine and I could feel the hardness of his anticipation against my backside. Breathing warmly against the back of my neck he began to lightly kiss along the top of my shoulder. Pushing my hips back tightly against him, I encouraged him to move his hands over me, to find the sensitive core between my thighs. He stroked gently until my breathing increased and I squirmed against him with eagerness. Pushing into me little by little until he was fully enclosed within my gratifying confines, I forced my hips back to meet his thrusts. Soon he felt the pulses of my stretched body tense around him and his release came. Once again we lay snuggled together in each other's arms and sleep crept over us.

When I awoke again the light was filtering in around the closed curtains and I wondered what time it was. Shane was still asleep; his arm lying across my side protectively. I studied him as he slept peacefully, his skin and hair a dark contrast against the pale sheets. Smiling, I silently acknowledged the magnificence that lay in the bed beside me; he was intriguingly handsome and I couldn't help but wonder why he didn't already have a lover or wasn't married.

The thought caused a twinge of jealousy and I scowled. I didn't want to think of him touching another as he touched me. Carefully, I moved his arm and slid slowly off of the bed but not before I bent over him and lightly kissed his rough cheek. He stirred for a moment but his eyes didn't open so I turned and padded quietly towards the bathroom. Looking in the mirror, I traced the two splotches of dried blood with my fingertips. They were merely scratches but I felt a shiver of apprehension wash over me.

The hot water was a welcome feeling as the shower drenched my hair and body, my mind reflecting on past night and I smiled. Lost in thought, I failed to hear the shower curtain open as Shane slipped in behind me. With eyes closed against the suds as I soaped the shampoo through my hair, I was startled when his hands took over the task. I didn't turn around but instead allowed him to lather my hair and run his soapy hands down my body.

"Good morning," he murmured against my ear as his body pressed up against mine from behind. His soapy hands moved down the front of me, over my breasts, across my stomach and beyond. I turned to face him; a smile gracing my mouth.

"Good morning," I replied, reaching up to kiss him. Picking up the bar of soap, I smoothed it across the breadth of his chest; surprisingly, it was covered only scantily with dark hair. Foaming the soap into lather, I covered his upper body as his hands continued to work over my slippery skin. My eyes moved down the length of him and lingered on his full erection before returning back to his face.

"You're beautiful," he said while his eyes raked over her wet skin. Shane enclosed her in his arms and moved her underneath the full force of the shower head, rinsing them both as he leaned down and kissed her. As his body compressed into hers she responded by pushing herself against him, letting her hands travel the span of his sides to his hips, pulling him closer. He growled low in his throat and closed his eyes; ravaging her mouth with his own. Shifting his hands down across her back side, he cupped her cheeks and lifted her up against him. Settling her on him, he supported her weight as he slowly lowered her until she engulfed him. She gasped against his neck, her arms clinging to his broad shoulders while he lifted and lowered her tirelessly; her legs wrapped tightly around his hips. The water pummeled over them as they shared the release together.

As we dried and dressed, my stomach suddenly grumbled. "I'm starving," I said, "Do you want some breakfast?"

Shane flashed a toothy smile, "I'm ravenous," he answered as he swept a kiss across my forehead, "I could eat a horse this morning."

I smiled back and lightly punched him on the arm, "I'll make us something," I said leaving the bedroom. He followed behind me and went to the coffee maker to get a pot of coffee started while I moved about, gathering a skillet along with bacon, eggs and biscuits.

"How is it that being however old you are and looking like you do, that you're not married?" I boldly asked as I leaned against the counter. He appeared to be surprised at my question and moved toward me.

"I never found the right one," he said as he pulled me close again and breathed softly against my ear, "And I'm thirty-four." Kissing me on the cheek he moved back to the table and sat down. He took out his cell phone and noticed that he had one missed call.

"Looks like Jeremy tried to reach me late last night," he chuckled, "guess I was too busy to hear it."

I shot him a devilish look, "Busy would be a good way to describe it," I said, my face turning slightly red.

"It was an unbelievable kind of busy," he grinned, "I'd better give him a call and see what he wanted."

Grabbing a mug of coffee he sat back down at the table while thumbing the phone and lifted it to his ear. "Hey, saw you called last night...what's going on?" I could only hear one side of the conversation which was enough to make me realize that Jeremy was inquiring about our night. "Really?" Shane asked and then paused, "Well, good luck with that one," he laughed. "You'll need it."

I moved over toward him and mouthed the words, "Does he want to have breakfast?"

"Hey, Elisa is making breakfast. She wants to know if you're hungry," another pause, "All right, see you in a bit." he said as he punched the end call button on his phone. "Yep, said he'd be over after a shower," Shane responded as he looked over at me.

He started laughing, "You know what else?" he paused as if waiting for me to ask, but then he continued. "Andrea showed up over there last night to see how I was faring with the renovations," he cackled, "Seems that Jeremy has a acquired a new fan."

I turned from the stove to look at him, a flare of loathing crossing my face, "That woman………." I began, "I'm glad that you weren't there."

Shane laughed again, "You don't care for her much…..do you?" he asked sarcastically, egging me on.

"No, I don't. And she's only interested in Jeremy for one reason……."

He grinned slyly and laughed, "Jeremy's only interested in *her* for that same, one reason."

I turned back to the stove giggling, "Well, if he's just looking for that then he's found it." As I continued preparing our breakfast, Shane retrieved another cup and poured it full of coffee, handing it to me. We talked more about Andrea and laughed together as we predicted the outcome between her and Jeremy.

Abruptly, I changed the subject to a more serious discussion. "Can I ask you a question?"

Shane looked toward me inquisitively, "You can ask me anything."

"Tell me about the biting," I said and turned to look over my shoulder at him before concentrating on the breakfast again.

Shane's eyes caught mine for a brief moment over the top of his coffee cup before he set it down on the table in front of him.

"Let me start from another point and move into that," he answered.

I nodded, "Okay."

"First off," he began, "You know how you are uneasy about how much you feel for me in just the short time that we've known each other?" he added.

"Yes," I replied.

"There's a good reason for that Elisa," he paused, "My *kind* finds one mate in their lifetime. When we find our true mate……..we know." He stopped again before continuing, "It's the same with the other individual involved……….they feel the pull but most humans don't understand it."

He stopped so the information had time to sink in before continuing, "It's why you feel so connected and close to me in just this short time."

I turned from the stove to stare at him, "You're saying that I'm your *mate*?"

"That's exactly what I'm saying," he got up from his chair and moved over to where I stood and grasped my hand, "You were meant to be mine. It's why I ended up here," he said as he lowered his head to kiss her. When he backed away she was just staring at him, "Are you freaked out?"he asked.

For a split second I just stared into his tepid blue eyes, they were not unlike viewing the ocean from somewhere high above with its dark and light contrasting depths. I drifted on the absolute wonder of his words realizing that the feelings that he roused within me were anything but ordinary.

"I'm not freaked out……...I don't really know what I am."

"So…." he continued, "When a wolf has found its mate it is instinct for it to put its mark on her; it's called bonding," he hesitated, "As a man, I have put my mark on you by……well, our activities last night…and this morning," he grinned, "But the wolf also needs to put its mark on its mate and it is made with a bite to the neck," He paused again, "not the accidental scrape that happened last night……..but a full bite where blood is actually……taken," He finished.

"The wolf wanted it last night but you had no idea what to expect. I didn't want to scare you and even fighting as hard as I could," his fingertips traced the wounds on her neck, "This still happened," he stopped for a moment. "During bonding, each takes blood from the other. It opens up a mental connection."

This was a lot of information to process and I turned quickly away to tend to the breakfast before it burned to a crispy offering. His hand rubbed across my back warmly and with affection and comfort.

"Mental connection? What exactly does that mean?"

"We can communicate without speaking," he stated simply.

I persisted, "Jeremy said that some werewolves are made............he said he wasn't sure how exactly," I paused, biting my lower lip, "Do you know?"

He stared at me for a moment before he spoke in a low voice, "Yes, I know."

"Tell me how it happens," I said.

"You don't really need to know Elisa...........you never have to be what I am," he answered.

Her brow creased, "I just want to know, Shane."

He saw the determination on her face and knew that she wouldn't let it rest until he told her; but still he hesitated, "It can be...........violent," He said as he waited for her reaction. She continued to stare into his eyes, waiting for answers.

He inhaled deeply, debating on the best way to explain this to her. "Werewolves are not usually mistakenly created," he murmured, "it isn't as simple as a bite on the night of the full moon," he paused, "Although the full moon does play a part in it........... it doesn't happen so...........effortlessly."

He waited for her to question, but she didn't; her eyes watching him closely, "For the few hours during the full moon night, a werewolf can be made but it involves the wolf itself......not the man," he hesitated again, "What I'm saying is that the man must relinquish all control to the wolf; he has no control over the beast during those few hours." He sighed, "That means that the person who is to become the werewolf is at the mercy of the beast..........."

Her unflinching gaze was locked on his eyes as he continued. "There must be an exchange of blood." He began again, "The wolf wounds the person and brings first blood.........and the other must make the wolf bleed." He stopped, watching her unchanging expression, "It isn't easily done Elisa, and many don't survive."

I finally spoke, mesmerized by the vivid images in my mind. "Exchange of blood? How does that happen exactly?"

"The wolf's blood has to enter into the other's body through a wound," he answered, "It's complicated......." His voice faded and when he spoke again, it was low and barely audible. "The wolf wants to kill………and the mixing of blood that has to take place is difficult to accomplish when one is fighting for their life," he finished, his eyes penetrating hers.

"You never have to be what I am Elisa………not to be with me."

I brought the bacon to the table and sat it down, my gaze unfaltering. I placed a reassuring hand on his shoulder, "I know you would never hurt me," I said as I rubbed down his arm before turning back to finish up breakfast.

He shook his head as she moved away. No*, he* would never hurt her but she didn't comprehend the violent nature of the beast. She couldn't fathom the brutality that went along with the creation of one of his kind. He had witnessed it; even in a controlled situation it had failed miserably. His human friend, Paul had begged him for it; wanted more than anything to live as he did and be a part of their pack. After developing a romantic interest in one of the females, Jasmine, Paul was convinced that their life would be better somehow if he could live as she did; experience her life. Even through his tearful pleas, Shane had refused and attempted to persuade him differently. It was someone else who agreed to Paul's appeal.

He remembered recoiling as he watched with horror the bloody battle that waged below from where he stood on the top of the pit. Paul was given weapons to protect himself but even with those, he was at a great disadvantage. He wasn't a large man, but he was young and physically fit which served to preserve is life for the first few minutes.

Under the light of the full moon, Shane gaped helplessly as Paul was slaughtered. The sound of Jasmine's screams filled the night before altering into a long howl as Paul's entrails spilled from his body. Within moments, her silver wolf stood protectively over his still, bloody form; teeth bared and although much smaller than Paul's killer, her intent was clear. The massive deep brown wolf growled and lunged toward her. She met him in mid air and they tumbled into a pile of claws, teeth and fur. Shane's body urged him forward; to join her in seeking retribution deep in the pit, but within the blink of an eye, the Alpha was among them, tearing his way through fur and skin until they were separated.

Shane would never forget the distraught look in Jasmine's eyes. She was never the same afterwards and over time, fully retreated from pack society. The sadness consumed her until she finally vanished. He had observed firsthand the tragedy and loss that she had endured and continued to suffer until she disappeared.

I remained quiet for a few minutes noticing how Shane seemed to be lost in his own thoughts. Both of our eyes turned toward the window at the sound of gravel crunching before the expected knock on the door. I walked over and opened it, smiling warmly as Jeremy came inside.

"Man, its cold out there this morning!" he declared, shivering for the extra affect. He met my friendly gaze, "Thanks for having me over for breakfast." Removing his coat, he hung it on the back and settled into a chair.

"Want some coffee?" Shane asked as he got up and went to retrieve a cup before allowing Jeremy to answer.

"Love some," he responded as Shane handed the steaming cup to him. Reaching over, he stole a piece of bacon from the plate, shoving it into his grinning mouth quickly before he thought I would notice.

"So, how did y'alls evening go?" he inquired playfully, looking at Shane first and then at me. I immediately felt the warmth move up into my face so I turned away, my attention back to the stove. Shane shot him an annoyed look which he returned with a mischievous grin.

I turned back around suddenly and addressed him.

"So……..Andrea, huh?" I asked, my own face lit up with mischief.

Jeremy stared at me, his face revealing surprise that Shane had shared that anecdote, but he smiled. I could tell that he wasn't about to allow me to get anything over on him.

"Well, you know…………." he said, "She showed up yesterday evening looking for Shaney boy," he said smiling over at his friend, "but she found me instead. She didn't stay too upset about missing him though…….." his voice trailed off as he laughed.

I couldn't contain a giggle as Shane shook his head at him from across the table.

"How do you guys want your eggs?" I asked, attempting to detour the conversation.

"Over-easy?" Jeremy inquired.

"Over-easy would be good for me too," Shane replied.

"Over-easy it is," I said while listening attentively to their conversation as I finished preparing the breakfast. Sitting a plate of eggs in front of each h of them I then put the biscuits and gravy on the table. Sitting down in the chair closest to Shane, I picked up a fork.

While waiting for them to finish talking, my own mind was lost in the past few months. Grabbing a biscuit, I pulled it in half and covered it with gravy and snatched a couple of pieces of bacon. When I looked up both of them were staring at me; I looked from one to the other.

"What?"

"Where'd you go?" Shane asked; concern in his voice, "I asked you a question…….twice."

"Sorry……..I didn't hear you; my mind was elsewhere," I replied. "What did you ask me?"

He reached his hand over and placed it on her arm, "You okay?"

"Oh yeah, I'm fine," I replied, raising my fork to my mouth.

"I asked if you wanted to ride in with us to town later," Shane asked again.

I shook my head, "I don't think so," I paused, "I'd just like to hang around here today. Plus, I'm a little tired."

Jeremy sniggered to himself but loud enough for them both to hear it. Shane sat down his fork and stood up, "Well, I'll be right back," he said as he ambled off toward the bathroom.

Once he was gone, Jeremy looked over at Elisa. Brazenly, he reached over and pushed her hair back away from her neck revealing the faint marks on her neck.

I was startled by his forwardness as his thumb moved lightly across the area before he drew back; his gray eyes boring into mine.

"Andrea is to never know….anything," he said matter of fact, seriousness in his tone.

I gazed at him questioningly, "Do you think that I would tell her? I don't even like her."

Jeremy shook his head, "No, I'm not worried about you telling her. I know that our secret is safe with you," He replied as his eyes traveled back to her neck and then locked on her eyes again.

"She isn't anything to me…………it's not like….," he paused uncomfortably, "Sometimes a guy just needs companionship… you know?" he grinned.

Smiling back, I responded, "I get it, it's just about sex, right?"

He laughed at her directness as he nodded and pointed his finger at her, "Exactly."

As Shane returned to the table he looked skeptically at both of them, "What's so funny?" he asked as he sat down and picked up his coffee.

Jeremy chuckled, "Oh nothing……..just laughing at the frankness of your…….of Elisa," he quickly added.

Shane met his eyes, "We have no more secrets between us Jeremy," he said as he looked over at her, "Including Canada."

"Really……………"Jeremy said, not so much as a question but as an acknowledgment, his eyes moving from Shane's to Elisa's. A stormy look passed through his clouded gray eyes.

"How do you feel about all of this new commotion in your life?" he asked.

I could fell Shane's eyes on me; anticipating my answer. I shrugged, "I'm not sure," I paused, my eyes moving from Jeremy to Shane's probing gaze, "It has been a lot to take in."

Shane's face fell slightly as he looked back down at his plate, let down by my response.

"But I haven't run away screaming yet," I added, grinning.

He raised his head and looked back at me, a smirk on his face.

"I think I would have by now if I was going to."

"Maybe you should reconsider," Jeremy said sarcastically as Shane scowled in his direction.

"I thought it would be best if she knew why we left and why we ended up here…….other than for the obvious reason." Shane reached over and took my hand, rubbing his thumb across the top of it.

I beamed at his affectionate gesture, "You said you were planning on starting a pack here……"

"Yes, that's the plan," Shane replied as he exchanged a quick look with Jeremy, "We still have a lot to do before that happens though."

Jeremy smirked in response, "I think that's the only reason you let me come here," he laughed, "To be the manual labor."

They all laughed together, a welcome sound in the coziness of the little cabin. I smiled to myself as I felt the easy and comfortable atmosphere envelope me. It had been a long time since I had felt the feeling of family; the support and love had been absent from my life since my parents died other than the stableness of Edna and Dan. They meant well but they couldn't substitute for the family that I once knew. But now, these two new companions with their crazy secret lives had allowed me to be part of their world; giving me a sense of belonging to something again.

Finishing breakfast, both of the men helped pick up the dishes and assisted with the clean up. I was pleasantly surprised at their assistance.

"Wow..........thanks for the help," at the same time, they both flashed their charming smiles at me and my heart leapt in my chest. They were both so surprisingly handsome, both large, strong and powerfully built; either one could have any woman that they damn well wanted.......how in the world did I ever snag one of them?

"Thank you for breakfast," Jeremy said as he flipped the dishtowel good-naturedly in my direction catching the side of my hip with a loud pop.

His eyes widened, "Shit, I'm sorry........I didn't mean to really hit you," he apologized.

I rubbed the spot with the palm of my hand and shot him a disparaging look but grinned, "That smarted!"

Shane watched the scene unfold in front of him with a look of doubt. In a way he wasn't crazy about the closeness that the two of them had seemed to have developed but yet in another way, he was glad that they got along. "Well Jer," he said, "Let's get rolling and get back." He wandered off into the bedroom to find where his coat had ended up from last night's activities.

"Sure you don't want to ride in with us?" Jeremy asked.

"No, thanks, but I don't really want to. I'm going to be heading in myself in a few days to spend Thanksgiving with Edna and Dan. Since my parents died they insist that I come and stay a couple of days over the holidays with them," I paused, smiling, "Their kids come in from Colorado and Wyoming with their families. It's a pretty big ordeal."

Jeremy nodded, "It's great that they include you in their family," he said, his voice soft and sober.

Shane returned with his coat as Jeremy finished speaking. "What is this?" he asked, "Every time I leave the room I come back in the middle of a conversation." he teased, but Jeremy's façade remained solemn.

"Elisa was just telling me how Edna and Dan kinda took over as her family when her folks died," he said, "Just made me remember how your parents included me in all of your family stuff," he replied looking at Shane and then added, "I need to go see Mother."

"I need to go see her too," Shane replied solemnly, "I haven't talked to her since before I left Canada."

"Maybe we should plan a trip," Jeremy stated, "She'd be glad to see us.......alive."

Shane dipped his head in agreement, "Maybe we'll plan on a spring trip," he replied indifferently as he pulled on his coat.

He walked over to me and bending down, swept a kiss across my lips, "I'll give you a call when we get back," he paused, a sinful grin played across his mouth as he moved it close against my ear, "Maybe we can have a replay of last night....and this morning," he whispered.

I grinned in response and kissed his stubbly cheek. "Maybe," I teased.

Jeremy shook his head, "Geez......come on," he said rolling his eyes as pulled on his coat and moved toward the door.

"Later Elisa," he said as he stepped out the door.

Shane lingered for a moment more, his eyes locked to mine before he turned and followed Jeremy out across the yard.

Chapter 17

Hearing the sound of the vehicles come to life, I listened until the motors faded away before moving back into the bedroom. My intention was to make the bed and tidy up but it was so inviting that I couldn't stop myself from crawling back into it; snuggling up under the thick, heavy softness of the blankets. Closing my eyes, I inhaled the smell of Shane that still lingered on the linens while my mind played over the past evening. Finding myself looking forward to another night in his arms, sleep gently washed over me.

The sound of the phone ringing jolted me out of my slumber and while still half asleep, I jumped up from the bed and ran into the living room snatching the phone from its cradle.

"Hello?" I muttered, my voice groggy from my nap.

I exchanged pleasantries with Edna for a few minutes and the discussion turned to the advancing holiday, "Can we expect to see you on Thursday dear?" she asked.

"Yes, I've been looking forward to it," I answered, "But what can I bring?"

"Just yourself honey, nothing else," Edna answered.

"No, you never let me bring anything Edna; I will make a side dish or a dessert or something. What are you already planning?"

"If you want to make a dessert, that would be wonderful honey, but you don't need to do that," the older woman answered.

I paused, "I do have a question though........would it be alright if I brought a couple of people with me? We won't stay the night, we'll just drive back," I said, "I have a new neighbor that doesn't have any family close around and his friend has come for a visit and they will be alone for the holiday...is it alright if I bring them?"

Edna's voice was excited on the other end, "A new neighbor, huh?" she chuckled, "The more the merrier Elisa! You know that is my motto!" She laughed loudly on the other end of the conversation, "We always have plenty of food....please extend my invitation to them!"

I smiled to myself, Edna was always accommodating, "I think that you will like him," I said, "And he'll get along well with Dan."

Edna giggled, "If you like him honey, I'm sure that we will as well. I can't wait to meet your *new neighbor*."

She paused for a moment, "You know Elisa, ol' Edna wasn't born yesterday," she laughed.

I followed with my own laughter.

"I know Edna, and I appreciate you allowing me to bring them to the family's holiday celebration."

"Oh!! It's really no problem Elisa, you're part of our family too," she chuckled again, "There will be plenty of food!"

After a few more comments back and forth, we said our good-byes and I placed the phone back in the cradle. Well that was that. I would ask Shane later if he and Jeremy wanted to go. They may very well say no, but at least I had cleared it before mentioning it to them.

Glancing at the time, I realized that I had been asleep far longer than I had wanted to be. It had already been five hours since they had left and depending on what they were doing, they would be back before too much longer.

Climbing into the water's stream, I let it wash the sleepiness from my body. Once finished, I climbed out and while still towel drying my hair, padded into the bedroom to dress. Passing by the window something caught my eye and my head jerked sideways to look out. At the edge of the woods was an unmistakable form just within the shadows….a wolf. Narrowing my eyes, I attempted to get a clearer observation but it was gone; or was it really ever there?

Pulling on a pair of jeans, boots and a sweatshirt, I grabbed my cell phone and walked out on the deck. I studied the wood line and in every direction as far as I could see but found nothing. Punching Shane's number, I lifted it to my ear. He answered after the second ring.

"Hey, what's up?" he asked, a chipper note in his voice.

"Where are you?" I asked.

"Oh, just about 10 miles from home," he answered, "Why?"

"Jeremy with you?"

He hesitated; slight confusion in his reply, "Yeah, he's right here…..what's going on?"

"I saw something out here and I thought it was one of you," I answered, "But I don't see it now."

When he spoke again his voice was edgy, "What do you think you saw, Elisa…..a wolf?"

"Yeah, but it must've been…………." he cut me off quickly.

"Elisa, if you're outside……get inside," he said sternly, "Lock the doors and I'll be there in just a few minutes."

Suddenly feeling vulnerable, I immediately moved back inside the cabin and pushed the door shut, locking the deadbolt. "Okay, you're scaring me," I muttered.

I could hear Jeremy's voice in the background demanding to know what was happening.

"I'll be right there," he said again, "Stay inside," and then the call was ended. I moved the phone away from my ear and stared at it.

Feeling ill at ease, I moved to retrieve the pistol. Once I held it in my hands I felt somewhat better and protected, but still nervous. With my mind racing, I instantly understood that if I had really seen something, and it was neither Shane nor Jeremy it could only mean one thing…..there was another one. The cabin was too quiet and only added to my anxiety. Listening closely for any sound or movement, I still heard nothing. Moving back toward the window I peered out; searching the shadows of the woods but still failed to locate anything there. In the living room I finally settled onto the sofa, holding the pistol in my hands.

It felt like hours passed while I sat there and before I finally heard the undeniable sound of Shane's truck and the gravel spinning beneath the tires. Jumping up, I almost ran toward the door, flinging it open as I saw Shane and Jeremy bounding out of the pickup. They both stopped midway to the door and looked at one another at the same time.

Jeremy nodded his head, "Someone's been here," he said as he looked at Shane, "I'll go."

Immediately, he began removing his clothing, leaving them where they fell until he was completely naked. I was once again shocked as I witnessed the blurred transformation from man to beast. The large mahogany wolf bounded hastily away into the woods in the exact location where I had thought I'd seen something.

Shane bent down and picked up the clothes that Jeremy had so quickly discarded and carried them up the steps where I was waiting, my mouth ajar.

"Come on," he said, his voice tense, "Let's go inside." He opened the door and let me go first and then followed closely behind.

"So I did see something?" I asked as he set Jeremy's clothes down on the kitchen chair.

"You did," he confirmned.

"How do you know?" I asked shakily.

"Scent," he answered, "We could smell it as soon as we came across the yard," he paused, "Jeremy will know more when he comes back." His tone was a mixture of concern and anxiety.

"What does this mean?" I questioned, my worried gaze fastening onto his.

He shrugged, "Could be just an isolated incident…..or maybe a rogue," he answered, "Or something entirely different." He then paused, "What color was it?"

"Dark… maybe black or brown…..I'm not sure. It was just for a split second and when I looked again, it was gone." He nodded as if acknowledging his own thoughts.

"What's a rogue?" I inquired, breaking through his concentration.

"It's when a wolf leaves its pack and travels on its own; becoming more wolf than man, " he answered, "They become a danger to all that they cross paths with. Often, a rogue wolf will become a killer….I was nearly rogue."

My eyes widened. "You never tried to hurt me." I said softly.

"No," he responded, "but you don't understand how hard it was for me to keep that from happening the first time that we came across you," he hesitated, "I still had some control….many rogues have none and are at the mercy of their wolves."

"You could've killed me then…." my voice waned.

He nodded, "Yes, I could've…but I didn't," he smiled uncertainly.

Minutes ticked by slowly before we heard the distinctive thump of something outside the door. Shane moved to peer out and then opened it, allowing the huge mahogany wolf inside. Raising his immense head, he looked at Shane and then at me.

I was uneasy until I saw the recognizable gray eyes set into the dark fur of its face. The wolf stretched its head over to the chair and took hold of Jeremy's clothes in its jaws and trotted out of the room. Jeremy returned only minutes later and sat down in the kitchen chair to pull his boots on.

"Sorry about the nudity once again, Elisa," he chuckled but I noticed the slight flush of his own face. "Did you see anything you liked?" He laughed as he looked at me and my cheeks reddened.

He turned to Shane who had quirked an eyebrow at his silliness, "It's definitely male," he said, "He's been all around here today…..I guess after we left."

I shuddered, thinking about something lurking out there in the woods sent shivers through my body.

"I followed the trail about a mile through. I didn't pick up where he had veered off in any other direction," he paused, "Like he was on a mission straight here."

"This is freaking me out," I interrupted, "I don't know what any of this means but its scaring me."

Shane reached his hand up to my shoulder reassuringly and rubbed it. "You won't be left alone anymore," he said.

"I just don't understand....why would it have even been here?" I asked.

"He smells us," Jeremy answered, "He knows there are others like him in the area because we've been here and he detects our scents," he paused, "He may just be looking for his own kind....we're going to find out why he's here, don't worry."

"I'll bet he's been at our place too then," Shane said, "I guess if he hasn't then we'll know there's something else going on."

Jeremy agreed, "I'll take your truck and run home and check things out," he said as he stood up.

Shane shook his head, "No..........I think we all need to stay together until we figure out what's going on. We'll all go." He turned to me, "Gather up anything you need to take with you, I want you to come home with us." He could see the fear in my face as I nodded and moved into the bedroom to pack a bag.

He turned back to Jeremy, "What do you think this is.......seriously?"

"I don't know Shane. Like I said, its male but I couldn't get a feel for anything else about him. The scent isn't familiar," replied Jeremy.

Shane dropped his head and looked at the floor before returning his gaze to his friend, "It's just odd," he began, "I've been here for a few months and have never come across another one of our kind......I'm not sure what to make of this."

Jeremy patted Shane's shoulder affectionately, "Don't get all uptight and worried about it yet," he said, "We'll figure it out and then do whatever we have to."

Shane accepted his response knowing that he was right. This could all just be a rare occurrence that never happens again.......or at least he hoped that was what it was.

I returned quickly with a bag and grabbed my coat and purse off of the rack behind the door. Forgetting something that I felt was ultimately important, I disappeared into the living room and came back with the pistol in my hand and stuck it inside my purse. When I looked up, both of them were staring at me, slightly amused.

"What are you going to do with that?" asked Jeremy mockingly, but smiling.

"What do you mean? I'm going to protect myself with it if I have to," I answered smugly.

Shane's eyes caught Jeremy's but he continued anyway, "You know that you can't hurt one of us with that………right?"

Blankly, I stared at him and then at Shane who didn't speak but nodded in agreement.

"Sorry," said Shane, "I never told you about that."

"What are you saying?" I asked, "If I shoot you…nothing happens?"

"Well, something would happen," Jeremy replied, "But not what you want to happen," he paused, "It hurts like hell, might be laid up a day or so…………but those wounds heal."

I looked at Shane who averted his gaze from my penetrating stare. "So……." I said as I picked up the pistol and held it in my hand, "This would have done nothing to you that day at the lake?"

Sheepishly, he shook his head, "It would have hurt me; maybe even cost me an eye," he paused, "but kill me? No."

"How does someone like me kill someone like you then?" I asked, not attempting to keep the frustration from my voice.

Jeremy and Shane exchanged an uneasy glance before Shane spoke, "If the injury is severe enough, we can bleed to death…no matter what form we're in," he answered but his answer didn't sway my perseverance.

"How can a normal person kill one of you?" I asked determinedly, my voice wavering. "How do I protect myself if I am attacked by whoever is roaming around out there?"

Shane exhaled loudly in an attempt to relieve the increasing tension, "Silver," he said, "You can kill us with silver…..or behead us. Either of those two things would do it."

"It has to be in the heart though," Jeremy intervened, "You can't just stab us and kill us with something silver….or shoot us with a silver bullet in some random area of the body….has to be in the heart." He paused, "Or if a silver bullet hits us in another part of the body and it can't be removed in time, it will eventually kill us."

"Oh," I said thoughtfully, "I don't own anything silver."

Jeremy grinned, "Elisa, you don't need to worry about it," he countered, "We're going to figure this out….come on, let's go."

As we stepped out the door onto the deck, I noticed that both Shane and Jeremy lifted their noses to the air before continuing down the steps and across the yard. There was a great sense of security and safety as I walked between them and I felt even more protected centered amidst them in the cab of the truck. Leaning my head against Shane's shoulder as we drove, he turned and kissed me lightly on the forehead.

When we reached his house, I was told to stay in the truck for a couple of minutes how they checked things. Watching them move about the yard, they paused and raised their heads searching for a telltale scent. Soon Shane turned and headed back toward the truck and opened the passenger door. He picked up my bag and took me by the hand as I slid out.

"Did you find anything?" I immediately asked.

"No……..he's not been here," he answered uneasily. He escorted me to the cabin and upon entering he flipped on every light in the vicinity.

Jeremy ambled in behind us and flopped down on the couch. I addressed him as he settled, "Anything?"

Jeremy shook his head. "Nope. Nothing," he replied.

"What do you two think about this………really?" I asked, certain that they weren't being totally honest, "I want the truth."

Jeremy answered, confirming what Shane had already told me.

"It's probably just a fluke; someone passing through that scented us," he hesitated, "We'll know more in a day or two…if the scent stays strong; he's still around. If it fades out then he's moved on. We're just going to wait it out and see what develops," he finished.

Shane agreed, "That's about all we can do right now……..wait and see," he said. "Meanwhile, I'll show you where you can keep your things."

Taking me by the hand again, he led the way into his bedroom.

Once alone, Jeremy sighed. He felt an odd sense of impending doom but he dared not say it out loud around Elisa. She was worried enough as it was and Shane's overprotective mode wasn't helping much either. He didn't want to jump to conclusions but in the back of his mind he had to wonder if this didn't have something to do with Canada. They had all scattered so quickly that no one really knew who was responsible ….but he knew the reason behind it all was the mixed blood that existed in their pack. He knew that one key detail was the one that weighed the most heavily on Shane's mind.

Shane and Elisa returned from the bedroom and moved past him into the kitchen. He could hear their muffled conversation and the sound of dishes rattling as he absentmindedly picked up the remote and flipped on the television. Slipping his boots off, he stretched his tall frame out on the couch, rolling up the afghan for a pillow. Although he allowed his body to relax his other senses were alert in foreboding anticipation of things to come.

I awoke sometime later that night with a dire need to use the bathroom. In an attempt to not disrupt my comfort and warmth, I moved about restlessly in hopes of going back to sleep. No matter what I tried, it didn't work and I knew that there would be no more sleep until I relieved my bladder.

Shifting slowly away from the protective clutches of Shane's arms, I eased off the side of the bed; trying not to make too much of a disturbance and wake him. My feet hit the cold floor and I shivered; immediately missing the warmth. I padded across the bedroom floor and cracked open the door and slid between the small available space I had allowed. The living room was illuminated with the soft glow of the television and I noticed Jeremy's form still on the couch. My footsteps were silent as I moved past to the bathroom.

I was careful to turn the light off before exiting the bathroom so it didn't blare into the darkened living room where Jeremy was asleep. Passing by, I grabbed another blanket and cautiously laid it over him, trying not to wake him.

"I'm not asleep," he said softly.

The unexpected sound of his voice was alarming in the silence and I nearly stumbled backwards. If it hadn't been for his quick reflexes I would have been piled in a heap on the floor.

"Damn!" I whispered breathlessly, "You scared the crap out of me!"

He laughed quietly, "Sorry." he said, releasing his hold on my arm.

Clad only in a pair of shorts and t-shirt he at once noticed that I was shivering.

"Cold?" he asked as he sat up and offered me the blanket, "Or are you heading back to bed?"

There was a certain melancholy tone to his voice that made me suddenly think that maybe I shouldn't hurry back, "I don't have to," I said, "You feel like company?"

He smiled and pushed the blanket into my hands and then patted the couch beside him, "Yeah."

Curling up next to him, I snuggled underneath the warmth of the heavy cover; warming my ice cold feet beneath me. We both sat silently for a while with our eyes on the muted television screen, neither speaking but instead just sitting in comfortable silence. I remembered a time not too long ago how he had made me feel uneasy but it all seemed much different now. He was my protector….just like Shane; and I trusted him.

After a few minutes, he finally spoke. "I know you're scared about this whole deal," he began, his voice low and hushed, "But Shane won't let anything happen………..and neither will I."

I smiled, "I know," I whispered, "But I'm still scared. Especially since I know that I can't do anything to protect myself."

"That's what we're here for.," he uttered, "Not that I think anything is going to happen….just sayin'."

Quietness overtook me again for a moment before I spoke. "Out of curiosity, what if I was……….like you and Shane?" I paused, "Could I protect myself then?"

Jeremy stared at me directly, his eyes guarded, "What is rolling around in that head of yours?"

I shrugged, "Shane told me how it happens…..I just wondered if I would be better off to know what you know….be able to smell, see and hear all of the things that you do. I might not be so scared if I could tell if someone was around."

He shook his head, "I don't think that is what you really want to do," he paused, "It's too risky."

My eyes narrowed suspiciously, "You said you didn't know how it was done……." I said accusingly.

Crap, Jeremy thought to himself before responding, "I don't really………..I've just heard…….. things," he muttered as he looked away.

"You're so full of it," I snarled and glared at him, "Why'd you lie?"

He shrugged, "I thought Shane should be the one to explain that to you….not me."

My anger softened and I couldn't help but agree, "I guess that was probably the right thing to do," I answered.

"It was," he paused, "But I guess if he didn't answer all of your questions I'm at liberty to do that now," he grinned as he playfully jabbed my arm. I laughed and then we both realized how loud we were getting and shushed each other at the same time, invoking another round of giggling.

"We're going to wake Shane up if we don't keep quiet!" I whispered hoarsely, giggling.

"Shane's already awake." His voice boomed loudly; we both jerked our heads toward the sound. Walking out of the bedroom, he pushed his hand through his tousled hair with a look of displeasure on his face.

I felt a sudden twinge of guilt as his eyes traveled from my face to Jeremy's and then back to mine again, "I woke up and you were gone," he stated, his voice tense, "I see that you didn't go far though."

Jeremy intervened, fully aware of Shane's annoyance, "It's my fault," he said, "She was on her way back from the bathroom and I stopped her."

Shane's eyes lingered on the pair as he surveyed the coziness that the two seemed to be sharing. His eyes locked on Jeremy's and I could see the warning in his stare before they returned to me, "Let's go back to bed," he said as he extended his hand towards me. I hesitated before taking it, but under his scrutinizing gaze I felt compelled. As I was hoisted from the couch, I turned to glance over my shoulder at Jeremy who gave me a crooked smile and a nod.

"Good night," he said softly as Shane pulled me back toward the bedroom.

Once in the confines of the dark room and the door pulled closed behind us, Shane dragged me down on the bed against him. He wrapped his arms possessively around me, holding my body close against his. My voice faded when I spoke, "He's lonely Shane."

His body stiffened for a few moments before it relaxed against mine once again, "I know," he confessed, "But I don't like that you're the solution."

I shifted restlessly in his arms and pushed him away with my hands, searching for his face in the darkness, "Are you *jealous*?"

I couldn't see the scowl on his face but somehow, I could feel it.

"Jealous?" he asked, "I just feel that you two are getting too close, considering..."

"Considering what?" I asked, irritated.

"He would eat you alive if I wasn't around," he snapped back.

"What exactly does *that* mean?"I demanded, "Jeremy's been nothing but sweet to me once I got past the sarcasm."

Shane chuckled softly then but it was a cynical sound to my ears, "You don't know Jeremy very well," he answered, "Your first impression of him made you feel unsettled and intimidated….it was the right impression."

"Are you going to keep beating around the bush? Why don't you just say whatever it is that's on your mind?" I replied, slightly angry.

He pulled me tighter against him although I tried my hardest to maintain the distance between us. "Jeremy acknowledges very few boundaries, Elisa," he breathed into my neck as I struggled against his unyielding hold, "And I haven't marked you………you're fair game in his eyes."

"How could you think that of him? He's your best friend," I snapped back.

Pulling back, Shane could see the frustration on her face and hear it in her voice, "Why are you so defensive?"he asked impatiently.

"Why are you so suspicious?" I retorted as I continued to struggle from his grasp. He didn't allow me to wriggle free which angered me further. With his superior strength he instead crushed me back against his body.

"Shane, let me go," I demanded.

"No," he growled as he buried his face once again in my neck, his mouth scorching a heated trail along my skin.

"Shane, stop….." I ordered, "I want to talk about this."

His voice was muffled when he replied, "No more talking." He moved his hands over expertly over my body, setting my skin on fire and stirring my senses until helplessly I began to respond to his touch. His mouth devoured me; roughly, and demanding. I found my clothes stripped forcefully from my body as his form hovered over me. The gentleness of the intimacy we had shared and that I was accustomed to had vanished; replaced with his primal need to possess. He plunged into me again and again until his eyes burned with an eerie glow as I attempted to continue to meet his thrusts. When my body finally quivered beneath him in spasms, his fangs lengthened and penetrated my skin.

Shane's release came as the taste of her blood flooded his mouth, rolling across his tongue and trickling from the corner of his lips.

He heard her faintly gasp while his mind and body reeled with waves of pleasure at the taste and warmth of her life oozing into him. He was jerked back to reality when he felt her body go limp underneath his mouth and he quickly withdrew from her, his eyes seeking her face in the dim light.

Her eyes were closed, her skin pale and her body lifeless. Placing his hand against her neck he was relieved to feel a strong pulse at his fingertips. "Elisa," he murmured. She roused groggily at the sound of his voice lifting her hand to her neck.

"You bit me….again," I uttered drowsily. I knew what had happened and I felt the pain but my mind was so light and fuzzy that I just wanted to sleep.

"I know…..I'm sorry," he said regretfully, "I'll be right back." He grabbed his lounge pants and slipped them on before leaving the room.

Finding the first aid kit in where it was stashed in the kitchen pantry, he returned quickly to her side. He gently cleaned the puncture wounds on her neck and secured a bandage to the area. She barely stirred during his care and once he was finished, he sat on the bed beside her for a long while just watching her sleep. The guilt flowed through his mind when he thought of the way he had forced himself on her and ultimately had ended up causing her pain. Sighing deeply, he stood up and left the room.

Jeremy was still reclined on the couch, the television emitting a faint light but the sound had remained muted. His eyes were closed but Shane knew he wasn't asleep. He knew that with the sharp hearing that was common to their kind that Jeremy had heard everything through the walls. He opened his eyes as Shane shifted his feet to the side so he could sit down.

"We need to talk," He said as he settled on the opposite end of the couch.

"You're right about that," Jeremy stated frankly as he raised himself to a sitting position, "What in the hell has gotten into you?"

Shane sighed deeply while his eyes locked on Jeremy's, "You two seem to have developed quite a cozy relationship."

Jeremy held his gaze, "It's nice to have *female* companionship in the family again," he responded. "Why is it that you have such a problem with it?"

Shane sensed that he was confrontational and he advanced cautiously. "*My* problem," he began, "Is that when my back is turned you make it a point to be more than just amiable towards her. I know how you roll Jeremy. I just want to be clear that she is mine."

"Are you fucking kidding me?" Jeremy replied angrily, cocking his head slightly as if trying to comprehend. "What are you saying? You think that I'm trying to pull something over on you?" he hesitated as he tried to maintain control of his temper. "I don't know what has happened to you but you need to get a grip….I'm the one that took the initiative to make sure you two hard headed fools got together!" He stood up, his body tensed in anticipation of the impending argument, or fight.

Shane read the defensive movements of his body and understood that their dispute was headed into something more aggressive if he pushed further. "Calm down, we're just having a conversation."

"No, we're not……..You're *accusing* me of something. That's not a conversation," he growled, his eyes intensely bearing down on Shane. Feeling threatened, he stood up to his full height in front of Jeremy, only a few inches between their bodies.

"Let's sit down and talk," Shane said impatiently through gritted teeth, "We don't want this." His eyes fastened on Jeremy's and for a few moments neither moved nor spoke; a wrestle for power evident in their unrelenting stares. The tenseness in Jeremy's body loosened and he diverted his eyes as he sat back down.

"You're right, this is stupid."

Shane's form relaxed as well and he moved back to the couch. "We're all on edge," he said.

"I know…..but to accuse me of doing something behind your back is just….wrong," Jeremy replied mockingly, "I can't believe that as long as you've known me and everything we've been through that you would even entertain the thought of anything but my best intentions where you're concerned."

Shane ran an agitated hand through his thick hair, "I don't," he noted, "Not really. I guess I just feel overprotective," he paused, "the closeness between you two doesn't help."

Jeremy shrugged, "What do you want me to do about it? Avoid her? Going to be kinda hard since she's staying here."

Shane shook his head, "No, of course not," he answered.

"Well then, looks like we got nothing resolved with this *conversation*," Jeremy said smartly. They sat and stared at one another from opposing sides of the couch; and of the dispute.

"So now what?" Jeremy proposed.

"I need to know that you have my back…..no matter what," Shane reciprocated.

"I've always had your back……."Jeremy's voice trailed off as his eyes searched Shane's face for answers, "I don't know where you're going with this."

"I marked her tonight," Shane said flatly watching for Jeremy's reaction.

Jeremy lowered his eyes to the floor in deliberation before he spoke, "Yeah, I know. I smelled the blood," he said; a hint of disappointment reflected in his words before he raised his eyes to Shane's.

"It was time."

Shane swore that he had noticed a glimmer of sadness pass across Jeremy's face and then it disappeared just as quickly. Getting up, he turned away and then proceeded toward the bedroom to check on Elisa, leaving Jeremy to his own musings.

She still slept soundly. Shane discarded his lounge pants and inched into the bed next to her; nuzzling up against her sleeping form and placing his arm protectively across her torso. The bond was partially established now; she was linked to him forever……

Chapter 18

The early light of dawn emitted a dim glow as it passed through the frosted pane glass into the darkened cabin. In his position on the couch, Jeremy stretched his legs and sat up. If he had slept any, it was only for a few minutes at a time and although his body was tired, his mind continued to wield its influence. He rubbed his hands across his face and up through his hair as he stood up and went into the kitchen. Coffee was a must have this morning. He busied himself moving about as noiselessly as possible preparing it and while it brewed he determined he had time for a shower.

Early morning was his favorite time. Every day held the potential for a new, fresh start when there was only stillness and tranquility for early morning companions. He unwound as the hot water flowed along the length of his body in a series of snaking rivulets. The water took with it the tightness of his muscles and dissipated it into a tumultuous stream that disappeared down the drain. As he dried himself he felt oddly refreshed for having had such a long restless night but then his mind drifted to Elisa and his gray eyes darkened.

He replayed the heated exchange with Shane in his head as he sipped his first cup of coffee in the silence of the kitchen. Shane had been right…..he did feel a strange pull to her but he didn't understand it or know what it was. Having been confronted with it the first time they had met; he had touched her and there had been a trace, something that lingered. She belonged with Shane; it wasn't jealousy that ruled his thoughts or his feelings. It was something else-something he couldn't wrap his head around.

He heard someone stirring and within a few moments Shane appeared. "Morning." He mumbled as he moved past and poured a cup of coffee before sitting down at the table across from him.

"Mornin'." Jeremy answered.

They sat in silence, both lost in their own thoughts as they ingested their morning caffeine. Neither made a point to look at the other and the space between them became thick and strained with avoidance.

Shane took a deep breath and then released a long, heavy lungful of air, "Did you sleep?"

"Not really," Jeremy said.

"I got a couple hours…..maybe," replied Shane.

An uncomfortable lull followed their short exchange during which time Jeremy got up to fill his cup again. When he turned to walk back to the table he looked at his early morning companion.

"Are we going to have an issue this morning? Cause if so, let's just do it and get it out of the way," he said with a hint of disdain in his voice.

"I don't really feel like it…………you?" Shane raised an eyebrow in question.

"Not really," Jeremy came back with, "But we need to clear the air between us."

He waited for Shane to respond but he didn't so he continued, "You're right," he paused again, "Her and I….. there's something."

Shane's eyes narrowed but he didn't speak so Jeremy persevered, "Whatever it is, I don't think you should feel threatened by it."

"You're too close," Shane replied, "I can't help but feel threatened."

"Nothing has ever happened that would be a good reason for you to feel like that," Jeremy interjected, "She's yours," he paused, "And with that being said, you trust me – and you'll always be able to."

"I know that Jeremy. I really don't know why I question your loyalty now," said Shane, "I just feel protective where she's concerned."

Jeremy held his gaze from the opposite side of the table, "Me too."

They both turned toward the sound of my movement as I padded into the kitchen, clad in Shane's robe, the bandage still clinging to my neck. They both stood up I entered.

"Feeling okay?" Shane asked as he pulled out a chair for me to sit down. Jeremy moved to retrieve a cup of coffee.

I nodded, "Yeah, I'm fine." I said, "A little tired."

Jeremy sat the steaming cup in front of me and I thanked him in a soft tone before raising it to my lips. They both sat back down and then traded a fleeting look between them from across opposite sides of the table.

"I'll fix some breakfast," Jeremy said, moving toward the stove.

He busied himself making sausage and eggs and later, as we ate, the conversation returned to the infiltrator. Shane pushed back from the table and extended his long legs with his cup in his hand. "I plan on making a run over there sometime this morning to see if I can pick up the trail."

My eyes settled on him while Jeremy nodded in agreement, "I'll go with you. We can split up that way and cover more ground."

"You're going to leave me here………alone?" My voice quivered, betraying my underlying fear.

The shrill ringing of a phone broke in, leaving the question dangling and unanswered. Jeremy dashed from the room and I could hear his muffled voice as he answered and moved into the confines of his room to continue his conversation.

Shane laid a comforting hand on mine, "I'll stay with you and let Jeremy go."

I nodded.

"Hey," he spoke softly as he diverted the subject, "I'm sorry about last night – I was wrong to treat you that way." His blue eyes mirrored his remorse while his fingers caressed my arm, "Are you upset?"

"Not upset," she answered. "Just a bit taken back," My voice faded to a whisper.

"I know…and it shouldn't have been like that," he replied, "I felt insecure."

"Jeremy?" I asked directly.

Shane nodded.

I smiled halfheartedly but spoke directly and to the point. "This new pack you want to build?" I paused, "I don't know much about it but I'm certain that it won't work if you two don't trust each other."

"I do trust him," He answered, "Just not necessarily where you're concerned. Last night I was compelled to reinforce that you belong to me."

"Shane, I already knew it……Jeremy's knows it. He's your brother," I delayed, "And the kind of friend to you that cared enough to come to me and convince me what I already knew in my heart…..the kind of friend that I feel lucky to have and you should too."

Shane smiled and leaned over to brush a soft kiss across my lips. "I know that I'm lucky," he murmured, "lucky to have him and even luckier to have you."

"So….we're done with this then, right? You're finished questioning, being suspicious….and jealous?" I asked.

"I'm done," he whispered against my mouth. I smiled and placed my hand against his unshaven face affectionately.

"Good."

Jeremy came back into the kitchen, an impish smile playing across his face, "Well, looks like I've got company coming later…..Andrea wants to have a *visit*."

"Well, that works out then," replied Shane, "You and Andrea can stay here with Elisa while I make the run."

I rolled my eyes at him revealing my obvious disgust with his proposition while Jeremy laughed.

"She should be here in a couple of hours," Jeremy said and then looked at me, "You won't have to spend too much time with her………..I have plans for us," he snickered.

"I think that I'll just hole up in Shane's room until he gets back," I countered, "That way I can avoid even seeing her."

Shane and Jeremy both chuckled.

"You may still *hear* her………."Jeremy said as he grinned wickedly.

I rolled my eyes again but this time at him, "Great," I muttered sarcastically under my breath as I stood up. "I'm going to take a shower, do either of you need in the bathroom?"

"Nope," Shane replied as Jeremy shook his head, "It's all yours."

Retreating from the kitchen, I left the two of them to clean up the breakfast dishes. Upon peering at my reflection in the mirror, I carefully pulled the bandage off of my neck anticipating a nasty wound. But as the tape released and my skin was exposed I was shocked at the insignificant damage that was revealed. Expecting two very distinct rips in the skin, only two small holes remained.

I finished my shower, dressed and combed my hair. After gathering my things I left the bathroom and was met halfway across the living room by the large, black, blue-eyed beast that I instantly recognized. Suddenly tearful at his reappearance, I dropped to my knees in front of him and wrapped my arms around his massive neck. "I have missed you." I whispered into his fur. He rubbed against me, pushing his head against my neck, his body leaning into mine. I caressed the dark fur with my fingertips.

I'll be back soon, I heard his voice clearly in my mind. Startled by the unexpected lucidity as if he stood there in the room alongside me, my eyes widened. The wolf's mouth opened in what looked to be a smile and then he turned toward the door. Getting up to open it, I watched as he trotted past me into the yard and toward the wood line.

He turned for a moment and looked back at me before he disappeared, becoming hidden among the tree trunks and darkness of the forest.

I continued to watch after him for a few moments and then I shut the door. When I turned back, Jeremy was observing me from his position leaned against the kitchen countertop. Our eyes met and there was a strange unspoken exchange between us before I went into the bedroom to put my things away.

Jeremy's voice startled me as I busied myself making the bed and tidying up Shane's room. He leaned casually against the bedroom doorframe, "You alright, Elisa?"

"Yeah, I'm fine. Why?" I asked.

"Just wondered," he admitted but I could sense that there was more to his inquiry.

"What's up with you?" I asked him as I sat down on the edge of the bed and began folding some clothes to put away in my bag before glancing up. His eyes were narrowed as he assessed me from his place by the door.

"Shane thinks that there's something between us," he said bluntly.

"I know," I replied half laughing, "It's crazy, isn't it?" Expecting his laughter to follow, I raised my eyes to his face when the sound didn't come.

He wasn't smiling and his expression was a mask of seriousness. "Is it...crazy?" he asked soberly.

I wasn't sure how to answer or what reaction he was fishing for so I cocked my head in question.

"I think he might be right," he responded while moving towards me. Reaching his hand out, he touched my arm. Feeling an immediate reaction between his fingertips and my skin, his eyes locked hard on mine.

"That's happened before......"

I stood quickly and attempted to put some distance between us, suddenly uneasy in his presence.

"Don't freak out," he said.

I shook my head, "I'm not *freaking* out," I answered, "I just don't understand. I felt that with Shane but I thought it was because..."

He cut me off before I could finish, "Because he said that you're his mate?"

I nodded again.

"Huh," he grunted, "It's strange."

He looked away as if deep in thought, "I don't get it," he said, "There's something......I just don't know what it is."

"Obviously so," I admitted, "but I'm not sure what it is either. This is all brand new to me and if you don't have any idea what it could be, then I sure don't."

Jeremy shook his head, "I've never had that happen before. I haven't told Shane about it...." he paused uncertainly before continuing, "The thing with Shane is, he doesn't believe in coincidences."

"How do you mean?" I probed.

"He thinks there's a reason that everything happens. He's sure that he ended up here because he was meant to find you. If I tell him about this....."

"He'll believe that it means something," I said, finishing his sentence and Jeremy agreed and then shrugged.

"Maybe it does," he commented.

I looked at him warily, "I don't think it's a good idea to mention it to him. Not now."

Out of the blue Jeremy turned away and looked toward the front door, "Andrea's coming up the driveway," he said as he turned back to me. "You going to hide out in here?" he grinned, his mood lightening drastically.

"Uh huh." I answered. "For now, anyways."

They exchanged a silent, knowing glance before he left the bedroom, closing the door behind him.

Chapter 19

It wasn't long before I heard Jeremy's low muffled voice through the wall followed by Andrea's exuberant laughter. The dulled tones of their conversation continued for close to an hour before they moved into the privacy of his bedroom and I heard the distinctive closing of his door.

Thank goodness, I thought as I quietly opened the door, peering out to make sure it was clear. I couldn't stand the sensation of being trapped inside the cabin with what I knew was happening behind Jeremy's closed door. I found my coat, scarf, and gloves and quickly donned the extra apparel needed to stay warm outside.

The immediate cold air took my breath as I closed the cabin door behind me and stepped out on the newly constructed porch. Shoving my gloved hands into my pockets, I searched the surroundings woods for any sign of Shane or anything else for that matter. Once convinced I was safe, I moved off the porch and crossed the yard. Deeply inhaling the fragrance of winter, I mentally noted the faint scent of snow in the air. It felt good to be outside, to stretch my legs and be alone in solitude for a few minutes.

My mind began to wander back over the conversation with Jeremy and the odd incident that had happened between us. What did any of this mean or did it mean anything at all? Maybe it was just a werewolf thing and it would occur if I was in contact with *any* werewolf. I didn't know enough about any of it to form an opinion or try to find the explanation.

I looked up at the sky and reveled in the beauty of the full moon on the far horizon; sitting elegantly at the top of the tree line. It would be a beautiful moonlit night if the clouds didn't cover it before it had fully risen. As if prompted by my thoughts, the first few snowflakes began to fall. Smiling to myself, I watched their imminent journey from the sky to the frozen earth where they left small, white imprints as each came to rest.

Jeremy abruptly lifted his mouth from Andrea's painted lips; his body suddenly on high alert. Even with her obvious disappointment he withdrew from her, moving quickly away, "I'll be right back," he said as he pulled on his jeans. The displeasure was apparent on her pouty face, "I promise," he added, "And I'll pick up where I left off," he grinned.

"I guess I have no choice but to wait for you….." she said provocatively, her voice thick with arousal as she lay twisted in his dark sheets.

He pulled the bedroom door closed behind him. Someone was here; he had sensed it. Moving to Shane's room, he found the door open and Elisa gone. "Elisa!" he whispered as loudly as he felt he could without alerting Andrea to her presence. There was no answer. "Elisa!" he said a little louder but there was still no response.

Shit! He thought to himself. He lifted his nose to the air and searched for her scent which led him to the outside door. Jerking it open, his eyes fell upon her in the yard as she stared up into the sky, oblivious to the danger that lurked somewhere out there. "Elisa!" he said sharply. She turned at the sound of his voice and when she saw him, she smiled.

He stepped out on the porch, the frozen wood cold against his bare feet. "Elisa! You need to come in here…now!" he bellowed. Her smile faded as she looked at him with confusion. At that moment, he watched as it materialized from behind Shane's truck; a huge brown creature with black tinged fur. A thunderous, deep growl radiated from its throat as it moved forward.

She jerked her head around in time to see it lunge, its wide gaping mouth prepared to slice her into pieces. It hit her and toppled her easily to the ground, the weight of it bearing down on her fallen body. Its claws pierced her skin, leaving deep slits that immediately flowed crimson. Lowering its snarling snout toward her struggling body, it plunged its fangs into her shoulder as she shrieked in pain and began to pummel at its head with her bloody fists.

In an instant, Jeremy shifted and the monstrous mahogany wolf charged, roaring a warning to the intruder. He leapt and collided into its side full force, knocking it off balance and away from her. Standing protectively over her fallen body, Jeremy waited until the trespasser regained its footing and wheeled back around. Hurling himself at the scourge in mid air, they crashed together to the ground in a growling mass of snapping jaws and spattering blood.

I pulled myself away from the violent battle the waged only a few inches from my side. What I felt was beyond any fear that I had ever experienced. My injuries were deep and they throbbed with each deafening beat of my heart but my eyes searched for something; anything to defend myself with. Seeing the pile of unburned lumber , I withstood the onslaught of pain that dragging myself to my feet caused, and made my way towards it. The old boards were riddled with nails and splinters and as I grasped one and yanked it from the heap, I winced as one of the nails pierced through my palm. That pain was nothing compared to the sharp ache of my existing wounds. I turned back toward the grisly scene with the board clasped tightly in my hands.

Jeremy felt the toll on his body as each of them grappled for control. He had already suffered several bites and had started to pulse with agonizing exhaustion. The killer was unwavering and continued to assault his battered form unrelentingly, drawing blood with every strike. Jeremy felt the advancing weakness and wasn't sure how much longer he could sustain the fight. Finally, his energy depleted, the beast stood above him, bracing itself to make the last tearing snap that would end his life. Jeremy's mind couldn't accept that he was beaten and he continued to struggle beneath the heavy weight; not for himself, but to save Elisa.

I swung the board down with every ounce of energy inside me onto the beast's broad back, the nails puncturing the hide in several places. It howled in pain and spun its massive head towards me, its blood swathed teeth bared. The look in its eyes was murderous as it howled with fury and rushed at me. I met it with another swing of the board which delivered a merciless blow to the side of its head. The blood flew and it roared in agony but it immediately recovered and continued its menacing approach toward me, backing me toward the cabin.

Jeremy wrestled with unconsciousness. Its intentions were clear and it wouldn't stop until it had killed them both. Using his last shred of energy to pull himself to his feet, he stood on trembling legs and tried to make out the scene before him through the blood that clouded his vision.

I swung again but this time the monster side-stepped and the blow connected with nothing, causing me to stumble off balance, stagger and fall backwards. The brute seemed to smile as it slowly moved toward me, blood dripped from its wounds and I could see that I had destroyed its left eye; it hung loosely from the socket, dangling on thin, wispy tendrils. When it jumped toward me I raised the jagged piece of lumber above my body, placing the other end against the frozen ground. As it bore down on top of me I was ready for it; the board plunging deeply into its abdomen.

The crushing weight of the beast fell upon me and I couldn't breathe as it wheezed its last, dying gasp. I lie there for a few moments before attempting to drag myself from under it while the blood that drained from the gaping hole in its stomach covered me with thick, heavy warmth.

Jeremy teetered unsteadily towards them and heard the agonizing wail of the wolf; he watched as it fell on top of her, burying her body beneath it. Elisa slowly struggled to free herself from its lifeless form and stood above it on shaky legs. The blood poured out of its body and pooled on the ground. She turned to look at him, her eyes full of terror. As their eyes met, his legs gave out from under him and he fell against the hard, cold ground.

Rushing to his side, I placed an unsteady hand on his ribcage; he inhaled sharply and closed his gray eyes. Letting my eyes travel over his body I shivered at the amount of blood that covered his fur, realizing that most of it was his. "Is it dead?" I whispered.

The blood tinged brown wolf beneath my hand opened his eyes and attempted to struggle to his feet. Immediately, I wrapped my arms around his broad, broken body to help steady him as he moved toward the still form of the intruder. He lowered his nose to the lifeless shape for a moment and then raised his eyes and nodded.

In an excruciating transformation the wolf disappeared and Jeremy's naked form stood in its place. He was plastered with blood, one eye was swollen shut and the telltale bite marks covered his body. Although always astonished at the change, I moved without hesitation to his side and encircled his waist with my arms to support him. His one good eye moved over my body, taking in my various injuries.

"We need to get out of the cold," I said, my voice trembling.

"Andrea," he stated wearily in a deep whisper, giving a warning look toward the cabin.

"Shit," I mumbled having forgotten that she was inside, "What do we do about her?"

It was a moment before he answered, "Shane will take care of her......let's just go in."

I didn't know what he meant and right now didn't care. My only goal was to get him inside and get him warm. My own throbbing pain was forgotten when I noticed the coldness of his skin and realized that it was from blood loss; it was only a matter of time before he lost consciousness and then I wouldn't be able to move him at all.

Managing to help him to the door I shoved my body hard against it, slamming it open against the inside wall behind it. Andrea stood in the doorway of Jeremy's room wearing only his shirt. When her eyes took in the sight of the two of us bathed in blood and Jeremy naked, her earsplitting scream filled the cabin and she stood frozen in place.

"What is this?" she shrieked; a horrified tone to her shaky voice, "What happened?"

I threw an unsympathetic look in her direction as Jeremy and I hobbled towards his bedroom. Andrea veered hastily away from us as I pushed past her and got Jeremy onto his bed. His battered body had begun to shake uncontrollably. Covering him with the thick comforter, I tucked it snugly around him while attempting to ignore Andrea's frantic questions. When I turned, she was hovering behind me, chattering in an unnerving tone.

"Shut the hell up!" I screamed in her face. She retreated backwards, her eyes glued to me but she didn't utter another word. Her eyes darted hysterically from my disheveled appearance to Jeremy, naked and covered in blood. Clutching her stomach, her faced whitened and she bolted to the bathroom, finally leaving me a moment of peace to think.

Miles away Shane had picked up the trail of the unwelcome guest, following it for several hours in a clearly identifiable loop that headed back toward his cabin. As he moved silently through the woods he noticed a few small snowflakes drifting down through the openings in the forest canopy. It was then that he heard the distinctive scream. Stopping abruptly; his body stiffened as he realized the location from where it came from.....home. He began to run hard through the woods, dodging and ducking the limbs and trees, leaping over ravines and downed logs in his haste to reach the cabin.

He smelled the intruder and the blood before he came upon the gruesome scene in the yard. The dead wolf lay in a puddle of its own blood with a jagged fragment of a 2x4 sticking out of its gut. Splatters of scarlet covered the surrounding area and it was clear that there had been a horrific struggle. His heart lurched at the instantly recognizable scent of Elisa's blood and he scrambled up to the door of the cabin, bursting through it and skidding to a halt in the living room floor. Elisa stood at the entry way to the kitchen, blood soaking her clothes while Andrea was just coming out of the bathroom. Upon seeing him, she shrieked and then looked as if she melted to the floor in slow motion.

Shane swiftly shifted and progressed toward Elisa on two feet but stopped mid-way as she met his eyes.

"Jeremy," I said softly, motioning toward his bedroom.

Hastening inside, he rushed to the bed with me close behind carrying the first aid kit.

By this time Jeremy had slipped into unconsciousness. Shane surveyed the damage to his friend and quaked with anger, "What happened?" he growled.

"I'll tell you...but we need to get rid of Andrea," I answered in a hushed tone, "Jeremy said you would take care of her."

He stared at me for a moment before nodding, "Ok," he answered simply.

Disappearing momentarily, he returned with the clothes that he had shed earlier and pulled them on followed by his boots. While he was dressing he watched as I began to carefully clean Jeremy's face and then start on the wounds that covered his body. When I pulled the covers away he saw the extent of the injuries that were spread over him and a low growl escaped his throat. Storming from the room, he slammed the door closed behind him.

I removed my blood soaked coat slowly. A dull ache engulfed my entire body and I yearned to just lie down and curl up. After removing my shirt, I peered down at the long gouges that extended from my shoulder to my elbow and another set of deep scratches that crossed from one side of my rib cage to the other. The flesh was laid wide open and the blood continued to seep from the openings. The bite on my shoulder had bled the least amount but throbbed worse than the others.

I could hear Shane's voice through the wall followed by the thankfully muffled sound of Andrea's shrill tone. They entered the bedroom and she gathered her things quickly, her eyes momentarily shifting across the bloody sight on the bed before exiting hastily, followed closely by Shane who once again closed the door behind him. A few minutes passed and I heard the cabin door open, close again, and the sound of Andrea's car starting. The hum of the motor faded as she drove away.

Jeremy's weak grasp on my wounded arm jerked me back to painful awareness. I looked down at him but both eyes were closed as if he wasn't really awake and his hold on my arm suddenly fell away, leaving his bloody handprint across the torn skin. The bedroom door opened and Shane entered; gasping when he saw the gashes across my bared abdomen. Helpless anger flashed across his face before it softened and he moved to my side.

As I cleaned and doctored Jeremy's wounds, Shane tended to mine. We worked in silence, neither speaking until Jeremy and I were cleaned and bandaged. I finished undressing and threw the blood soaked clothes in a pile on the floor. Leaving, I returned wearing a pair of pajama bottoms and a clean t-shirt.

I moved back to Jeremy's side and tucked the comforter securely around him. "He has lost a lot of blood, Shane, I'm worried," I said.

"It will take him a few days but he'll be fine," he answered, "We heal quickly."

I nodded, but became suddenly overwhelmed by the incident. My face twisted into a release of emotion and the tears flowed freely. Shane tenderly pulled me into his arms and held me tightly while I cried. "I was....so scared."

"I shouldn't have left," he answered, gently rubbing my back trying to ease the fear that engulfed me.

"You couldn't have known he'd come," I said, wiping my face with the back of my hand. "You wouldn't have left if you had," I sobbed.

Shane shook his head, "No, of course I wouldn't," he paused, "You killed him...didn't you?" he asked. It was more of a statement than a question because he already knew the answer.

I nodded and the tears flowed heavily, "He was going to kill us," I gurgled. He stood and held me for a while, letting me release the distress that was built up inside. When I calmed, I told him exactly what had happened.

"It's over now," he reassured me, gently pushing his hand through my tangled, matted hair. "I'm proud of you."

"What did you do about Andrea?" I suddenly questioned, "She was in a panic."

He smiled weakly, "I can be very....persuasive," he said softly.

"What does that mean?" I asked, "I don't think you could convince her to keep her mouth shut about everything she just saw here today."

He smiled, "I inherited a special gift from my mother," he began, "the ability to fog – for lack of a better word- people's minds."

"Fog?"

"Andrea will remember what she saw ....but only vaguely. It will be hazy like a dream. She will never mention it because she won't be able to fully grasp that it actually happened…….she'll think she dreamt it," he explained.

I studied him for a couple of moments and then averted my gaze back to Jeremy. "There's a lot more to you that I don't know, isn't there?" I asked, knowing that there was indeed, "You can tell me how you do it……one day," I said.

We stood together in silence and watched Jeremy's chest move with every labored breath. I felt certain that at any moment he would fail to inhale and just fade away but Shane assured me that he would live. There was nothing else that could be done for him until it was time to clean the wounds and reapply fresh bandages again so we left him to rest.

Nightfall had come and I could see that the clouds hadn't hidden the full moon from the dark night sky as I passed by the window. Its glow edged in around the drawn curtains and beaconed to me to get a closer look. A skiff of snow had fallen and hidden the remnants of the gruesome bloody incident beneath its crisp, clean whiteness. I didn't have to squint to make out the form that lay covered by the new snowfall; it was the only evidence that something had taken place there…other than my soreness and Jeremy's tattered body.

As if reading my mind, Shane's hand came to rest on my shoulder as his body pressed protectively against mine "I've got to get rid of it."

"The ground is too frozen to bury it………" I stammered as my voice faded.

"I'll burn it," he stated and without delay pulled on his coat and went outside.

Returning to Jeremy's room, I sat down on the edge of the bed touching his face gently with my fingertips, hoping that he knew he wasn't alone. He moved slightly in response to my touch, "Jeremy?" I said quietly as I smoothed his hair from his forehead.

"I need water," he croaked.

Instantly, I left the room and returned with a cup of ice water. I helped him lift his head and placed the cup against his lips, allowing him a small sip before easing his head back to the pillow.

"Better?" I asked.

"Yeah," he responded hoarsely. He started to say something more but I quieted him.

"Save your energy………we can talk later."

He didn't try to speak any more but instead moved his hand to cover mine with his own. The warmth was starting to return to his skin and I could feel it radiating into mine. It was a good sign. I sat with him there silently as outside, Shane ignited the monstrous pile of broken lumber he had torn out of the cabin.

He stood and stared into the flames as they swirled and danced before he heaved the lifeless form of the wolf into the center of the inferno. Watching as the blaze devoured the fur and blistered the skin of the beast, he could hear the sizzle and hiss as its flesh began to liquefy into the fiery sea of flames.

"Go back to hell where you came from," he growled under his breath.

Chapter 20

By the next morning Jeremy was wide awake and able to open the eye that had been swollen shut only a few hours before. He demanded a shower so Shane assisted him to the bathroom, got the shower regulated and managed to get him under the stream of water without getting totally soaked himself. Once reassured that he wasn't going to fall, he left him to finish and went back to his bedroom.

Elisa was still asleep, turned on her side with her dark hair fanned out across the pillow. He wanted to let her sleep but couldn't stop his fingers from gently tracing the line of her cheekbone. She stirred, opened her green eyes and sighed drowsily. Leaning down, he kissed her lightly on the lips as he smoothed his hand across her hair.

"How do you feel?" he asked softly.

Suddenly, I became aware of the overpowering smell of soap mixed with his strong scent, "Did you just shower?"

"Last night, late," he answered, "After I……..I smelled like smoke."

"Oh."

"Let me see what this looks like this morning," he mentioned as he began removing the tape and loosening the bandage on my upper arm. As it fell away, he looked up into my face with a troubled expression.

Glancing down, I gasped.

Where the wolf's claws had ripped deep, wide gashes, my flesh had strangely pulled together overnight into rough, scabbed seams. The redness had disappeared, leaving the lesions to look as if they were days old….not hours. Quickly, I tore the dressings from my ribcage and observed those injuries as well. They were the same; my tissues unexpectedly repairing themselves in the brief amount of time that had passed.

"How…….." I began, alarm in my voice.

Shane stared at me in disbelief, "It's almost like………," but he stopped himself before he said it aloud. Our eyes locked and neither of us spoke as if by saying something aloud would imminently make it the truth. We both silently acknowledged that the conversation was over.

Shane rubbed his hands through his hair in exasperation as he tried to fathom how this might've happened; if it had happened. He wasn't here when everything had transpired but what he did know was that the fullest phase of the moon…..had been yesterday. Could she have been infected?

"Should you check on Jeremy?" I asked in a controlled voice as I attempted to hide the true emotional turmoil that seethed inside. He glanced at me for a moment and then stood up and left the room, his thoughts clearly wreaking their own special kind of havoc.

Jeremy had made it out of the shower by himself and wore a towel around his waist. Shane didn't knock but instead barged right in.

Jeremy's eyebrows rose with surprise, "Damn," he muttered, "Could've knocked or something."

Shane's eyes surveyed the injuries that covered the exposed parts of his body and how the deep punctures had already began to fill in and lighten. "Glad to see your humor's returning," he replied, "And you're healing up," he added.

Jeremy's eye was still swollen although no longer clinched shut and a deep gash stood out on the top edge of his cheekbone. There were various bite marks along his shoulders and neck and scratches that stretched from his chest, down his abdomen and disappeared beneath the wrap of the towel. There were very few areas on him that didn't bear witness to yesterday's vicious attack.

"Wish I'd have been here, Jeremy," Shane said stiffly.

Jeremy braced himself against the wall and sighed, "Well, you weren't," he responded. "No matter how much you wished you had been."

He managed to hobble over and sit down on the toilet to rest. He felt the exertion from just taking a shower and trying to dry his body.

Hell with it, he thought to himself, *I'll just sit here until I drip dry.* "But," he continued, "We're going to be okay."

Shane wondered if he should tell Jeremy what he suspected but decided against it. He would know soon enough if Elisa had been infected with the werewolf's blood. They would both know.

"Would you grab my pajama pants out of my room?" Jeremy asked, "And maybe a shirt."

Shane nodded, "Sure."

By this time Elisa was already in Jeremy's room pulling the stained sheets off of his bed and remaking it with fresh ones. He knew she was achy and stiff as he watched her stop and rest periodically before carrying on with the task.

"I'll help you with that as soon as I get him some clothes," Shane told her.

I looked up and smiled half-heartedly, "It's ok. I've got it."

He left with the clothes in his hand and in a few minutes returned with Jeremy, his arm around his waist for support. Jeremy's eyes fixed on Elisa as Shane helped him sit down on the freshly made bed and she returned a weak smile.

"How are you feeling?" Jeremy asked me as he motioned for me to come closer, "Are you alright?"

I moved to stand in front of him and placed a reassuring hand on his shoulder, "I'm fine."

Jeremy instantly positioned his hands on my waist and pulled me to him, pressing his face gently against my stomach. Normally I might have felt uncomfortable with his gesture, but somehow now, it seemed appropriate.

Shane stood back and watched the scene unfold before him; his displeasure obvious yet he didn't move or say a word. He hadn't been a part of the suffering or the brutality that they had experienced together the previous day and he knew from experience that those kinds of emotions needed released.

My eyes threatened tears as I rubbed my fingers through Jeremy's hair while he held onto me firmly, his grasp uncompromising.

When he spoke, his voice was strained with emotion, "I'm sorry that I failed you," he uttered.

The tears overflowed and cascaded down my face. "You didn't fail me," I managed to say, my voice trembling; "You saved me."

At this point Shane moved forward and rested one hand on Jeremy's shoulder and the other on Elisa's back. He felt suddenly overwhelmed with the realization that he could have lost both of them in a matter of only minutes, the blink of an eye. Elisa responded by wrapping her arm around his waist and his heart wrenched in his chest when he glimpsed the sorrow in her eyes.

"You saved each other," he said softly, "I'm thankful."

Jeremy's hand reached up and grasped Shane's forearm firmly.

The three of them held on to one another in grateful silence, each reflecting on the devastating loss that could have prevailed after yesterday's unexpected attack. Shane realized in that moment that his loyalty and devotion to these two surpassed what he had ever experienced before. Together they were a pack.... his new pack.

I felt that I was part of a family again; enveloped in the strong, protective arms that encircled me. I knew that either of these two men would fight for my safety or die defending me; I would do the same for them without hesitation. My intimate relationship with Shane and the close friendship that I shared with Jeremy meant more to me than anything else in my life. They were my family now...the three of us.

Jeremy's body ached but he denied the pain; he dared not break the connection with their comforting support. He could feel the healing capabilities of their affectionate touches upon him; not repairing his flesh but instead restoring his faith. He and Shane had a long history, as close as brothers could be. They had shared their childhoods, wreaked havoc during their teenage years together and grew into respectable men side by side. And now, because of him, Elisa had walked into his life. In her, he had discovered a friendship and closeness like none he had known with any female, even his mother. He was secure within these walls that they built around him and he felt confidence in the stability of his newly established pack family.

Chapter 21

I watched in disbelief with each passing day the substantial difference in my injuries. Before my eyes, they had healed and were now only barely noticeable marks upon my skin. The pain was nearly nonexistent with only some slight soreness at the wound sites. Shane had noticed as well but he refused to acknowledge my quick recovery as anything but good genetics. Try as he might to conceal it, I could see the worry shadowed in his eyes when he spoke. To shield him from the truth that he already knew, I avoided mentioning anything else that was happening.

Jeremy, however, had very little concern for my privacy.

Jeremy made the dreaded phone call to Andrea to feel out the situation and see what she might remember. Luckily, she seemed to be her normal, pretentious self with no mention of what she had witnessed. She did however; invite him to spend Thanksgiving with her and some of her friends in town. Although less than excited about the idea, he coolly accepted her offer; justifying it as a means to further his investigation about what she might remember. As he began to pack his overnight bag he noticed Elisa heading towards the laundry room with a full basket of laundry.

"Hey!" he yelled, startling her and causing her to drop the basket and spill its contents. She whirled around to look at him.

"You don't have to do our laundry you know."

I cocked a disapproving eyebrow, "Yeah, I know," I told him as I bent down to gather the bloody clothes and sheets and stuff them back in the basket, "Some of these are mine though." Jeremy kneeled down beside me to help as I continued to speak, "I want to get this stuff washed up before I head home."

He stopped and looked at me, concentrating on my face until I felt his penetrating stare and finally looked up. "Do you think that Shane is just going to let you go home.... by yourself, and with everything else going on?" He asked cynically and then laughed in a mocking tone.

I scrunched my eyebrows together, "I need to go home," I said, "The place is probably cold and I need to turn the heat up. Plus, I have my own things to take care of there," I argued. Looking down, I resumed gathering the laundry. Jeremy reached over and grabbed my hand causing my eyes to jerk back to his face.

"If Shane wants to deny it, that's his problem, but you need to talk about what's happening to you," he paused, "You don't need to be alone right now Elisa."

My face fell suddenly and I could feel the tears forming, "Shane won't talk about this," I sobbed, "and I don't understand how this could've happened!"

Jeremy rubbed my hand reassuringly, "Shane feels responsible since he wasn't here to protect you," he said, "And as far as how it happened.....I don't really know ...we were covered in each other's blood."

"He made it sound so complicated," I cried, "Like it was almost impossible to happen or live through!"

Jeremy's expression softened before he spoke, "You almost didn't live through it," he reminded me, "If it hadn't been for your quick thinking neither of us wouldn't have." His eyes hardened with regret, "I couldn't have saved you."

My tears slowed and I stood, picking up the once again full basket. Jeremy rose up in front of me, "Shane will come around," he said, "Talk to him."

I nodded and moved away toward the laundry room.

Jeremy headed back to his room to continue packing and then to the bathroom to get his toothbrush. He met me again on his way through with his toothbrush in hand.

"Are you going somewhere?" I asked.

"Yeah," he said reluctantly, "Andrea's. She asked me to come in for Thanksgiving so I was just packing a few things," his voice conveyed a less than enthusiastic tone.

My eyes widened, "Oh!" I exclaimed, "I was supposed to ask you and Shane to go with me to Edna and Dan's tomorrow! I totally forgot!"

Jeremy laughed out loud, "You've had some *other* things on your mind....."

"I'm supposed to make a pie or cake or something....I don't even remember now, " I stuttered.

He placed a steady hand on my arm, "Calm down.....take a breath."

We both jerked our heads toward the door as Shane came in. The blast of cold air he brought with him cooled the interior of the cabin quickly; bringing a chill to its warm occupants. He had been for a run and his bare human skin goose pimpled as he quickly closed the door behind him. He grabbed the robe he placed on the back of the door and pulled it on as he turned around.

I immediately advanced toward him, "I need to go home today," I said as I wrapped my arms around his waist, "I have to make a pie."

Shane was confused as he looked from me to Jeremy who met his questionable gaze with a shrug and a grin. He held me out away from him at arm's length and studied my serious expression, "A pie?"

"Or maybe a cake, I don't really remember," I replied, "I have to go to Edna and Dan's tomorrow for Thanksgiving. I forgot about it and I said I would bring something. Would you go with me?"

From behind her Jeremy chuckled, "Breathe.........."

I ignored him and continued to wait for Shane's answer.

"I don't want to intrude on their family holiday," he said, "Didn't you say their kids come from other states?"

I shook my head, "Edna specifically told me to extend the invitation to you and to Jeremy." I turned to look at Jeremy accusingly, "But he has *other* plans." I peered back up into Shane's eyes.

"They have two sons that live out of state. Michael and Jeanette live in Wyoming and Brandon and Susan live in Colorado."

"Do you really want me to go?" Shane inquired.

I nodded excitedly, "Yes, I want you to go," I paused, "Unless you are strictly against it for some reason."

"No, no," he answered, "If it's important to you that I come with you, then I will."

I smiled broadly and pulled myself against him, hugging tightly. He looked at Jeremy who was smiling ear to ear and he grinned in response. "Well, I'd better get dressed if I'm going to take you home to make pie....or cake....or maybe a pie....," he joked.

We immediately missed the warmth of Shane's truck as we stepped inside the cold cabin. Having not been there for a few days to turn up the heat it had regulated back to a balmy 50 degrees. I set the thermostat on 75 and threw my overnight bag down in the kitchen chair.

Shane removed his coat and hung it on the back of the same chair. When he looked up, Elisa was staring at him, shaking her head.

"I can't believe you're not cold," I said, "I'm freezing!"

He held out his hand to me which I automatically accepted, and he pulled me to him. Wrapping his arms around me he teased, "I'll keep you warm."

"You're really not cold?"

Shane smiled, "No, I don't normally get cold...I'm from up north, I'm quite used to it."

I pulled away from him and grabbed my overnight bag, "I'm going to put this stuff away how I'm warming up. Should we make coffee or something?"

Shane nodded, "I'll make some," he said as he watched me pull some of the items out of my bag. My toothbrush and shampoo in hand, I headed toward the bathroom; he followed me inquisitively.

"Won't you need that stuff tomorrow?" he asked, his eyebrows pulled together questioningly.

"What do you mean?" I asked innocently, "Of course I'll need it."

Shane immediately realized I was trying to pull something over on him. "It will be hard to use that stuff if it's here," he motioned with his head the direction of his cabin, "and you're there."

The conversation with Jeremy flashed through my mind. He had told me quite frankly that Shane wasn't going to just let me mosey on home. I sighed heavily and looked up into his intent stare. "I've got to come home sometime," I replied, "I can't stay over there with you forever."

"Why can't you?" he quickly responded and then waited patiently for me to answer; his eyes twinkling with amusement.

"Because that's your home, and Jeremy's home; I have a home already...*here*," I paused, "Everything that I own is *here*....all of my things are *here*."

"*Wherever I am* is your home," he said softly, "I had hoped you understood that."

I suddenly felt guilty, "I *do* understand that Shane, but I don't want to keep living out of my suitcase."

He smiled with understanding, "I know that feeling all too well." He hesitated, "But were going to have to remedy this one way or another....I don't want you to be alone," an unexpected shadow passed across his face and settled in his eyes.

Was he finally going to talk about what might be happening? I asked myself. I tried to structure a reply that would urge him into that conversation before I spoke again, "I'm use to being alone Shane."

"I know that," he replied, "It's a little different now though," he stopped and studied me; the uncertainty and question expressed in my face, "You need to have someone around."

"But I'm safe now, right?" I baited him, "The danger is gone."

Shane sighed and took my hand in his large, warm grasp, "Yes Elisa," he began, "*That* danger *is* gone but that isn't what I'm talking about," he said simply, "I haven't been the most open to the possibility that you could be....like me."

His face was solemn as he spoke, "It will be a very tough time for you," he paused, "That's what I'm worried about most."

I smiled and squeezed his hand reassuringly, "It doesn't seem like a horrible thing...to be like you."

"I know no other way of life," he replied softly, "but *you* do. There will be changes and you will have questions...concerns.....it changes you emotionally, not just physically."

He paused and then added, "I just don't want you to be alone if something does happen and it scares you and no one is around."

"I know you're just looking out for me," I responded, "But we don't know for sure if anything is going to happen. I'll stay with you if it will make you feel better, or you can stay here...but for how long are we talking?"

"You'll know within a month," he replied delicately, watching for my reaction.

"How?" I asked inquisitively.

"Your senses will drastically improve....you'll be able to smell, hear and see things much better than you ever did before," he stated. "What concerns me is if the wolf comes out and you don't know how to control it...."

"Well, I'm not going to let this worry me." I sighed, "Nothing spectacular has happened yet. When it does, I'll tell you."

"Good," he smiled, "That's what I want you to do."

"But, what if I am.....?" I waited earnestly for an answer.

Shane smiled; it was the brilliant smile that I had first seen when we had met and the one that I had learned was his most jovial. He reached up and swept his fingers across my lips before stepping forward and brushing across them with his own.

"We will share everything," he whispered against my cheek.

I didn't grasp the concept of what he truly meant but it seemed to me that he actually *wanted* me to be like him.

"And if I'm not?" I asked softly, somehow now afraid of the answer he might give.

But as he pulled away, his smile remained unfaltering, "It doesn't matter to me Elisa. If you are ......if you're not. It will *never* change that we are supposed to be together."

I wrapped my arms around his large frame and pulled him close. His body was comforting as he held me tightly, locked in an unyielding embrace for what seemed like minutes. I felt the security seep from him into my every pore and fill my heart until it overflowed. He allowed me to pull away but his face reflected the disappointment.

"I have to make a pie," I grinned.

"Yes you do," he smirked, "Or maybe a cake," he joked.

I spent the next couple of hours going through recipes and searching through the cupboard trying to come up with the right ingredients to make something sensational. Once I found something I set to work and when I was finished a delicious apple pie was cooling on the table. After being ran out of the kitchen for trying to help out, Shane had reclined on the couch watching television and had dozed off.

While he slept, I went into the bedroom and started refilling my overnight bag. Clean underwear, clean socks…..shirts….jeans….*crap.* I went to the closet and pulled out a much larger suitcase and began taking the clothes out of the overnight bag and stacking them in the suitcase.

Now, what about tomorrow? Wanting to dress a little nicer for our visit, I retrieved a sweater, skirt, black tights and tall black boots from the closet. I also grabbed my makeup bag and curling iron from the bathroom and packed in away to take as well. Within a half hour I had everything ready to go.

Deciding that I would drive the SUV in tomorrow, I went ahead and loaded it with my clothes. Shane had gotten up when he heard me go outside and was standing in the doorway when I came back across the yard. I smiled at him as he held the door open.

"Have a nice little nap?" I joked as I sauntered in beside him.

He laughed as he rubbed his face with both hands, "You wouldn't let me help so…..what else was I supposed to do?" He asked cynically, "What are you doing any way?"

"Were going to take my car tomorrow so I'll follow you over when you're ready," I returned. I glanced at the clock on the kitchen wall and was surprised at how late it had become. Shane's eyes followed my gaze.

"I guess I'm ready," he said after seeing the time. He picked his coat up and shrugged his shoulders into it and noticed the pie on the table. "That looks good…..you should have made an extra."

"I only had enough stuff for one….and thanks for reminding me to grab it," I said as I pulled on my coat and then picked the pie up.

"I guess were ready then?"

Shane nodded as he held flipped off the light and held the door open. I passed by with the pie in hand and proceeded down the steps. Hearing Shane pull the door closed and rattle the knob to make sure it was locked made me smile. In two strides he was beside me, opening the car door.

Chapter 22

    The next morning I awoke early. Too early. Glancing over at the digital clock on Shane's nightstand I sighed; 5:43 A.M. The strong scent of coffee wafted through my nostrils and I knew that Jeremy must be up. For some reason that I hadn't figured out yet, he couldn't ever sleep in.

    I turned on my side to face Shane, shifting slowly from underneath the weight of his arm. Although the room was dark, I could make out the distinct profile of his handsome face on the pillow beside me and I smiled. He was a beautiful, strong man…and he was mine. Leaning forward carefully, I kissed him lightly on his stubbly cheek before edging off of my side of the bed.

    I retrieved Shane's robe off of the hook and pulled it tightly around me; it smelled like him. Cracking the door open, I squeezed out and shut it silently behind me and then padded quietly into the kitchen. Jeremy was sitting at the table with a cup of coffee in his hand and a magazine opened up before him on the table. He seemed to be intently reading but without looking up spoke softly.

    "Good morning."

    "Good morning." I responded quietly, "Do you have something against sleeping late?" I kidded.

    He looked up grinning, "No sense in sleeping my life away."

    I moved to the coffee pot and filled a cup and as I looked down, I noticed a plate and fork in the sink. The food fragments that had been left on the plate looked strangely like…..pie crumbs!

    I wheeled around, my eyes searching the table and counters and finally settling on the pie pan. I strode over and looked down reluctantly, then turned to stare at Jeremy's back.

    "Jeremy," I whispered loudly, the agitation obvious in my voice. When he didn't respond I spoke louder, adding fuel to the flickering flame of anger that had been lit. "Jeremy!" He pivoted in his chair and met my fiery green gaze, "Did you eat my pie?" I growled

    Holy shit, Jeremy thought to himself as he saw the emerald glow in her eyes and heard the low growl in her throat.

    I ate the pie and awoke the beast, "I'm sorry…..was I not supposed to? It was really good pie," although he grinned, he was uncertain if now was the time to tease her.

    "I made that to take with us today," I said flatly, the gleam fading slightly.

"Really, I'm sorry," Jeremy said warily, "I thought since you left it on the table it was fair game." He got up from his chair and advanced cautiously toward her, careful to avoid eye contact as he held his hand out.

The rage diminished as quickly as it had come over me and I spiraled downward, my emotions raw. I gratefully accepted the hand that he offered and when he finally allowed his eyes to settle on mine, he realized that the wolf had retreated. He pulled my trembling body into his arms, holding me tightly and stroking my hair.

"I'm really sorry that I ate the pie...I didn't know," he apologized. He was unsure if he was apologizing for the pie as much as apologizing for what just happened. She allowed him to hold her for a few moments before she backed away, the counter preventing further retreat.

"Are you ok?" he asked softly.

"I think so.....I just got so...angry," I whispered.

"I know," he replied, "I could tell...and all about a pie," he chuckled in his attempt to be humorous but she continued to look at him blankly.

"I've never felt anything like that before," my voice seemed small in the early morning silence.

"This is exactly why you don't need to be alone, Elisa," Jeremy said soothingly, "Shane and I can handle you no matter what happens....and help you." He urged her toward the table, "Why don't you sit down for a minute."

She did as he asked and he sat the cup of coffee down in front of her. Absentmindedly, she lifted it to her lips and took a small sip, her eyes emotionless. He permitted her to sit silently for a few minutes before he spoke again, "Do you want to talk to me about it?"

Turning my head to look at him, I nodded but didn't begin to talk immediately. He waited patiently for a few additional minutes before he encouraged me.

"What did you feel...besides anger?"

"Tingling," I replied quietly, "and a million tiny needles poking me," I paused, "From the inside."

"Was it painful?"

I shook my head, "Not painful, just uncomfortable."

He laid a consoling hand across mine, "One day," he said, "You will look forward to that feeling, and it won't be uncomfortable anymore," he hesitated, "It will feel like being set free." He smiled at me as he rubbed my hand in an attempt to reassure me.

"I'm scared," I admitted.

Jeremy chuckled lightly, "You'd be crazy not to be," he joked.

Elisa sat in silence, as if concentrating on the coffee cup before her, her fingers fidgeting with the handle. Jeremy casually resumed reading the magazine spread out in front of him but he wasn't absorbing the information. Instead, he kept a vigilant eye cocked in her direction as he tried to determine if he should say or do anything more.

Suddenly she stood up, sighed, and dismissed herself. Jeremy's eyes followed her as she headed toward the bathroom. He waited until he heard the shower turn on before he attempted to resume his early morning reading, but his mind just wasn't in it any longer.

"Good morning," Shane's voice startled him back to reality and he pitched back in his chair. He chuckled as he passed him on his way to the coffee pot, "Jumpy much?"

Jeremy didn't comment. Not even a sound escaped his lips until Shane seated himself on the opposite side of the table and looked up over his coffee cup, "We've got a problem," he said.

Shane's cup lowered and his brows knitted together, "What kind of problem?"

"Elisa had a, uh, ...an episode this morning," he answered flatly.

Shane sat his cup down. His voice concerned when he spoke, "She in the shower?"

Jeremy nodded.

"What kind of episode?" Shane questioned.

"It all started with damn pie," Jeremy replied sarcastically, "I thought since it was sitting in the middle of the table that I could eat it," he paused, "Apparently, I was wrong."

Shane cocked and eyebrow, "You ate the pie and it caused an...*episode*?"

"Uh huh," he nodded, "She got pretty upset," Jeremy declared. "So upset that I could see the wolf in her eyes."

Shane felt a chill pass up the length of his spine and his eyes narrowed, "Are you certain?"

"I'm certain," Jeremy answered, "And then we talked about it a little bit. She told me how she had felt," He waited before continuing, "Its coming Shane. We need to be prepared."

Shane nodded, and exhaled sharply, "This trip may not be a good idea today."

"Maybe not, but you're not going to convince her of that," Jeremy returned smugly, "Just be ready."

Shane walked purposefully toward the bathroom and disappeared inside, shutting the door softly behind him. When she stepped out onto the plush bath mat, he was sitting in the chair where she had thrown his robe randomly. His eyes traveled over her wet body hungrily as he picked up the towel and wrapped her snugly within it before embracing her in his arms.

"Are you alright this morning?" he asked, his voice silvery and low.

"Jeremy told you what happened?" I inquired, already knowing that he had.

Shane nodded as he sat back in the chair and pulled her onto his lap. Elisa could see the intent in his eyes as he moved his hands up and down her back and then kissed her lightly on the neck.

"What do you think about the trip today?" he mumbled against her skin as he continued to move his mouth over her without waiting for her answer.

I couldn't answer, concentrating on the touch of his lips as they journeyed up my neck and settled on mine. He kissed me tenderly while he removed the towel and let it fall to the floor. His warm hands traveled over my body, caressing and stroking until I trembled with anticipation. In a few moments he had stripped away his lounge pants and pulled me down to straddle him on the chair. My wet hair draped across him producing cold, wet droplets that spattered on his face as he raised me above him. When he lowered me, he allowed me to take over and ease myself onto his shaft. My body greedily devoured him and set the pace that brought us both close to release.

Shane shifted forward causing her back to fall into his waiting arms and while he held her, his mouth and tongue ravaged her breasts. He continued to thrust into her bringing her closer and closer to liberation. Beginning to moan softly, a low guttural sound resonated from deep in her throat that grew louder with each shove. He was fully aware what was happening and wasn't alarmed when her eyes changed to an eerie green glow as the waves of pleasure racked her body. Just as he reached his own fulfillment a loud hammering arose on the bathroom door.

"There's like *one* bathroom in this whole freakin' place," Jeremy's voice was muffled by the wooden door but Shane could hear his agitation, "You guys *could* do that somewhere else."

"Hang on," Shane answered with a grin as he lifted Elisa to a standing position in front of him, "We're getting ready to come out."

"Don't take too much longer," Jeremy warned.

Shane heard his footsteps retreating and then turned his attention back to me, watching as I wrapped my long dark hair up in a towel. He reached out and ran his fingertips lightly between my breasts and down across my flat abdomen.

"I think Jeremy needs in here."

I nodded and retrieved his robe from the back of the chair, wrapping it tightly around me while Shane pulled on his pants. I opened the door and exited with Shane close behind. Jeremy abruptly got up from his position on the couch where he had been waiting, entered the bathroom and slammed the door behind him in disgust.

I picked up my cup off of the table and refilled it before sitting back down. I suddenly remembered an initiated conversation cut short. "What did you want to say about the trip?"

Shane was amused at how quickly she picked their conversation back up where it had been left off. He chuckled softly before his countenance turned more serious, "With what's going on....maybe we should forego the holiday with your friends."

"No," I answered quickly, "I don't want to miss Thanksgiving." My eyes expressed the disappointment at his suggestion.

"I know you don't, but I don't think it's a good idea," he disclosed, "I'm concerned."

I sighed and sat down, "Come on....it's just for one day," I pleaded, "It will be alright."

Shane moved to stand behind my chair and placed his hands on my shoulders. With skillful motions he massaged the tension from my neck and back and then leaned down close to my ear, "And what will we do if something does happens?" he whispered.

A bit more relaxed, I replied calmly, "Nothing will happen," I said, "And if it should, you will be there to take care of me."

Shane turned away and refilled his cup before returning to the table. He sat down across from her and immediately noticed the questioning gaze as she waited for his consent. On one hand, he understood the consequences he faced if he refused to allow her to go. But on the other, he also knew the chaos and disorder that would prevail if a problem should present itself. He was damned if he did and still damned if he didn't.

"We'll go," he finally agreed, "But we leave when I say."

I nodded with a grin. "It will be ok." I chirped, "I promise."

Shane nodded hesitantly. I got up and retrieved what was left of the apple pie off of the counter. Along with two forks, I returned to the table and sat down. I held one fork out to Shane.

"We may as well eat this," I laughed.

Shane grinned and together they ate half of the pie before Jeremy returned from the bathroom. He stopped, scowling with his hands on his hips when he saw what they were doing.

"Isn't that nice?" he said sarcastically, "Hell gets called down on me when I eat the pie but look at this!" he joked.

"We saved you the last piece," I said as I handed the pie plate towards him. Without hesitation he took it and sat down at the end of the table. Not even concerned with a clean fork, he began shoveling the remainder of the pie in his mouth, scoop by scoop until only a residue was left in the bottom of the pan. He leaned back in the chair and extended his legs out in front of him and rubbed his stomach.

"Great pie," he reiterated.

The morning hastened by as the three prepared to go their separate ways for the holiday. Jeremy's overnight bag sat on the floor by the couch as he finished gathering any final items that he thought he might need. Shane had dressed, and he now lounged on the couch with a cup of coffee in black jeans, black boots and a blue button up shirt that matched the striking hue of his eyes. Elisa had been in the bathroom getting ready and when she finally stepped out, Shane allowed a low growl to vocalize.

Her dark hair hung in long loose curls that cascaded in graceful waves over her slim shoulders. There was the hint of purple above her green eyes and the whisper of deep rose that she had applied to her invitingly plump lips. He smiled as he let his eyes travel down her dark purple, snug fitting sweater. The deep neck opening allowed just a suggestion of cleavage but yet was fully concealing. She wore a black, velvet skirt that stopped just past mid thigh paired with black pantyhose and boots that came nearly to her knees. He stood up and walked toward her but stopped before reaching the place that she stood. He smiled broadly.

"You look.....beautiful," he said huskily as his eyes consumed every inch of her.

"Thank you," I said softly.

A low whistle came from behind her as Jeremy came out of his room, "Damn!"

Shane witnessed Jeremy's eyes travel over her, head to toe just as his had done. He quirked an eyebrow when their eyes met but Jeremy quickly averted his gaze back to Elisa. She was grinning, a slight flush on her cheeks.

"You clean up nice!" he teased.

Shane advanced and moved his hand up to tangle gently in my hair and then leaned in to brush a light kiss across my lips, "You do look beautiful," he whispered.

"You look quite handsome yourself," I replied, letting my hands smooth down the front of his shirt.

I immediately turned to look at Jeremy and noticed that he too was impressive in dark jeans, a form fitting deep burgundy button up shirt and tan loafers, "You look very nice too Jeremy."

He smiled, "Thanks," he picked up his duffel bag and turned to face them. "Well, I'm heading out," he said coolly, "You guys enjoy your day."

I walked over and wrapped my arms around him affectionately, "Happy Thanksgiving, and be careful," I said softly.

He returned my embrace, "Guess I'll be home sometime tomorrow."

Shane nodded and grinned, "Have fun," he ribbed.

"Yeah," Jeremy smirked, "See you two later."

He opened the door and stepped out. Shane and I heard the echo of his footsteps across the porch and the sound of his truck starting.

"Are you ready to go?" he asked, looking over at me.

"I believe so," I answered, "I'll get my coat."

Within a few minutes, we were on the road headed toward our destination.

Chapter 23

I smiled with anticipation as we pulled into the driveway at Edna and Dan's. The unfamiliar vehicles with out of state license plates indicated that the boys I grew up with were already there. I looked forward to seeing them every year during Thanksgiving and I was grateful that Shane had understood. After we parked the car and we got out and walked toward the door. Shane absentmindedly placed his hand on the small of my back as we ascended the steps. It was a gesture that I had become accustomed to.

My knock was answered by a short, friendly faced woman who smiled brightly as her eyes fell upon me. Her salt and pepper hair was pulled up in a loose bun on the back of her head which loosened even more as she grasped me and hugged me tightly, squealing with delight.

"It is so good to see you dear!"

Over my shoulder, her eyes took in the tall stranger standing slightly behind. Shane smiled brilliantly as their eyes met.

I stepped back from Edna's embrace quickly, "This is the neighbor that I told you about," I said, "Shane. Shane, this is Edna."

Shane immediately extended his hand which Edna seized with both of hers warmly, "So nice to meet you Edna," he said politely.

I saw that even at Edna's age she wasn't immune to Shane's handsome face and brilliant, friendly smile. I began to think that no woman was.

"So nice to meet you Shane," she said cheerfully, "I'm so glad that you could join us today," she grinned, "And I must say what a handsome *neighbor* that Elisa has acquired."

She chuckled softly as she turned and winked at Elisa, "Come in, come in!"

Shane's senses peaked as he picked up the many different pleasant odors of food wafting past Edna from inside the house but among them was something that wasn't food. The strong scent of wolf mixed in with the pleasing aromas that his nose detected. His nostrils flared and his body tensed as they entered the house behind the woman. He placed a protective hand on Elisa's shoulder as they moved into the living room full of people.

His eyes searched the group within as Elisa made her way to a man that stood and advanced toward her, his smile broad and inviting. Three children played in the center of the room where a tall woman with long blonde hair was bending over to scoop up a smaller child in her arms. Suddenly she turned her head, her eyes meeting Shane's from across the room. She seemed startled as her brown eyes locked on his and for a brief moment she held his gaze. Flipping her hair back, she angled her chin slightly, exposing her neck before averting her eyes from his. When she looked back at him, his slight and approving nod went unnoticed by anyone else in the room.

    In those few seconds of exchange, Shane already knew quite a bit of information. The woman understood the order of the pack and had unconsciously gestured her submission to him. This meant that she had obviously grown up as a part of pack life. With no detection of another wolf scent in the room, he also knew that she belonged to one of the human males there.

    He was first presented to Brandon, Susan and their two sons; Damon and Wyatt. He learned that their family was in from Colorado and Brandon was the eldest of Dan and Edna's sons. He was of average height with dark blonde hair and glasses and seemed to be a bit on the shyer side but grasped Shane's hand firmly when introduced. Susan was petite with red hair and a boisterous character who smiled pleasantly as Shane extended his hand to her.

    The youngest son, Michael was the man who had met Elisa enthusiastically when she had initially entered the room. He was taller than Brandon at a bit over 6 foot with light brown hair and an athletic build. Confidently, he took Shane's hand in a firm greeting and then turned to the tall blonde woman who stepped forward, the child still balanced on her hip.

    "This is my wife, Jeanette," he said.

    Jeanette extended her free hand to Shane who accepted it as his eyes locked on hers. She smiled timidly as he acknowledged her, "Jeanette," he said cordially, nodding.

    "And this," Michael said, reaching over to rough the white blonde hair of the child that Jeanette was holding, "Is our daughter Abby."

    "And I'm Dan," a booming voice accompanied by a slap on his shoulder caused Shane to wheel around defensively to face the source. Elisa, who had come to his side, placed a calming hand on his arm indicating that he needn't be alarmed.

    Dan was a large, silver haired man who towered above nearly everyone in the room...except for Shane. They stood eye to eye with one another, the older man smiling broadly. He stretched his large hand out to Shane who immediately accepted it.

"Good to meet you...Shane, is it?"

"Yes sir," Shane replied respectfully, "Glad to meet you."

"Are you taking care of our girl here?" he asked, affectionately rubbing my arm. I instantly moved to embrace the big man.

"I'm doing my best," Shane replied honestly.

Once the introductions were complete, Shane and Elisa found empty places to sit among the family. Shane listened intently while Michael and Elisa talked about old times and he soon discovered that they had dated in their teenage years. Brandon added his memories to their stories as well and even though he had initially seemed timid, Shane couldn't help but laugh at his humorous views on past events.

Soon, Edna came from the kitchen to corral everyone for dinner and the group moved into the kitchen. Jeanette ended up sitting next to Shane when they seated themselves at the table and he sensed that it wasn't a complete accident that it had happened that way. Elisa was seated to his left and she reached over and patted his leg reassuringly.

"You okay?" she whispered.

Sensing her concern that he might feel out of place, he nodded and smiled; strangely, he didn't.

Pleasant small talk was exchanged over dinner along with conversations about Elisa's deceased parents that brought with it a sense of melancholy. Shane realized that they had all been and still remained a tightly knit bunch. It was no wonder that Elisa felt close to them and had not wanted to miss this day. From the corner of his eye, he noticed that Jeanette kept glancing over at him periodically. When he finally looked over, she again smiled timidly.

"Where are you from Shane?" She asked softly as she took a small bite of turkey. It seemed the entire table had quieted, waiting for his answer.

He cleared his throat uncomfortably, "Actually, I was born in Boston but I grew up in Canada," he answered.

Jeanette's soft-spoken voice seemed loud in the now silent room, "And you live by Elisa now?"

Shane nodded, "Yes, I bought some property just down the road from her place."

"The old Hawkmeyer place, right?" Dan asked, his voice carried above everyone else's.

"I wanted to get hold of that place years ago," he said, "But they wanted too much money for it."

"I got a pretty good deal," Shane answered.

"He's done quite a few renovations to it already," I added.

"What brought you all the way from Canada down this way?" Dan inquired.

Shane suddenly got the feeling he might be getting grilled....for Elisa's sake, something similar to protective parents.

"I was looking for some investment property initially," he paused, looking over at Elisa and then back to Dan. "But it's a nice area out that way and I may just stay."

After a few more questions, the conversation veered to other topics and Shane mentally sighed in relief. He leaned over to Elisa and asked her where the bathroom was. Overhearing, Jeanette immediately volunteered to show him since she herself was headed that direction as well. They excused themselves from the table and Shane followed her from the room. He had the distinct feeling that there was a reason she wanted to get him alone.

He was right.

As they climbed the stairs to the next floor, she hesitated at the top and turned to face him. When she spoke, it was in a low, soft voice that was barely above a whisper.

"It's been a long time since I've come across one of my own," she said.

"I'll admit that I didn't anticipate running across you here either," he responded, his own voice just barely audible.

"Does the family know?" Shane inquired.

"No. Michael of course, but no one else," her smiled was guarded, reserved, "Elisa?"

"Yes," he replied then changed the subject, "You don't see any of your family?"

"No," she said bluntly, "I was forced from the pack when Michael and I….." her voice trailed off. "My pack didn't believe in mixing with humans. I haven't seen any of them since I left."

Shane heard a hint of sadness in her voice although she was proficient in masking her emotions.

"I've always felt like an outsider here."

"I'm not sure how anyone could feel like an outsider here," Shane chuckled softly, "Everyone is quite friendly."

"Oh, no……Edna and Dan are great," she responded. "It's just being different……no one to share that part of my life with other than Michael," she hesitated, "I miss the feeling of having someone to run with."

Shane understood all too well what she felt. The sense of belonging to something bigger than you was something a wolf craved; it was pack stability. The feeling of running headlong through the forest with wolves beside you, in front of you and behind you; secure and protected in their midst.

As if she read his thoughts about getting back to everyone, she continued down the hall and stopped in front of a door.

"Here's the bathroom," she said, "There's another in the spare bedroom that I can use."

"Thanks," he said as he closed the door behind him.

Returning downstairs he took his place next to Elisa. Jeanette hadn't come back yet and he noticed Michael's gaze upon him from a couple of chairs down. Glancing over, he smiled but Michael's body language indicated that he was uneasy. Had something happened while they were gone? Jeanette returned and seated herself between Shane and Michael, who immediately put his arm possessively across the back of her chair.

They finished dinner and dessert without incident and as the hour grew late, Elisa began to say her good-byes. Once they had their coats on getting ready to walk out the door, Michael stepped forward.

"I'll walk you guys out," he said, grabbing his coat.

Sensing the tension in the man's body, Shane suddenly felt the edginess creep up his spine and move into his muscles with anticipation.

"Susan, would you please watch Abby for a minute?" Shane heard Jeanette's voice as they were walking out the door.

Reaching over, he took Elisa's hand in his, uncertain what was getting ready to transpire. Her fingers intertwined with his tightly, easing his mind momentarily. He stopped and waited for Michael to get to them but he had paused as Jeanette was coming down the steps. Once she was beside him, she walked stride for stride beside her husband until they stopped and stood in front of Shane and Elisa.

"Jeanette told me," Michael said as he gazed directly at Shane.

"Told you what?" I intervened.

Michael's eyes darted toward me but Jeanette was the one to speak, "He's a wolf," her voice was low and hushed.

I jerked my head toward Shane and then back to Jeanette.

"What's going on?" I demanded. It was obvious that something had occurred somewhere during the course of the afternoon.

"Jeanette and I have something in common," Shane said. His voice had taken on the unease that his body already felt. His eyes met hers before he warily looked toward Michael.

"Jeanette's a....." I stuttered before I could finish the question.

Jeanette smiled the sweet smile that matched her quiet disposition as Michael nodded, "Yes, she is a werewolf...just like Shane."

"When did you guys figure this all out?" I asked, still confused and wondering where I was when it had all come about.

"Shane and I sensed each other when you two first walked in the door," Jeanette calmly told me.

"Well regardless of all of that," Michael said, his voice agitated, "Against my better judgment, I have a favor to ask." His eyes locked on Shane's, "Jeanette has asked me if she could run with you....if you will allow it."

Shane felt a huge sigh of relief. He now understood why he had sensed that Michael was ruffled. His mate had asked him to run with another male....it was jealousy.

Shane looked at Elisa who seemed to still be confused and then back to Jeanette and Michael. "Do you mind if Elisa and I talk about this on the way home and I call you later tonight?"

He saw Jeanette's face slightly fall with disappointment.

"No, that's fine. I understand," Michael said gruffly. "I'll give you my cell number," he rattled off a number as Shane programmed it into his own phone.

"I'll call you either way," Shane said as he held out his hand to Michael. He hesitated before accepting it but finally did. Shane then turned to Jeanette who smiled half-heartedly. She held out her hand out and he took it without faltering.

"It would mean a lot to me," she said softly before allowing his hand to withdraw from her own. Shane nodded in acknowledgment and he and Elisa walked the short distance to the car and got in. As they pulled away, Shane could see them still standing where they had left them, their eyes watching the tail lights of the SUV as they pulled away.

"What happened in there Shane?" I asked. "How did I miss all of what was obviously going on?"

On the drive home, he explained how at the very moment we walked into the house he knew that another of his kind there. Realizing that there wasn't a threat, he didn't concern me with it and planned on telling me about Jeanette later. Apparently she had the mental connection with Michael to forewarn him about Shane, resulting in the change in Michael's entire demeanor.

Shane clarified that it wasn't normal once a pair was mated, for either to run with a member of the opposite sex alone, hence Michael's hostility. In this case though, Jeanette hadn't been in contact with another of her kind for years and she yearned for it. Shane admitted that it took a strong man to ask for such a favor for his mate….and then deal with the feelings that resulted.

"And so now that leads me to our present dilemma," he said. "How do you feel about Jeanette running with me?"

I scowled, "Is there a reason that I need to be concerned?"

He reached over and placed his warm hand on my knee, "No."

"Why do you think that Michael is so upset about it?"

"I know exactly why. It's the one thing he can't give to her," Shane answered, "He can be a mate, a husband and a father. He can share every aspect of her life…..except this one. He's bitter about having to ask another male to do this in his place."

"Is this why you said if I end up being like you, then we can share everything?"I inquired.

"Yes," he answered.

"Do you feel that it's that important to her?" I asked softly.

"Yes, I believe that it is very important."

"Then its okay with me Shane," I said.

He patted my leg reassuringly and then leaned over and kissed my cheek gently, "I'll call."

Shane hit the button on his phone and within a couple of seconds he was already having a conversation with Michael. They settled on the next day since they would be leaving to go home on Saturday.

"Tomorrow, then." Shane clicked the button and laid his phone on the console,

I nodded silently, lost in my own thoughts as I drove toward home. For all of this time, year after year I had visited with Edna, Dan, the boys and their families. And all of this time, Jeanette was right under my nose and I never had a clue…none of the family had any idea that she was any different. She and Michael had done a good job of keeping her secret and I couldn't help but wonder if he had even shared this information with his own brother.

That night, as Shane held Elisa in his arms he knew that he dare not vocalize his excitement and anticipation for the upcoming day. She snuggled in close to him and he found himself longing for the time that she would be able to accompany him on his runs; side by side. He drifted off to sleep hoping that she would embrace their new life together when the time finally came.

The morning light seeped in around the curtains urging Shane out of his slumber. Elisa still slept peacefully beside him but his eagerness to start the day prompted him to crawl from within the warm comfort of her arms. He pulled on his lounge pants and padded barefoot into the kitchen to start the coffee. He heard the unmistakable sound of a vehicle motor coming down the driveway and immediately recognized it as Jeremy's truck. He glanced at the time. 8:23 A.M. He was surprised that he was back so early.

Hearing the jingle of keys in the lock as Jeremy quietly opened the door, Shane moved to the kitchen entrance, "You're home early," he said.

"Yep," Jeremy answered, "It was time for me to get out of there," he answered as he walked into his room with his overnight bag, returning empty handed. Kicking back in a kitchen chair extending his legs out in front of him he sighed.

Shane filled up a couple of cups and handed it to him, "Bad night?" he asked as Jeremy carefully accepted the steaming cup he was offered.

Jeremy shrugged, "No, not really," he answered. "Just don't fit in with a bunch of hoity-toity people."

He took a sip of the coffee, "How did your day go?"

"Pretty good actually," Shane answered, smiling, "In fact, were going to have some company today."

He filled Jeremy in on the unexpected events from the day before with his new acquaintances over their first cups of coffee.

"That *is* an interesting turn of events," Jeremy said thoughtfully after Shane had finished, "It's a wonder that this Michael fella is going to let it happen."

"He knows she needs the interaction," Shane answered. "Wolves are sociable....she hasn't had that," he paused, "But it isn't as if he's jumping for joy over it, let me tell you."

"Hostile?" Jeremy asked.

Shane nodded, "It wouldn't take much for him to be provoked, "he responded. "But he understands what's happening between Elisa and me, and they're mated so it isn't as if there's another agenda."

"So….. I guess if I wanted to go along it might be a problem?" Jeremy wanted to know.

Shane shrugged, "I can't really say for sure. Since you're unattached, maybe….." he hesitated, "But, there are ways around that problem," he grinned.

Jeremy smiled back. He knew that Shane was indicating that he could just meet up with them in the woods but it seemed too sneaky. It also might startle the female and end up causing a much larger issue.

"I'll try to get the feel from the guy when they get here," Jeremy said, "If it's going to be a huge issue, I'll just hang here," He waited, "But it would be nice to run with a pack again."

"I've not told Elisa how excited I am about this," Shane admitted, "And if you go too, it will like old times," he smiled eagerly.

"I don't think that I would mention it to her either," Jeremy agreed as he sipped his coffee. He now felt a growing sense of anticipation. His only hope was that this Michael guy would allow him the opportunity to once again feel the companionship of wolves.

Chapter 24

When I awoke I could hear the soft muffled voices from the kitchen. I distinctly heard Shane's tone along with the familiar sound of Jeremy's. They spoke soft and low so I couldn't tell what they were saying but as I rolled over and looked at the clock, I wondered why Jeremy had come back home so early. Rising from the warm bed, I pulled on Shane's robe and padded into the kitchen in my sock feet.

"Good morning," I said cheerfully as I entered the kitchen and filled a cup of coffee before sitting down.

"Good morning," Shane and Jeremy answered at the same moment.

"I see you cut your time short?" I inquired as I looked at Jeremy.

"Uh huh," he said, "I'd had enough."

I chuckled, "I'd have had enough long before now," I joked.

Jeremy smiled in response but didn't expand on it any further.

"So what time did you say that Michael and Jeanette were coming?" I asked as I turned my attention to Shane.

"I didn't," he answered, "I just told them any time today since I wasn't planning on going anywhere."

"I hope that Michael will have loosened up a little bit today," I said, raising the cup to my lips as I eyed him over the brim.

"No kidding," Shane agreed, "he was pretty uptight last night," he paused, "I take it that you and he were once an *item*?"

I laughed, "I don't know about an *item*," I giggled, "But we dated for about a year during high school. Our parents were always planning vacations and outings so the boys and I were always thrown together."

"Nothing serious then I guess?" Shane pried a bit further.

Jeremy raised an eyebrow in question at his motive for the continual inquiry.

"It could have been," I said, "But it just didn't work out," I paused, "We were better at being friends than at being anything else."

Jeremy laughed at Shane's obvious concern over Elisa's past with Michael. "Sounds like you two have some history," he instigated further. He could see Shane eyeing him from his peripheral vision. It was always so much fun antagonizing the man.

"Yeah," I said, "But now I see all of them about once a year....at Thanksgiving."

I stood up from the table, "I'm going to take a quick shower and then if anyone wants breakfast I'll make something," I sat my cup down on the table and walked out of the room.

"Satisfied with her answer?" Jeremy inquired after she was out of hearing distance.

"Yeah, I'm satisfied," Shane said, "Just trying to get a feel for the past," He defended.

Jeremy snickered, "Leave the past in the past where it belongs Shane," he said, "It's a hell of a lot easier that way."

After breakfast was over I was clearing the dishes away when I heard Shane's cell phone ring in the other room. In a couple of minutes he came into the kitchen.

"They're just turning on the gravel road," he said. I detected the excitement in his voice that he desperately had tried to disguise and I smiled.

"You're really going to enjoy this, aren't you?" I asked softly.

He smiled and looked at me shamefully as he walked over and wrapped his arms around me. He couldn't lie when I had so openly asked.

"I am," he admitted with just a hint of regret in his tone, "But I will enjoy it much more when it is you and I," he said truthfully as he held me tightly against him.

"How much time do you think….until I can be with you like that?" I asked, my words muffled against his chest. He pushed me out to arm's length and studied my face.

"Elisa, if it *never* happens, it makes no difference to me," he said, "You're mine and I'm happy with however I have you."

I nodded and smiled, "I know that," I said, "But I also know that I want to share everything with you. As scared as I am of what is going to happen," I paused, "it is overshadowed by my thoughts of being utterly and completely yours."

He pulled me back against him and wrapped his protective arms around me, "You are already utterly and completely mine," he said softly against my hair, "And I love you."

Even though I had thought I knew how he felt, I had never yet heard the words uttered from his lips. They were like a soothing and reassuring heat that traveled from my heart up to my brain in a wave of pure happiness. My arms tightened around him and I buried my face against his broad chest. I could hear his heart beating and it seemed to carry the same rhythm as my own. For a few moments, I refused to loosen my grip but when I finally did, I stepped back and took his hand in mine.

"It's going to be a good day for you," I said.

We both turned toward the window at the sound of a vehicle slowly maneuvering around the potholes in the driveway. Jeremy had heard it too and came from his room. The three of us stood in the kitchen entryway, awaiting the anticipated knock on the door. When it came, I looked from Shane to Jeremy and then moved to the door and opened it.

Michael and Jeanette stood before me, a broad smile graced Jeanette's normally reticent face but Michael's was drawn with concern. Upon seeing me, he forced a smile as he and Jeanette entered the cabin. Michael's eyes first fell on Shane who stepped forward with his hand extended in greeting as he addressed him.

"Michael."

Michael shook it firmly before his eyes settled on Jeremy who stood slightly behind. Jeremy's eyes were already trained on Jeanette who had in turn, acknowledged him with her returning gaze. Shane could sense the tension building in Michael as he released his hand.

"Who is this?" he asked his voice slightly strained.

Jeremy immediately stepped forward and reached out his hand.

"Jeremy."

Michael didn't accept it but instead averted his eyes back to Shane questioningly. Jeanette had moved to his side and placed a reassuring hand on his arm, her face taking on a look of distress that replaced her previous cheerful demeanor. Jeremy let his hand fall back to his side and sensing the tension, I moved to stand between them.

"What's going on here?" Michael asked; his voice cracking as he looked at Jeremy, "Are you…..?"

Jeremy rudely cut him off, "I am," he said arrogantly and winked.

Great, I thought to myself, Jeremy's sarcasm could only make things worse right now. I stepped forward and stood just inches from Michael

"Can I talk to you?" I asked, "In there?" I motioned toward the bedroom. For a moment it seemed that he was going to ignore me but then he looked down and nodded.

Starting to follow me, he stopped and turned back, "Jeanette?" He said when he noticed that she wasn't following.

"Jeanette will be fine, please…."

Only after his eyes judgmentally shifted from Shane and then to Jeremy did he reluctantly followed me from the room. I shut the bedroom door softly behind us.

"Sit down," I demanded.

Michael immediately sat, dropping his head into his hands in frustration, "Damn, Elisa…."

"Listen to me," I said, sitting down beside him, "I know you're nervous about all of this…and you feel threatened by those two huge men out there," I said, "But neither of them poses any risk to you or Jeanette."

"She's everything to me," he said softly.

I nodded, "I know," I said, "Shane and Jeremy both know it too."

"Who is this Jeremy any way?" he asked gruffly, "Where in the hell did he come from?"

"He and Shane were in the same pack," I replied, "They grew up together. He has been here for a few months," I paused and then quickly added, "He has a tendency to express himself with sarcasm….don't take it personally."

"He isn't mated?" Michael said as he exhaled sharply, already knowing the answer.

"No…..he isn't," I confirmed, "But he would never…….."

Michael eyed me suspiciously, "How do you know Elisa? How do you know when they get out there what might happen?"

I challenged him with my eyes, "*I don't* know," I said, "But what I do know is that either of those two men out there would do anything for me," I paused, "and that makes me defend their integrities. If you have faith in Jeanette that is all you need."

"I do have faith in her," he answered, "I understand her motive and I only want her to be happy."

I smiled again, "*This* will make her happy," I said, "And I know that both Shane and Jeremy are excited, I've felt it in them all morning even though they've tried to hide it."

Michael was silent for a few moments before he spoke again, "I trust you," he said when he turned to look at me again. "If you're telling me this will all be alright, I'm going to choose to believe you."

"It will all be alright Michael," I said softly, "I promise."

I put my arm around his shoulders in a gesture of comfort.

"Ok," he said, "Let's get to it." He stood up from the edge of the bed and walked over to the door.

Shane and Jeremy had taken a seat on the couch while Jeanette nervously paced the floor. She had disclosed her concern with them about Michael's hesitation to allow her to run, sharing with them how after discovering that Shane was one of her kind, she had begged him for his approval. Finally caving in after much deliberation, she now feared that Jeremy's presence may have been the final straw that would to cause him to refuse. Jeremy had apologized to her and even told her that he would forego joining them if it would ease Michael's mind.

Her eyes jerked upward to Michael as he and Elisa came from the bedroom and she moved stealthily across the room to him. Smiling, he embraced her. She knew at that moment that whatever Elisa had said had convinced him. Jeanette's brown eyes settled on Elisa's as she looked over his shoulder. She mouthed the words *"thank you"*.

Elisa smiled and nodded in acknowledgment.

Michael released her and moved to stand in front of the couch where Shane and Jeremy sat. He looked from one to the other and then settled his eyes on Jeremy.

"Sorry for acting like an asshole," he said as he reached his hand toward him. Jeremy stood up. He was only slightly taller than Michael but his height combined with his confidence was intimidating combination. For a moment he just stared into his eyes but then grasped Michael's hand strongly.

"I understand," Jeremy said. "If it were me in your place, I'd act like an asshole too."

"Are we all okay then?" Shane asked from his position on the couch before he rose to his feet.

Michael nodded and simply replied, "Yes."

"Well then," Shane said, "My wolf is anxious…..let's go."

"Jeanette, you can use the bedroom," I said and motioned toward the room that Michael and I had just exited.

As she began to walk toward the door she turned to look at her mate, "Are you coming with me?" she asked in her normal, soft-spoken voice. Michael followed, and the door clicked closed behind them.

Shane strode over to me and hugged me before he swept his lips across mine, "Jeanette was worried that he would change his mind," he said.

"I think he was on the verge of it," I answered, "I told him that everything would be okay."

"And it will," Shane replied, "thanks for whatever you said."

"The guy is a bit uptight," Jeremy added from behind them, "I guess I must just have that "up to no good" look," he chuckled as he moved off into his room.

Shane and I both laughed, "I'm going to go……" he said as he once again leaned down and kissed me. I watched as he turned his back and walked away.

For the first time since I had met Shane, I felt completely alone.

Jeanette was the first to emerge and Elisa was in awe at her beauty as she timidly entered the room with Michael not too far behind. Her fur was a golden hue tinged black at her muzzle and ears. She looked at Elisa with familiar dark brown eyes.

The other two wolves materialized quietly at nearly the same time. Shane, as black as midnight with his startling blue eyes advanced toward Jeanette first. She immediately laid her ears back against her neck and began to rapidly wag her tail in a low, sweeping submissive manner. He approached her, his head high and ears pitched forward, tail raised high and slowly swishing back and forth. He extended his nose to hers in greeting.

The large mahogany wolf pushed in beside the black one and carried the same alert stance as he too reached his nose forward in greeting. They stood in silence for a few moments with the two males standing over the passive female and then she suddenly stood to her full height and shook herself. Although she stood a bit smaller than the others, Jeanette was in no way dwarfed by their larger size.

As the huge black wolf turned and walked toward the couch, he sensed Michael's unease and he steered clear while he concentrated on me, laying his massive head across my leg. I smiled down at the familiar beast and got up, moving to the door. When I opened it, Jeremy trotted out first and then Shane. When I turned, Michael was holding the yellow wolf's head in both hands; stroking her gently. When he spoke, it was barely audible.

"Enjoy your run baby," he said. Turning, she bolted out the door past me.

I watched as they quickly disappeared among the trees before shutting the door. Michael was still sitting on the couch and he sighed deeply before speaking.

"How long do you think they'll be gone?"

"Given the excitement that seemed to be anticipated by all….I'd say we have a few hours," I answered.

Chapter 25

Shane led the way deep into the woods. The sound of the other wolves beside him empowered him and he lengthened his strides in response. No matter how much he increased his speed, the others kept with him as they wound their way through trees and brush. In one long effortless bound, they cleared the dry creek bed and continued on until they came to the edge of a field. The pack slowed and hesitated on the fringe of the clearing.

Shane turned to look at the blonde wolf beside him. Although smaller, she had proved she would not be left behind. She had matched him stride for stride and kept with him as he dodged and darted through the forest. Jeremy stood a few feet to his left and Shane noticed his eyes also scrutinizing her form.

Perhaps it was to interrupt their assessment of her or possibly just because she was excited, she began to jump around playfully coming first to Shane, energetically nipping lightly at him and bounding around. He raised his head but didn't respond to her so she moved to Jeremy circling around him a couple of times and snapping at his flank, urging a response.

A low growl formed in Jeremy's throat and in an instant he had turned and collided with the tawny wolf, knocking her to the ground. She was immediately on her feet and back for more. Shane knew that Jeremy was playing even though his idea of playing was a bit rougher than hers. Instead of coming back at him directly, she again circled, looking for the best opportunity. When she lunged, Jeremy sidestepped but caught the back of her neck with his teeth. She yelped and turned back to face him. The mahogany wolf seemed to laugh as he opened his mouth, tongue lolling out the side.

Shane watched the scene intently. He had known Jeremy long enough to realize that he was greatly enjoying the physical aspect of the confrontation. But he also knew Jeremy well enough to know that at any moment his playfulness could turn into something entirely different.

Jeanette continued to provoke him and each time, Jeremy responded accordingly, but not gently. On her final pounce, her canine tore across the sensitive skin of his muzzle. He yelped as an immediate line of blood quickly rose from the long gash and dripped to the ground.

As if Jeanette had realized her error, she slowly backed away, eyes locked on Jeremy's. Shane tensed and moved forward but in the few seconds it took him to travel the short distance, Jeremy was upon her.

Small tufts of tawny fur floated in the air as the mahogany wolf fiercely attacked while the smaller wolf howled under his crushing weight. Shane charged and hit Jeremy full in the side, dislodging him from his assault. He sprung back instantaneously and Shane was ready, teeth bare and stance unyielding.

Jeremy stopped nose to nose with him, snarling and snapping while Shane stood his ground, his lips drawn back over his fangs in warning. Jeanette had crawled away and now stood only a few feet from the faceoff, her tail drooping and head down. The two large males continued to snarl and growl but there was no physical contact between them. In a few moments they both calmed and turned away from one another.

Under Shane's watchful observation, Jeremy moved toward the yellow wolf that cowered and rolled to her back passively, exposing her neck and underside. The mahogany wolf nuzzled her, urging her to her feet and once she stood, he circled around her, rubbing his body against the length of her side. Shane knew it was his way of smoothing over the conflict and gratefully, she reciprocated the gesture and all was right again.

Even though Michael had allowed Jeanette on the run, I could still sense the apprehension in his voice when he spoke. After a couple of hours passed, he began to move about nervously as he anticipated their return. I allowed him to pace for about ten minutes before I couldn't take it any longer.

"Would you just sit down?" I demanded, the agitation clear in my voice.

Michael's eyes jerked toward me, "I can't just sit," he answered, "Not knowing what is going on out there."

"There's nothing going on," I said, sighing heavily, "They're running together, that is it," I reiterated. "What is *really* going?"

Michael looked at me for a moment before he spoke, "What if she decides that she has missed pack life and chooses………."

I cut him off before he finished.

"She wouldn't decide that," I answered, "You two are meant to be together, she's not going to run out on you."

Michael sighed heavily, "I just know how much she wanted this today. After she met Shane, there was a different look in her eyes.....a look that I haven't seen before."

"I think you're reading too much into it," I replied bluntly, "She hasn't been around her kind for years; she's excited."

"I know, I know," a frustrated tone evident in his voice, "I just wish that I could be a part of it," he admitted.

"That's what bothers you the most...." I mentioned, "I figured as much."

"We're so close, "he paused, "But I can never share that part of her life. You do realize that don't you Elisa?" he hesitated, "You'll never share that with Shane and it will eventually pull you down."

I held his gaze for a moment before looking away, "I *will* share it," I uttered as I met his eyes again.

Michael's eyes narrowed, "What do you mean?" he asked.

I hesitated before answering, "I am...I've been....um...infected, "I confessed, "If that is even the right word to call it," I paused, "I just haven't fully transformed ....yet."

"How?" he asked, suddenly very interested in what I was saying, "How did it happen?"

I told him the entire story about the rogue wolf. He listened with intent as I described what had happened to me that day.

"Was it the rogue or Jeremy?" Michael asked when I had finished.

I looked at him questioningly.

"Which one ...infected you?" he wanted to know.

Michael had raised a question to me that I had previously tried to dismiss, but here it was again.

"I'm not sure," I conceded, "It could have been either."I had never voiced the possibility before now, although it had always been there; looming in the back of my mind like a dull ache.

"Shane said that the wolf had to be totally in control," I said in the attempt to ease my own mind, "But Jeremy was in control that day....not his wolf."

Michael shook his head, "I'm not sure how all of that works," he said, "Jeanette has told me that it is when the blood of the wolf and a person mixes....that's when it happens. She never said anything about the wolf being in control."

"If that's the case, then why haven't you allowed Jeanette to change you?" I asked, "If you want to share that part of her life, then that would be the easiest answer." I paused, "If that is how it happens."

"She says that the females aren't able to do it," he replied as he shrugged his shoulders. "The males are the only ones that have the ability."

For a moment, Michael's eyes searched mine as if looking for an answer before he ever asked the question that was on his mind, "Do you think that Shane would......"

I cut him off again, fully aware of where he was headed, "No," I said abruptly, walking away from him, "I don't."

I heard Michael's footsteps behind me and the painful grasp on my arm, "Why?" he probed, "Why wouldn't he?" His voice was almost desperate.

"He says people die," I gritted through clenched teeth, "he says that most don't survive."

"Isn't it *my* choice?" he said angrily.

My face grew suddenly solemn, "It wasn't *mine*."

Michael's grip fell from my arm, his eyes apologetic, "I'm sorry," he said softly as he took a step back. "But it is something that I want," he paused, "And I'm going to ask him."

"You have a family Michael," I argued, "If things were to go bad you might never see your daughter grow up. That's exactly what Shane is going to tell you...and why he will refuse."

After about four hours had passed, I heard the unmistakable light thuds of the returning wolves on the wooden deck. Opening the door, they entered in single file; Shane, Jeanette and then Jeremy. I immediately noticed the dried blood across Jeremy's muzzle and dropped my hand to run my fingertips along the top of his head as he passed. Pausing, he looked up before trotting off to his room. Shane returned to the bathroom and Jeanette immediately went back to Shane's room. For the few minutes they were gone, I let my eyes settle on Michael's face. He was smiling until he raised his eyes to mine, his elated behavior at their return fading quickly under my gaze.

Shane was fully dressed when he emerged from the bathroom except for his boots that he carried loosely in his hand. I met him as he crossed the floor and wrapped my arms around his waist and looked up. He bent and kissed my forehead lightly.

"Was it good?" I smiled.

He nodded and smiled, "It was," he answered.

Michael's eyes followed them across the room until he was disrupted by the bedroom door opening and Jeanette walking out. Her normally reserved personality now seemed to be bubbling over with delight as she walked over to Michael and embraced him.

"Thank you," she whispered softly in his ear.

The four of them were silent as they waited for Jeremy's return but he remained behind the closed door.

"Let's go into the kitchen...Elisa, would you make some coffee?" Shane asked as he began to herd everyone into the kitchen. I looked at him skeptically but did as he asked, Michael and Jeanette following close behind. Shane immediately turned and went to Jeremy's door, knocking lightly.

"Yeah," Jeremy grumbled.

Shane opened the door and stepped inside, shutting it behind him. Jeremy had dressed and was sitting on the edge of the bed, a deep gash started under his left eye and traveled across the bridge of his nose. The blood was dried but it wasn't something that would be easily hidden.

"I didn't realize she got you so good," Shane confessed.

"I thought maybe I should just hang back," Jeremy said, "Didn't think that I wanted to explain this."

"No," Shane said, "I don't want you to stay in here."

"It might be the best thing; that guy is already edgy...." Jeremy argued.

"I know, but things happen.....she needed put in her place and you did, end of story. Just clean it up a little and come in, huh?" Shane asked.

Jeremy nodded, "Alright....I'll be in."

Shane turned and left the room. Jeremy followed but veered off toward the bathroom. When he entered the kitchen, everyone was looking at him, expecting an answer for Jeremy's absence.
Shane sighed and looked immediately over to Jeanette. He could see that she understood what was going on and immediately spoke up.

"I may have injured Jeremy.....a little," she uttered, holding Shane's gaze.

Instinctively I thought of the dried blood across his face when they had first come in.

At the same moment, Michael and I both looked at her, but I vocalized my question first, "Injured?"

Michael stared at Jeanette as he waited for her response.

"I was a bit overzealous," she admitted, "And I may have left a sizable scratch....on his muzzle..er, his nose."

Michael's eyebrows rose in question and Shane intervened quickly.

"It was all in play," he defended, "Not a big deal."

Jeanette nodded in agreement, "My excitement got the better of me and I was too rambunctious."

She reached her hand over and laid it on Michael's in a gesture of reassurance, but his eyes narrowed suspiciously.

Shane wondered if she would mention Jeremy's retaliation to her playfulness later. For now though, she seemed to want to accept full blame.

"Jeremy will join us after he cleans up a bit," he said, "Anyone want coffee?" He looked at Elisa who was peering at him, waiting for the truth while he tried to avert everyone's attention.

We'll talk in a little bit…., he told her. She reluctantly nodded up at him from her seat at the table although he could see in her eyes that answer would only appease her for a short while.

Everyone's gaze turned to Jeremy as he entered the kitchen, and feeling as if he was in the limelight, he spouted off with his normal cockiness.

"What's everybody looking at?"

He had cleaned the dried blood off of the scratch and it now looked surprisingly less serious that it had previously, but still deep.

"I'm so sorry Jeremy," Jeanette said softly.

His eyes jerked toward her voice, "It will heal," he snapped, "Let's not make a big deal over it."

She quickly averted her eyes at the gruffness of his voice. Michael tensed when he saw her reaction and glared at Jeremy from across the kitchen table. Jeremy met and held his gaze, a flash of warning crossing through the clouded gray. When Michael stood, Jeremy advanced purposefully towards him but before they could reach one another, Shane moved between them.

"Let's have none of this," he said harshly as he looked at Jeremy and then back to Michael.

Once the tension had seemed to evaporate, a light conversation developed. Jeanette spoke of her adventure with a newfound passion that I had never seen before. Her smile was no longer just a distant indication but now seemed genuine, an advocate of the happiness she felt. It faded when Michael stood and asked Shane to walk outside with him and then motioned for her to stay behind. Her eyes followed them until the door closed, erecting a barrier between them. She then looked to me for her answer.

"He's asking him... isn't he?" Jeanette's soft voice echoed in the now silent kitchen as her eyes firmly held my gaze.

I nodded while Jeremy's eyes roved back and forth between us.

"What's happening?" he finally asked.

It was Jeanette who answered, her voice just above a whisper. "Michael wants Shane to make him....one of us."

"I told him that Shane wouldn't do it," I added, "But he was dead set on asking."

"He does know how it happens, doesn't he?" Jeremy inquired.

"He knows," Jeanette sighed, "I've tried everything to convince him that it doesn't matter to me. He was only human when we met and I've never expected more."

I stared across the table at her with regret, "I can see that you're different and happier ...Michael can see it tenfold."

"I should have never asked him for this," she replied as a tear trailed down her cheek.

"For what it's worth," Jeremy interrupted, "We all understand...even Michael, or he wouldn't have let you come."

Jeanette looked across the table at him, her dark brown eyes brimming with tears and Jeremy felt his heart soften for her circumstances. Although he disguised his feelings with cynicism most of the time, deep down, he understood the longing.

"I'm going to see what's happening out there," he grabbed his coat and walked through the living room out the front door.

Jeanette had gotten her bearings back and now sat silently, the reticent manner that I was familiar with had returned. Her detached emotionless eyes turned to me when I spoke.

"Tell me what happened out there today with Jeremy," I said.

"I was excited," she said softly, "I played too rough."

"Shane told me something else happened."

"You have to understand the structure of the pack," Jeanette paused, "Females aren't to provoke males....not in the way that I goaded Jeremy. He put me in my place, that's all."

She hesitated for a moment more, "I hold no grudge against him."

"No," Shane said sharply, "And that's the end of it."

He had listened to Michael's request, his reasoning behind it and now he had tired of the argument. Shane was suddenly in no mood for further justification of his thoughts on the subject. During their conversation, his mind had drifted back to circumstances years earlier when he had been asked for the very same favor. After refusing, another wolf was sought out and the ending had been deadly.

"Can't you at least give it some thought?" Michael requested.

"No."

Shane could see the frustration written on his face, and feel the desperation that seeped out of his pores. He openly admitted that he sympathized with the guy...he really did. He was almost relieved when the door opened and Jeremy stepped out on the porch.

"What's going on out here?" he asked as he sauntered up next to them. Michael glowered in his direction and then looked back at Shane.

"I'm not sure what I've done to you, man, but I get the distinct feeling that you really don't like me," Jeremy growled.

"This is a private conversation," Michael replied cynically, "A good indication might have been when we came outside ......alone."

"This conversation is over," Shane said gruffly looking at Michael, "And you two need to cool it." He turned and walked back across the porch to the door and disappeared inside. Right now he didn't really care if they annihilated one another.

Jeanette met his icy stare as he entered the kitchen and immediately looked away. Elisa watched as he sat his coffee cup in the sink and turning around, leaned his body against the countertop.

"So, did you know this was coming?" He asked, looking directly at her.

Her brown eyes rose to meet his, "No," she said apologetically.

"I'm sorry Shane; he told me how you were gone," I replied, "I tried to tell him that you would say no."

"He should have listened to you," he said coolly.

Michael and Jeremy glared at each other as Shane walked away. Only after the door was closed behind him did Michael finally avert his eyes.

"You're an asshole," he said matter of fact as he looked away.

Jeremy smiled obnoxiously, "I know, I don't try to hide it."

"You couldn't even if you tried."

"Why such dislike for me Mike?" Jeremy inquired.

"It's Michael," he barked.

Jeremy laughed loudly which only succeeded in infuriating him further, "Look asshole, I've got nothing to say to you."

Jeremy's face turned serious, "Yeah, I think maybe you might want to reconsider."

Michael's eyes narrowed, "I doubt it." He turned and started across the porch but was stopped by the steely grip of Jeremy's fingers biting into the flesh of his arm. He spun around, geared up for the altercation that was sure to follow.

"I'll give you what you want," Jeremy said flatly, his piercing gray eyes locked on Michael's.

Michael's eyes squinted with distrust as he stared back, "How do you know anything about what I want."

"You have a beautiful mate," Jeremy began, "And you'd do anything to make her happy…wouldn't you?" he smirked. "There are parts of her life that you'll never know and it's festering inside you - killing you from the inside out." Jeremy could see the anger he was initiating flash across Michael's face but along with it, the hard cold truth flickered in his eyes.

Michael clenched his teeth against the smartness of Jeremy's grip before jerking his arm away and for a moment just stared him as if he was trying to figure out what to say. Jeremy knew that he wanted to accept his offer but was hesitant due to their obvious personality conflict.

"It's an open invitation," Jeremy finally mumbled as he walked toward the cabin door leaving Michael to his own internal conflict.

"Is he very upset?" Jeanette inquired in a quiet voice.

"Yeah. He's pissed," Shane said, "But he can get over being pissed, he can't get over being dead."

"I wish that it could be easier for him," she replied softly, "We have been together for six years and it was effortless at first," she paused, "But as time has passed, I've found that part of my life is missing. I know that he feels it."

"Do you feel guilty?" I asked.

Jeanette nodded. "I do….it causes him pain."

Shane sighed and turned to look out the kitchen window. It was clear from the way she talked about Michael and put him before herself that she genuinely loved him. She had devoted her life to him no matter what and Shane respected her for it. He turned when he heard the door open.

Jeremy ambled into the kitchen after removing his coat and sat down in the kitchen chair next to Elisa. Meanwhile, Jeanette immediately pulled on her own jacket and went outside with purpose.

"You're torn, aren't you?" I asked as I studied Shane's features; I could see the indecision in his face.

He scowled, "No, I'm not doing it."

"I'll do it," Jeremy piped in. Both Shane and I looked at him skeptically.

"That's ironic," Shane countered, "You two can't stand each other....you'd definitely kill him. Or if he got lucky, he'd kill you."

"I didn't see this coming," I said in a surprised voice, "Did you tell Michael that?"

"I told him but he didn't seem convinced that I was sincere."

Shane laughed, "Hell, *I* don't even think you're sincere!"

Jeremy chuckled half-heartedly, "Seriously though, I'll do it," he paused, "Not for him....but for her."

He and Shane locked eyes for a moment, "I don't think we should get involved in this," Shane remarked.

"Isn't there some way to restrain a wolf? An easier way to do this so no one really gets hurt?" I asked.

"You too?" Shane grumbled. "Are you kidding me?" His voice mirrored his exasperation.

I shrugged, "Well, isn't there?"

Jeremy gave me a sideways glanced and grinned, "It could be done."

Shane shook his head and left the room scowling. In a few seconds the bedroom door slammed as he sought solitude within its confines.

I looked at Jeremy, "I'd better go and talk to him."

"Maybe you should give him some time to think."

The door opened and Jeanette came back inside, "We're leaving," she said simply as she walked over to me and embraced me warmly. "Dan and Edna are watching Abby and we need to get back. It was very good to see you again."

I returned her hug, "It was good to see you too Jeanette. Will Michael be coming in to say good-bye?"

"I don't think so," she muttered before turning her gaze upon Jeremy and extending her hand, "It was good to meet you Jeremy."

He took her hand politely, "Pleasure was mine," he said, "Good luck."

"I'm sorry about what happened today." she apologized again.

"I shouldn't have reacted the way that I did," he replied with a sincerity that almost shocked me.

"It's alright," she answered, "I won't hold it against you."

I headed out the door and found Michael already in the car. He rolled the window down when I got to the door beside him.

"Not going to say good-bye to me?"

"I'm just …..pissed. I finally found a person that can give me a complete life with Jeanette," he paused in exasperation, "But he refuses."

I sighed, "I told you he wouldn't do it."

"I know, I know. My only option now is Jeremy….and that isn't much of an option."

"Jeremy can be hard to take," I agreed. "But most of the time his heart is in the right place."

"The guy is a prick," he paused, "But if he's my only option…"Michael's voice tapered off as Jeanette came down the porch steps and headed toward the car. She got in and pulled the seatbelt around her.

I took a step back from the car, "Be careful," I said. Michael nodded while Jeanette gave a brief wave before he put the car in gear and began to back up.

Suddenly the cabin door flew wide open and Shane moved quickly across the porch, down the steps. "Michael!" he shouted as he covered the yard in lengthy strides. The car tires skidded to an abrupt stop as Shane came up to the window, "Come back when the moon is full."

Michael gazed up at him unbelievingly, a smile lighting his face, "You serious?"

Shane nodded, "Yes."

I looked at him in bewilderment but didn't speak. I couldn't believe what I was hearing after his unwavering decision from earlier.

"I'll make it back here one way or another," Michael said softly, "You don't know what this means to me."

Shane turned to look towards me and then back to Michael, "Yeah I do."

"Thank you Shane," Jeanette uttered breathily from the passenger side of the car, "You're an alpha. I had hoped that your leadership might make you reconsider."

He didn't reply but instead backed away from the car. We watched as it disappeared down the driveway and only then did he turn and look me in the eye.

"What changed your mind?" I demanded to know.

Shane pulled me into his arms, "You," he said, "I count the days until you and I are the same. I understand the longing between them."

I pulled away. "And what if things were different? What if I wasn't on my way already….would you want me to change?"

"Perhaps if *you* wanted it," he hesitated, "but I would never have forced it on you."

"But now, after seeing this happen between Michael and Jeanette I would have known that it *does* matter whether you would have admitted it or not."

"You're my mate. It doesn't matter either way. We will be together regardless of what we are," he paused, "Come on; let's go in, it's cold out here." He took my hand and led me back inside.

Chapter 26

As the days passed, winter's bitter bite settled on the land. Temperatures dropped and even the sun couldn't break through the harsh cold that December and January ushered in. Elisa's behavior seemed to morph with the onslaught of the frigid air and each day proved to be a new test for Shane and Jeremy. They understood what was happening and the up and down roller coaster of emotions that she was riding. Yet even so, both had grown weary of her constant mood swings.

After one particular heated incident, Shane decided that it was time for him to take the matter into his own hands. The cold had kept the three of them trapped inside for days and it was early evening, when darkness had started to fall that Jeremy voiced his need for an outing. He returned from his room already shifted into the mahogany wolf and Shane opened the door to let him out.

Elisa was busy in the kitchen when Shane retrieved her, "Come with me," he said softly. She looked at him reluctantly.

"I have things to get cleaned up in here."

"They will wait," he urged her along with his hand on her back toward the bathroom.

When we went in, I gasped; the tub was filled with water and thick with bubbles. He had lit several candles around the edge along with others on the countertop that illuminated the bathroom in soft, calming light. He turned me to face him and brushed my hair off of my shoulders before sliding his hands beneath my shirt. He pulled it gently up over my head and let it fall to the floor. After leaning over and sweeping a tender kiss across my lips he finished undressing me before I stepped into the tub.

"This is nice," I sighed as I reclined with my head to rest against the back of the tub, "Thank you. I needed this."

"I know," he said softly. *Believe me……..I know,* he thought to himself.

With very few spoken words, I allowed Shane to wash my hair and then my body. He paused periodically to place a kiss on my shoulder or neck affectionately before continuing. When he was finished and stepped out onto the plush bath mat, he wrapped me in a thick, warm towel.

"Tonight is the night," he muttered as he rubbed me dry with the towel.

"The night for what?" I asked curiously.

His blue eyes met my gaze, "Tonight you will meet your wolf."

I couldn't hide my skepticism, "How do you know?"

"I'm going to help you. You're fighting it and neither Jeremy nor I can take many more of your moods," he grinned.

I scowled, "Has it been that bad?"

Shane couldn't help but laugh as he continued to wipe the towel over me, "We knew why, so we dealt with it but it is time that you meet her."

Shane found a comb and began to work it through my long dark hair until it was free from tangles. He plugged in the hair dryer and let it blow through my tresses until they were only barely damp. I put up no resistance when he picked me up effortlessly and carried me out of the bathroom and to his bedroom. Pulling the comforter and sheet back, he laid me gently in the comfortable softness before removing the towel and throwing it to the floor.

The sheets were cold against my bare skin as I lay there watching quietly as he shed his own clothes and climbed in beside me, pulling the comforter up over us as he moved his body close to mine. His warmth was welcome as he drew me to him with one powerful motion and his breath came hot against my neck, "I need to tell you some things," he murmured into my skin.

"What things?" I whispered.

"You need to know how to get back," he said as he lightly moved his fingertips down the length of my arm, "And how to control it."

I turned my head to look worriedly into his eyes.

"Don't fret, I'll be right here with you," he said.

His large warm hands softly stroked my skin causing gooseflesh to rise over my entire body as his lips brushed mine tenderly. I turned to face him with urging lips demanding more while I let my hands wander across the expanse of his hard chest. His hands moving over my body inflamed my passion even more and I pressed against him in need.

"Listen to me," he breathed against my mouth, "When you feel it beneath your skin, don't fight it, embrace it. If you let her out it will be much easier for you."

I kissed across his strong jaw and tasted his skin as I let my lips move down his neck. My fingers trailed across his stomach and then moved lower. He shuddered when I grasped him in my hand, encircling my fingers around his erection. Drawing me tighter against him in response I lifted my knee up the length of his leg to rest on his hip, opening myself up to him. His fingers found the swollen, eager wetness and as he accessed the waiting warmth I pushed readily against his hand, demanding more.

The smell of her arousal was intoxicating and he had a difficult time concentrating on what he needed to do instead of what he wanted to do. Shane knew that if he got caught up in the moment he would never be able to push her to the edge and then not fulfill his own need. In order to bring the wolf to the surface he would have to provoke it and that was something near to impossible, at least in Shane's eyes.

Next to him Elisa coaxed impatiently. Her body's movements pressed into him, her hands stroked the length of his arousal as she urged him to respond to her touch. In one swift motion he flipped her over on her back and poised himself above her on his hands and knees. As he kissed her, she tried to pull him down against her but he resisted; only with great difficulty.

Confused by his reluctance, she stared up into his eyes questioningly when he pulled away. Plainly seeing the passion in his gaze, she could feel it in his body but yet she was denied.

"Why?" She asked softly. As if the words had turned a switch, he lowered himself and thrust inside, filling her completely. Body screaming at the initial shock, she quickly adjusted and the intense needy ache returned. He pushed into her again and again until he started to see the soft glow in her eyes.

He was fighting. Shane wanted to continue relentlessly, wanted to take his own pleasure in the moment but he couldn't allow it. He had to stop. Already his fangs had dropped as his body prepared to be liberated. The glow within her eyes grew brighter and her body swept closer to the edge of release and it took everything that he had to pull away. It was at that moment that he sank his fangs into the soft flesh of her shoulder.

Seeing the shock and sudden anger flash through the burning green of her eyes he hovered above her, blood trickling from the corner of his mouth. It was then that he realized he had made a foolish mistake.

The fire that swept through my body was no longer that of passion. Rage began to fill me to the point that I felt ready to explode. It pushed against the inside of my skin demanding an outlet. I gave into it freely and let it rip upward through my flesh, converting smooth skin to dark fur, teeth into long, sharp fangs.

He hadn't expected her to change so quickly....the first time was never usually swift, or easy. But as the short moments passed during her transformation, he had no time to retreat. The chocolate wolf rose up from the bed in its anger and seized him by the throat before he had time to respond. Her fangs sank into him and he felt the sting as they punctured the skin.

Stop! He growled at her, *Elisa, stop!* He felt the wetness of his own blood before she paused, allowing him just enough time to set his own wolf free.

The wolf carried the outlet of her anger as she hid within the dark shadows of its thoughts, frightened. She felt the long unfamiliar teeth embed themselves in Shane's throat and the iron taste of his blood as it seeped across her tongue. Through the fury she had heard his command clearly and she fought to control the wolf that he had released. In the few seconds that she was able to disrupt it, the sensation of his throat in her jaws changed and in response, she let go.

The black beast stood over her, his glaring blue eyes demanding submission. A low warning growl rumbled deep within his throat. The rapid change had allowed the wolf to come to full control leaving Shane struggling to maintain some rationale within the animal's brain. It glowered down at the brown wolf, its lips pulled threateningly back over deadly fangs. He grimaced from his buried place inside when he saw the snarling and snapping that met his wolf's forewarning. He felt its body stiffen when it realized her defiance.

Elisa's wolf cringed back against the mattress, her eyes boring into the looming form above her. She was scared and her feelings of fear transferred into the wolf creating a distress in the creature that resulted in it to feel threatened, baring its teeth in defense. In a flurry of fur and fangs, the black wolf powered down on her.

The struggling mass rolled from the bed and fell to the floor with a heavy thud, claws gouging deep grooves across the wooden floor planks. Shane could feel the slight pressure of his wolf's jaws on her throat and realized that it didn't seek to hurt her....just overpower and force her to submit. Once she did, the confrontation would end.

Be still and it will be over, he said. *Don't be afraid....*

Strangely, he heard her reply come quickly before fading away, *But I am afraid!*

Unintentionally, during the course of freeing her wolf they had completed their bond....all due to Elisa's abrupt transformation and his near deadly mistake.

She quieted with his words, her sides heaving as she lay beneath him. The challenge still in her eyes, she finally broke their gaze and stretched out. The black beast continued to stand above her for a moment longer before he lowered his nose to her muzzle and nudged tenderly. Shane was aware of an overwhelming sense of delight washing though the wolf's body. She was his mate and he had waited a long time for her. Now that she knew her place, he would protect her with his life. She was his.

The brown wolf relaxed with the tenderness that the other offered and I felt calmness settle throughout. The feeling of being in a body that wasn't really mine was a disturbing and strange experience. It was almost as if there were two personalities trapped inside my mind. Although I survived in the conscious of this animal, it was clouded with uncontainable and uncontrollable urges that I couldn't resist or fight.

Shane's wolf moved and stood a few feet away. It whined softy with encouragement and in response, she struggled to stand, her legs splaying out in all directions. Once fully on her feet, she swayed unsteadily but managed to remain upright. The black wolf moved back to her side and leaned slightly against her, offering his own sturdy frame as a means of support.

My wolf took advantage of the reinforcement that the black beast presented. I inclined my body toward his just enough to steady the new, shaky legs beneath me. The strangeness that I felt could not be formed into words and there was no way to describe the notion that my body was not responding to my own thoughts and commands. My voice was only a distant echo to the animal that I had become and I was confused about how to reach it.

Are you alright? I heard Shane's unmistakable tone coming through to me.

I managed to turn my head and look at him, *I'm scared*.

When I spoke it was a whimper that filled my ears, a foreign sound that came from my own mouth.

Come, follow me, he said as the black wolf turned and moved toward the door. It pushed its muzzle through the slight opening and widened it enough to allow his body to pass through before he turned to wait, whining softy.

The brown wolf lifted her paw and stepped forward with uncertainty toward the door. In slow motion and with labored steps she was soon standing in front of him. He responded by flattening his ears against his neck and wagging his tail fiercely with elation before turning and moving farther out into the living room and then waiting.

His game soon had Elisa's wolf trotting across the floor behind him. He stopped occasionally and circled her, brushing his body against hers and nuzzling her face. Abruptly, the chocolate wolf moved toward the cabin door and then turned to look at him, a low whine emitting from her throat.

In an instant, Shane shifted and opened the cabin door granting me access to the new world that waited outside that door. Walking timidly out onto the deck, I managed to make it down the steps to the frozen ground and across the yard before stopping completely. I raised my nose to the air and inhaled deeply, devouring every new scent that filled my nostrils. Some of the odors were easily identifiable while others sparked my curiosity as nothing I had ever noticed before.

I turned to look back at Shane who still stood in the doorway in his human form, a broad smile gracing his handsome features as he watched me from his position. In one swift motion he closed the cabin door and ran across the deck. Leaping from the top step, he shifted to the wolf in mid air and landed gracefully near me on the frozen ground.

My wolf turned and broke into a run, the first steps irregular before lengthening into long even strides. I had never felt as alive as I did at that moment. With paws moving swiftly across the crisp frozen grass that crunched beneath my weight, I breathed the cold air deep into my lungs. With keen eyesight I scanned the path ahead and found it easy to leap over the obstacles as I wound through the forest. So many sensations flooded my newly receptive senses; the smells, sights and the sounds all amplified in my brain. I could plainly hear the black wolf keeping pace a few yards behind, allowing me to run but keeping a watchful eye. When I finally stopped, he paused beside me for a moment before flattening his ears and swishing his tail back and forth ecstatically. He circled me again, rubbing his body against the length of mine.

The rush of emotion that Shane was getting from his wolf was overwhelming. In his life, he had never experienced the euphoria that flooded his senses as it did now. The wolf had always been a creature of strength and power to be respected and feared and here it was now, acting like a frisky pup. Shane couldn't see past the happiness it felt to find any fault with its actions.

Shane's voice was soft as it drifted into her thoughts, *I love you Elisa,* when her eyes met his, his gaze was strong and unfaltering.

Her mouth widened in what might have been a smile and she returned his affection by rubbing her head against his.

I love you, she answered.

At the same moment, both were distracted by the crunch of leaves off to their left and the unmistakable scent of another wolf. Jeremy stood several yards away, observing them through the gray eyes of the mahogany wolf from a safe distance.

She immediately recognized her pack member and even though Elisa struggled to stop her, she continued to move away toward him. The black beast tensed protectively as she left his side and he followed just a few feet behind, hackles raised slightly as he prepared for a confrontation. Jeremy trotted toward them and stopped nose to nose with Elisa's wolf. His ears were pitched forward inquisitively and he held his tail rigidly upright in a slow sway. He walked around her on stiffened legs, nostrils flaring as he inhaled her scent. For a moment his eyes locked on Shane's before he continued his assessment and came back to a halt in front of her.

Shane cringed inside when he saw Elisa's wolf take on the same stance that Jeremy's had done. He knew that her demeanor would mean insubordination to the other male wolf and he had witnessed Jeremy's wrath before. The smaller brown wolf's ears pitched forward and with tail held upright, she slowly moved around the large beast.

They gray eyes followed her movements but he remained motionless. Once her circle was completed, she locked her green eyes on those of the large brown wolf. For a few seconds they stared at one another and as each one passed, Shane's wolf readied itself to protect its mate.

Suddenly, the smaller wolf flattened her ears and lowered her head beneath the larger wolf's neck. She rubbed her body against the front of him and under his neck as she slowly walked passed him before turning to look at him once again. Shane nearly stumbled in disbelief as Jeremy's wolf returned her gesture by wagging his tail and rubbing his head against her neck. He turned quickly then and trotted away before stopping to look back at them. It was an invitation that both Elisa and Shane accepted. Together they ran; Jeremy leading their pack and Shane protectively bringing up the rear.

As the darkness began to settle in, the three made their way back to the cabin. Elisa's wolf trotted up the steps and was first at the cabin door. She pondered how she might open it and as quickly as the thought had passed through her mind, her human hand was upon the doorknob. She realized at that same moment that she was standing naked when the cold evening air touched her bare, human skin. Shuttering, she turned to look at the other two who were staring at her in disbelief. Darting inside, she grabbed Shane's robe from the back of his door and hastily pulled it around her, embarrassed.

"I didn't expect you to shift back so easily," Shane's voice echoed in the empty room. Jeremy entered and stood a few feet behind him.

"I uh.." I stuttered, still feeling ashamed at being caught naked, "I just imagined myself opening the door…..and then my hand was on it."

Jeremy stepped forward, comfortably naked and seeming to be in no hurry to cover himself, "Listen," he started as he put his hand on Elisa's shoulder. "I can see that you're unsettled with the being naked thing. But, we are all going to see one another naked from time to time and you might as well get used to it," he paused, "And from what I've seen…you needn't feel insecure about It," he grinned.

I returned a shy grin, my face turning an even darker shade of red, "It is just a little weird."

"You'll get used to it," Shane interjected, "It's going to happen."

As he spoke, Jeremy noticed the bloody marks on Shane's neck and a puzzled expression crossed his face, "What's up with the, uh…." he motioned with his fingers to his own neck.

Shane laughed uneasily, "I misjudged her….things could've gone south really quickly."

The images flashed through my mind of the situation that Shane was referring to. I vaguely remembered the taste of his blood on my tongue and my teeth embedded in his flesh. My eyes widened, "I could have killed you?"

He smirked and then nodded, "Yes, you could've. I've never known anyone to shift so quickly their first time….or shift back either. It was easy for you and I don't understand it."

"Everyone is different," Jeremy said, "Maybe she has been fighting it for so long that it was just time."

"Maybe," Shane answered but his tone sounded unconvinced, "Guess we'll just see how it goes the next time."

"I can't believe that I could've killed you," I said softly.

Shane moved to my side and wrapped his arm around my shoulders, "But you didn't, and I wouldn't have gone down without a fight." he teased, pulling me close against his side, "Come," he said, "Let's get dressed."

I looked up at him hesitantly, "Do you mind if I just lie down for a while?" I asked, "I'm pretty tired...it's been a big day for me."

Shane smiled down at me and hugged me tightly, "I'll call you when dinner is ready."

I nodded and turned to walk away and as I did, he snatched hold of the robe and pulled it away from my body, leaving me once again naked. I squealed and ran into the bedroom slamming the door behind me.

Smirking, Shane pulled the robe over his arms while Jeremy chuckled at his playful antics.

"You probably shouldn't aggravate her like that," he laughed.

"I know. I just can't help myself," Shane chortled, "I'm going to make some dinner...I'm starving."

Jeremy readily agreed, "Yeah, me too," he paused and stared at Shane, "But it was a great day."

"Yeah it was," Shane answered, "It was perfect. I was a bit concerned how your wolf was going to take to her though," he paused, "I was surprised by its reaction."

"He felt no threat from her," Jeremy answered, "Because he already knows her," his eyes remained locked on Shane's.

Shane's forehead wrinkled and his eyebrows drew together, "Yeah, maybe so."

Jeremy studied him for a moment before answering. "Shane," he said, "It wasn't the rogue that made her."

"Huh?" Shane asked, staring at him with a blank expression.

Jeremy stepped closer towards him, "It was me...I made her."

It took a moment for Jeremy's confession to sink in but once it had, Shane stared vacantly, not knowing how to respond. Jeremy's blood ran through Elisa's veins and he realized deep down, what it could mean to their relationship and their future.

As if Jeremy read his thoughts he spoke again, "Listen, don't get weird on me," he said, "I have no intention of using my influence on her. She's yours..... I would never betray your trust."

Shane nodded in slow motion as he took in what Jeremy had said, "Wow," he muttered, still shocked by the revelation, "I didn't expect this. For some reason, I always thought it was the rogue."

"Maybe you just wanted it to be," Jeremy answered, "That way it would be over.... not something you'd have to deal with....forever."

"Are you certain?" Shane questioned.

"I'm sure," he answered, "I feel it," he paused, "Beneath my skin when she's close to me."

"Does she know?"Shane inquired.

"We've never talked about it. I don't think that she is familiar enough with all of these new feelings that she suspects it or knows what it means."

"Do you mind if we keep this from her for a while?" Shane posed the question.

"Indefinitely," Jeremy agreed.

In Shane's mind it was as if fate had somehow woven an invisible bond between the two of them. From the very beginning there had been some kind of connection that had evolved into an unnatural closeness. At times he had felt threatened by it while at other times he was secure in the thought that Jeremy would always protect her with his life. He had proved it with the rogue…and now the bi-product of it, however unfortunate as it seemed, was that he was Elisa's creator. Time would tell if destiny had other plans but for now he would hold tightly to her and trust Jeremy as he had always done.

Chapter 27

The long cold winter gave way into early spring and periodic bouts of warmer weather brought back the chirping songs of the birds along with a few of the insects. Michael had decided to hold off on his change until warmer weather was in full swing. It would make it easier for their travel plans and for arrangements for the care of their daughter. Jeremy stayed true to his word as Shane had expected and their lives moved forward without incident….at least for a little while.

Jeremy awoke in a cold sweat before the sun had broken through the horizon. The sky was just beginning to lighten and it seeped around the curtains into his room. He wasn't sure what had roused him but he was wide awake.

He flipped the covers off of his body and felt the delicious cool air sweep across his wet, sweaty skin. He sighed deeply and it was then that he sensed what had awakened him. His wolf lurched forward as it too recognized the scent that filled his nostrils.

Spending the next hour struggling to keep the wolf down, he realized that he couldn't maintain it for much longer. Storming through the cabin to Shane's bedroom, he slung the door wide open, slamming it into the wall behind it.

Shane straight upright in bed and Elisa bolted to a sitting position beside him, her eyes wide.

"What the hell?" Shane demanded, noticing the glow lit behind Jeremy's eyes. Before the words had fully left his lips he quickly sensed Jeremy's quandary and turned to look at Elisa.

"Get her out of here," Jeremy growled, "Now."

Shane nodded and immediately jumped out of bed, "Get some clothes," He slung the words toward me, "We have to go."

"What is going on?" I asked, my voice shaky and frightened by being roused so abruptly from sleep.

"Just do it," Shane commanded, "I'll explain when we get out of here."

"I've been fighting this thing for over a hour," Jeremy continued, "I won't last much longer."

"We're going, give us a minute," Shane said.

I suddenly noticed the glow in Shane's eyes as well, a low light seeping in behind the blue.

"What is happening?" I asked again, the fret obvious in my voice.

"Just gather what you need from here…..we're going to your house for a couple of days," said Shane, a low rumble emitting from his chest. Walking past Jeremy he reached out and grasped my arm roughly.

"I'm apologizing now for anything that might happen later on," he whispered hoarsely into my ear, his breath hot against my neck. His eyes bore into mine before I yanked my arm away. Confused wasn't even the right word to explain how I felt.

I did as I was told, moving as quickly as I could and within a few minutes Shane and I were in the truck headed toward my house.

"Tell me what is going on!" I demanded, my voice no longer scared and uncertain but instead, angry and frustrated.

"Why was Jeremy so mad?"

"It isn't that he's mad," Shane said, "There's something that I didn't think to tell you; something that is pretty important."

"He seemed very mad," I answered.

Shane held back a chuckle. The situation wasn't funny but he needed to laugh. They pulled into Elisa's driveway and he quickly corralled her inside. Once gathering up everything they had brought, he sat her down gently in the kitchen chair pulling another up in front of her and eased himself down in it to face her.

"How do you feel?" he began.

I looked confusedly at him, "I feel fine."

"Nothing weird?"

"No."

"Ok, here's the thing," he said, patting my leg, "You're in heat."

I could see his surprise when I laughed heartily, "What? That's ridiculous!"

"That is what's happening," Shane answered, "You might not feel it just yet, but you will."

I rolled my eyes, "Just explain what is going to happen and quit making me beg for information," I said shortly, "Just say it."

Shane cocked an eyebrow, "Ok," he answered. "Have you noticed that you haven't gotten your period for a few months now?"

I nodded, "Of course I noticed, but…"

"That's because your body was getting ready for this," he paused, "Here's a little history lesson. Females come into heat one time a year. It last for about 2 to 3 days. Every male in a 10 mile radius is going to show up for the big event," Shane watched as her eyebrows scrunched together in concern.

"Ok, so that's it then?"

"Oh….I'm not nearly finished," he answered as he shook his head. "The heat cycle ensures the future of the pack. If you don't feel the effects of it yet, you will soon," he hesitated again, "Your body is going to betray you Elisa….and if given the opportunity you will betray me as well."

"What do you mean? I don't understand!" I cried out.

Shane reached across and grasped my hands in his own, "Listen to me," he said as his glowing blue eyes pierced into mine. "You're giving off pheromones that drive males crazy…including me….and Jeremy. That is why he demanded that I take you and leave there. He will mate with you if given the chance…and you will allow it."

"No!" I shrieked, "I would never…."

"Calm down …listen. I'm not going to leave you so we don't have to worry about that….but in a few hours your will feel the effects and you will want to mate. If I wasn't here for some reason, you will search out a male. That is just how it works Elisa….It's the nature of animals."

"You're basically saying that I am going to turn into some kind of sex-crazed maniac and if you're not around anybody will do?"

"That's exactly what I'm saying. It ensures the future of the pack."

"And you're okay with that?"

"No, I'm not *okay* with it. I have no plans on leaving you for any reason. I just want you to realize that when you feel out of control, its normal…..it is supposed to happen."

"This is unbelievable," I said, shaking my head with skepticism.

"When Jeanette gets here she can fill you in on what to do. There are herbs that can be taken close to the heat cycle that can stop it. I just don't know enough about all of that," he said.

"So what do I do now? Just wait?" I asked in frustration.

"Basically," he answered softly, "Soon enough we will have something to do," he smiled, the blue glow illuminating his eyes.

"Let's find something to eat," he said, "We will need the energy."

A few hours later, I realized that Shane had been right. He had done his best to keep his distance from me within the tight confines of the cabin but as the heat came into full swing, my body began to sweat profusely, stirring the strength of the pheromones to a level he could no longer resist. As I began to shed clothes, he came from the shadows to embrace my body against his. His eyes glowed unnaturally.

"My wolf will take over soon," he whispered softly against my skin, "I'm not sure how long I can delay it...."

"Should I shift?" I asked breathlessly.

"Not yet," he breathed, "Not yet." His hands roamed over my slickened body evoking an orgasmic reaction from his touch alone. While I shuddered with the release he thrust into me, quickly finding his own.

Outside the cabin walls the low wail of a lone wolf echoed through the stillness. Breathing heavily, Shane lifted his head and then stood up moving away toward the window. He could see the mahogany wolf pacing back and forth at the wood line. It paused when it saw him at the window and for a moment their eyes locked in a challenging stare before it looked away and continued its vigilant trot. It wouldn't leave until this was over and Shane knew it. Yes, he would fight him if the need arose but he couldn't be angry. Shane understood the wolf's instinct and if the situation was reversed, it would be his wolf outside that window looking in....waiting for his opportunity.

When he looked from the window back to Elisa, she was standing quietly in the doorway watching him. Already he could see the heat building her back up from the release only minutes before. His wolf lurched forward, demanding to be let out. Shane couldn't fight it any longer and gave in. In an instant the black beast stood in his place.

Elisa let the change come over her swiftly and met the black wolf as he made his way across the floor to her. After a small show of affection at their reuniting, the black beast mounted and mated with her. The rest of the night progressed in a similar manner. After each union the wolves would snuggle together for an hour or perhaps two before the heat would again demand their mating.

The next morning, I shifted back to my human form and left the black wolf asleep on the floor as I sought the hot stream of the shower. Not really believing Shane when he told me that my body would betray me, I admitted that he knew what he was talking about. Attempting to fight it, I found that I wasn't able to, especially when he touched me, it was pretty much over at that point.

After finishing my shower, I wrapped up in my favorite robe. I found Shane sitting on the sofa halfway dressed with his feet propped on the coffee table when I returned. He smiled and held out his hand to me which I took without hesitation. He pulled me down onto his lap.

"You okay this morning?"

"Yes," I answered, "Just a bit tired."

Shane's laughter filled the room, "I'm afraid that it isn't quite over yet," he said as he wrapped his arms around me.

"Is Jeremy still out there?" I asked.

"I haven't looked this morning but I'm sure that he is," he responded as he lifted me to my feet and moved to the window; I followed a few steps behind.

Shane peered out toward the trees where he had seen Jeremy the evening before but couldn't locate him. Moving to a different window he continued to search but what he found wasn't what he expected. Out the north side of the cabin stood a gray wolf staring openly toward the cabin. Its eyes settled on his silhouette framed in the window before it took a couple of steps forward hesitantly.

"Who in the hell is this?" Shane said as he studied the gray wolf. I pressed up against him to see out. Once my eyes fell upon the stranger I glanced back to Shane.

"I told you…..they come out of the woodwork," he said, "I just didn't know that there were any others around," he paused, "I'm concerned about Jeremy though. I don't see him anywhere." He continued moving to different windows, peering out.

"Do you think something's happened to him?" I asked with quiet concern.

"I don't know," said Shane, "I'm uneasy. Especially since there is another wolf out there that we didn't know existed." Shane started removing his clothes, "I have to check on him."

I nodded. "Wouldn't we have heard something if there had been a scuffle?"

"I would think so, but I'm nervous about this. I'll be right back as soon as I see who this is and find Jeremy." He opened the door, shifted quickly and moved down the steps and out into the yard. The gray wolf scurried away immediately at the sight of him and disappeared into the woods with the black wolf in heavy pursuit.

Left alone, I suddenly felt vulnerable. Although the shower had delayed the effects of the heat I could feel it starting to creep back into my senses. I stared out the window, hoping that I would see the black wolf returning from where it had disappeared, but as I continued to watch the woods, I saw nothing. My skin had already taken on the sheen of moisture beneath the robe as I turned and headed toward the bathroom. Maybe another shower would slow it down.

Nearly across the living room, the cabin door burst open. I wheeled around to see Jeremy's frame silhouetted in the doorway before he moved inside pushing the door shut brusquely behind him. Striding across the room, his intimidating behavior should have frightened me but instead it bewitched me, and I stood trancelike and frozen. In the back of my mind somewhere a voice resisted but when he wrapped his arms around me and buried his face against my neck, the voice was lost in the sound of his labored breathing.

Stripping the robe from me, it fell in a pool to the floor as he pressed his naked body against mine. A smoky fire smoldered behind his gray eyes that matched the green embers that glowed within mine as he pulled me down to the floor and positioned himself between my willingly open legs. I lifted my body towards him and as he was moving forward with intent, a strong hand on his shoulder jerked him sprawling backward onto the floor.

Shane stood above him, his chest heaving. An inhuman roar of rage filled the cabin and continued even after he shifted into the black wolf. Beneath him, Jeremy's wolf snarled upward from its disadvantaged position. Shane glanced at Elisa who had shifted as well and watched from a safe distance. Although the confrontation between the two beasts sounded serious, both Shane and Jeremy's wolves wielded more bark than they did bite. The black beast withdrew from its position over the other male and moved back toward the female, standing protectively in front of her. Jeremy's wolf glanced back only once as it made its way back to the door and outside down the steps. Only then did the black wolf turn its full attention back to the female.

Once our mating was once again complete, we shifted back to our human forms. Tears welled up in my eyes as I confronted Shane with what he had witnessed.

"I am so sorry," I sobbed, "I couldn't stop."

He brought me against him and held me tightly, stroking his fingers through my dark hair.

"It's okay," he said reassuringly, "That sneaky bastard set me up," he chuckled softly.

I pulled away and looked at him through misty eyes, "You aren't mad….?"

"I'm not mad," he answered, "I told you what could happen. I also told you that I wouldn't leave you alone….and I did. It's as much my fault as anybody's."

"I feel terrible," I said, "what if you hadn't showed up when you did and we had….."

"You would have mated with Jeremy," he said matter of fact, "Or that kid."

"What kid?"

"The gray wolf," Shane said, "Is just a kid. Well, I say kid but he's probably 20 or so."

"Where did he come from?" I questioned.

"He hasn't been around here long." Shane answered, "Apparently he has a couple of sisters as well. We'll be seeing some out of them as soon as this is over."

The second day seemed to drag but as it crept by, the bouts of heat grew farther and farther apart until they were able to sleep the full length of the night. The next morning, embraced in Shane's arms, I felt that I must be one of the luckiest women in the entire world. By no fault of my own, I had come close to betraying our relationship and yet he wasn't upset or even angry. Now though, as I thought back over what had happened, I didn't know how I could look Jeremy in the eye again.

As Shane urged me to gather my things so we could return home, I hesitated, "Maybe I should just stay here for a while."

Shane stopped dead in his tracks and stared at me, "Why?" His voice held a tone of authority that I had heard very rarely.

"I feel odd with what has happened. I think I'd like some time…alone," I answered.

He absorbed her words shook his head, "No," he said bluntly, "You're coming home with me."

"Shane, I'm tired of living out of my overnight bag. All of my things are here," I argued.

Again he nodded but this time more slowly and thoughtfully.

"Okay," he said thoughtfully, "Give me some time and we will remedy that," he paused, "But please, don't argue….come home with me now."

"What about Jeremy?" I asked, slightly embarrassed to have brought up the situation again.

"You and Jeremy can talk about what happened," he answered, "If that will make you feel better. But you're the only one concerned about it. Jeremy will tell you the same thing." He seemed set in his thoughts about it which made me feel more comfortable even though I still felt the pang of guilt deep in the pit of my stomach.

"Okay," I simply agreed. I finished gathering a few things and as we stepped out on the deck, I locked the door behind me.

I missed home.

Chapter 28

Jeremy heard Shane's truck long before it rumbled down the driveway so there was ample time to prepare for the confrontation that was sure to come. He kicked back on the couch and turned the television on just to appear relaxed although he wasn't feeling relaxed at all. It had been a long couple of days without eating or sleeping for him; his wolf hadn't allowed it. He had spent those two days pacing around the outside of Elisa's cabin in complete and utter torture. The appearance of the gray wolf had been a distracting surprise.

At first encounter, Jeremy had asserted his dominance and he had willingly and quickly submitted. Once shifted, Jeremy easily determined the reason for the wolf's hasty submission….he was young and inexperienced. They had talked for a couple of hours and Jeremy learned that he was new to the area and had only been there a couple of months. His name was Tristan and he had also learned that the boy had a couple of sisters which immediately sparked his interest.

Shane was the first inside when the door to the cabin opened and their eyes met briefly

"Hey," said Shane.

"Hey," Jeremy replied.

Elisa followed behind juggling a few items she had brought with her. When she looked up she found Jeremy's eyes settled on her. Smiling shyly and without saying a word, she quickly moved to the bedroom to put her bag away.

"Go talk to her if you want," Shane said as he watched Jeremy's eyes follow until she disappeared within the bedroom walls. "She feels it's important that you two talk."

Jeremy nodded and got up from the couch. He turned to Shane for just a moment, "Thanks," he muttered.

"Oh, we're not done you sneaky son of a bitch," Shane snarled in reply, "But I'll wait my turn."

"Oh," Jeremy grinned, "That."

"Yeah…that."

As Jeremy walked into the bedroom, I was unpacking the clothes from my bag. I looked up nervously as he shut the door behind him, confining us alone in the room.

"You know," he began, "I apologized beforehand for anything that might happen so I hope you aren't expecting anything like that."

His cocky attitude was in full swing and my eyes narrowed at his blatantly careless tone. "You certainly know how to open up a conversation asshole," I replied sharply.

Jeremy settled on the corner of the bed opposite of where I was unpacking my things and grinned. I could feel my face reddening with anger and embarrassment as I waited for his next snide remark.

"Nice," he said motioning his head toward my hand. I had forgotten that I was still holding some clothing and as luck would have it, it happened to be a particularly lacey pair of red underwear. Quickly, I flung them down on the bed.

My sigh was filled with frustration, "Okay Jeremy. Shane told me you wouldn't have anything to say about this and I am guessing that he was right….as usual. So, if you're finished tormenting me you can just go," I snapped.

"Listen," he said, his tone strangely milder and considerate. It was almost shocking to hear the difference from what it had previously been. "If you feel that you need to talk about what *almost* happened to feel better about it, I'm here to listen."

"Am I the only one that finds my behavior and yours to have been …inappropriate?"

"Here's the thing," Jeremy answered, "You're looking at this whole thing like a *human*. Yes, for human standards what *almost* happened could be considered very, very bad," he said, "But therein lies the problem, Elisa. You're not a human *anymore*."

"I understand that," I interjected, "But I'm still *me* and I can't help but feel that it was wrong."

Jeremy stood up and moved closer. He rested a reassuring hand on my arm, "You're right, you are still you……but now you're also much more."

Jeremy's touch was a sense of comfort to me and for some reason my mind was immediately put at ease. "So you're telling me that you don't feel weird at all about what happened and I shouldn't either?"

He grinned before he answered, "Weird? No," he said, "Although I do wish that Shane could've waited at least a couple of more minutes before he decided to show up."

My face flushed at what he was insinuating but I knew he was only teasing. He stood up and moved toward the door. He had an odd look on his face when he turned back towards me.

"I'm really not," he said as he passed through the open door and left me standing with my mouth gaping. Finally regaining some sort of composure, I slammed the door behind him, creating a barrier between us.

"What is going on?"Shane demanded as he stormed out of the kitchen at the sound of the banging door, "Didn't it go well?"

"You know me," Jeremy chuckled, "I know how to get a rise out of the best of them."

"You do have a certain suave quality," Shane joked, "But, speaking of getting a rise,you were pretty sneaky over there," his tone turning suddenly somber.

Jeremy nodded, "That new wolf's appearance did prove advantageous for me," he paused, "But don't act like you wouldn't have done the same."

"I'm not sure you would have left your mate to check on me," Shane answered, "So I wouldn't have been offered the same opportunity."

"Yeah, you're probably right. I don't think I would have trusted you…especially if you were anything like me……….." Jeremy laughed, "You should have known better."

Shane gave a short chuckle, "You can be such an arrogant, selfish and somehow generous bastard all at the same time. I don't know how you do it."

"Lots of practice," he chortled, "Lots of practice," he paused and then changed the subject, "Okay, let's talk about this kid…Tristan."

Shane nodded.

"I told him after the deal with Elisa was over, we'd all get together. We spent a couple of hours talking there in the woods how we were walking around with hard-ons and he seems like a real nice kid," they both laughed.

"Yeah, I talked to him too. Just briefly though. He let it slip what you were up to so I had to cut our conversation a little short," said Shane.

"He's just an inexperienced kid. Elisa drew him in but he really didn't know what to do once he got there," snickered Jeremy.

"Well here's what I am thinking," Shane began, "In a week or so I'm going to ask them over here for a BBQ or something so we can get to know them. It sounds like he has a couple of sisters as well," Shane paused, "We've talked about building a pack here and I think this may be our opportunity. They are new, young blood….they may be looking for the security of a pack."

Jeremy nodded, "We've already got a foundation and the larger we can make our pack the stronger we will become. Plus, the safer we will be."

"I agree," Shane responded.

"There's something else we need to talk about too," said Shane, "Elisa misses her things and she doesn't feel like this place is hers. I want to fix this… make her feel like she belongs here. I hope that if I build her a home that she can have a hand in, she will feel more comfortable here."

Jeremy cocked an eyebrow, "Really? A house huh?"

"Yeah, I think so. I would appreciate your help in planning it out."

For about an hour they sat and discussed the possibilities of building on the property and the best way to go about it. They would need a place large enough for everyone to gather for meals but they would also all need their own sleeping quarters. They debated about building one big house with several rooms and a large kitchen/dining room, living room or perhaps several separate dwellings.

They both brought up good and bad points about each idea until their conversation began to idle and they decided they had plenty of time to talk about it later. Jeremy then brought up the fact that children could very well be in Shane's future, especially now given the events of the past couple of days. They would need to think about the additional room needed for nurseries and playrooms.

"We've never talked about a family," said Shane softly, "I don't even know how she feels about that."

"Might be too late for talking," Jeremy grinned, "You could quite possibly be on the road to fatherhood right now."

"Huh," Shane grunted as he let that thought weave throughout his brain, "You know though….we've been together for a while and nothing has come of it."

"She's been through quite a bit Shane," Jeremy interrupted, "The shock of learning about us…the rogue and all that followed that whole ordeal. She recently learned that close family friends are werewolves….I think that all of those things would cause enough stress to deter a pregnancy," Jeremy added, "Don't start doubting your masculinity," he teased.

Shane seemed lost in his thoughts as he stood up, "I'd better go check on her…..see if she's cooled down since you pissed her off." He strode toward the bedroom while Jeremy watched and chuckled to himself. Shane was so predictable.

"Elisa?" Shane said softly as he cracked open the bedroom door. His eyes fell across her sleeping form curled up in the middle of his bed. Moving closer, he pulled the comforter up over her as he took in the way her dark hair framed her face. He sat down easily on the bed and gently pushed a stray strand of hair away from her cheek as he admired her. She was beautiful and she belonged to him. Together, they would build a strong pack.

Chapter 29

A week passed by and Shane decided it was time to pay a visit to Tristan and his family and thought it might be best to go alone. The early April weather had turned warm enough to don only a t-shirt and Shane was relieved at not having to wear the extra clothes. Although naturally hot natured, the cold Missouri winter had proven to be a little more than he could bear without the additional wardrobe.

Although Jeremy had been ready to accompany him, he was wary that his roughshod attitude might quickly put the new family on edge. He wasn't necessarily worried about Tristan, but the females might find him a bit too much. They would meet him soon enough.

Shane wound his way along the gravel road toward his destination. He hadn't ventured this far before so he was unfamiliar with the landscape. Passing by several houses on the way, he couldn't help slowing to watch some children enjoying the warmer temperatures.

There were two boys and a smaller girl playing on a swing set next to a run-down looking trailer, their faces flushed from their activity as they chased one another around the yard. Shane's thoughts wandered as he watched them but suddenly noticed that he was being watched as well. A woman had come out onto the rickety deck attached to the trailer and was eyeing him suspiciously. *Crap*....she probably thought he was some kind of pervert. He pushed down on the accelerator and moved on down the road.

Finding the driveway that he thought belonged to Tristan, he maneuvered his truck around the pot holes. Pulling up in front of a small, but well kept house he immediately noticed the silhouette of a woman peering out the window between the curtains. As he stepped out of the truck, the curtains fell closed and Tristan appeared in the doorway smiling. He strode toward him.

"Tristan?" he said as he extended his hand, "Remember me?"

Tristan smiled, "Sure I remember you...Shane, right?" He grasped Shane's offered hand firmly, "Tristan Taylor."

Tristan stood at least a foot shorter than Shane's towering height. He was of medium build but Shane remembered that he was well muscled beneath his long sleeved shirt and he could feel the strength in his handshake. His hair was a tousled mess of darker and lighter shades of blonde and his pale blue eyes stared back at Shane intently and unwavering. Shane observed his strong features and could foresee a future alpha...once he matured.

"It's good to see you again," grinned Tristan.

"I told you that I would catch up with you," Shane said chuckling, "Once the air cleared."

Tristan's laugh was soft but genuine, "I apologize for ….uh…imposing," he paused, "But I wasn't myself."

"It seems to have that affect on us, doesn't it?" Shane laughed heartily, "But, I'll get to the reason for my visit," he paused, "I wanted to come by and invite you and your family over for dinner tomorrow. I would like you to meet my mate Elisa, and of course you have already met Jeremy."

"Jeremy's the sneaky one, right?" Tristan inquired.

Shane chuckled, "Yeah, exactly."

"I've already talked to the girls about you," Tristan replied, "Lena will be on board and will demand to bring something…..you might as well tell me something she can bring," he grinned. "She loves to cook," he paused a long moment before continuing.

Shane could see his unease.

"Zoey is my younger sister. She……is a handful."

Shane wondered if he should ask but Tristan had already opened that door, "A handful, huh?"

Tristan nodded, "She's sixteen. Do I need to say anything more?"

Shane smiled and shook his head, "Nope, nothing else needed," he laughed. "So, can I tell Elisa she will get to meet you tomorrow?"

Tristan smiled again, "Sure. We'll be there even if I have to drag Zoey by her hair. What time?"

"Four o'clock." Shane said, "Looking forward to it." He flashed a wide smile and extended his hand again. Tristan shook it eagerly.

"Thanks Shane."

As Shane turned to head back to his truck, a movement in the window caught his eye again. Before the figure could retreat, he clearly took in the pale blonde hair with bright streaks of pink before she disappeared from his view. "Hmm……that's interesting." he said to himself as he settled on the truck seat and headed for home.

When he got back to the cabin and walked in the door he found Jeremy and Elisa standing over the kitchen table with a huge paper stretched out on the surface. They both looked up as he entered and Elisa's eyes lit up as she rushed to him and jumped into his arms wrapping her legs around his waist. He looked at Jeremy with surprise and was met with a smirk.

"You're building me a house!!??" I said excitedly. It was more of a statement than a question.

He glowered at Jeremy.

"Didn't know it was a secret……….." Jeremy uttered.

I rained kisses on his face from one side to the other before his mouth finally found mine, halting my thrilled assault. After a few moments he eased me back to the floor.

"Yes, we are going to have our own house."

He couldn't help but laugh at my overly eager antics. I was smiling ear to ear as if I couldn't help myself.

"So….what are you two doing over here?" He asked as I took his hand and led him to the table.

Shane was in awe as he looked down at the detailed prints that Jeremy had created of their future home. He had seen Jeremy's work but had no idea that he was capable of such intricate detail on paper.

"I wasn't sure what you had in mind," Jeremy said, "So I made this as one huge house."

Shane shook his head slowly in astonishment, "When did you do this?"

Jeremy looked up and smiled, "After you guys went to bed. I've been working on it since we talked about it."

"I'm just….amazed." said Shane as his eyes raked over the forms on the paper.

Jeremy began to point out where bedrooms were, with adjoining bathrooms and living/recreational rooms on the first and second floors. The kitchen and dining room would be on the first floor.

"And here," he continued as he pointed out the empty spaces that he had left, "are the rooms where the nurseries and play areas for the kids will be." He stopped and looked up at Shane, "What do you think?"

"It's awesome," Shane answered right away. "It's like you read my mind." He looked over for Elisa's approval but she was openly staring at him and then back to Jeremy, her excitement having suddenly disappeared. "What?" he asked her.

"Nurseries and playrooms?" I asked curiously.

Shane glanced at Jeremy who took that as his cue to find an excuse to exit the situation.

"I uh….I need to…..well hell, I'm just going to walk out of this." He finished as he strode past them through the living room and out the front door. The sound of the screen door closing brought Shane's eyes back to Elisa's.

I watched as he fumbled for something to say.

"I'm just going to say this," he finally said, "You could be pregnant....we will need those rooms for our children."

He was surprised by my laughter, "I'm not pregnant Shane. Why would you think that?"

"The heat," he said, "that's normally when it happens," he answered, openly confused by my obvious certainty.

"I take birth control...I can't get pregnant," I said, "I thought that you knew that."

He shook his head slowly, "I didn't." I could hear the disappointment in his tone.

"Are you upset?"

It took a moment before he replied. "No, not upset," he paused, "I just thought......" His voice trailed off.

"What?" I paused, "What did you think?" I asked softly, somehow feeling that I had betrayed him in some way. When his eyes met mine again I saw a flicker of sadness in them.

"Do you want a family.....with me?" he murmured.

"Of course I want a family with you," I countered, "Just not ...yet."

"I see," was all that he could muster to say before he turned away to hide the sting that I had apparently caused.

I watched his broad back as he walked away and cringed when the cabin door slammed. Confused and hurt by his reaction, I didn't know what to say or do to make him understand that I wasn't ready for another change in my life....not yet. I hadn't had time to settle into the one that I had just recently acquired. Surely he could understand that.

Jeremy watched Shane storm from the cabin from his position under the hood of his truck. Since he had the time to kill he figured he check all of the fluids until their conversation was finished. He sighed heavily as Shane made his way over to him as he really didn't need to be a part of this, but if Shane wanted to talk, he'd listen. He was able to tell from Shane's stiffened posture that it hadn't gone well.

"So......didn't go well?" he asked as he continued pulling out the dipstick to check his oil.

Shane growled in response, "No."

Jeremy tried to change the subject, "So, how was Tristan today?"

Shane scowled, "He was fine. They're coming for dinner tomorrow." he paused, "She takes birth control."

"Oh yeah?" Jeremy replied, trying to appear indifferent.

"Yeah," Shane muttered.

"Well, at least you know it isn't you," Jeremy's chuckle was met by another low growl. He stared at his friend from across the Ford's engine.

"Come on Shane. It isn't that big of a deal." Instantly he could see that voicing his opinion hadn't been what Shane had wanted to hear. If looks could have crippled him, Shane's would have.

"I thought that she ...." Shane started but Jeremy cut him off before he could get the complete sentence out.

"That's the problem." Jeremy interrupted loudly, staring at his friend from across the truck's engine, "You *thought*," he paused, his voice taking on a condescending tone as he continued.

"Okay, okay, here's a little scenario for you to think about since you're already pissed off," he said, "Okay.....let's see," Jeremy said thoughtfully as he looked up at the sky, "What was it....like six months ago that she first met her neighbor Shane?"

Shane glared at him but he continued, "Now, *six* months later, Shane wants her to have his babies," he hesitated, "It doesn't seem to matter to him that she's trying to adjust to being a new wolf herself or that she has been thrown into a brand new life that she didn't know existed or was even possible."

He stopped before sarcastically adding, "Go Shane," and raising his fist for a fist bump he didn't expect in return.

Shane's eyes narrowed and his lip quivered into a snarl before he turned to cross the yard. He tore the t-shirt he wore into two pieces and threw it to the ground. When he got to the deck steps, he kicked off his boots and stripped his jeans off. He headed toward the woods in a run and shifted to the wolf in mid-stride before he disappeared among the trees.

Jeremy watched for a few moments after he disappeared. He closed up all of the open compartments under the hood of the Ford before he slammed it closed and headed toward the house. Going into the bathroom, he washed the grease and oil from his hands and then drifted into the kitchen to find something cold and wet to drink.

Elisa sat at the kitchen table. She had rolled up the house prints and secured them neatly with a rubber band. Neither spoke as he rattled around in the fridge and pulled out two bottles of beer, one which he sat in front of her on the table.

"You alright?" he asked as he reached over and unscrewed the cap on her beer.

I inhaled sharply and exhaled a long, slow breath, "Yeah."

We sat in silence for a while, sipping beer before I spoke again. "Where'd Shane go?"

Jeremy shrugged, "Ran off in the brush."

A few more quiet moments passed. "I upset him," I added.

"And I pissed him off," Jeremy responded as he took another long drink. He could feel her eyes on him and knew the questions were coming; he'd put a stop to it before they got started.

"I don't enjoy being the devil's advocate between you two but there's no one to do it," he said as he peered into her green eyes. "He told me about the birth control."

"He doesn't keep anything from you, does he?" I said sharply.

Jeremy glared back at her. "No, not ususually, but I wasn't finished."

He noticed the thin line of her lips as she fought the urge to respond, but didn't. Inwardly he giggled to himself, he would have them both pissed off before it was all over.

"I was going to say.....I agree with you. I can fully understand your position. But," he added, "Shane's an alpha and used to getting things his way without a debate. He won't tolerate insubordination for long.....even from you."

I glowered at him, "I'll not be forced into something like this," I growled.

"No, I don't think you will," Jeremy agreed, "But I'm going to share a little piece of important information with you," he paused, "Pack law allows a mated pair to reproduce outside of their bond if one of the pair can't....or won't procreate," he paused again, "Do you catch on to what I'm saying?"

With that said he subtly got up from the table and walked out of the kitchen not waiting for her response. Yes, he was an asshole....

The afternoon passed quietly for Jeremy. Shane hadn't yet returned from his run and Elisa was working off her frustration by cleaning the house. Thankfully the weather was nice and he was able to spend his time outside. The warm weather always put him in the mood for planting so he began to scope out the best places for some raised flower beds next to the deck. He stepped off an area on each side of the steps and placed markers in the ground, studying it for a while befoe finally coming up with a plan.

He glanced down at his watch, 2:00 PM. He really didn't feel like going to town to get the landscaping supplies he needed today so he'd make a list and go in the next day or two. His mind wandered off suddenly to the BBQ that Shane had promised their company. Did they even have a pit?

"Hey Elisa," he yelled as he stepped in the door. The smell of cleaning supplies was overwhelming to his senses so he couldn't imagine how she was standing the fumes. She came out of the bathroom when she heard him.

"Don't you have a BBQ pit?" he asked. He was surprised when she answered without a hint of anger in her voice. He had just assumed that she'd be mad at him for the rest of the day.

"Yes, I have one at home," I answered softly.

"Well, Shane promised the kid a dinner tomorrow evening...we don't have a pit. Can we get yours?"

"Yeah, you can go get it," I answered as I turned back toward the bathroom to finish that chore.

"Come on," he said, "Ride with me."

I turned and studied him for a moment before nodding, "Okay."

Shane returned how they were gone, picking up the remains of his shirt, his boots and jeans on the way in. He had heard Jeremy's truck start even at the distance away that he had been and he could tell by the scent that Elisa wasn't inside the cabin. He had run most of the anger out of his system and now he was just tired and felt like a selfish fool. Jeremy had a way about him that infuriated him. On more than one occasion he had wanted to put his fist through that arrogant smile of his but he never had. Jeremy knew the buttons to push to get the desired response and he never failed to disappoint. But Shane had to admit that most of the time; in the end....Jeremy was always right.

Damn him.

"I figured you'd be pissed off at me," Jeremy said without glancing over as we drove toward home to get the pit.

"I am." I said, "But I will get over it...just like I always do."

Jeremy grinned. "You can't stay mad at me for long," he teased.

"You're just such an asshole," I replied, "I should be immune to it by now."

Jeremy laughed loudly.

We loaded the BBQ pit and grabbed an extra bag of charcoal that I had in the pantry before heading back. The silence was comfortable between us as we maneuvered the rough driveway but yet Jeremy felt the need to disrupt it with small talk.

"So......I guess you'll meet Tristan tomorrow."

"I guess." I responded thoughtlessly, my mind obviously somewhere else."

"He seems to be a nice kid," he added.

"I'm surprised you didn't piss him off in the first 5 minutes."

Jeremy chuckled, "There's always tomorrow."

I couldn't help but giggle. The worst part was that he was probably telling the truth.

Jeremy unloaded the pit after we parked and carried it up the deck steps. I grabbed the charcoal and carried it inside. Shane was reclined on the couch when I walked through the door. He got up and walked toward me and removed the load I carried from my arms. Sitting it on the floor and without speaking, he pulled me close and embraced me within the welcoming warmth of his arms, holding me for a moment before he spoke.

"I'm sorry," he said simply, "I never want you to feel pressured...especially by me."

I pulled back and looked up into the startling blue of his eyes, "I want a family with you Shane.....it is something that I have thought about." I said, "Just not now."

He nodded, "I know. I understand...you don't need to explain."

Jeremy walked in and saw the two of them embracing and smiled. "And all is right in the world again," he joked.

They both just looked at him without a comment, "Good then," he began, "We need to figure out what we're doing tomorrow for this dinner you've schemed up."

Chapter 30

Thankfully the weather cooperated while Jeremy stood behind the hot grill flipping burgers the following afternoon. I had baked an apple pie and chocolate cake for dessert along with a generous potato casserole that was staying warm in the oven until our guests arrived.

Shane had set up a couple of tables out on the deck. He was secretly looking forward to a quiet evening learning to learn about the newcomers. He had opened all of the windows and a refreshing spring breeze seeped from outside, freshening the cabin's interior.

He noticed that Elisa had taken advantage of the warmer temperature and dressed in a pair of capris and flip flops. Her long dark hair was pulled back in a low pony tail. Wearing a form fitting, low cut pink t-shirt that hugged her curves, it allowed just a hint of cleavage. Although she hadn't ever gained back the weight that she had lost during their separation, she filled out the shirt nicely. Feeling his eyes on her, she looked up. He smiled approvingly.

"I see you're planning on impressing our male guest," he teased.

I grinned back. "Couldn't hurt," I said slyly. Shane wrapped his arms around my waist and kissed my exposed neck.

"Just remember who loves you baby," he growled.

"Hey! I need a pan....or a plate....or bowl or something out here!" Jeremy's voice cut in loudly from outside, "I'm going to burn this shit up if I don't get some of it off here!"

Breaking away from his arms I rushed to grab a pan out of the cabinet. Hurrying outside I pushed it into Jeremy's outstretched hand.

"Thanks," he muttered.

Our eyes were immediately drawn toward the sound of a vehicle turning from the county road onto our driveway. Shane heard it as well and stepped out on the deck beside us.

"Well, here they come," Shane stated, a hint of excitement in his voice. Jeremy and I looked at him questioningly. He shrugged in response before turning to watch the advancing SUV.

Tristan stepped out of the driver side of the vehicle as a woman exited the passenger side holding a large bowl. Shane and Elisa moved toward the steps while Jeremy continued his vigilant watch over the meat that was still on the grill. There was no denying the similarity between the two siblings. The woman had the same tousled dark and light blonde hair except that hers was long and wavy, cascading just past the top of her shoulders. Her eyes were the same pale blue as Tristan's and when she smiled, it was the same mouth...only feminine.

"Welcome," Shane said as he took a step forward and held his hands out to take the bowl that the woman carried. "I'm Shane," he said, accepting it from her outstretched hands.

She smiled shyly, "I'm Lena," she responded, "I brought some pasta salad."

Shane gave his famous brilliant, toothy smile as he extended his hand to her. Lena slipped hers into the large warm grasp that he offered.

"It's nice to meet you," she said timidly.

"It's a pleasure to meet you as well," Shane replied before turning to introduce his mate, "This is Elisa."

I immediately stepped forward and smiled pleasantly at the blonde woman extending my own hand. Lena took it and smiled back. We exchanged pleasantries while Shane disappeared inside to set the pasta salad on the kitchen table. When he returned, Tristan had already introduced himself and was holding my hand in his own. Shane could see the flush of red on his cheeks and chuckled to himself at the youngster's inexperience.

"Let's go meet Jeremy," Shane said as he led them across the deck toward the grill where Jeremy was engulfed in a thick cloud of smoke.

He spoke but apologized for not being able to leave his post long enough for a more formal introduction. His eyes traveled over Lena with curiosity before returning to the chore in front of him.

"We can get to know each other a little more once this part is finished," he said as he motioned toward the grill. "Nice to see you again Tristan."

"Your other sister....didn't she come?" Shane asked.

Tristan laughed uneasily, "Yeah, she's out in the car," he paused, "I warned you yesterday....she's a handful."

Lena's soft voice cut in, "A handful?" she said, "I can think of a much better word....." Her voice trailed off as Tristan flashed a warning look in her direction.

"Will she be joining us for dinner?" I asked. "I hope that she doesn't sit out there the entire evening."

"No." Tristan said rather strongly, "She'll be getting out and joining us whether she likes it or not. Right now she's on the phone so I said she could have a few minutes."

I led Lena into the cabin and thanked her for bringing the extra dish.

"Pasta is one of my favorites," I praised, "I'm glad that you brought it, now I don't need anything else!" We both laughed and it wasn't long before we were getting along like we had known one another for years.

I found out that we had much in common and were only a couple of years apart in age. I also learned that Lena had full intentions of returning to their pack to be reunited with her mate. They had never gotten to complete their bond, she told me, and he would be waiting for her return. It was at that point that my curiosity got the best of me and I had to find out why the family had left their home in the first place.

"Can I ask why you left your pack?" I inquired lightly, "You don't have to say but I can't help but wonder what happened that you would leave your mate."

For a moment Lena was quiet, "It's Zoey," she said softly, "We had to leave because of her." She looked at me as I watched her inquisitively, "She's…….trouble."

"Trouble? What kind of trouble?" I asked, "She's just a kid."

Lena chuckled softly. "Yeah, just a kid," she said sarcastically, "That kid has no respect for pack hierarchy and has gotten us all in deep water with the elders and our alpha," she stated. "She's our sister, so of course we want to protect her but it has gotten to the point that it is easier to just leave."

"Will your pack accept you back…when you decide to go?" I inquired.

Lena nodded, "As long as Zoey doesn't come back with us… Tristan and I can go back any time."

"Wow," I replied, "She must've done something pretty bad."

"Uh….yeah," Lena answered.

I decided to leave it at that.

Jeremy opened the cabin door and strode across the living room to the kitchen carrying the last pan of meat.

"It is finally done," he said as his eyes fell on the two girls standing in the kitchen. "I think we can eat when everyone is ready."

Lena smiled timidly as their eyes met and then she quickly glanced away. Jeremy looked at Elisa who in turn held his gaze and smiled pleasantly.

Two very different females there, he thought to himself. Elisa wouldn't ever back down from eye contact while this new female didn't dare hold his gaze. He studied her for a moment since he wasn't lingering over the grill any longer, taking in the wavy blond curls that framed her face and her pale blue eyes. She was of medium height with a curvy build and attractive.

There was an insignificant nudge deep in the back of his mind as if a memory existed on the edge of his conscious but couldn't quite fall over the rim into something recognizable. The line of her cheekbone and the pale blue eyes seemed slightly familiar.

Strange, he thought to himself before dismissing it. But that was it…. she didn't give off a scent that affected him in any way nor did his body stir at their close proximity. She was just another wolf, nothing more. A little disappointed he turned and made his way back across the living room and outside.

Elisa and Lena followed him out with Lena carrying the pasta salad and Elisa retrieving her casserole from the oven. Jeremy held the door as they exited and sat the dishes down on one of the tables that Shane had set up. He and Tristan were leaned against the deck railing lost in a quiet conversation of their own.

"Let's eat!" Jeremy's loud voice broke the quietness of the warm afternoon, "I'm hungry!"

Everyone laughed as Tristan moved off the deck and toward the car to retrieve his other sister. Everyone could hear her before they saw her.

"I don't want to!" The girl's voice echoed through the sensitive ears of the company of wolves. Shane and I exchanged a look from across the deck, his eyebrows rose in quiet amusement.

"I said get out and meet these people…Now!" Tristan's voice was edgy and rough; a complete change from the seemingly docile tone of earlier.

"This is stupid Tristan," she snapped. "I don't care about them and couldn't care less if I meet them or not."

"If you don't get out of this car and spend an evening like a sensible, respectful person I will not be held accountable for what I am going to do to you," Tristan growled, "You've ruined our lives for the last time." He turned away from the car and headed back toward the cabin, his face ablaze with anger.

Lena's soft voice broke the awkwardness, "I apologize for my sister…." she started but Shane cut her off before she could finish.

"No," he stated simply but firmly as he looked at her over the table. "She's obviously not a child any longer and needs to be responsible for her actions," he said sternly, "she'll apologize for herself."

Lena laughed uneasily, "I mean no disrespect when I say this Shane," she paused, "but good luck with that."

Shane didn't laugh and I could see the serious set in his eyes. I had quickly learned that he had very little patience with some things and disrespect was at the top of that list. Tonight might not be as pleasant as we all had initially hoped.

Tristan made his way back up the steps and took a seat beside Lena. She placed a supportive hand on his arm.

"Let's just eat," Tristan said.

I nodded in agreement, "Yes, let's eat."

Beginning to fill our plates, the conversation finally picked up again. As Jeremy took a bite of his food he looked across the table to the SUV that was directly in his line of vision. He paused with the fork midway to his mouth, his eyes wide.

"Holy Mother of............" he uttered.

Zoey had gotten out of the car and was now making her way slowly toward the cabin while she busily looked down, texting on her phone. Her straight, pale blond hair hung below her shoulders and bore a couple of bright pink streaks down each side. She wore some kind of black, holey leggings beneath an inappropriately short denim skirt and boots that hit slightly above her knees. Hooker boots as Jeremy fondly liked to call them. Her pale blue eyes were outlined in thick, black liner and he immediately noticed the pierced bolt through her eyebrow.

Shane had caught sight of her as well and choked on the food he was trying to swallow and began to cough uncontrollably. Finally looking up as she began to climb the steps to the deck, she took a seat directly across from Jeremy as she continued to move her fingers across the keypad of the phone.

Tristan growled, "This is my sister...Zoey."

When she finally did look up, Jeremy was staring openly at her and she met his eyes defiantly.

"What in the hell happened to you?" he asked sarcastically.

Zoey glared at him for a moment before answering, "Nothing happened to me asshole."

Jeremy laughed in response and I shot him a look but he didn't seem to notice. The girl obviously didn't need to be antagonized.

"Here Zoey," I said as I handed a plate toward her, "Get some food, there's plenty."

Zoey scowled back at me but took the plate that I offered. "Thanks," she grunted, barely audible. She sat the plate down in front of her on the table and continued texting. Everyone exchanged glances with one another nervously but continued eating, leaving Zoey to her own devices. The silence was awkward between the group and no one knew what to say or do to make things better. I could see a nerve beginning to tick in the side of Shane's face.

After a few minutes of complete silence, Shane had tolerated quite enough. He abruptly stood, leaned across the table and snatched the phone from Zoey's busy fingers. She looked up in shock.

"Hey!" she barked, "Give that back!"

"We can't get to know you if you have your nose in this." Shane said calmly as he held up the phone.

"I don't want to get to know you asshole. Give me my phone!"

Lena cringed in her chair as she watched the scene unfold. She glanced over at me, also wide eyed as I waited to see what would happen next. For a moment we caught each other's eyes and exchanged equal looks of uncertainty before looking back at Shane. It was like a train wreck....neither of us could find the ability to look away.

Jeremy had kicked back in his chair with his legs stretched out under the table in front of him watching with an amused expression as the episode developed in front of him. He had to admit, the girl had spunk. She was thick-headed......but she had spunk. She kind of reminded him.....of himself!

Tristan sat stiff in his seat and Jeremy could see the protective stance in his posture. He hoped that this wasn't going to turn into an all and all out brawl; if it did he was more than ready.

"The phone is yours when we finish our evening of getting to know one another....and only then," Shane said coolly, still managing to keep his temper in check.

"You son of a bitch," Zoey snarled, "You can't do that! Give me my fucking phone!" she shrieked as she stood up and made a swipe in attempt to retrieve it. In one quick motion, Shane caught hold of her wrist, his fingers biting into the flesh.

"Let go of me!" She screamed.

"Come with me," he growled as he pulled her around the end of the table by her arm.

"Let go! You're hurting me!" she cried, suddenly looking to Tristan for help, "Are you going to let him treat me like this??"

Jeremy watched Tristan's reaction, expecting any moment to have to defend Shane's actions but he held fast even though his body language betrayed his desire to defend his sibling.

"You're on your own Zoey," he uttered.

Shane pulled the wriggling teen by her arm into the cabin. Her resistance was no match for his strength but her vulgar mouth was close to infuriating him. He found it difficult to maintain some level of calmness since she had called him every name imaginable and even some that he hadn't heard of before.

Jeremy could see the uneasy looks between the remaining siblings at the table. He pulled himself upright in his chair and picked up his fork. He looked across at Tristan and Lena who were exchanging nervous glances.

"He won't hurt her," Jeremy said, "Just give her a firm talking to." With that, he continued eating.

I looked over at him. "You shouldn't have antagonized her," I said, "She might've been okay otherwise."

Tristan broke in, "In Jeremy's defense, she wouldn't have. If it hadn't been him, something else would have set her off."

"We would have just left her at home," Lena added, "But she's never shifted yet and we're concerned what is going to happen when she finally does."

"How old is she?" Jeremy asked, suddenly curious.

"Sixteen," Tristan replied.

Jeremy nodded, "Should be any time now. Looks like puberty has already paid her a visit," he said as he thought about how her breasts had been pushed up in the tight shirt that she wore. His body responded to his thoughts and he shifted to a more comfortable position in his chair.

Hmm.. well that was interesting.

Shane pushed the girl down on the couch and stood in front of her. She automatically tried to spring back up to her feet but he caught her shoulders and pushed her down again forcefully. The string of obscenities that followed rolled off of him and he smiled in return which only seemed to make her angrier.

"Are you finished?" he asked when it seemed that she had finally run out of breath.

"No, I'm not finished! I want my phone and I want it now!"

"Are you ready to listen to what I have to say?"

"I don't care what you have to say!" she screamed, "I just want my phone!"

"You'll get your phone before you leave here tonight," Shane said calmly, "Not before." He paused, "It would be best if you would listen to what I have to say instead of me forcing you to behave."

"You can't force me to do anything!" she retorted, "You alpha bastards think you can tell me what to do but so far none of you can enforce it!" she said smugly. "I'm not scared of you!"

Her expression was one of surprise when Shane laughed heartily. He leaned down only inches from her face and stared into her eyes, his own slightly emitting a bluish glow.

"You should be scared of me little girl," he returned, "I'm like none you've ever met before."

For a moment she was still, silently staring as if she suddenly realized the uncertainty that she faced.

"You use your family Zoey," he continued, "You've destroyed their happiness because the only person you think about is you. You think that they are always going to save you………but one day, they will no longer be able to," said Shane, "and today is that day."

"What do you mean, you crazy fuck?" she growled, her voice a slightly softer tone than before.

"Here are your choices," he said, "You either act like a normal, respectful person for the rest of this evening or I will make you." He smiled, "Either way, I get what I want," he paused, "You have ten seconds to decide."

Her eyes narrowed and Shane could sense that she was searching for the right smart ass remark. Somehow though, he had bluffed her and she wasn't sure if he was for real or feeding her a line.

"Five seconds Zoey," he said.

"Alright, alright," she said in a defeated tone.

"Alright, what?" Shane asked, his eyes drilling into hers.

She sighed heavily, "Alright, I will behave the rest of this evening."

Shane nodded and held out his hand to her. She looked at him skeptically before placing hers timidly in his.

"Good, let's eat." He helped her back to her feet and followed her out the cabin door.

The conversation outside hushed as the two of them reclaimed their chairs from earlier. Shane picked up his fork and continued eating while Zoey began to fill her plate. I smiled across the table at Lena who raised her eyebrows questioningly; I shrugged in response.

"Lena, do you like wine?" I broke the silence.

"I do," she answered.

"I'll get a couple of glasses. Do any of you guys want a beer?" I asked.

"I'll take a beer if you're going that way." Jeremy replied, "Tristan?"

Tristan nodded, "Sure, thank you Elisa." His eyes followed her toward the door and then they came back to rest on Shane. He was puzzled to say the least and couldn't help but wonder what he had said to his sister; whatever it had been had obviously worked. She was now sitting quietly and eating.

Suddenly noticing that Jeremy seemed to be interested in his youngest sister, he scowled as he watched how his eyes hungrily devoured her petite frame. Surely the guy did realize she was only sixteen.....

Returning, I balanced two glasses of wine in one hand with three beers cradled in the crook of my arm. I had automatically brought Shane one even though he hadn't said either way. I figured he might need it after his stressful evening so far. I sat a beer in front of him, then Tristan and Jeremy before moving over and taking the empty seat next to Lena. She immediately picked it the glass of wine and sipped the contents.

"Mmmm Elisa, what is this wine? It is very flavorful," Lena said.

Elisa told her what it was and soon the two of them had lost themselves in conversation. Zoey had finished eating and took a drink of the soda that she had taken out of a nearby cooler and let her eyes wander the new group she'd been forced to spend time with.

Shane was definitely the alpha of the bunch, strong-willed and with a voice full of authority. There was something in his eyes that made her believe that he would do what he said. She didn't know him well enough yet to decide if he was bluffing.

Her pale eyes then traveled to the woman of the group, Shane's mate...Elisa. She was pretty with long, dark chestnut hair and bright green, kind eyes. She seemed nice and had apparently hit it off with her sister. But when her eyes moved to the other male of the group, she found that he was staring directly at her with cloudy gray colored eyes. He was big, just like Shane, with chiseled features and hair about the same color as Elisa's.

"Problem?" she asked smartly as she held his openly amused stare.

"Nope, no problem." he answered but continued with his scrutinizing gaze, "Zoey, huh?"

"And I assume your name isn't really asshole…..although I would have almost bet on it," she answered smartly.

He chuckled. For a kid she had a smart mouth…..they had that in common.

"Jeremy," he snickered.

He found the young girl interesting in a peculiar sort of way. The pale blue eyes and blonde hair that the siblings all shared were dimly familiar along with the distinctive shapes of their noses and high cheekbones. There was something about this family that he just couldn't put his finger on.

Tristan and Shane had moved away from the table and stood back against the deck railing a few feet away. Again they seemed lost in their own private conversation as they sipped their drinks. Elisa and Lena were giggling like young girls together as they drank their wine and then Elisa looked over and noticed Jeremy's leisurely posture and mile long stare.

"Zoey?" Elisa said softly, "Would you like to go inside with us?"

Nodding, she stood up from the table, breaking the intent gaze that Jeremy had fixed on her. Moving around the table, she followed her sister and Elisa inside.

"You can go play with the boys," Elisa said with a slight tease to her voice as she looked back at Jeremy. He scowled but got up and moved toward Tristan and Shane.

The rest of their evening went amazingly well. There were no more issues from Zoey and she even seemed to open up a little bit. I began to think that she was just a misunderstood teenager. When our time together came to a close, Shane recovered Zoey's cell phone that he had stashed and as they said their good-byes, he held it out to her. For a moment she just looked at it and then raised her black lined eyes to his. She was petite and he seemed exceptionally intimidating as she stared directly up at him. She took it from his outstretched hand without a word.

"Good job, kid," he said softly and was met with an uncertain smile that made him grin in return.

Elisa hugged Lena goodbye. They had already made plans to get together the following week. It felt good to have a female companion after being in the company of only men for so long. Lena would be a valuable source of information when it came to questions about her new life.

    Jeremy shook hands with Lena as well as Tristan before they exited the cabin. As Zoey walked by, he held out his hand to her. She looked at him cautiously before extending her own. The moment their fingers touched, a slight shock traveled up his hand into his arm causing his wolf to stir. Zoey jerked her hand back and scowled at him before following her siblings out the door.

    "I'll walk out with you," Shane said as he followed them out the door.

    "Well, I guess I'll start picking some things up," I said grudgingly.

    "I'll help." Jeremy muttered, uncertain about the response that had just been elicited from his wolf. He was lonely....that had to be it.

    The two of us cleared the dishes and folded up the tables in silence. I was grateful for the help but couldn't help wonder about Jeremy's somber mood.

    "You okay?" I finally asked.

    He nodded and when he answered, his voice a tone of seriousness that I wasn't use to hearing, "I'm fine."

    "Hmmmm….." I paused, "Not sure that you're being truthful."

    He moved to stand beside me then, draping an arm across my shoulders and pulling me against his side.

    "You always worry about me, don't you?" He asked softly as he leaned his head against mine.

    Jeremy was never surprised at the stirring that he felt when he was next to her. He had grown accustomed to it as being something normal that they shared whether it was really normal or not. He knew she felt it too, the immediate warmth that spread down the entire length where their bodies touched.

    "I do," I agreed. "You can sure be a prick but I know there's more to you than that," I laughed.

    "Run with me tonight," he said softly as he turned to look at me. My wolf stretched against my skin at the opportunity but I wasn't sure if I should go without Shane. I knew that I was safe with Jeremy but that wasn't what gave me pause.

    "I'll ask Shane if he minds," I said as I turned to walk away from him.

    He gently grabbed my arm, stopping me, "No. Just come," he said.

For some unknown reason his words seemed to have control and I paused, searching his eyes.

"I need the gentle companionship of a female tonight," he said softly as he pulled me back toward him, "Please," he begged, "Come with me."

The sound of his voice seemed to melt my resolve as I stared into his eyes. He pulled his shirt off over his head in one swift motion exposing his broad muscular chest before he reached toward me, fingering the bottom hem of my shirt.

"I….uh…." I struggled but he cut in before I could get any words out.

"You don't have to," he said, his voice betraying his disappointment.

"I want to," I replied, "But I need to say something to Shane first."

"I'm not waiting for you to ask him." He responded sharply, "I'm going now." He turned and headed toward the door but stopped suddenly and whirled around to look at me. "Do you ever wonder why you react to me like you do?"

I felt a sudden flush in my cheeks. I hadn't expected that question so blatantly thrown out there. A slight pang of guilt twisted in my stomach, "I have," I paused, "Often."

Jeremy's eyes bore into mine for a few seconds longer before he nodded and walked out the door. Only minutes later, Shane came inside whistling cheerfully.

"Did you finally get them on their way?" I joked.

He smiled broadly, "Yep. I like them," he paused, "I think that…"

I interrupted, "I'm sorry Shane, but do you mind if I go after Jeremy? He really wanted the company on his run tonight."

Shane's eyes narrowed in annoyance at my interference but softened as he looked down into my imploring gaze, "What's the matter with him?"

I shrugged, "I don't know…..lonely I think." I watched as Shane began to untuck and unbutton his shirt. I placed my hand on his to still their busy task., "Just let me go," I said softly, "Just me."

"You don't want me to go?" He asked, a hint of injury in his voice a slight suspicion in his eyes. We had not run separately since my first transformation. He looked into my eyes, waiting for his answer.

"Do you mind if I go…alone?" I swallowed, afraid of his answer, "I will make it up to you," I teased softly.

He grinned a crooked smile with one eyebrow raised in curiosity, "I can't say no when you put it like that," he said as he pulled me into his arms. "Go," he said simply, "be careful."

He moved his hands down my sides and slid them beneath my shirt, lifting it smoothly up over my head. He then went to work on the button of my capris and pushed them down easily over my hips to the floor. When I stood in front of him naked, he pulled me against him once again and whispered into my ear.

"Go."

Chapter 31

I followed Jeremy's scent through the woods. It weaved and twisted a winding path that seemed to purposefully elude me at times. It would take a few moments but I would soon pick it up again and continue on my way. I could see where he had paused now and again to sniff the ground and to rake his claws across the earth and I would lose his scent momentarily in the freshly upturned soil. It was as if he was trying to make it difficult for me to follow. Suddenly his scent became strong in my nostrils and I knew he was close.

I heard a branch snap off to the left and before I could turn to look, I was hit broad side. The weight knocked the wind out of me and threw me roughly to the ground. In an instant, I was on my feet, defense mode in full force. The mahogany wolf stood a few feet away, his mouth formed into what appeared to be as close to a smile as a wolf could get.

I could swear I heard him laughing.

Staring at him I growled a warning but he continued his gaping grin. He lowered to a pouncing position and leapt at me. The two of us rolled about playfully in a mass of fur before I broke free and ran into the darkness.

I could hear Jeremy's wolf only a few yards behind. Even though I ran at my fullest and hardest, I could sense the distance being closed between us. Soon I could feel his hot breath on my haunches as I struggled to push ahead of him. My body began to deceive me with its exhaustion while we ran side by side across the clearing and up the bank of the lake. When we finally stopped, we both stood on top of the dam, sides heaving.

We were silent except for the panting that filled each other's ears. I turned suddenly and looked at the big brown beast beside me and when his eyes met mine, I bolted away and ran toward the floating dock. My paws hit the wooden planks and in three bounds I was sailing through the air off the end of it, a gigantic splash indicating that I had landed. Coming back to the surface, I heard the unmistakable thuds of Jeremy's wolf across the planking and the few seconds that passed before he splashed into the lake beside me.

Laughing hard inside, I wasn't sure how I paddled my way back to the dock. Jeremy followed and came up on the bank beside me; we both shook ourselves sending excess water spraying in all directions. Jeremy loped back toward the dock and I was surprised when I heard the sound of his laughter echoing through the stillness of the night. He had shifted and was now lying on his back across the wooden dock planks, laughing as he peered up the stars. I moved up on the dock and sat down beside him, looking out across the lake. I felt his fingers run down my side, sinking into the thick brown fur.

"Talk with me Elisa," he said softly, his voice still holding a note of humor.

I peered at him hesitantly from the corner of my eye.

"I won't look at you," he said, "If that is what you're concerned about." To prove his point, he rolled over on his side facing away from me.

I shifted quickly and turned my back toward him as I sat, pulling my knees up close and wrapping my arms around them. "Okay," I said. I heard him reposition and secretly wondered if he had thought that I would be standing there brazenly naked for his viewing pleasure.

"I didn't expect that out of you," he chuckled, "Jumping in the lake." He laughed again, "That was great."

I couldn't help but laugh too. His light, playful mood was contagious. It felt good to laugh out loud in the cool dark where I was surrounded by the wide open empty night. It was a joyful sound that resonated through the obscurity of the shadows and filled my ears and heart with delight.

If someone would have told me a few months ago that I would be sitting here on this very dock naked, in the middle of the night with a handsome nude man; I would have laughed in their face. The thought made me laugh even harder.

When our amusement finally subsided Jeremy cleared his throat before he spoke, "So what did you think of the newbies?"

I shrugged in the darkness, "I like them. They seem nice."

Again, Jeremy laughed, "Even Zoey?"

"She's just a kid trying to find herself," I replied, "We've all been there."

"I guess," said Jeremy, his voice suddenly a more drastic sober tone.

I turned and looked at him over my bare shoulder, "Why so serious?"

"I'm not sure, but I felt something." he said softly, "When we touched."

My eyebrows shot up inquisitively, "Like...?"

"Like maybe……she might be something ……"Jeremy responded. "I don't know for sure, it was strange."

I felt excitement rush through my body, "You mean….like your mate?" I adjusted my position to look fully at him, not thinking any longer about being naked.

His eyes met mine and I saw the smirk on his face, "Hell I don't know Elisa. She's sixteen….."

"It's only 2 years until she's 18. That's not very long," I said elatedly.

Jeremy's gaze hardened beneath his dark lashes, "It is a very long time if you're waiting."

We were silent for a few moments, me not knowing what to say to lighten his mood and he lost in his own thoughts. The song of the frogs and crickets surrounded us in the night and a hoot owl murmured in the distance. Its question was answered by another from farther away and together they carried on a private conversation that only they could understand. I gazed out across the lake. The reflection of the stars mirrored in its still surface along with the partial moon that hung low in the sky.

"Jeremy?" I said softly.

"Yeah?" he answered dreamily, his mind trying to sort out the possibilities that crowded his mind.

"Why did you ask if I ever wondered about…….you and I?" My voice was low and thoughtful. I heard his lengthy sigh as if he needed the extra room in his lungs.

"Hmm." he grunted. "I just wondered."

"There's some reason you asked." I said, "What was it?"

Jeremy mentally kicked himself that had brought it up earlier. He should realize by now that Elisa didn't forget much. He turned on his side to face her even though her back was still toward him.

"I just wondered. You never mention it….but it's there."

He saw her nod her head, "What do you feel that it is? Don't lie to me either or tell me only what you think I need to know."

He reached his fingers out and trailed the tips from the top of her neck down her spine. He felt her body stiffen as the touch ignited the spark that traveled from his fingers through his hand and up his arm, knowing that she felt it the same as he did.

"I made you," Jeremy's voice was soft and smooth, "It wasn't the rogue…it was me."

I turned quickly and stared into his face. Although not surprised by his confession, my heart had skipped a beat at hearing the words actually spoken aloud.

"I've wondered about this," I uttered, "Why haven't you said before now?" I paused, "Does Shane know this?"

"Yeah, he knows, didn't want me to tell you," he answered. His words were met with a low growl and exasperated sigh.

Anger reared its ugly head within me. I was growing tired of being left in the dark.

"Why is it that you two always discuss and decide what's best for me but don't bother to care what I think?" I snarled as I shifted back into my wolf and jumped off the dock onto the grass. Winding my way along the lake dam, I broke into a lope as I crossed the open field headed toward the woods. I heard the unmistakable sound of the other wolf gaining on my position but I didn't care, this wasn't a race.

I was angry.

As soon as he caught up with me, Jeremy brandished his much larger size as he jumped ahead of me and allowed my body to crash into his, bringing me to an abrupt halt. I growled a warning but he stood his ground defiantly. In my mind, his words echoed and I shivered in surprise.

You can't outrun me.....we aren't finished.

What was happening? How did he do that? His words were met by my growls and snarls as I maneuvered around him and continued at a full run.

Jeremy shook his head. He could see that she wasn't going to make this easy for him and he was quickly losing his patience. Following her scent back towards home, it wasn't long before he could see her retreating form through the darkness a few yards ahead. Rushing onward, a blast of energy fueled his speed until he was nipping at her furry flanks. Biting deeper than he intended, he felt the flesh beneath give way beneath his teeth. As he tasted blood she whirled around with unexpected fury and viciously began her assault.

Jeremy hadn't had any intention of hurting her but as she mauled him; inflicting bite after bite over his body he quickly became irritated. He gave a low growl that quickly advanced into a thunderous roar as he issued a final warning. As if a switch had been flipped, she stopped. Panting, she glared at him, the fur tinged red around her jaws.

Shifting quickly under her scrutinizing gaze, he stood before her. Even as the wolf, she turned her head away from his nakedness which allowed him the opportunity to seize the fur around her neck with both hands roughly, pulling her to him.

Elisa growled, her lips pulled back over her bared teeth but she didn't offer to bite.

"Change so we can talk," he demanded. His fingers had no choice but to loosen their grip as her fur disappeared but they remained upon her. She stared up at him in defiance even as his fingers bit into her bare shoulders.

"This is bullshit," he said forcefully, "There's no reason to act like a little bitch."

I didn't answer right away. Instead I studied the bloody punctures on his skin…..the abrasions that I had inflicted, and I felt guilty. My own ass cheek bore the brunt of his aggression from earlier when he had nipped me but it was one bite, not numerous as I had inflicted on him.

"Listen," he began, "We didn't keep this from you. You already knew it," he grumbled, "But we keep things from you to protect you."

"Protect me?" I asked breathlessly, "From what? Myself? Don't you think that the more you tell me, the more prepared I will be when things happen?"

"And if they never happen, we've worried you for nothing," he said smartly as he let his hands fall from my shoulders. Rubbing one hand across his own shoulder, he grimaced as his fingertips grazed an open wound.

I sighed, the anger still heavy in my voice, "So why was this a huge secret? Why didn't anyone voice this possibility instead of letting me just wonder about on my own?"

"We thought it would be best if maybe you never knew," he said. "It could change things between all of us."

My eyes narrowed. "What things?"

Jeremy struggled with whether he should say anything or not. She was already pissed off because of what had been kept from her, so he continued.

"I will always be able to control my blood."

"Control your blood….what does *that* mean?" I asked sarcastically. "Just say what you mean."

"My blood runs through your veins," he said, "In a nutshell, I can control you………..if I choose to," he paused, "Is that clear enough for you?" he said mockingly.

"It is why you respond to me when we touch…It's because of my blood."

"Control me?" I asked, my eyes narrowing.

"Influence you more than anything else, not really control you." he said, "but I don't want to do either one," he added. "I never have and I never will."

"And Shane knows all of this?" I inquired, somehow disbelieving that he hadn't ever talked to me about it.

Jeremy nodded.

"No," I said simply, "This isn't true. We've had a connection before….before all of this." I turned to walk away but Jeremy's steely grip on my shoulder made me stop.

"I still don't know why that is," he said. "Maybe Shane is right……there are no coincidences, maybe this is just the way it's supposed to be." He released her and she continued walking.

In front of his eyes she shifted back to the wolf effortlessly and trotted off slowly toward home. He watched her go, his lip pursed together in indecision. If he went home now there was bound to be some kind of conflict with Shane. They both bore the brunt of their disagreement; he would no doubt question what had happened between them.

Or, he could lay out most of the night and come in later when they were asleep. He could slip in and at least get some clothes on before the telltale signs of their encounter was exposed to Shane's eyes. Closing the distance to the cabin, he heard the confrontation from where he stood and decided to just wait. Lying down on the ground he listened to the argument that continued inside.

"I can't believe that you would keep this from me," I said boldly, my voice condeming, "You didn't think that I had a right to know?"

"Elisa, calm down," Shane's voice urged, "Let's talk about this."

I picked my clothes up from where they had been discarded earlier and stormed from the room.

Shane's eyes traveled to the bloody mark on her rear as he followed her into the bedroom, "What is that?" he said accusingly as he pointed to her backside.

In my anger, I had forgotten about the bite. "It's nothing," I returned quickly as I struggled to pull my clothes back on. Shane moved swiftly across the room and grabbed my arm, jerking me roughly around to look at him.

"What happened tonight?" The authority in his voice demanded an answer.

I looked at him insolently, "What? You don't like when things are kept from you?"

I saw the nerve tick in the side of his jaw as he clenched his teeth and his grip tightened on my arm, "Don't," he said plainly but with force.

I looked down at where his fingers were pressed into my flesh bringing about a whitish appearance to the skin. Following my eyes, he immediately eased his hold and watched as I gathered up my suitcase and began to cram clothes into it.

"What are you doing?" he growled.

"I'm going home," I retorted.

"No," he said bluntly. "You're not leaving before we resolve this."

"I no longer want to have this conversation," I said, "I'm finished talking."

Shane sighed deeply in an attempt to exhale his frustration. He threw his hands up in disgust, "Fine, go then," he said as he stormed from the room. I heard the cabin door slam and his footsteps as he stomped across the deck.

Why did everyone insist on controlling me? Wasn't I a big girl that could handle the truth? With everything that had happened in the course of the past few months, I hadn't run away screaming yet so why did they still insist on keeping things from me? I continued gathering up the items that I had in Shane's room and then moved into the bathroom picking up anything that I could see that belonged to me.

Jeremy watched as Shane ran frustrated fingers through his hair while he walked out of the shadows towards him. The rage was apparent on Shane's face as he turned in his direction, his eyes glaring accusingly.

"What happened out there?" Shane growled as he took a few towards him. It was then that he saw the various marks on Jeremy's bare skin and stopped, his blue eyes piercing into Jeremy's.

"What in the hell?"

"It looks worse than it is," he said defensively.

Shane fingers bit into his shoulders and he grasped him firmly; his voice was low and deep as it left his mouth.

"Tell me what happened," he commanded.

Jeremy growled and jerked away from his grip, his eyes issued a warning. "She walked away from me and I tried to stop her," he paused, "This is what I got." He indicated the abrasions all over his body, "She's tired of us keeping things from her."

"I know," Shane replied smartly, "I heard," he paused, "She's leaving."

"Yeah," Jeremy responded in the same tone, "I heard."

The two eyed each other as Elisa came out of the cabin and moved across the yard. She flung her belongings inside the SUV and got in. In a few short strides, Shane was beside the car, his fist pounding on the window. She rolled it down hesitantly.

"Get out and let's talk about this Elisa," he said coolly, "Don't leave here like this."

From behind him, Jeremy's voice broke in, "Come on Elisa, let's all go inside and talk."

I sighed and looked first at Jeremy and then back to Shane who could see the betrayal in my eyes. "Look, I need some time to be alone."

"Let's talk and then if you still want to go, you can." Shane responded, his anger gone, his eyes now pleading.

"There's nothing left to talk about," I said earnestly, "You know how I feel. No amount of talking is going to change that," I paused, "You said no more secrets."

"I know," said Shane.

I eyed him doubtfully, "I want some time…..alone."

The anger rose up in him as he backed away from the car, "Just go!" He bellowed, his voice starting out as human but the tone quickly changing to a deafening howl that wasn't.

I put the car in reverse and backed out. The gravel spun from beneath the tires as I sped away down the uneven driveway, the tears welling up and spilling down my face.

From behind him, Jeremy chuckled uneasily, "Not sure that I would have handled it quite that way."

Shane whirled around, "I think you've done enough." He snarled as he walked past him toward the cabin, bumping intentionally into his shoulder.

Jeremy winced. He had made direct contact with one of his injuries but he was no longer in the mood for confrontation and instead held his tongue.

I pulled into the driveway and sat silently in the car for a few moments before climbing out. Coming home in the dark used to make me uneasy but now that I could actually see in the dark, it no longer was a cause for hesitation. Mounting the steps, I pushed my key into the door lock and flipping on the kitchen light, I threw the suitcase down in the floor. Fuming mad but hurt at the same time, I hadn't expected Shane to be so gruff. I had seen him upset before but he had never yelled at me that way. The emptiness of the cabin encased me in immediate loneliness and I couldn't stop the tears that came.

Crawling into my empty, cold bed later that night, the quiet engulfed me and I found myself yearning for any sound that might bring comfort. There was nothing except the soft ticking of the clock and the low hum of the refrigerator that did little to put my mind at ease.

Maybe I had been wrong to have left the way that I did and I discovered that I sorely missed the sound of Shane's breathing beside me. I managed to fall asleep after what seemed like hours and was awakened when the sun peeked over the horizon as Shane's voice echoed in my mind.

They're coming for you, get to Tristan.

Chapter 32

Shane couldn't sleep at all. Instead he tossed and turned and then gave up all together. It was nearly 3:00 A.M. according to the microwave clock when he started the first pot of coffee. Jeremy soon joined him at the kitchen table and they sat in silence; Jeremy reading the paper and Shane lost in his own thoughts.

"I'm going to get her," Shane's voice broke the ongoing silence after being up for almost 2 hours.

Jeremy looked up from his newspaper and nodded, "I can see that neither one of us are going to get any rest until she's back here," he chuckled jokingly.

Shane shook his head, "Nope," he paused, "It doesn't feel right. I'm going to get a shower and then I'm headed over there."

He stood up but suddenly stopped, his eyes on the door. He glanced at the clock again, 5:00 A.M. before glancing back to the door. Someone was outside.

Looking over at Jeremy, he met his eyes in acknowledgement and nodded. It was human scent. A knock on the door abruptly jarred them both from their trance like states. Shane moved toward the window and looked out........no strange vehicle in the driveway. He parted the curtains slightly so he could see out.

"Caleb…..?" he whispered.

Jeremy was soon beside him peering out the window as well.

"It *is* Caleb," he murmured in return.

"How did he find us?" Shane asked quietly before placing his hand on the doorknob. Opening it slightly he looked out into the eyes of the familiar human.

Jeremy stood a few feet behind, his brow creased with concern.

"Shane?" Caleb said, his voice excited and friendly.

Shane opened the door wider, allowing his entry, "Caleb…..what are you doing here?" he asked and then added, "at 5:00 in the morning?" He was unable to mask his surprise or distrust.

Caleb strode inside with confidence. He was familiar with both Shane and Jeremy and he had little reason to fear entering the wolf's den, "I can't believe I finally found you guys!"

"About that…." Jeremy said roughly, his eyes squinting in suspicion, "How did you?"

Caleb smiled warmly. "I've been searching for you two for a while; especially this guy." he said as he motioned toward Shane. "I never heard back from you after I brought the stuff that you wanted."

"Sorry about that," Shane said, "I've had quite a bit going on." He felt ill at ease for some reason as he studied Caleb. He had never been given a reason to doubt him, but something didn't feel right about his presence here….not at this time of day and certainly without warning. He could vaguely pick up the scent of metal wafting from him as he moved about.

"Care for coffee?" Shane asked hesitantly.

"Yeah, sure, "Caleb replied cheerfully, "Maybe you can get me up to speed with what has been going on with you."

As they turned, Shane caught Jeremy's eye and they exchanged a look of doubt. There was something off about Caleb's visit and Jeremy was now on alert. He too could scent the metal that came from Caleb and something else distantly familiar besides his own human odor.

"So…..how exactly did you find me?" Shane inquired, his eyes narrowed.

"Circle Reality," Caleb answered as he sipped his coffee. "There's a gal that works there that said she dealt with you on this place," he paused, "nice," he said as his eyes surveyed the interior around him.

Shane nodded. Well, so much for confidentiality. "Huh," he grunted, "I shouldn't be surprised about that I guess."

Caleb's face clouded for a moment, "What? You didn't want me to find you?"

"No, no. It isn't that," Shane lied, "I just didn't expect you to show up here is all. Call maybe…but not show up."

Jeremy stayed leaning against the kitchen door frame sipping his coffee and listening to the conversation. He felt more secure at a distance, being observant.

"Oh, good," Caleb sighed with relief, "I thought maybe you didn't want me here."

After talking for about an hour Jeremy immediately noticed that although Shane was being cordial, he wasn't giving up too much information. Nothing was mentioned about Elisa, Tristan or the others. He also didn't mention the episode with the rogue or the plans he had for the property. Jeremy silently approved that it was a wise decision on his part as he listened to the discussion progress. When Caleb asked to use the bathroom, Jeremy pointed him in the right direction and then moved closer to Shane.

"I don't like this," Jeremy said in a low tone. He could feel Shane's unease oozing into the space between them.

Shane nodded, "I know. Something isn't right."

A short few minutes passed and Caleb returned from the bathroom and leaned against the doorframe that Jeremy had just left. He sighed as he surveyed the two men and as Shane felt that he was suddenly being size up. As he eyed him, he had the fleeting thought of how similar he was to a weasel with little beady eyes.

With that thought still fresh in mind, Caleb reached into his jacket pocket slowly and withdrew a gun prompting he and Jeremy immediately to their feet.

"Whoa boys," he said as he waved the gun towards them, "Just take your seats and relax."

"What is this Caleb?" Shane said, his surprise evident but yet at the same time not totally unexpected.

"This," he said sarcastically, "Is a pistol that contains some potent ammunition for taking down your kind," he paused as he pulled out a couple of syringes from the other jacket pocket.

"And this," he hesitated again, "is filled with drugs to help you relax….and to insure that you don't shift."

"What are you up to you little bastard?" Jeremy snarled, stepping forward menacingly.

"Don't make me kill you right off the bat," Caleb grinned and pointed the gun in his direction. "What fun would there be in that? Just sit down, both of you."

They hesitantly sat back down but continued to glare at the human in front of them.

"So, here is what is going to happen," Caleb smirked, "You're going to give each other these," He said, indicating the syringes. "If you don't do it to my satisfaction…I have more."

He slid the syringes across the table towards them.

Shane glowered at the little man. He could feel the rage building inside, "I don't get it Caleb. Why are you doing this?"

Caleb smiled slyly, "We'll talk once you're more relaxed. Shane, you do him first," he said, motioning toward the syringes.

"Why don't you come a little closer and do it yourself?" Jeremy snarled.

"Now why would I do that?" Caleb sneered. "I can see you both plainly from here. If you try to shift I can use this," he waved the gun, "Now do it, Shane."

"And if I refuse?" Shane's eyes narrowed with defiance.

"I don't think that you want to do that," he paused, "If you care anything about the girl."

His comment immediately caused Shane and Jeremy both to stare in his direction.

"What does this have to do with her?" Shane's voice was edgy, but remained calm.

"Just take the syringe and do what I told you," Caleb answered. "We'll talk more afterwards."

Shane glowered at him but picked up one of the syringes and looked at it. Jeremy slowly pushed his sleeve up over his shoulder revealing the bared muscular form of his upper arm, his eyes never diverting from Caleb's.

"No, no," Caleb said, shaking his head, "In the jugular."

Shane clenched his teeth. He wanted to rip this man into a thousand little bloody pieces at this very moment.

Jeremy looked over at Shane and nodded, "Go ahead, stick me….give the little fucker what he wants."

Jeremy then looked back to Caleb from his seat at the table. His gray eyes boring into the humans with such intensity that Caleb was momentarily forced to look away. "You'd better enjoy this," he growled, "because when I'm finished with you, there won't be any parts of you to put back together."

Caleb laughed and nodded. He knew he would be no match for either of them. Even now he could see the rage building inside them and the distant glow in their eyes. As long as he had the gun, he was in control. Once the fear of them being able to shift and tear him apart was alleviated, he would let them in on exactly what was going to happen.

Shane gripped the cap of the syringe in his teeth and spit it out on the floor. Carefully, he pushed the needle into the side of Jeremy's exposed neck, emptying the contents into the flesh.

In turn, Jeremy picked up the one that remained and did the same to him. They traded a look between them and within a few minutes the effects of the drugs had began to seep into their muscles.

Shane found his vision becoming clouded and he fought to focus on their captor. He sent a warning to Elisa hoping that she would hear it across the distance that separated them.

"How much of that drug was in there?" Shane slurred.

"Enough for me to know that I'm safe," Caleb replied.

He moved across the room and pulled a wad of wire from his back pocket, "Put your hands behind the chairs....Both of you," he instructed.

Moving slowly, both men did as they were told and Caleb bound their hands, securing them with the wire while watching intently for one of them to make a move. It wouldn't take much prompting for him to pull the trigger on either one of them. The drug had the desired effect and was beginning to cause them to slump slightly in their seats, relaxed and sluggish.

He moved back into their lines of vision, "Can you hear me?" he asked as took advantage of their helplessness and slapped each one against their faces.

Jeremy roused and jerked forward in his chair. His movement elicited a defensive response causing Caleb to bash the handle of the pistol against his forehead. A resulting trickle of blood ran down into his left eye.

"You little bastard," Jeremy slurred, "When I get my hands on you....."

Before he could finish, Caleb hit him across the mouth with his fist. The blood flew from his lips. Jeremy's eyes blazed with hatred as he spat a mouth full of blood on the kitchen floor. He peered up through the red haze at the human before him and muttered softly but with purpose and intent, "I *will*....kill you."

Again, Caleb's laughter filled the kitchen. "I'm sure you will," he said snidely before turning his attention to Shane.

"Shane, are you still with me?" Shane's head rolled to the side as he looked up.

"Yes Caleb," he said breathlessly, "I can hear you," he mumbled.

"Good," Caleb said as he squatted in front of Shane's chair, the pistol pointed directly at Shane's chest. "Here are the answers you wanted," he said, "At this very moment, the girl is in the same predicament as you are."

Startled by this revelation, Shane pushed against the wire that bound his wrists; he could feel it cutting into his skin and the blood that began to dribble across his hand and down his fingertips.

"As long as we have her, you'll do what we want."

"What is it that you do want you scrawny little fuck?" Shane roared, his voiced laced with rage. He was met with rebuttal as Caleb's fist found contact with his face, leaving a red line across his temple.

"Leave Elisa out of this...whatever *this* is," Shane managed to mumble.

Caleb placed his hands on Shane's shoulders and leaned close; a few inches from Shane's face he whispered his intentions, "You will do what I tell you or you will watch her die."

Without warning, and so suddenly that he could see even see Jeremy's surprise, Shane forced his head forward making direct contact with Caleb's face. He felt the give of bone and flesh against his own skull as Caleb stumbled backwards howling in pain, his hand covering his face, blood oozing between his fingers. In his peripheral vision he saw Jeremy struggle against the wire binding that held his wrists.

"I should just kill you now!" Caleb shrieked, his hand now covered in his own blood, the pistol shaking in his grasp. Through his blurred vision Shane could make out the twisted form of Caleb's nose.

Good, he had broken the fuckers' nose.

"Then just do it," Shane said, struggling to form the words, "If you're going to kill us, just do it," he paused momentarily, "But if you have hurt Elisa in any way...."

Again, Caleb laughed as wiped the blood from his face, "I'm not going to kill you Shane. That isn't the plan, " he paused and looked over at Jeremy who growling and clenching his teeth, continued to wrestle with the wire around his wrists.

It cut painfully into his skin but he was determined. Shane hadn't inserted the needle into his vein like he had been instructed but instead had pushed the drugs beneath his skin, drastically slowing their effect on his system. He was fully alert and had the ability to shift if he could free his hands, and when he did, he was going to kill Caleb......as soon as he was free he was going to tear him into bloody shreds.

Chapter 33

I bolted upright in bed. I had dreamt of Shane and his voice had been urgent and worried. Who was coming for me? I scrambled from under the blankets and pulled on the same clothes that I had taken off the night before. Shane had said to get to Tristan; but why? I pulled my hair back, grabbed my keys and headed towards the door. Suddenly, I sensed a presence before I opened it. Backing away, I retrieved the pistol from my purse and eased back toward the door. A sudden knock sent a shiver of anticipation through my body. Pulling the curtain back slightly, I peered from behind its shield.

A woman stood at the door, her back to my curious view. Her long dark hair hung loosely halfway down her back. When she turned, I noticed her dainty features and eyes the color of coffee set beneath thick, black lashes. She reached forward and knocked lightly again.

I glanced uneasily at the clock.....6:45 a.m. Something was wrong with this scenario. I cracked the door open, my hand gripping the pistol handle.

The woman smiled sweetly as she met my eyes, "My car broke down," she said as she tilted her head toward the road, "Can I use your phone?"

I scented the wolf just as the woman pushed against the door, forcing her way inside. Behind her, two men appeared from the shadows. Defensively, I raised the pistol and pointed it directly at her head. She smiled and began to laugh. Her amusement spread contagiously to the men that were standing now behind her inside the kitchen.

"Please," the woman said sarcastically and with a sudden wave of her hand knocked the pistol from my surprised grip. It clamored to the floor and slid a few feet away. Her eyes then came back to rest on me, "You're surely not that stupid, are you?"

"What do you want?" I stuttered, searching her face.

She smiled, "I want you," she answered coolly before turning to the men behind her, "Tie her."

The two men advanced and even though I fought against them, I was no match for their superior strength. Soon I was slammed roughly down in a kitchen chair with my arms pulled smartly behind me, wrists bound tightly. I continued to struggle but the bite that the wire inflicted was enough to silence my efforts.

I eyed my abductors warily, absorbing their features as well as their scents. The woman stepped forward purposely and without hesitation jabbed a long needle into the side of my neck.

Wincing in pain, my eyes began to water as I felt the burn of drugs entering my body. I squirmed against the restraints.

"Awe, don't cry," the woman regarded me with cold brown eyes, "It won't do you any good."

"What do you want?" I asked shakily.

"I told you, I want you," she replied, "My name is Jasmine."

I continued to stare at her.

"You've never heard of me?" She demanded.

"No."

Jasmine's demeanor quickly turned from cool to edgy, "Shane never mentioned me?"

"I've never heard of you ....what's this have to do with Shane?" I probed with confusion. My voice was beginning to slur slightly as the drugs began to affect me.

Jasmine gritted her teeth, obviously offended that I didn't know who she was. She nodded grudgingly in acknowledgement, her eyes squinted in contempt.

"Shane betrayed me," she growled, "for which he will now pay."

What was she, a jilted lover or something? My clouded mind whirled with questions before I could no longer resist the darkness. It settled over me and dragged me down into nothingness.

Jeremy glanced over at Shane who was becoming increasingly drowsier by the minute. He seemed to have now dozed off, his chin resting uncomfortably on his chest.

"Kill me Caleb....if that's what you need to do," Jeremy sneered in a low, tired voice as he turned his eyes back on Caleb's. He felt a bitter sense of satisfaction as he gazed upon his now distorted and bloody face...thanks to Shane's hard head. He'd always known he was hard headed for a reason.

Caleb glowered through half squinted eyes as he made his way toward Jeremy, the gun still held tightly in his trembling fingers. Instead of walking around the two bound men, he maneuvered his body between Shane's slumped form and the kitchen table on his way towards him. All at once, Shane's slack figure sprang into motion. He kicked out swiftly, his foot making direct contact to the inside of Caleb's knee bringing him to the floor in front of him. Deafened by the roar of the gunshot and the searing pain that followed, he only faltered momentarily before wrapping his legs around Caleb's body; he began to squeeze with everything he had left.

Once he saw Shane's attack, Jeremy managed to shift his chair around so that he was within legs length of Caleb's body. He wasn't quick enough to kick the pistol from his hand before it fired but soon after, the gun skidded away in circles across the kitchen tile. With both of Shane's legs compressing Caleb's torso, only gasps were escaping from his lips. He continued to struggle in Shane's grip, his fists making useless strikes as he tried to free himself.

The searing pain in his side was worsening with every passing second and his strength was quickly deteriorating. Shane could feel the effects of the silver burning through his system and the weakening of his legs as he fought to maintain his crushing hold. He wasn't sure if he could keep the pressure up for much longer but as his strength began to falter, Jeremy landed a kick to Caleb's head that quickly quieted his struggles. As soon as Shane felt the slackness of Caleb's body, he relinquished his hold and allowed him to slide to the floor.

Jeremy's attention turned quickly back to Shane. He could see the blood soaking through his shirt and the painful grimace on his face.

"I'm going to get over there so we can get this damn wire off," Jeremy mumbled, "And then we've got to get that out."

"I know," Shane breathed heavily. He was still affected by whatever drugs had been in the syringe and now the silver creeping into his bloodstream. The unconsciousness had begun to flood the back of his eyes, the darkness crowding into his vision from the edges. He was fighting; he had to get to Elisa.

He heard the scraping of the chair legs across the floor as Jeremy scooted closer until he was back to back with him.

"Undo me first," he said sharply, "before you're out of it."

Shane felt Jeremy's wrists thrust amongst his fingers and he began to work laboriously on untying the wire that bound them. After what seemed like forever that he fumbled, Jeremy's hands were finally free and he heard him stand abruptly and throw the chair roughly to the side.

He was only slightly aware of Jeremy's fingers skimming across his own wrists and the wire falling free as he battled against the aching torture moving through his body.

"Come on, we've got to get that bullet out, "Jeremy urged, grabbing Shane's arm and hoisting him upward.

"Elisa." he gasped. "I have to....."

"We'll go together. You'll feel better once the silver is out of you....come on," he pushed.

Jeremy looked down at Caleb who was still unconscious; possibly dead if they were lucky, before helping Shane lay down on the kitchen table. There wasn't time for the formalities of sterilizing the tools or washing and cleaning the wound. If the silver didn't come out soon, it would kill him. He pulled up Shane's shirt and looked at the damage, grabbed the dish towel and wiped a large portion of the blood away from the wound. Rummaging through the utensil drawer, he found the sharpest knife that they owned.

"I'm sorry buddy," he said softly as he pushed the blade down into the gaping hole the bullet had created.

Shane's painful bellow filled the kitchen, his knuckles white as he gripped the edges of the table. Jeremy continued to dig until he hit the bullet with the knife blade and then hesitated when Shane's body went limp. Looking at his face he realized he had passed out.

"Just as well," Jeremy mumbled to himself before returning to his bloody task. In a few minutes he had pulled the bullet from Shane's side and sighed deeply with relief as he let it along with the knife fall to the floor. Without a sound he stood there, taking in Caleb and Shane's unconscious bodies and the blood that covered his hands.

He let his mind reach out to Elisa...hoping he wasn't too late.

After finding the peroxide and bandaging the area, he bound Caleb's hands and feet with the wire that had once bloodied his and Shane's own wrists. Once satisfied, he went in search of Shane's cell phone and found the number in his contacts. He punched the dial button and waited for the answer.

"Tristan, its Jeremy. Something has happened and I need your help. Can you be here in a few minutes?" He waited for the reply and then spoke again, "Yeah, hurry....and bring Lena with you," he ended the call.

Shane still lay lifeless on the table. Caleb was unconscious but secure. Now he could only wait. He paced the floor, back and forth while his mind worked through the morning's events scanning for overlooked details that he may have missed. It had to be Canada since Caleb was involved but who had Elisa? Caleb certainly wasn't the mastermind behind the plan....but who was. He recalled the vaguely familiar scent that he had noted when Caleb first arrived. Were the others involved someone that he knew?

He heard the speeding vehicle before it turned off of the gravel road onto the driveway. Jeremy walked to the door and watched as the SUV skidded to an abrupt halt and the doors opened simultaneously. Tristan and Lena bolted in a run across the yard to the house followed by Zoey a few steps behind.

"What's happened?" Tristan asked breathlessly.

"I'll fill you in on the way," Jeremy answered, "Lena, would you come with me?"

He led the way into the kitchen and motioned toward Shane, "Can you stay here with him?"

Her eyes traveled from Shane to the man lying bound on the floor, "What happened here?"

"Silver bullet," Jeremy responded bitterly as he eyed Caleb's still form, "I dug it out but I don't want to leave him alone."

Bending down, he picked up the pistol that was still on the floor, "If that guy moves, just kill him." He handed the gun toward Lena who hesitantly took it from his fingers.

"Where's Elisa?" asked Tristan in a concerned tone.

"That's why I need you. They have her," he answered softly before his voice hardened, "Look; I don't have time for questions right now. I've got to get to her before.........."

"I'm going with you," Lena said softly, "Maybe I can help."

"I need you to stay with Shane, Lena. Please, don't argue," Jeremy said gruffly.

A soft voice spoke from behind them. "I'll stay here with Shane."

They all turned to look at Zoey. Jeremy hadn't really noticed her standing there but she was without the eye makeup and the bolt in her eyebrow. Her pale blonde hair with the pink streaks was pulled back in a ponytail and she appeared to be just a normal, regular teenager.

He immediately took the gun from Lena's hand and shoved it toward her, "Can you use this?" He asked as she took it from his hand.

"Yes," she answered, "Tristan taught me."

Jeremy nodded. "Good. Don't be afraid to use it if you have to."

He turned back to Tristan and Lena, "I'm ready, let's go. We'll figure out a plan on the way."

He made it to the cabin door before turning back to look at Zoey, standing innocently in the kitchen doorway; the gun dangling in her hand.

Don't be afraid to use it," he said again.

Zoey nodded and they walked out the cabin door leaving her alone with the two unconscious men.

Chapter 34

The muffled voices edged into my conscious as I struggled to wake. My eyelids fluttered until I was finally able to hold them half open, my vision as cloudy and unclear as my mind. I couldn't move. My hands and ankles were bound tightly and I winced at the cutting pain of the steel wire into my skin. I could barely make out the bulky form of someone standing over me, leering down.

"I see you've decided to wake up," said Jasmine calmly as she pushed her way up next to the man hovering over me. "Welcome back," she said snidely.

I continued to blink, trying to clear my vision and realizing that they had moved me from the chair to my own bed. The lights weren't on, but the early morning sun was streaming through the curtains creating its own dim lighting. The bed shifted next to me and I was startled to turn and look into the ominous eyes of one of Jasmine's male sidekicks lying next to me on the bed. A wicked smile crept across his face as he moved his fingers lightly up my arm. My skin prickled beneath his touch and I could see the coldness in his eyes.

"Don't touch me!" I growled and shrank from him.

All three of them began to laugh. It wasn't the laughter of happiness but instead that of despicable intentions.

"Brett, leave her alone for now," Jasmine cooed sweetly, "You'll have your opportunity."

Jasmine sat down gently on the edge of the bed next to me. She smiled pleasantly but the smile didn't touch her eyes.

"I can scent that you're one of us," she said softly, "Did Shane do it?"

Elisa glared up from her compromised position, "No."

Jasmine's eyebrow quirked as if she was puzzled, "Hmmm. Who then?" She asked thoughtfully, "You're supposedly Shane's mate, and I know you weren't born to it."

She waited for my answer and when it didn't come quickly enough, she slapped me hard across the face. A low growl formed in the back of my throat as I stared at her coldly, the reddened handprint emerging brightly on my cheek.

"I expect an answer when I ask you questions."

"It was Jeremy," I muttered through clenched teeth. I had a growing hatred for this woman, whoever she was.

Jasmine laughed loudly in surprise, "Really!? Well, isn't that quite interesting!" She chuckled, "Do tell how that happened!" She flipped her dark hair away from her face, her eyes remaining on mine.

"It doesn't matter *how* it happened…..it just did." I replied bitterly, keeping the information simple and to the point. There was no reason to give this woman details.

She slapped me again and I lurched upward from the bed, my eyes blazing and the wolf pushing to be freed.

"Answer the question," she demanded.

"There was a fight……with a rogue," I growled with loathing.

"He wasn't a rogue," Jasmine remarked, her face now serious. "His name is Stephen, and I sent him," she paused, "Tell me what happened.

"What happened to *him*?" I asked.

Jasmine nodded.

I suddenly felt a sense of power and wielded my words like a double edged sword, "I *killed* him."

Jasmine looked at me with disbelief etching her refined features, "You're lying."

There was no way that this inexperienced woman could have beaten Stephen. He was a skilled fighter, a seasoned wolf; born and bred to this life.

I slowly shook my head, a look of satisfaction traveled across my features. My eyes glanced over at the two men standing in the bedroom doorway.

"And then……..he burned."

For a brief moment, Jasmine appeared distraught, her smooth forehead wrinkled with doubt. Her eyes seemed to grow distant, a slight hint of tears adding sheen. Sighing, she stood up but before turning her back she spoke, her voice soft and calm.

"Shane and I were once friends. I don't know what he's told you about our life, if anything," she paused, "But now has to pay for what he did," she said.

"When I located him, I sent Stephen ...."Her voice trailed off. "He failed. But now, as long as I have you, Shane will do whatever I ask." She turned and left the room pushing her way between the two men.

I began to think back to the story that Shane had told me about the eradication of his pack. His voice echoed the brutal details in my mind and now I believed I had met some of those responsible for the massacre. I pushed against my restraints, feeling the biting sting of the wire into my wrists.

Jeremy's voice unexpectedly cut into my thoughts, *We're coming for you Elisa.*

Brett and the other man had moved from the doorway and left me alone in silence. I could hear their mumblings from the other room but couldn't distinguish the words that were being said until Jasmine's voice cut clearly through the muffled tones.

"We have company."

After the door slammed and she was left alone, Zoey stood silently in the kitchen with the gun still in her grasp. She nervously eyed the man on the floor. His face was barely visible beneath the blood that covered it and his nose leaned unnaturally to the side, obviously broken.

Allowing her eyes to settle on Shane, she moved with hesitation toward the table, her eyes skimming across the bandaged area on his side. There were deep lacerations around his wrists that were caked with dried blood. His forehead bore the brunt of some type of injury and he was still unconscious. She looked around the kitchen noting the bloody towel, knife and the mushroomed remnant of the bullet that Jeremy had severed from Shane's body.

Zoey opened several drawers and finally found a clean dishtowel. Dampening it, she moved back to the table, timidly wiping Shane's forehead with the cool cloth. A low moan escaped the man on the floor, startling her. She picked up the pistol and turned her full attention to him. He rolled his head from side to side as if he was in pain before he opened his eyes and stared at her.

"Who are you?" he muttered.

"Doesn't matter who I am. I have instructions to kill you if I feel the need, just so you are aware," Zoey said smartly.

The man seemed to study her for a moment before he spoke again, "Can I have some water?"

From behind her, Shane's weak voice interrupted, "No. Give him nothing."

Zoey turned toward his voice. Shane was still lying on the table, his eyes closed but one foot now rested on the edge of the table, his knee bent.

"Where's Jeremy?" he asked without opening his eyes.

"They went to Elisa's," she said.

Shane turned his head to look at her through half closed eyes, "They?"

Zoey answered, "He, Tristan and Lena."

Shane rolled his head back and closed his eyes, "That lying bastard said we'd go together."

All at once he sat up and the room began to spin; he felt Zoey's hands on his arms, steadying him.

"You can't," she said, "You aren't strong enough."

"I have to get to her……I don't know what is happening," he said weakly.

Zoey looked into his Shane's eyes. His concern was apparent but his body wasn't cooperating. She loosened her hold on his arms trying to determine if he was stable enough to sit on his own. Once convinced that he was, she turned and walked back over to the man on the floor.

"Tell me how many there are."

Caleb smiled, his white teeth a striking distinction compared to his blood stained face. Zoey raised her foot and placed it above his broken nose.

"You tell me now or I will smash what is left of your nose straight through your worthless head," she growled.

If he hadn't been so worried about Elisa and the rest of his family, Shane might have laughed. Zoey wore jeans and black combat boots that laced up midway to her knee. To see her petite frame complete with the pink streaked hair balancing on one leg over Caleb's body might have otherwise coerced a chuckle from him.

But, this situation was far from being funny.

When Caleb still didn't speak, Zoey lowered her foot onto his face, applying pressure. He howled in pain until she relented.

 "Tell me now!"She barked.

"Three!" Caleb shrieked, "There are three of them!"

Zoey turned back to Shane, "It's even then."

Shane shook his head slowly, "Could you get me a glass of water?"

Zoey did as he asked and handed the glass to him. He brought it to his lips slowly and took a long drink, refreshing his dry mouth and throat.

"Elisa needs me….they all need me. I might make the difference in whether they all live or die," said Shane.

Caleb snickered from across the room, "You can't help them Shane, not in the shape you're in."

His laughter seemed to enrage Shane's caretaker and Zoey moved quickly back across the room and planted a well placed kick to Caleb's ribs.

"Shut up!"She yelled. He immediately curled up in a fetal position, groaning in pain.

"Not that I'm agreeing with him, but he's right," she said as she moved back to Shane's side. He edged himself off of the table using the small girl as his support. He towered over her but she proved strong enough to hold up some of his weight.

"I'm proud of you," he uttered while he attempted to find the strength to stand.

Zoey smiled at him timidly, "I told Jeremy I'd take care of you…I intend to."

"But you understand that you can't stop me…"

"I understand that I shouldn't try alpha…..but it wouldn't take much at this point," said Zoey smartly, "If you go, its suicide. That won't help Elisa or anybody else."

"My wolf may be stronger," he reflected his inner thoughts as he turned his attention to the girl, "If I can shift, you'll drive me there, alright?"

Zoey frowned in disapproval, but nodded. She picked up the pistol and stuffed in the back of her jeans.

"What about him?" she asked, motioning toward Caleb.

Shane glared in his direction then back to Zoey, "He can't go anywhere…after you take me, I want you to come back here. If none of us return, I want you to kill him. Can you do that?"

"You might as well kill me now!" Caleb shouted, struggling against the wire binding.

Shane turned all of his rage toward the bound man. He stumbled across the room with Zoey's help until he towered over Caleb's helpless form.

"I will come back," he said through gritted teeth, "and when I do, I will set you free…..and then, I will hunt you."

He turned his concentration back to Zoey, "But if I don't, can you do it?"

She nodded slowly, "I can, and I will."

"Help me with this….." Shane said as he attempted to pull his shirt off. Zoey grabbed the bottom of it and stood on tiptoes to help him get it off over his head. She gently tugged the bandage off of his side and grimaced at the raw wound in his flesh. Shane told her where his truck keys were as he unbuttoned his jeans and tried to push them down over his hips. His side ached and he stiffened. Zoey moved to help him, oblivious to his near nakedness. He felt suddenly awkward, this sixteen year old girl helping to undress him.

"Wait, wait….I'll do it."

Zoey had lived in a pack where it was a normality to see people naked from time to time. It wasn't something that she had ever given much thought to.

"Just let me," she demanded as she continued to pull his jeans down and then held them while he freed each foot, "I've seen naked men before."

She stood up and without making eye contact, turned to find the truck keys. When she returned, the big black wolf stood in his place on rigid legs.

"Ready?"

The wolf's bright blue eyes met hers and he walked slowly past her toward the cabin door. Zoey eyed Caleb one last time before she turned and followed him, closing the door behind her.

Lena was nervous as she walked toward Elisa's cabin after leaving Tristan and Jeremy in the parked SUV on the gravel road. She knew that whoever was inside had already scented her and knew she was close. Hesitantly climbing the steps toward the door, she knocked timidly. When no one answered, she knocked again.

"Elisa?"

When the door opened, a large dark haired man stood in the doorway. Lena wasn't able to hide the surprise as she backed away.

"Who are you?"

The man cocked one eyebrow, "Daniel. Who are you?"

"A friend," Lena stuttered, "We have plans today…."

The large man laughed as he stepped out the door menacingly toward her, "I don't think Elisa is going to make it."

It was the opportunity that Tristan was waiting for. The moment that the giant stepped fully out of the cabin toward his sister, the gray wolf hit him broadly in the side, knocking him down. It wasted no time and before the man could shift, the wolf latched onto his throat. Daniel thrashed about trying to dislodge it from on top of him but its teeth were already deeply embedded in his throat quickly shutting down his ability to breathe. The blood spewed, covering the wolf's face as the man's struggles slowed and eventually ceased altogether.

As soon as Tristan had ambushed, Jeremy slipped inside behind the commotion coming face to face with another oversized ruffian. Without hesitation, Jeremy threw the first punch that made direct contact with the man's nose. He stumbled backwards, covering his face with Jeremy closing in. He continued his assault until the man was down.

A woman's voice rose above the disorder that stilled Jeremy's battering strikes. Turning, his eyes fell on the voice's source and then the familiar face. *Jasmine*. He remembered the recognizable scent that he had noticed on Caleb and all of the pieces suddenly fell into place. She smiled at him sweetly from behind the safety of the gun she held in her hand. Jeremy gritted his teeth.

"Jasmine," he growled with contempt.

"Well, well," she said as she sauntered up to stand in front of him. The man beneath Jeremy pushed him aggressively to the side as he clamored to his feet. He made a low, rasping grunt before he buried his fist in Jeremy's stomach.

Doubling over from the blow, his insides felt like jelly and the urge to vomit pushed up in his throat. He wouldn't give them that satisfaction so instead he swallowed hard and slowly stood fully upright. He was certain that he had heard the cracking of bone but a broken rib at this point was nothing.

"Where's Elisa?" He snarled.

Jasmine waved her hand toward the bedroom in a carefree gesture and then turned to the other man.

"Check on Daniel."

He nodded and pushed past Jeremy, ramming his shoulder into him on his way by. When he got to the door he paused, surveying the bloody scene on the deck. Daniel's throat was laid open, his eyes staring blindly to the sky. He turned his head to look at Jasmine.

"He's dead."

"Go find them," Jasmine barked sharply, "Kill them both."

Brett followed her orders without delay. He stripped his clothes off and before their eyes shifted into a massive brown wolf that trotted out of their vision and down the deck steps. Jasmine's attention turned back to Jeremy.

"I've been waiting a long time Jeremy. Now….what am I going to do with you?" She said, waving the gun in his direction.

"I want to see Elisa," Jeremy said, his voice low and harsh.

"You're in no position to make demands," Jasmine retorted, "But, I suppose you might want to see how your protégé is holding up."

She paused for a moment as if evaluating the scenario in her mind. "Its odd that she is s Shane's alleged mate and you are the one that created her. Doesn't that put quite a strain between you two?" she chuckled.

"Just let me see her," he demanded.

He didn't owe her an explanation and had no intention of explaining their relationships. Jasmine motioned toward him indicating that he was allowed to move and he walked swiftly toward Elisa's bedroom. Jasmine trailed closely behind, her hand gripped tightly on the pistol.

When Elisa's eyes fell on him he could see the look of surprise that quickly turned to relief and then finally distress. Her hands were bound with the same injurious wire that his had been and he could see the dried blood on her wrists from her struggles. Her feet were wired as well.

"Jeremy," she said despairingly. He immediately moved to her side and sat down on the bed. Jasmine remained in the doorway from where she accessed the situation closely. Jeremy knew that if he made any rapid movement, he would lose his life. He smiled down at her and gave her a quick reassuring wink.

"It's going to be okay," he whispered and nodded.

"Isn't this sweet?" said Jasmine sarcastically from her place in the doorway, "Does Shane know?"

Jeremy turned to stare angrily at her, "Unlike the pack from where I once came, we have no secrets between us here."

Jasmine laughed again, a menacing sound in the quiet of the bedroom, "Except for one," she cackled, "But you know as well as I do that this situation," she waved a hand toward them, "is a disaster waiting to happen."

"What is it that you want Jasmine?" asked Jeremy, already quickly tiring of her games.

Her smile quickly faded, "I want my revenge."

"For what?" Jeremy growled, "You knew about me……….You're the cause of your own agony you stupid bitch, and Shane did nothing but try to protect you."

She laughed again, "Protect me?" She managed to say amidst the hysterics, "Shane stood by when I needed him the most and you………" her face quickly became a mask of hatred.

"Paul understood the risks……..Do you think that he would be happy about this??" Jeremy asked, facing her and nodding toward Elisa.

"I took care of the others and now there are only you and Shane left,"Jasmine finally answered.

All of the blood suddenly drained from Jeremy's face as it fell, void of all emotion. When he spoke his voice was low and deep.

"It was you?"

Jasmine took a few steps until she was face to face with him, the pistol barrel buried against his chest. She smiled as she looked into his eyes.

"Yes, we killed them all."

I watched helplessly as the situation unfolded before me. I began to struggle against the restraints but didn't continue for long, my wrists were already painfully sore. A movement at the door caught my attention and I saw Lena there with her finger against her lips, urging my silence and in the other hand she held a metal pipe. If Jeremy noticed her there, he gave nothing away.

All of the violence and brutality of that night in Canada flooded back to Jeremy's thoughts. A torrent of emotions spun out of control within his brain. The whirlwind of surprise, sadness, deceit and finally rage created a burning sensation that traveled down his arms to his clenched fists.

"The family," he said lowly, "you killed the family."

Jasmine snickered and pushed the barrel harder against his chest, "Not *all* of them."

Out of the corner of his eye Jeremy saw Lena swing the pipe. As soon as it neared Jasmine's head, he lunged to the side hoping to put himself out of the deadly range of the gun. A look of surprise crossed Jasmine's face as the pipe made blunt contact with her head. Slowly crumbling to the floor, the gun fired before falling from her hand next to her body.

The gunshot was deafening in Jeremy's ears as the painful bite of the bullet tore through the flesh of his upper arm. He turned quickly around to look at Elisa. Her eyes were wide with terror. The bullet hole in the pillow was only a couple of inches from her head and the soft downy feathers floated gently in the air above her.

Lena rushed to the bed, "Oh Elisa! Are you alright?" She whimpered, pulling her up into her arms.

"I'm okay," I said shakily. Jeremy began to unwire my ankles and then freed my hands.

"Lena, grab that pistol, would you?" asked Jeremy. Lena did as he asked, picking it up from next to Jasmine's unconscious body.

My eyes met Jeremy's and he saw the fear and the tears that began to well up, threatening to fall. He grasped me in his arms and pulled me close, his breath was hot against my ear.

"Are you hurt?"

"No," I answered.

Tristan led the brown monster away from the cabin down the winding trails of the forest. It was easy to stay a good distance ahead of it as he was much younger and more agile. As he rounded the trail and climbed the ridge he was halted in his tracks by the immense black beast that stood before him, blocking his path. When the wolf met his gaze and Tristan scented it, he knew immediately that it was Shane.

The fur around the gray wolf's jaws and face was tinged red, so Shane knew that there had been bloodshed. He was anxious to reach the cabin, to find Elisa, make sure that she was safe and hold her in his arms. They both turned as the huge brown wolf crested the ridge. It stopped a few yards away, looking over them, evaluating what chance it might have between the two of them.

A loud rumbling growl erupted from Shane's chest that reverberated through the forest. He started forward, his limbs only cooperating with constant prompting but he refused to let the pain slow him. Tristan followed at his heels. As they drew closer to their adversary it suddenly tucked its tail and barreled off through the woods away from them. Shane watched it go until it disappeared from his sight. He then trotted off with difficulty toward the cabin with the gray wolf at his side.

Jeremy helped me off of the bed to stand. My legs trembled beneath me but his strong arms held me stable. Lena had taken the wires that had been removed from my wrists and ankles and was now bent over Jasmine, securing her. When she finished, she stood up to survey her work. As if she was satisfied, she turned back to me and quickly moved in my direction, embracing me once again.

"I'm so glad you're ok. I was so worried when I saw Shane and............" My voice interrupted before she could finish, pulling away from her arms to look her in the face.

"What's happened to Shane?" I asked my voice full of alarm.

Lena's eyes moved from mine to Jeremy's nervously and then back again.

"He will be alright." said Jeremy, "Zoey is with him."

Turning, I eyed him suspiciously, "Tell me."

"Please Elisa...just trust me. I have to go find Tristan......he may need me," he paused, "Lena, can you stay here with her?"

"Sure, I will," said Lena.

Jeremy headed toward the door but then suddenly turned.

"Oh, and Lena? Kill the bitch if she bats an eye."

Lena nodded as she watched him turn back toward the door and then stop. He pushed the door open and held it there allowing a massive black wolf to enter, followed by her brother. In moments they had both shifted and were standing naked in the kitchen. Shane's eyes scanned the room and with one deep breath he moved toward the bedroom. His brow furrowed when he realized who the woman was on the floor but he didn't stop walking until he had Elisa securely wrapped in his arms. Lena smiled shyly and drifted noiselessly out of the room, leaving them a private moment.

I felt as if I might be crushed but I didn't fight him. I finally felt safe, wrapped within the warm confines of Shane's grasp. He pushed me out to arm's length to look at me and I instantly saw the bloody bullet hole in his side.

"Are you alright?" he asked.

"I'm okay....you?" I said as I touched his side with gentle fingertips. He winced and I withdrew my hand but he stopped me, placing my palm back against his skin.

"I'll live," he answered.

He wanted nothing else but to feel her skin on his, to reassure himself that they were really together. He could take the physical pain that her touch caused him, but he couldn't have dealt with the mental anguish of losing her. Only a short time ago, he had wondered if he would find her alive.

Jeremy stalked back to Shane's side, "Did you see? Did you see who is responsible?"

"I did," Shane answered, refusing to give up his hold on Elisa. He felt Jeremy's grip on his arm and he turned to look into his clouded gray eyes.

"Canada," he said softly, his eyes betraying the emotion that churned underneath.

Shane's eyes narrowed, "What do you mean?"

"*She* is responsible for what happened in Canada," Jeremy said in a harsh whisper as if the lower he spoke the less true it would be.

Shane's response had been the same as his. His face paled and became a blank canvas with no touch of color. His eyes moved to the woman that was bound and unconscious on the bedroom floor and she slowly disappeared from his vision replaced by the rage that crept in and turned everything red. He felt Elisa's calming hand on his arm, he heard her voice and then Jeremy's but they seemed distant and he couldn't decipher what they said. His wolf reared its massive black head from deep inside and in an instant had taken his place. He walked stiffly over to where Jasmine lay.

"Jeremy… what do we do?" I stuttered, "He will kill her."

"We let him," he said coldly as he slowly turned to look at me, "It was *her* plan for you. If she lives, we will never have peace."

By this time Tristan and Lena had come to stand in the bedroom doorway watching to see what the alpha would do. As if feeling the eyes upon him, the black wolf paused. His eyes scanned the room and the man deep inside realized that they were all holding their breaths, anticipating his actions.

This one decision could determine his place as alpha or crush it if they lost faith in his ability to protect the pack. He wanted to kill Jasmine, he wanted so badly to avenge the deaths of his family, his friends…his pack; those helpless victims that were never given a chance. He uttered a low growl and stared down into the face of the woman that he now felt nothing for but hatred.

Jasmine groaned and stirred, her eyelashes fluttering open to stare up into the face of the black beast. Seeing her cold brown eyes renewed his rage and he had to fight to stop himself from grasping her head in his jaws and shaking her like a rag doll. Backing away from her slowly, he continued to growl and bare his teeth. He felt the soft caress of fingertips along his back and knew it was Elisa attempting to calm and soothe him. He allowed himself to relax and in a few minutes, and in the silence of the room he shifted back to a man.

"I see you still have no backbone," Jasmine's voice cracked through the quiet.

With his back still turned toward her, Shane closed his eyes and breathed in deeply through his nose.

"We'll take her back with us and decide her fate along with Caleb's……together, as a pack." He turned and made eye contact with everyone in the room leaving Elisa for last. When his eyes settled on hers, he moved forward and wrapped her within his arms again, placing his lips against her forehead.

"Come, let's all go home. We have a lot to talk about."

"What about the mess outside?" Jeremy asked. "Do you want me to stay and take care of it?"

He nodded, "Yes, I guess that does need cleaned up. Do you mind?"

"Nope. I'll start the fire and if you leave her here," he nodded toward Jasmine, "I'll throw her on there too." He growled as he scowled down at her, "Her screams would be music to my ears."

Shane smirked but didn't respond. He took Elisa's hand and led her toward the door past Lena and Tristan.

"I'll stay here and help you," Lena directed at Jeremy as he was leaning over unwiring Jasmine's ankles.

He nodded. Truth be known he'd be happy to take care of her now without anyone else's influence and if he had been alone here with her, he would have. But, Shane had chosen the course of action to take and he would now have to abide by it.

Jasmine watched his every move as his fingers moved quickly. When her legs were finally free, she took the opportunity to lash out at him, directing a kick between his legs. Jeremy had expected her to retaliate and he easily knocked the blow to the side with his hand. He laughed callously as he looked down at her.

"You'll have to do better than that bitch."

Jasmine struggled as he grabbed her bound arms and jerked her upward to her feet and then pulled her roughly toward the door. She continued to lash out with her feet and refused to go along with him. The nerve began to twitch in the side of his face as his teeth clenched in anger. He turned to glare at her.

"Stop," he said in a low voice, "Or so help me God I will finish you now."

"You can't," she snapped back smartly, "Shane won't allow it."

Shane turned suddenly and stared at her shaking his head, "My mind can change....rather quickly."

Jeremy grinned ominously, "And I'd love nothing more."

He grabbed her aggressively and pushed her out the door in front of him. Her eyes absorbed the gore of Daniel's corpse as he pushed her past and toward the deck steps. For a moment her eyes rimmed with tears but she held them back, determined not to show her weakness.

"We can take my car," I said once I discovered no other vehicles were in the driveway.

"Lena, are you staying to help Jeremy then?" Asked Shane as he turned to her.

"Yes, I'll stay."

"Why don't you ride with us down to where we parked the SUV and you can bring it back here for you and Jeremy," he said.

Lena nodded.

The group left the cabin in silence, walking past the dead man lying in a pool of his own blood as they crossed the deck. Shane shielded Elisa from the view of it with his own body, knowing in his heart that it would affect her the most.

The mid morning sunlight streamed through the newly leafed trees and fell upon them as they moved across the yard in a line. A melody produced by songbirds resting in the nearby trees floated over them creating a false sense of just another ordinary spring morning.

Chapter 35

Zoey sat on the kitchen table swinging her legs back and forth, the pistol lying casually across her thigh. Caleb had maneuvered himself around so that he sat propped against the refrigerator, his eyes studying the girl. He had tried to talk to her, win over some sort of sympathy from her young, inexperienced mind for his predicament but she was uncaring and snippy with her remarks. He had asked for water again but she had refused him, reminding him coldly that Shane said he was to have nothing.

"He can deal with you when he gets back," she said.

"He isn't going to come back," Caleb replied, his bloody mouth contorted into a wicked smile.

Zoey glared at him, her blue eyes narrowed, "He left me with instructions if that's the case."

"Instructions that you think you can carry out?" He inquired.

"Look, there's no reason that you and I need to talk. Just keep your mouth shut," she snapped.

Caleb shrugged, preparing to make another attempt to play on her sympathy when they heard the footsteps on the deck. The girl slid off of the kitchen table and moved to where she could see, the gun in her hand and her finger on the trigger. When she saw Elisa a wide grin spread across her face and she rushed to the door.

"Elisa, I'm so glad you're alright," said Zoey ecstatically.

Her eyes then fell on Shane and her brother, who drug behind him a dark haired woman whom she had never seen before.

She had never been an affectionate person so her voice carried all of the weight of her excitement, "I'm glad you are all back."

"How are things?" Shane questioned, not waiting for her answer. He moved past her to retrieve his clothes from the kitchen. Caleb looked up as he entered, a dark shadow of fear creeping across his face. Tristan dragged the woman brusquely by her arm behind him to the kitchen where he pushed her down on the floor next to Caleb. The two communicated an unspoken exchange between them with their eyes before Jasmine settled against the refrigerator next to him.

Shane pulled on his jeans slowly, the ache in his side slowing his progress. He noticed Elisa's eyes scan the bloody floor, ending their search on the knife and blood soaked towel that was now on the countertop, her face reflecting her horror. Zoey stood beside her, unreadable, one hand restimg on her hip, the gun still hanging from the other and her eyes trained on him as if she was awaiting her orders.

Tristan had dressed and also stood in the kitchen doorway. His features betrayed his anger as he regarded the two on the floor with a look of disdain. Shane could already predict that the pack would decide they should die but he must wait for Jeremy. He needed to hear the physical vote from each of them. He turned his attention to those on the floor.

"Once Jeremy is back here, we will decide what happens to both of you," he paused, "If I was to have my way, I would end it now. Not only did you both betray our Canada pack which is worthy enough cause alone to kill you, but you had the intention of destroying the family that I have now."

He shook his head slowly in disbelief looking at Caleb first. "You… we took you in when you had no place left to go. We brought you in to our family, kept you safe. And then you betrayed us?" He turned to look at Jasmine then, "And you," he paused, "you were family. We grew up together from childhood. You turned on your own blood?"

Jasmine's face was dark, her lips forming a taut line, "You deceived me Shane," she answered, her voice barely audible, "I begged you, and you refused me. And then you did nothing!" She cried out. "You did nothing but watch as Paul was slaughtered in front of us! No one did anything but watch….and then you ran, ran like a scared little pup."

Shane's eyes suddenly softened and when he spoke, his voice was calm and low, "You're wrong Jasmine. You knew the law…..you knew what could happen. Paul knew what could happen."

Jasmine shook her head, the hatred evident in her eyes, "You and I both know that there's more to this story Shane….more than you will let yourself remember."

Shane's eyes narrowed as if a passing memory had surfaced, "I refused because I didn't want to be the one that killed him. I cared too much for *you,*" Shane said softly, "I was on my way into the pit when Kyle came in……..I was coming to help you take your revenge."

As I listened, I soon realized that this was why Shane had wanted nothing to do with turning Michael. He was afraid of what he couldn't control and of the consequences that might follow.

Jasmine's dark eyes bore into Shane's, "I don't believe you. You told me you would be there for me…and then you weren't."

Shane straightened and sighed deeply before nodding, "Enough. You'll both have a chance to speak before we make our decision."

With that, he walked toward the three standing in the doorway. "Come, we all need to talk," he said sternly. He took me by the hand and led me outside, Tristan and Zoey following behind us.

Once out on the deck, away from the keen hearing of the wolf inside he leaned against the railing in near exhaustion. He pulled me against his side and kissed me lightly on the forehead.

Zoey and Tristan stood before him and he looked at them, his eyes roving one to the other before he spoke, "You two as well as your sister have proven your loyalty." he began, "I was able to count on you when I needed you most. You were called and you didn't hesitate...you didn't ask questions, you just came. I am grateful and forever in your debt."

"I know that Lena has plans to go back to the pack and to her mate," he continued, "I understand her reasons to want to leave." He turned and kissed me again before proceeding, "But all of you are welcome in my pack. It would be an honor to call you family."

Zoey and Tristan looked at each other, a small smile edging to the corners of Tristan's mouth. Zoey's emotions remained unreadable, guarded. Tristan stepped forward with his hand extended toward Shane.

"It would be a privilege, alpha."

Shane grasped his hand warmly and then pulled him into a full one armed hug of appreciation. "Thank you Tristan. This day may have turned out differently if it weren't for you," he uttered.

Tristan backed away, smiling broadly. Shane's eyes then moved to Zoey as he waited for her reply. For a moment she stared at him suspiciously, as if assessing the honesty of his invitation. Still unsmiling, she stepped forward toward him, her eyes narrowed.

"How long do you think you can tolerate me?" she asked in the familiar smart aleck attitude. Shane smiled down at the girl before placing his large hands on her thin shoulders.

"Forever," he answered sincerely.

A timid smile curled her lips as her brother beamed with hopefulness from behind her. Maybe things would be different here.

"Good," Shane said. His smile was brilliant, even happy after everything that had occurred during the course of the morning. His body relaxed against mine.

"I have many plans," he said, "But first things first. We'll wait for Jeremy and then we'll make our decision about those two," he motioned toward the cabin.

Jeremy and Lena worked side by side, cleaning and scrubbing the blood stains from the deck. Jeremy had moved Daniel's body to the yard and together they began to gather up wood and whatever other burnable materials that they could find to start the fire. He rummaged through Elisa's shed and found a nearly full can of gasoline and a shovel.

Jeremy was surprised at Lena's helpfulness. She remained quiet and unquestioning and did everything that he asked, understanding that it was a serious situation and one that they needed to dispose of as quickly as possible. As far as an outsider would see it, it was murder and they were attempting to cover it up. The body would have to be burned and everything that was left would need to be buried.

As he doused the pile of rubble with gasoline, he glanced over at her. She had pulled her curly blonde hair back in a pony tail and the bloody smudge on her cheek was a telltale sign of the morning's activities. She was solemn but Jeremy could see the determination on her face.

"Thanks for staying," he said as he sat the gas can down several feet away from the pile, "You've been a big help."

Her blue eyes darted in his direction but didn't make eye contact, "You're welcome," she said softly.

Jeremy chuckled. She was so submissive. "How is it that you and your sister are so different?"

She laughed lightly, an uplifting sound in spite of the seriousness of the situation. "She has a different father than Tristan and I," she said, "I give him that due credit."

"You all look the same. Same blonde hair and blue eyes. Must be from your mother then?"

"Yes. My mother was….."Lena hesitated, "a beautiful woman." Recognizing her pause as a sign of something uncomfortable, he knew better than to push farther.

"Your last name, what is it?" He asked, trying to piece together the vague feeling of recognition that continued to preoccupy his mind.

"Its Taylor," she answered.

"And where is it that you three came from?"

"Minnesota," Lena said, "Little Fork."

Jeremy was quiet for a few minutes as he pondered about the area. He had been to Little Fork once as a teenager; it was a small, quiet town a few miles from the Canadian border.

"And Zoey's last name?"

"Its Taylor as well. Our father raised her as one of his own," she replied.

"You and your sister must take after your mother," Jeremy said, looking away.

Lena smiled timidly towards him, "Thank you."

Jeremy struck the match and threw it onto the heap. It caught instantly, a hot blaze that leapt into the air a few feet above their heads. They stood silently looking into the flames for a few minutes, a sense of foreboding in preparation of the next step of their clean up. To not delay it any further, Jeremy turned and grabbed the shoulders of the dead man. He was shocked when Lena moved to help him, bending over and picking up the man's feet. They made quick eye contact before they threw his body into the flames.

Returning to the cabin early afternoon, Jeremy and Lena found the others outside on the deck. Shane stood up, still shirtless, a large bandage wrapped around his entire midsection. The others followed suit. He and Lena climbed the steps and he immediately went over to a chair and collapsed in it.

"It's done."

Shane nodded, "Thanks."

He turned to Lena, "I've asked your sister and brother to join our pack here and they have agreed," he said, "I know that you have other plans but I want to personally extend the same to you Lena."

Lena seemed surprised as she looked from Tristan's smiling face to her sister's. Zoey had always been able to keep her emotions under wraps but even she had a slight smile on her face. She looked back at Shane.

"You don't know how much your offer means to me," she said timidly. "If it wasn't for Brian I wouldn't go back...but you understand...."

"I do," said Shane considerately, "When you find them, you have to do whatever it takes."

Shane's words struck him peculiarly and Jeremy found his eyes wandering over the group coming to rest on Zoey. Young, rebellious

Zoey. Pink haired, combat booted, teenaged Zoey. He chuckled softly to himself. *What was this feeling?* He must've laughed louder than he intended because suddenly everyone's eyes were focused on him. As casually as possible he stood up.

"Ain't that a bitch?" He said to no one in particular and went inside the cabin.

With lengthy strides Jeremy he crossed the living room and went into the kitchen. He was suddenly craving a drink but Jasmine and Caleb were leaned against the refrigerator. He sneered at them and then went over to the sink and ran a glass of water. He drank it thirstly and refilled it again, noticing that all of the blood had been cleaned up from the table and floor as he leaned against the counter and glared across the room.

"So," he said bitterly, "Does it feel like a good day to die?" He raised the glass and took another sip.

Caleb and Jasmine both regarded him coolly. It was impossible to know what they had discussed together while everyone was outside. If he could be left alone with them for just a little while, he would terminate this problem for good. The cabin door opened and the rest of the pack came inside walking single file into the kitchen. Elisa came to stand at his side followed by Lena, Tristan and Zoey. Shane stayed across the room by himself and Jasmine's gaze settled on him while Caleb stared down at the floor.

"Its time," said Shane. His voice was calm and even with no hint of emotion.

"Good, let's get this over with. I've not eaten today and all of that *burning* has made me hungry," Jeremy snickered.

Shane glared at him but there was no reprimanding gesture. He turned his attention back to the pair of traitors.

"Jasmine, do you have anything to say that might sway our decision?"

"Might I stand for my sentencing?" She asked sarcastically.

Jeremy stormed toward her jerking her up roughly by her bound wrists. She cried out as the wire dug into her flesh.

"Let me help you out," He sneered. He left her standing and retreated to his place against the counter. Elisa cast a glance toward him and he turned for a second to look at her before looking away.

"Go on," Shane said to Jasmine.

"There's nothing that I can say that will make you spare me," she said as she stared directly at Shane, "Killing me will finally end my suffering......" she paused, "these people know nothing of my situation or why I chose this course of action and yet you will have them be my judge, jury and executioners?"

"You're only chance of survival are these people," answered Shane, "If you would rather only Jeremy and I decide your fate I think they would understand," he paused, "And I think you already know the outcome."

Jasmine looked from Shane to Jeremy and then let her eyes scan the group in front of her, "I feel that the outcome will be the same no matter who is involved."

"Do you want to defend your actions Jasmine?" Shane probed, "It is now or never."

Jasmine tilted her head defiantly before she looked at Elisa and spoke, "My mate was a human," she began, "Paul was his name. He was beautiful, trusting and good." Her voice cracked but she quickly regained her composure and continued. "He wanted to be a part of every portion of my life and he felt strongly that I could never be entirely happy with a mere human as my mate."

Her eyes skimmed over Elisa again, "I had asked Shane to convert him but he refused me. Not that it was important to me, but because Paul wanted it and kept pressuring me to find someone that would do it."

Jeremy rolled his eyes and sighed heavily causing distraction from Jasmine's story. Shane regarded him with a cool gaze, "Do you want to say something Jeremy?"

"Yes, I would like to say something," he retorted bluntly, staring back at Shane, "Its coming down to this so I will just tell you...it was me, I'm the one that killed Paul."

Shane couldn't hide his surprise. The blood seemed to drain from his face leaving him pale. He steadied himself against the kitchen doorframe. "What?" he asked in disbelief, "How did I not know?" His voice was full of accusation.

"You thought I was gone. It was when I told you I had to go to Thunder Bay for the week," Jeremy answered, "I didn't want you to know in case things went bad.......which they did."

Shane shook his head slowly in amazement that he had never put the pieces together.

Elisa looked from one to the other. She could see the betrayal etched into Shane's features and felt the tension in Jeremy's body as he stood beside her. Tristan and his sisters remained silent, standing close together looking as if they might bolt if things went south.

Jasmine's voice broke the sudden stillness, "I knew that he was volatile," she explained, "I told Paul the same thing but he was demanding. He didn't seem to care that Jeremy was unpredictable."

"How did I not recognize, or scent that it was you?" Shane asked, still confused by the latest turn of events. Jeremy sighed again before he spoke as if trying to expel the sudden anxiety that now spread through his entire body.

"I was careful. I didn't want anyone to know I was around so I used scent-guard and stayed in the forest for that entire time....until that night."

"How did you keep this from me? You never said....anything - all this time," Shane's voice sounded hurt, betrayed.

Jeremy moved across the kitchen toward him but Shane held up his hand, indicating that he shouldn't come further.

"Look Shane, they both knew what could happen......I didn't know she was going to go bat shit and kill everyone....."

"Yes, they did know," said Shane, seeming to have gotten his bearings back, "But this isn't about you...or me right now."

He looked away from Jeremy and back to Jasmine.

As if she had been waiting for her cue, Jasmine continued. She told about that night, the horror as she watched Paul killed in front of her as the entire pack stood by. From that very moment she began to plan her revenge and eventually, she was able to find those that would help her make it reality.

Shane couldn't help but look away when she spoke about the slaughter. His eyes found Elisa's and his heart felt heavy as he watched the tears fall down her cheeks uncontrollably. Jeremy stood rigidly in front of him, his teeth gritted, his hands clenched into fists. His eyes were glued to the floor in between where they stood.

"Stop!" Shane had finally heard enough and could stand no more of it. His loud outburst startled everyone in the room, "Enough.... Jeremy, help Caleb to his feet."

Jeremy turned without question and hoisted Caleb to a standing position and then backed away. The stress of the situation was weighing heavily on his mind and he felt near the breaking point.

"She threatened my life if I didn't cooperate," said Caleb.

Jasmine's head spun and she glared at him, "You're a liar Caleb."

"Quiet Jasmine. I want to hear what he has to say," Shane said forcefully.

"She told me that she counted me as part of the pack," said Caleb, "but she would grant me amnesty if I agreed to help her."

"I don't believe you," Shane said, "You seemed to rather enjoy inflicting the pain on myself and Jeremy earlier this morning."

"I had to play the part...I had to make it convincing," he argued.

Shane shook his head, "No, I don't believe that," he hesitated, "I'm the one person that could've helped you...you didn't ask for my help."

Caleb seemed to grow angry. His face contorted into a hateful grimace. He surveyed everyone in the room and finally settled his eyes on Shane.

"Do you want the truth.....do you?"

"Yes, I would very much like to hear the truth," Shane replied, his eyes boring into the human's.

"The truth is.......I think that every one of you filthy animals should die," his voice was cold and unfeeling, the look on his face one of pure hatred.

The breaking point came and he found himself falling helplessly, a deep abyss rising up to meet him that was the scarlet color of rage. Control had vanished and in its place something was cultivated raw and primal, rising to blur his vision with unquenchable fury. Jeremy lunged forward and grasped Caleb's head between his large hands. His penetrating, emotionless stare pierced the depths of Caleb's terrified gaze while his grip remained powerful and unrelenting. Only vaguely did he feel Caleb's ears pressing into his palms, or the dried, hard blood in his hair.

"You first," he said raucously through clenched teeth as in one quick motion he twisted Caleb's head in his hands.

Shane lurched forward but not before he heard the sickening crack of bones and saw Caleb's limp body crumble to the floor in a lifeless heap. Elisa's distant gasps echoed in his ears and from somewhere far away he heard her footsteps as she ran from the kitchen. The pounding of his own heart and the blood in his veins roared in his ears.

"Jeremy!" he bellowed.

Jeremy spun to face him, his eyes a frightening mirror of the underlying brutality like nothing Shane had ever encountered in him before. His gaze was cold and heartless with only a minimal trace of the man that Shane thought he knew and for one brief moment Shane's body stiffened in preparation for the onslaught that was sure to follow.

But it didn't.

Instead, Jeremy clutched the neck of his own shirt and ripped it away from his body, the tattered strips falling as he stormed past. A deep wail was unleashed from his throat that was a mixture of man and beast; a deafening sound that was part frustration and at the same time... insanity. The front door of the cabin slammed open, and an uncomfortable stillness followed his departure.

Shane placed one hand on the kitchen table and the other on his thigh and leaned over, relieving the ache in his side and breathing heavily as if he had exerted every bit of his energy in those few moments. Closing his eyes against Caleb's dead stare he took several deep breaths, attempting to determine what had just happened and get past the shock.

He turned to look at Jasmine who had sank to her knees and was sobbing and then to Tristan and his sisters. Tristan was holding Lena in his arms stroking her hair and Shane could see that she was crying; her body shaking with every quiet sob. In Tristan's face he saw anger and perhaps a certain amount of fear. Fear of the situation? Fear of Jeremy? Possibly the fear of what might happen next?

Young Zoey stood a few feet away, her eyes glued to him. Other than her normal paleness, there was nothing remarkable in her manner, as if Jeremy's actions had no influence on her. There were no tears in her eyes, no expression on her face.

He held her gaze, "Are you alright?" he croaked, his voice strained. She appeared thoughtful, mulling over the events in her mind but gradually nodded.

Straightening slowly, he went in search of Elisa. Finding her crying, curled up in a ball on his bed; he placed a gentle hand on her shaking side.

"I'm sorry," he said softly, "I'm sorry you saw that."

I sniffed and sat up seeking the comfort that came with his nearness, wrapping my arms tightly around him.

"What's happened to Jeremy?" I whimpered, "It's like he.........snapped."

The pain in his side was excruciating but the reassurance that he felt in her embrace was worth enduring any amount of pain. "I've never seen it before," he admitted, in his voice a trace of bitterness from the newly discovered betrayal.

I pulled away and looked up, my eyes filled with distress, "Jasmine…..will you kill her?"

"She would have killed you Elisa. How will we ever live without looking over our shoulders if I don't?" He asked softly, but I could see the harshness and determination in his face.

"Please……" I begged, "I can take no more of the killing." Again, I broke into a series of uncontrollable whimpers and tears. Shane pulled me close again, soothing me with his gentle caresses.

"It's alright," said Shane tranquilly, smoothing my hair, "Please don't cry."

He stood up and moved away, opening the door, "Tristan, can you all come in here please?"

Elisa heard their footsteps and the moment that Lena laid eyes on her, she was soon wrapped tightly within the other woman's arms. Another round of tears ensued as they held on to one another.

Tristan stood quietly watching, his own raw emotion plainly etched across his face. Zoey stood slightly behind him, her hands pushed inside the back pockets of her jeans casually, her eyes remained cast uncomfortably to the floor. Shane pulled the door closed behind them and waited respectfully until Elisa and Lena's crying had subsided and their embrace had been broken.

"It appears that Jasmine is the only person that we need to talk about," his voice was low as he attempted to keep things as quiet as possible. Jasmine's keen hearing could pick up anything that they discussed with ease if they spoke with any volume.

"I want each of you to know that I had no prior warning that Jeremy would ….take matters into his own hands," he paused awkwardly, "For that, I am truly sorry."

His eyes wandered over the group as he spoke.

"With that said, I feel that I am being unfair in expecting any of you to pass judgment on Jasmine. It's my history…this should be my decision and mine alone…since Jeremy has gone."

Tristan's forehead wrinkled with sincerity, "I'm not judging her for what happened back then," he said, "I'm judging her for what she did *now*."

"I understand that," Shane said, "And you must know that your devotion will not soon be forgotten." He smiled warmly and clasped Tristan's shoulder in an affectionate gesture, "But this decision should not be on such young shoulders. I will be the one to bear it… alone."

He felt the heavy stares of everyone's eyes on him and although hesitant to look directly at them, an alpha must persevere. After seeing the accusatory stares of the two red faced, tearful women, he dared to steal a quick glance in Zoey's direction.

He saw what he had come to expect there... nothing. With pale blue eyes she regarded him carefully but in them, the lack of emotion remained startling. They were empty, her face blank. Briefly he wondered how the images she had seen would affect her…..so young and impressionable to have witnessed such brutality.

"If anyone has anything to say that I should take into consideration, now's the time," he murmured. The room remained quiet except from the occasional sniffle of his mate and Lena. Plucking a bit more courage from down deep he looked directly at each one of them, trying to put them at ease no matter the amount of pressure on himself. He allowed a few moments to pass before he turned away.

"Tristan, do you mind giving me a hand?"

He nodded and followed Shane from the room with Zoey on their heels until she was reprimanded.

"Stay with your sister," Tristan said gruffly. Shane had stopped as well, staring back at her.

Shaking her head, Zoey eyed him with contempt, "I'm coming too," she sneered.

Shane stepped towards her. He was already concerned with the fact that nothing seemed to faze her and when things finally decided to sink in, she may be scarred….for life.

"No, I want you to stay with your sister and Elisa," he said sternly.

Pausing for a short time as if she had accepted Shane's command or was considering what might happen if she didn't, the hesitation was short lived.

"I want to come," she said more respectfully this time, "I want to see how you handle this."

"Why?" asked Tristan.

"I want to learn how things are taken care of," replied Zoey, "If I ever need to know."

Shane tried to hide his puzzlement. This girl was different in every aspect of the word and there was obviously more to her than he had first imagined. Against his better judgment he agreed.

"If it's alright with your brother………"

Tristan seemed surprised by his answer but nodded his acceptance.

Jasmine had remained on her knees, crouched next to Caleb's lifeless form. Her crying had ceased and when she looked up, Shane recognized the veil of defeat that had settled onto her pretty, tear stained face. He had always thought her beautiful, even as teenagers he had fancied her dark hair and eyes. He had never pursued her though… she had not been for him.

He felt a stab of guilt deep in the pit of his stomach as he and Tristan drug Caleb's body past her, her eyes following the trail of blood that smeared behind them across the kitchen tile. Shane secretly prayed for the strength to finish out the deed that lay ahead.

A stray beam of afternoon sun glared down on him as he lay amidst the leaves and litter of the forest floor. He fisted his hands distractedly into the brittleness that surrounded him, only barely hearing the crunch that disintegrated the dry leaves within his grasp. The pieces fell away in small fragments that fluttered softly to the ground in the early spring breeze, but he failed to take notice. Staring upward vacantly, he was unable to see through the wall of rage that engulfed him to the brilliant blue sky above.

His madness had transported him for miles through the woods and across acres of pasture land until his body was near exhaustion. With only a fleeting concern for the danger that unfamiliar territory could hold for him, he had collapsed onto the forest floor. Chaos churned within his mind and he was unable to escape from its clutches while at the same time it wrung and twisted his very soul.

Before standing, Jeremy shifted back into the wolf; his redeemer, his savior. Imprisoned within the beast, deep in its dark pit he was protected from the turmoil of his human mind. The mahogany wolf shook itself to dislodge the leaves that clung to its fur and then lifted its muzzle toward the heavens. A mournful, long howl erupted from its lips and deep down within that dark shadowy place where Jeremy had retreated, it was only barely audible.

Chapter 36

Raking the last of the cooling coals into a smoldering pile, Shane's mind mulled over the current situation and the dread he felt heavy in his heart. Hurt that Jeremy had never shared the information with him about Jasmine and Paul, he was still unable to understand how he had been able to keep it hidden from him, but he also felt stupid. How was it that he hadn't recognized that the brown wolf in the pit had been Jeremy?

Disrupting his thoughts, Zoey shifted the wheelbarrow towards him and waited as he shoveled the remaining bits of bone and ash into the empty receptacle. With Tristan and Zoey's help they had incinerated Caleb's body and dug a hole for the remains. He admitted to himself the chore had gone more smoothly than he anticipated and he had developed a strange sense of respect for the teenage girl.

She was different than most of the females that Shane had ever known. While Elisa and Lena had allowed Jeremy's uncontrolled explosion to illicit irrepressible tears and suffering, Zoey hadn't. She had remained distant and detached from the situation, protected by the shell with which she had enclosed herself. He was deeply concerned about that part of it but he also knew that she could be a valuable element to the pack.

Making one last trip into the woods, he dumped the contents of the wheelbarrow into the deep grave that Tristan had hollowed out. The freshly turned soil smelled of earthy dampness as he and Tristan shoveled the dirt in over what remained of Caleb.

They had worked without speaking for most of the afternoon and once the hole was filled in, Shane leaned with a sigh on the shovel handle. His body ached and he was exhausted physically as well as mentally.

"I want to thank you both for your help," he said as he stretched slowly, trying to work the kink out of his side. The fresh bullet wound would be a slow recovery and the dull, painful ache demanded him to rest, but he didn't have time for it. The brother and sister each acknowledged his statement with a nod but neither spoke and together they gathered up the tools and made their way up the path back to the cabin.

Lena and I had gone into the kitchen a couple of hours after Shane's departure and cleaned the trail of blood from the floor. Turning, I found Jasmine staring at me.

"Could I have a drink please?" she asked civilly.

Locking eyes with Lena's warning glare for a moment, I moved toward the sink and filled a glass. Returning with it in my hand, I knelt beside Jasmine and held it to her lips.

She drank thirstily and after draining the contents of the glass, she leaned back against the refrigerator.

"Thank you," she said softly as she closed her eyes.

Standing, I started to move away but her voice stopped me.

"I heard what you said Elisa," her tone was quiet, her voice relaxed.

"What did you hear?" I asked, eyeing her suspiciously.

Jasmine opened her eyes and leaned her head forward again looking unwaveringly into my eyes.

Lena shifted from one foot to the other nervously.

"I heard you tell Shane that you wanted no more killing," she paused, "Even me?"

"I think you deserve to be punished," I answered, "But killing you isn't the answer."

Jasmine appeared thoughtful before she spoke, "After what I did ….and what I had planned for you?"

I shook my head, "But it isn't up to me."

Jasmine leaned her head back again and shut her eyes, "No, I guess it isn't, but there's more that you don't know."

I was left wondering what she meant as Lena grabbed my hand and quickly dragged me back toward the bedroom, shutting the door behind us.

"I think you should stay away from her," she said in a motherly tone.

"I know," I responded, "But she's tied up, she can't hurt me."

"No, she can't physically hurt you but she goaded Jeremy to the point that he…." her voice trailed off.

I accepted the position that she was trying to get across and placed my hand on her arm reassuringly. The two of us stretched out across the mattress and Lena began to talk about her pack and Brian and her excitement to return home. It was a way of stepping out of the situation for a few minutes and I was sure that Lena was trying to commandeer control of my mind so that I wasn't dwelling on the inevitable ending.

I listened halfheartedly while my mind wandered on its own back to Jeremy and all of my unanswered questions. I had felt overwhelming alarm and shock at his unpredictable cruelty. And while I had lain sobbing on Shane's bed, the tumultuous wail would forever be imprinted in my mind followed by the cracking of wood as the door splintered shut behind him. I was pulled from my thoughts when the bedroom door eased open and Shane stepped inside.

Sitting up, I was immediately pulled into his comforting embrace. He smelled of smoke, earth and sweat but I didn't mind. Lena left the room quietly to join her siblings and to give us a bit of time to be alone.

"Are you better?" he breathed quietly against my ear.

"I'm okay."

"Don't ever leave me again." I pulled back and looked deep into his blue eyes; there was pain inside.

"I will never."

His face solemn, he stood, "I will be gone for a while this evening. Do you want them to stay or will you be alright here alone?"

Shane saw the apprehension move across my face and he reached out and touched my cheek gently, "I have to take care of this. Don't you understand?"

I cast my eyes to the floor but Shane tilted my face up with his fingers so that I had no choice but to look at him. "We will never be safe as long as she is out there."

"I understand," I paused, "But I don't agree with it."

He smiled proudly. "You have a forgiving heart," he said as he stood up. He bent down and placed a tender kiss against my lips. "Do you want them to stay?"

"No. I'd like some time alone."

Shane nodded and extended his hand toward me and I slipped mine inside and together we walked into the living room. Tristan was lounged against the wall near the door while Lena sat motionless in the recliner. Zoey wasn't in the room and as Shane glanced toward the door, he caught just a slight glimpse of her outline though the window.

"I hope you all know what today has meant to me," he said as he opened the door and proceeded through it with me in tow. The others followed and Tristan pulled the door closed behind him. Zoey turned as we joined her on the deck.

"I am indebted to each one of you," Shane began, "There is no way that I can ever repay you for what you've done." He regarded each one of them briefly, "I have plans for *our* pack….not that it comes close to repaying you for your loyalty."

"We aren't looking for repayment, Shane," said Tristan.

Shane smiled at him. "I know you aren't," he paused, "That's what makes you so valuable to me not just as part of the pack….but as a friend." Tristan smiled in return.

Shane then turned to Zoey. She met his gaze defiantly and he couldn't stop a chuckle from rising in his throat. "And *you*," he grinned as he reached a hand out to muss the pale blonde and pink hair. Even though appearing annoyed, she tolerated his gesture.

"I have one last thing to do," Shane said reluctantly as his face sobered, "You guys can head home and we'll talk in the next couple of days."

"Do you need help?" asked Tristan, "I can send the girls home and stay if you need me."

Shane shook his head, "No. …..thanks, but I need to do this on my own."

Lena turned to me, her face one of worry, "Do you want me to stay with you?"

"Thanks Lena, but I would like some time alone."She appeared hurt but she said that she understood.

"If you need me you know that I'm just a phone call away, right?"

"I know," I smiled weakly, "At least for a little while longer….."

"For as long as you need me," Lena corrected as she grasped me in a hug good-bye.

Shane and Elisa watched the family as they crossed the yard and climbed into the SUV. As they departed, Elisa felt the weight of the day bearing heavily down on her shoulders. Reading her mind, Shane wrapped his arm around her and pulled her against hin while she peered up into his handsome, yet troubled face.

"I'll be back late, are you going to be okay here alone?" he asked again.

"I'll be fine. Maybe Jeremy will be back," I said hopefully.

"I'm not sure that Jeremy is coming back," he replied frigidly. "Once I get everything taken care of I will look for him….tomorrow."

I ran my hand along the length of his arm and tangled my fingers within his. "I know he's hurt you, I can see it and hear it in your voice."

Shane looked down, nodding, but he didn't speak.

"But don't give up on him."

Shane looked over at me and smiled faintly, squeezing my hand gently, "Like I said...you have a forgiving heart."

Leading me back inside the cabin, I felt the tension overwhelm me. The feeling of dread settled over me and the threat of tears became prominent once again.

"Stay in the bedroom Elisa," said Shane quietly, "We'll be gone in a few minutes." Kissing me lightly on the forehead, he ushered me toward the bedroom door. I paused there gazing at him for only a moment before I shut myself inside.

Chapter 37

Jasmine looked up as he walked into the kitchen, her dark eyes regarding him warily but in them he detected a trace of fear. Leaning down, he untied the wire that bound her ankles and pulled her to her feet.

"Come, its time." His voice was cool and unemotional as he grasped her arm and led her toward the door, pausing for a moment to pick up his keys, wallet and the pistol from the counter before continuing at a fast pace.

Jasmine recognized right away that it was the pistol with the silver bullets in the clip and realized that her own plan may now be her demise. He manhandled her roughly up into the passenger side of his truck and shut the door and in only a few minutes they were headed down the county road.

Jasmine broke the tense silence, her voice strained, "What are you going to do with me?"

Shane continued driving as if he hadn't heard her question. He just didn't feel that she deserved any kind of answer. Five minutes ticked by before she spoke again.

"Please Shane."

He glanced over at her accusingly, "I want to hear you beg," he growled, "I want you to beg for your life."

The truck veered over to the side of the road and skidded to a stop throwing a myriad of gravel forward. Leaping out, he came around to the passenger side and flung the door open wide. Grasping her violently by the arm, he jerked her out of the pickup.

"Walk," he demanded, motioning toward the woods.

Jasmine knew deep down that these passing few minutes were ultimately the last of her life. As she moved closer to certain death with each step deeper into the forest, she forced herself to think of the plans she had carried out heartlessly and without remorse to avenge her mate.

Planning and executing the destruction of her entire pack with only the help of a few others, she had been close to having fulfilled her promise to Paul's lifeless body. Caleb had failed her and he had more than paid the price...Jeremy had seen to that. But now, faced with her probable end, her footsteps were tentative as the sense of foreboding flooded over her. Suddenly her mind was jerked back to the present as Shane grabbed her by the shoulders and pushed her to her knees.

The gun was steady in his hand as he thrust it towards the back of her head, the barrel grazing her dark hair. "Beg me," he sneered, "Beg me for your life, Jasmine."

His voice boomed from behind and she dared not turn and look into the bitterness of his face when she spoke.

"I can't beg you for something that I no longer want," she said evenly, "Killing me is the only favor you can do for me now."

Shane was still for a moment, absorbing her words. "I won't make it quick ….not after all you've done. You have to suffer."

She turned then, and looked at him over her shoulder, "And what about you? When will you begin to remember so that you can suffer as well? You can't bury those memories forever Shane, no matter what you do to me."

Confused by her meaningless rambling, he grew angrier, "You're crazy. I don't know what you're trying to pull."

"Am I?" She said despondently. She lowered her head, scarcely noticing the small purple spring flowers that covered the ground upon which she kneeled as she cast her eyes to the ground.

What the hell was she trying to convince him of?

Shane had imagined doing horrific things to the person responsible for his pack's massacre. But now, face to face with the offender he was having difficulty persuading himself to carry out the torturous acts. He wanted to hurt her, there was no doubt in his mind about that but a small part of him, one deep down in the pit of his stomach, felt a strange sense of pity.

He walked around in front of her so she had no place else to look but directly into his face. The gun now hung loosely in his fingers at his side. "Why Jasmine?" he asked, "You knew the dangers, you knew what could happen…."

Lifting her head, her dark eyes peered up at him, "I've lived that night over and over," she disclosed, the pain evident in her tone. "From the moment that I wake up until I finally sleep at night I see Paul's mutilated body in my mind. And even when I do sleep, I have nightmares," she hesitated, "The killing eased the painful memories….if even for just a little while." Her deep brown eyes glistened with the tears that formed, "I'm ready for it to be over."

"And Jeremy? We all grew up together………..you said yourself that you knew you couldn't trust him."

"Paul insisted," she paused, "I told him it was a bad idea…….but he was determined."

Shane's eye narrowed, "You allowed a human to make a decision for you that you already knew was wrong," said Shane furiously, "You can blame no one for his death but yourself."

Her eyes flared heatedly. "This is more than just about Jeremy, more than Paul...this is about you. You and me."

Shane was convinced that she had indeed fallen off the deep end, "You and me?"

Jasmine dropped her gaze from his. "Maybe one day you will allow yourself to go back there Shane," she paused and looked down again, "Just do this and get it over with."

For a few moments Shane contemplated his next action, but instead of ending her as he had fully intended, he reached down and grasped her bound hands, hauling her upward to her feet and yanking her back toward the parked truck.

She didn't question his intentions but instead felt a small wave of relief that he had chosen to prolong her existence for whatever reason. He pushed her roughly into the passenger side of the truck and then looked over at her briefly before he started the engine, the loathing he felt for her evident on his face.

Standing in the kitchen my mind relived the tragic episode that had happened earlier in that very room. The emptiness that I felt inside was amplified by the stillness of the vacant cabin. I looked toward the kitchen table and across the floor and envisioned the blood that had been spilled there and then the image of Caleb's broken body collapsing...

Suddenly overpowered by tension and anxiety, I turned abruptly and ran out the cabin door. I stood out on the deck, my hands braced on the railing for support and took a deep breath to clear my head. But instead of breathing in fresh air, it was air that was sullied with the scent of fire and burnt flesh and the smell plummeted directly to my stomach, bottoming out before it coursed its way back up my throat. I doubled over clenching my stomach and heaved repeatedly.

Overwhelmed with the need to get away from this place and from the stench that invaded my senses, I quickly stripped away the clothes that bound me to my human shape and shifted effortlessly into the wolf. Taking a few short steps, I bounded off the deck and disappeared into the dark forest. It wasn't too long before I picked up a familiar scent and with my muzzle to the ground I followed it until I found myself in unfamiliar territory. Hesitating uncertainly at the edge of the wood, I surveyed the clearing that sloped upward before me. I sensed that I would find what I sought on the other side but I paced nervously, undecided if I should press forward.

Lifting my nose to the air, I howled softly, announcing my presence. If Jeremy was close, he would hear it. I scanned the crest of the grade in search of any movement and then I waited. Minutes ticked by and then an hour had passed. Lying down, I remained quiet, my head resting on my paws. I listened intently for the unmistakable stirring in the tall grass that would indicate that I was no longer alone, but it never came. Having become weary of the passing time, I finally rose to my feet. Stretching, I searched the horizon once more before turning and trotting back the way I had come.

Uncomfortable silence was the only indication that he wasn't alone in the cab of the truck as he traveled through the lighted streets of the city. Dusk had descended on them about an hour before and had dimmed the landscape to reflect his darkened mood. Jasmine had not spoken the entire drive and he had made no effort to encourage conversation. Finally arriving at his destination, he pulled into the parking garage and shifted the truck into park.

Jasmine glanced over at him questioningly as he leaned over and unwired her wrists. Digging through the console, he pulled out his checkbook and reached for the door handle before she spoke.

"What are we doing here?"

Shane slowly turned to look at her, the unmistakable animosity still etched in his face like a permanent disfigurement. "You are going to decide where you want to go, and I don't really care where as long as it isn't in this state," he paused, "Preferably somewhere far from here. I'm going to pay for a one way ticket and if I ever...*ever* find you near here again..........." His voice faded before he finished the threat knowing full well that she understood what he didn't need to say.

He opened his door and stepped out, stretching his aching back. The long drive had taken its toll on his worn out and sore body. Looking down, he noticed the dark traces of fresh blood that had soaked through the dressing and now through his shirt. He pulled his jacket around his frame tighter to conceal it.

Jasmine stood beside the truck and rubbed her stinging wrists where the wire had bound tightly against them for so long.

He glared over at her, "Come on."

Knowing she had no choice, she followed him through the maze of vehicles inside the garage. Once within the airport, Shane walked directly up to the ticket counter.

"Can I help you sir?" The young woman asked from behind the counter, her blonde hair pulled back in a loose ponytail swayed with every movement of her perky attitude.

Shane motioned toward the lit up destination flights and turned to Jasmine, "Pick somewhere," he growled.

Sensing the hostility in his voice, the young woman at the ticket counter looked from Shane to Jasmine skeptically.

Jasmine's eyes scanned the lighted board quickly, "Portland."

He nodded toward the attendant, "One, one-way ticket to Portland. I would prefer no stops or lay-overs."

The blonde woman's fingers moved with speedy accuracy across the keyboard, her eyes searching the screen. "I don't have any coach available......" she continued searching, "but, I do have a first class available with no stops or layovers."

She looked up, waiting for Shane's answer.

"Fine," he snapped, "Whatever the cost, put it on this," he said as he pushed a credit card into her waiting hand. She continued with the paperwork while Shane fingered a pen from the cup beside her computer. He went to work writing and in a few seconds had torn a check out of his checkbook.

"Please sign, sir," The assistant said as she handed a credit card receipt over to him and Shane scribbled his name across it. Smiling, she handed him the plane ticket, "Just give this to the attendant at the gate."

Shane turned and shoved the ticket into Jasmine's hand. He took the check in the fingers of his left hand and waved it near her face so that she was able to view what was written upon it. "This should be enough to get you settled." he said, his eyes boring into hers.

Jasmine saw the amount written out on the check and was astonished by the kindness of his actions when his eyes regarded her with such contempt. She realized that his intention had been to kill her earlier in the woods and she was still confused by what stopped him. Perhaps down deep somewhere, there were still some memories of her that existed. Taking the check from his extended hand, her eyes brushed across his face for an instant before she turned and walked towards the gate.

"Jasmine," Shane's gruff voice halted her and she looked back over her shoulder. "Don't ever come back here."

For a moment she stared into the bitter blueness of his eyes before she turned and walked away.

Shane watched as she made her way toward the gate. He moved to stand near the window, waiting to physically witness her boarding the plane. A couple of minutes passed and then he saw her among the crowd of other passengers being ushered toward the boarding ramp. She climbed the steps and disappeared inside.

He felt compelled to stand there until the plane moved toward the runway and took off, disappearing into the night sky. Satisfied that she was indeed gone, his body relaxed and he sighed, finally able to exhale some of the stress and tension of the day.

Chapter 38

Making my way back up through the forest, I was lost in my feeling of hopelessness. Worried about Jeremy, where he was and what he must be going through distracted my attention away from the trail ahead as I trotted along. I was suddenly overwhelmed with the scent of him in my nostrils and then there he was, standing ahead of me in the path. His huge, rich brown body blocking my way, his head lowered and assessing me through cool gray eyes.

I froze, unsure how he would react to me being there. Our eyes met and a low rumbling warning sounded from deep within his throat. Immediately, I flattened my ears against my neck and shrunk away submissively, whining faintly. He raised his head and moved toward me, his nose extended in greeting. His wolf recognized mine….but did Jeremy know I was here? He walked around me on stiff legs, sniffing along my neck before he circled around and came to stand in front of me once again. Pushing my muzzle up under his neck, I then rubbed against him in a gesture of affection, hoping that if Jeremy could sense me that he would respond.

Feeling his body become rigid against mine, I cowered away in an attempt to lessen our contact. The wolf allowed me to back away and I was thankful that there wasn't a conflict. I knew in my heart that Jeremy would never hurt me but after what I had witnessed this day I knew that his mind was unstable. My wolf would be no match for his if it decided to turn on me. I walked slowly around him with the intention of leading the way home but as I looked back, only his eyes followed and he remained rooted to where he stood.

I wanted to call to him, to encourage him to come home but only a distressed whine escaped me. The big brown wolf seemed untouched by my urging but in his unyielding gray eyes I saw a flicker of sadness. I turned and trotted away, pausing once more to look back through the darkness but he had vanished.

My eyes searched the surrounding forest for a glimpse of him but there was no sign that he had been there. Raising my muzzle to the sky, I allowed a long mournful howl to emanate from deep down inside my very soul. Helplessness stole quickly into my mind and replaced the flicker of hope that had grown at having found him.

Through the night I ran as fast as I could toward home hoping that I would find Shane there and he would drape me in reassuring comfort. But as I hurried down the long winding driveway, I saw that his truck wasn't there. Climbing the steps, I shifted quickly before gathering my clothes and retreating inside. The cabin was empty, just as I had left it.

Discovering that the stress and tension of the day had left me exhausted, I curled up on the couch with an afghan and closed my eyes. All that I could see behind my dark lids were the images I had witnessed; Jasmine's determined face, the blood that seeped between the wooden planks on the deck and Jeremy's brutal attack. It all played through my mind like some kind of slow motion, horror movie soap opera.

My imagination constructed the terrible end that Jasmine certainly met with at Shane's hand. Shane's gentle hands, hands that were capable of horrible deeds, yet I knew nothing of how violent they could be. They were the same hands that held me tenderly and touched me lovingly.

In the late hours of the night I was roused from sleep by the light sweep of his fingertips across my cheek as he brushed the hair from my face. Opening my eyes, I peered up into the welcome sight of his face as he kneeled beside me. He smiled but I could see the weariness engrained into his weary appearance.

"Hi," he whispered.

"Hi," I pulled myself into a sitting position and he at once enclosed me in his embrace, burying his face into my hair. Wrapping my arms around him, I pulled him as close as I could draw him to me. We remained that way, not speaking but instead only holding onto one another as time ceased to move.

When he finally did pull away, his deep blue eyes stared into mine, "Are you alright?"

Accepting my nod, he pulled me gradually to my feet and led me toward the bathroom, his fingers warm on my skin. He undressed me and then in turn, peeled the stained, fouled clothes from his body. Slowly he removed the saturated bandage from his side.

As he stood beneath the soothing hot water allowing it to wash away the tightness in his muscles I couldn't help but speculate that he also hoped that it might cleanse his mind as well. Perhaps wash the memories and images away that crowded together inside his head. He turned and knelt in front of me and folded his arms around my waist, his unshaven cheek rough across my stomach. I lathered the shampoo through his thick black hair as he kneeled before me, my fingers lost within the dark lather.

Feeling desperately as if I needed to comfort him, I peered down at his face as I prepared to say something... anything. His eyes were closed in repose, the dark wet lashes resting on his tanned face, and I refrained from breaking into his few moments of peace.

Neither he nor I spoke while we towel dried before leaving the bathroom; only the meeting of our eyes now and again indicated that there were many things to be said, but they could wait. After reapplying the bandage and still unclothed, his hand gripping mine gently, we made our way silently to the bedroom after extinguishing the lights. Crawling between the cool sheets, his body nested against mine and his arms wrapped around me. When he spoke, his breath was hot against my ear and his voice was soft and surrendering.

"I didn't kill her."

Sighing, I backed up closer against him extinguishing any existing space between us, "Where is she?" I spoke into the shadows.

"I put her on a plane. I told her that if she ever came back I would finish her."

I rolled over to face him. Even in the darkness I could see his beautiful face and I found him even more so now, "It must've been hard...to just let her walk away."

His fingertips traced down the side of my face, along my jaw and chin affectionately. "I wanted to kill her," he admitted, "But, I hope that she finds that living with what she's done is more severe than death." Even though his voice was unruffled the bitterness in his words was evident.

I didn't want to push him, not now. I let my fingers move down the length of his side and he flinched as they traveled across the jagged rough edge of the bandage. His honesty about Jasmine wrenched my insides and I was compelled to tell him about my own outing. His eyes were closed in rest again but split open slowly when I spoke.

"I saw Jeremy."

"Where?" He asked, his voice hushed as his eyes explored my face.

I hesitated to respond, maybe too long, "In the woods to the north."

Holding my breath I waited for the outburst that I imagined would come. Expecting the heated words in which he would express that my behavior had been nothing short of stupid, I waited. But when he spoke the words weren't as harsh as I had anticipated.

"You followed him?"

Seeing the disapproval sketched across his face I admitted it apologetically, "Yes."

His stillness evoked a feeling of guilt as I continued to wait for his reaction. It was as if somehow he secretly could know or sense that I was cringing inside. He took a deliberately slow breath, moving his warm hand across my bare shoulder and down my arm to where it rested.

"How far?" he calmly asked once he finally decided to speak.

"Farther than I've ever gone before," I paused, "but he wouldn't come back."

At that point I could see a slight agitation growing at the corners of his eyes. "You went to unfamiliar territory in search of a volatile wolf." It wasn't a mere statement but instead an affirmation. I looked away from his accusing stare but his strong fingers underneath my chin turned my face back towards him. "Do you not understand how truly foolish it was?"

"Jeremy would never hurt me," I defended, "And he didn't."

Quiet again for a few moments, I squirmed beneath his scrutinizing gaze. It disappeared as suddenly as it had materialized and then his arms moved around me, unyielding.

"I will look for him tomorrow," he said wearily, "For now, can we sleep?" I snuggled in close against his solid chest and closed my eyes.

Chapter 39

The sun was high in the midday sky by the time that I awoke no longer wrapped within the arms that had sheltered me in my slumber. Shane was gone, the bed cool where he had once lain. Wondering where he was and how long I had been alone, I pulled my robe on and padded into the living room. I could sense that I was alone inside the cabin so I bothered not even to look for him.

The coffeepot stood half full and still on so I knew he had been awake for a while. I imagined him sitting alone here at the table in silence, contemplating his next move over a steaming cup as I poured one for myself. Wandering around the cabin I could only pick up his faint scent so I stepped out on the deck, raising my face into the warm spring breeze. I knew then where he had headed.

The black wolf paced along the edge of the open field; back and forth, back and forth, his paws moving soundlessly through the thick grass. Just over the crest of the hill he knew he would find the other. Although inquisitive, he couldn't shake the menacing sense of danger that billowed towards him like a thick, intimidating wall cloud.

He could smell the weak scent of Elisa there, exactly where he stood. In fact, it had been her stronger scent that he had followed this far. Jeremy's scent was obscure, diluted by the light breeze and by time, but he felt his presence just over the knoll. Shane was uncertain what would happen if he did find him. His feelings of betrayal were fresh and raw and inside the beast they amplified and gained strength.

Raising his muzzle he released from deep down within the bowels of his heart a dismal wail that carried on the warm breeze across the countryside. He maintained his vigilance for only a few minutes longer listening intently, but there was no returned response, no distant answer that drifted back to his twitching ears. Turning then, he trotted back toward the way he had come and back in the direction of home.

Erratic spring rains came and went during the next two weeks that eased April into May. There were only two or three days during that span in time that the showers would let up and we could venture into the woods without being drenched.

Trapped inside, Shane was able to teach me more about the wolf than time had previously allowed. We spent many rainy afternoons tangled in the bed sheets together and afterwards we would lounge leisurely discussing past events and future promises. Tristan, Lena and Zoey visited a couple of days after the incident to see how everyone had fared but other than those times, Shane and I had been completely alone.

When the weather finally broke and the summer heat replaced the rain he would begin construction on the house and by fall, our new pack would be brought together as it should be. And although he seemed eager for what was ahead, at times I could see a distant, sad look on the surface of his eyes that quickly descended into the blue depths and was lost. In my heart I understood what it was that haunted him but I dared not ask, and he never spoke of it.

I quickly tired of the constant wet weather and my mood began to reflect the incapability to deal with much more. On one particularly drizzly day my reserve was met and even with Shane's objections I ran outside totally clothed into the pouring rain. It soaked through my clothes instantly, matting my hair to my head as water ran in thin rivulets into my eyes.

Shane stood in the doorway watching attentively, a smile touching the corners of his mouth. He was amused by my behavior as I tried to convince him to join me. I laughed at his reaction as I stood staring back at him, soaked to the bone. But in no time at all I watched as the smile faded and was replaced by his stony facade; his eyes moving past me, I turned around abruptly.

In the pouring rain, a few yards behind me stood Jeremy. At first shock and surprise bolted through me like a flash of lightning and I could do nothing but stare. He stood there, staring back at me, his face sober, and his gray eyes cold and unemotional. My surprise was quickly exchanged for a wave of relief and I found my feet moving by themselves through the rain towards him. Shane had disappeared inside but I wasn't aware that he had as I hadn't so much as even thrown a glance behind me as I advanced in Jeremy's direction.

I stopped at an arm's length away, gazing up into those stormy eyes through the rain that drenched us, searching within them for some fragment of the Jeremy that I knew. He regarded me coolly but even so, a slight smile touched just around the rigid edges of his mouth.

Motivated by the moment, I seized hold of him, circling my arms around his wet, naked body. For an instant he remained rigid, motionless; but then I felt his arms move stiffly from his sides as his hands rested upon my shoulders. He lowered his head and relaxed his chin atop my head.

    Through the window, Shane watched the scene play out in a dreamlike state before his eyes. Spurred on by Elisa's actions in welcoming Jeremy home, he felt the gnawing familiar jealousy return down deep in the pit of his stomach. He had missed him; he couldn't lie to himself even if he had convinced Elisa otherwise. Part of him wanted to follow in her footsteps and throw his arms around his friend, but the other part was bitter and demanded a reckoning. Retreating from the window, he disappeared into the bedroom, closing the door behind him. Surprised by Jeremy's reappearance, he wasn't prepared for the confrontation that would and must come.

    I took his hand gently in mine and pulled him toward the cabin but he hesitated, uncertainty written plainly in the grayness. As I urged him to follow, I couldn't help but notice that he had grown thinner during his absence and his face was tired; older.
    "Come...please." My words were muffled by the heavy downpour but he allowed me to lead him forward. Detecting then that Shane was no longer in the doorway; I wondered where he had withdrawn to and what would happen inside the dry confines of the cabin.
    Stepping inside, I could see that Shane's bedroom door was closed and he had retreated into seclusion. I knew that this was just a start to some difficult days ahead for all of us but I felt content to have my small family back together. I walked into the bathroom and returned with a towel that I pushed toward Jeremy as I used another to run over my wet hair. He stood there, holding the towel, his eyes boring into mine when I looked up. After a couple of weeks of not talking to anyone, when he spoke his voice sound hoarse and scratchy.
    "Can I shower?"
    "Of course you can," I answered, smiling.
    Immediately he headed off in that direction, leaving me alone in the living room where I stripped off my wet clothes. Wrapped in the towel, I quietly opened the bedroom door and peered inside. Shane was standing at the window, his back to me as I entered.

"Are you alright?" I asked as I moved up behind him, putting my arms around his waist. He sighed deeply but didn't turn around.

"Yes. I'm alright," he answered, still gazing thoughtfully out into the downpour. Not sure of what to do, I just stood there for a few moments with my face pressed against his back, my arms wrapped around him. He said nothing more as I gathered and changed into dry clothes. He remained there, staring out the window even as I left the room.

Inside the isolation of the bathroom, Jeremy stepped into the shower. The hot water steamed the mirrors quickly as he stood there silently, allowing the soothing heat to devour him. He closed his eyes against the beating spray and bowed his head into it. Only when the water had finally begun to lose its warmth did he open his eyes again. Stepping out, the wafting aroma of food penetrated his senses and his stomach gurgled in response, twisting in spasms of hunger. He couldn't remember the last time he had eaten.

Making my way into the kitchen I could still hear the water running in the shower. I pulled left over roast and potatoes from the refrigerator and warmed them in the microwave along with rolls that had been our dinner the previous night. When it was just about finished heating, Jeremy appeared, quietly padding into the kitchen. Dressed in light pajama pants, he was bare-chested, barefoot and looked as if he had only towel dried his tousled hair. His chin and cheeks were covered with a growth of beard.

I sat the plate down on the table and looked over at him. His eyes met mine for a brief moment before they veered away and he settled uncomfortably in a chair.

"Thanks," he mumbled.

"You're welcome," I said, watching him take a bite.

He closed his eyes and chewed slowly as if savoring the flavors that gathered across his tongue. Knowing by his appearance that he hadn't bothered with satisfying an appetite for food in his absence I wasn't surprised at the rate he consumed the contents on his plate. I felt joy in my heart for his return but deep down I wondered if any of us would ever be the same as before.

Upon finishing, he carefully laid the fork on the table but continued to stare down at the plate as if it might somehow inexplicably refill itself.

"More?" I asked.

Although he remained looking downward, he shook his head in refusal. Reaching to remove the empty plate, his hand shot out and grasped my wrist. Stunned, I looked down at him in an attempt to read his face but he remained gazing vacantly at the empty plate. When he spoke, his voice was a harsh whisper.

"There are things that I need to say."

The tight grip of his fingers caused the skin of my arm to whiten and I winced but he didn't seem to take notice. "You don't need to …. not right now," I replied uneasily and wondered if he could hear or sense it in my voice.

When he finally turned his eyes up to mine there was something cold and unfeeling that inhabited the unsettled gray that struck fear in my heart. Releasing my wrist he stood unexpectedly and towered above me, his chest rising and falling as if agitated. Confused, I stepped back but he was upon me rapidly, his hands like vices on my shoulders.

"Jeremy?" I uttered, the uncertainty obvious in the pitch of my tone. It was then that he released me and sank to his knees. I saw the unmistakable sobs that racked his body as he crouched there, his head hanging limply in his despair.

Overwhelmed by his sudden outburst of emotion, I fell to my knees and drew him into my arms in an attempt to console his distress. Pushing his face deep into the side of my neck I could feel the wetness of his tears against my skin, his body trembling. The hot tears fell from my eyes as well while I held him.

When finally his body calmed and he pulled back, I brushed away the tears that remained on his face with my fingertips.

"I'm sorry," he said softly, the deep shadows gone now from his face.

"There's no sorry," I answered, as I cupped his rough cheek in my hand. Looking down, he enclosed my hand in his and rubbed his thumb across my palm before standing and hoisting me upward beside him.

"Shane's here?" he said simply turning toward the closed bedroom door.

I knew it wasn't really a question. Jeremy's senses would have detected Shane's presence as soon as he came through the door.

"This will take time," I explained, "For both of you."

"He's hiding from me?" he responded with slight amusement in his voice although no satisfaction seemed to come from it.

"No." I defended shaking my head. "You know that's not the case."

Jeremy nodded, acknowledging that what I said held truth. He knew it wasn't fear that kept Shane concealed behind the closed door.

"I'm going to lie down for a while." he said as he walked away, leaving me standing alone in the kitchen.

I felt caught in a spider web where all of our emotions created the thin, wispy strands that could be easily destroyed by the powerful hand of reaction. All that I could do was wait, watch and hope that our lives could somehow return to normal...whatever normal might be.

Shane stood on the opposite side of the bedroom door, his hands gripping the edges of the frame, white knuckled as he leaned his forehead against the dark wood. It had taken all of his self restraint to not charge in and cut short the tearful reunion that was occurring beyond his realm of control.

Keen hearing had already confirmed what he had imagined. The soft thud as knees made contact with the floor, the muffled cries and sharp intakes of breath. He sighed and backed away until the calves of his legs hit the bed and then he sat. He wasn't hiding....no matter if Jeremy believed it or not. The truth was, he was fearful of his reaction when he and Jeremy finally came face to face.

Chapter 40

Nearly two full days passed while Jeremy remained hidden away inside his room. Concerned, I would occasionally crack open the door and peer inside and I would find him there, his long legs twisted in the sheets, his breathing steady as he slept out his exhaustion. I would back out and quietly pull the door closed. On the evening of the second day as Shane and I sat down for dinner, we heard the opening click of the bedroom doorknob. Our eyes met briefly across the table and I prepared myself for the worst.

Without speaking, I mounded a plate with food and sat in down in front of him. He looked up at me and nodded in thanks which I reciprocated with a nod of my own. Shane continued to eat without as much as a glance in his direction and the room became unbearably tense. I found that I had suddenly lost my appetite and got up to remove my plate to the sink, stopping midway as Jeremy spoke.

I felt my heart sink inside my chest.

"I'll have my things packed and be gone by tomorrow afternoon."

I whirled around, *No!* I screamed inside.

Shane had lowered his fork and for the first time was staring directly into Jeremy's face.

"No," he responded, one single syllable from deep down in his throat, "You're not going to run from this," he growled.

Jeremy glared back, "I *will* be leaving tomorrow."

Shane pitched forward in his chair, something wild and threatening in his face, "Just walk away...that's how you want to handle it? That's how weak you've become?"

Jeremy stood and picked up his plate in a calm effort to refuse to let Shane get underneath his skin; his decision had been made. He had made it the day he had returned and before he had lapsed into exhausted sleep.

Shane's fist slammed forcefully down onto the table as he leapt to his feet. In one quick movement, his hand swept the plate from Jeremy's hands and it crashed to the tile and skidded across the floor in shards and splinters of glass.

All that I could do was watch, powerless to derail the oncoming locomotive that I could see bearing down rapidly from the horizon. To add my perspective to the hostility that existed in the room would be to invite bedlam down on myself. I wanted no part of it.

All that I could hope was that they wouldn't kill each other.

The two stood toe to toe now, both men tensed and ready.

"You don't want this Shane," Jeremy said matter of fact. I could only detect a slight hint of agitation in his voice but he refused to let his gaze falter, only inches from Shane's face. I witnessed Shane's rapid intake of breath as the alpha in him demanded Jeremy's obedience, but Jeremy would have none of it.

"You're wrong," Shane snarled, "I do want it." With those words barely out of his mouth, he launched his body into Jeremy's.

I recoiled from the clash, backing away until the countertop dug into my back and blocked any further retreat. With each blow I watched with horror as the blood formed in lines across their faces and dripped from their noses and lips. I was incapable of turning away but instead watched helplessly as they continued their battery on one another.

They pushed and pummeled each other throughout the cabin until Shane's body was hurled against the front door, flinging it loosely from its hinges as he fell outside. Jeremy pursued him and I moved quickly to the gaping open hole just in time to see the two crash through the deck railing onto the ground.

The struggle continued for nearly a half hour until both were exhausted, bruised and covered in each other's blood. With chests heaving, body's weak and sore, the pace had ultimately dwindled and they moved now as if in slow motion. In one last indolent collision, they gripped one another by the shoulders and swayed there while each pushed for the upper hand.

As suddenly as it had been instigated, it was over. They broke apart, Jeremy leaning over with his hands on his thighs breathing heavily and Shane with his hands on his hips looking downward, appearing crushed.

Relief flooded over me and I prayed that this interlude was the end of it, but I was wrong. After a few moments of rest Jeremy straightened and with unexpected swiftness landed one last strike to Shane's face that pitched him to the ground. Lying on his back with his knees bent he gasped, trying to catch his breath while Jeremy stumbled over to stand above him. I felt a looming sense of dread and inhaled sharply, waiting.

When Shane opened his eyes he looked up into Jeremy's bloodily battered and beaten face, their eyes locked and for a few seconds, neither moved. They had scuffled in their younger days but nothing as serious as where this fight had taken them. He couldn't help but wonder if, in Jeremy's state of mind he would now intend to end him. But as he continued to stare into the tenacious gray eyes he saw a glimmer of humility there and a smile that barely touched the edges of his mouth. Jeremy extended a blood-spattered hand down toward him which he seized without pause.

    I turned back into the cabin relieved then and allowed them their privacy. Too many years and memories existed between them that I knew little about and should not expect to be made a part of. I started picking up some of the items that hadn't fared too well during the passing by of the brawl; some were salvageable but others were not. By the time I heard the footsteps on the deck I had most of the cabin back in order.

    Exhausted, they both stood and attempted to catch their breaths; powerfully lean bodies smudged and smeared with grime and blood, "Why didn't you tell me?" Shane managed to stammer between sharp gasps of air.

    Still clad in pajama pants and bare foot, Jeremy gazed over at him, "I didn't want you to know," he said between pants.

    Shane's eyes narrowed in a confused response, "Why is that, exactly?"

    Jeremy's face hardened and he stared at Shane. Feeling the eyes penetrating through his skull, Shane looked back at him, "It was letting you down," Jeremy said, "What you thought of me.... "

    Shane closed his eyes slowly and looked away, shaking his head, "You were afraid I would be disappointed...in you?"

    Still breathing hard, Jeremy replied, "You live your life in perfection Shane...... you rarely make mistakes," he said, "Every move you make is cool and calculated...thought out," he paused, "I'm not like that."

    "I've always known how you are. Why would you think it would ever make any difference?" Shane asked.

    "Jasmine begged you to change Paul, but you weighed it out and decided it wasn't worth the risk. Not just for you, but for her and for him....so you refused, "his face mirrored his inner turmoil, "I didn't care about the risk to either of them....even though I knew how you felt about it."

    Shane wasn't sure what he was supposed to say. It was true, he had refused Jasmine's requests and eventually had even refused her pleas. Did he think less of Jeremy for agreeing to do what he wouldn't?

    Perhaps.

"You think you don't live up to my standards, is that it?"

"I know that I don't," Jeremy replied, his voice calm.

Out of the blue, Shane's laughter filled the choked air between them. It was an obscenely strange sound that didn't fit in amidst the two blood covered men.

"Nobody does," he said, returning once again to a more serious tone, "I never expected you to live up to my standards….But I didn't think that you would keep something like this from me just because you thought I'd think less of you."

Minutes ticked by as the two tried to catch their breaths and allow time for the tumultuous beatings of their hearts to quiet.

"I think you broke my nose," Jeremy said suddenly, breaking the silence as his fingers moved carefully across the bony bridge. He wiped the blood from underneath it with a swipe of his hand.

"I'm pretty sure my ribs are cracked," Shane answered as he attempted to straighten his upper body but then bent back over slightly, hands on his hips and a grimace on his face.

Jeremy returned to their conversation as if he hadn't missed a beat, his eyes probing Shane's face, "Where does this leave us then?"

"The same place that that we always are," he responded, "brothers."

The door hung only by the top hinge at a lopsided angle and as they passed through. I should have been appalled by their appearances but after being a spectator of the beating that each had been subjected to, their bloody faces and bodies did little to have an effect on me. Shane headed toward the bathroom while Jeremy wandered into the kitchen and sat down next to the first aid kit that I had already retrieved. When he looked at me I could see the slightly contorted curve of his once perfectly straight nose.

Handing him a dampened towel, I watched as he moved it carefully across his cheeks and forehead avoiding the mid section of his face altogether.

"What are you going to do about that?" I asked.

"You're going to line it up so it heals straight," he stated, "I can't have a crooked nose…..not on *this* face," he chuckled.

I assumed then that the conversation had gone well between the two. His humor had returned in all of its wondrous glory and I found myself giggling in response…maybe giggling with relief as well.

Shane came in and settled in a chair on the opposite side of the table. He had cleaned his face and stripped off the torn, blood stained white shirt, exposing bruises that were already turning dark blue along the line of his ribs. The white of his left eye was speckled with red and the skin around it was beginning to darken indicating that a black eye was in his near future, but in all, he seemed...happy. A slight smile edged its way to the corners of his lips curling them upward in a barely noticeable manner as he started to bandage his midsection.

I wasn't sure if I should shatter the tranquility that now existed in the silence between them, but I also couldn't stop wondering. Gathering my nerve, I decided to just blurt it out.

"So....."I began, leaning as casually as I could against the counter in an attempt to mask my nervousness, "Is everything....good?" I felt the intense current of their eyes on my face and the heated redness that crept up my neck and into my cheeks. Turning and walking away quickly, I was instantly sorry I hadn't kept my mouth closed.

"Hey," Jeremy snapped toward my retreating backside.

Wheeling around, I saw the smug look on his face. He held out his arms and shrugged, "My nose?" He asked sarcastically.

My apprehension was promptly dashed and replaced with agitation. While glaring back at him and before I could reply with my own bit of attitude, his cocky demeanor vanished and he smiled.

"Could you?"

Sighing, I moved back across the kitchen, "I see the asshole has returned," I paused, "But I'm kind of glad to see him." I leaned over him and examined his nose, touching it gently causing him to flinch, "You know this is going to hurt, right?"

Shane shifted to my side, looking with concern down into Jeremy's face, "Do you want me to do it?"

Jeremy's eyes darted back and forth between us anxiously. "Look, I don't really care who does it, somebody just do it so I'm not stuck with this," he growled, motioning toward his face.

Grabbing the role of tape out of the first aid box, I cut off a strip long enough that it would stretch from one side of his nose to the other. Sticking it on the edge of the table so that it was readily available, I turned my attention once again to his nose. I was halted by Shane's insistent hand on my forearm.

"Do you want me to do this?" He asked.

I shook my head in refusal.

Jeremy was worried, I could see it in the concerned depth of his eyes as I deliberated on the best course of action to take. Placing an index finger on both sides of the nasal bridge, I looked again into his eyes.

"Are you ready?"

"Just do it," he snarled.

"Ok....On three."

I steadied my fingers firmly against the bone.

"One.......two......." and then I pushed in from both sides as hard and as quickly as I could.

Jeremy's eyes scrunched together and the blood began to pour from both nostrils as he roared with pain.

"What the fuck happened to three???" He screamed while I snatched the tape and pressed it onto his newly straightened nose. Shane grabbed a towel and held it carefully against Jeremy's upper lip in an attempt to catch some of the blood.

"I got it, I got it," Jeremy spouted as he reached up and took hold of the towel. Shane let his hand fall away and he took a couple of steps backward.

Caught up in the seriousness of the task at hand, none of them had heard Tristan's silent progression across the living room and into the kitchen where he had stood quietly; watching with concern. There had been no door on which to knock which had initially alarmed him, so he had cautiously made his way toward the voices.

We were startled when he spoke from his position by the entryway.

"What happened here?"

My head jerked in the direction of his voice and Shane reeled around to face him. It was then that I saw his eyes assess the beginnings of Shane's worsening black eye, the bandages wrapped tightly around his ribs and the full view of Jeremy's blood covered face.

"What *did* happen here?" He came in for a closer look, his face paling as he took in the damage, "Who got a hold of you two?"

It wasn't my place to explain what had happened and I averted my eyes from question. Shane met my gaze for a brief moment before he looked back in Tristan's direction but still didn't speak. I could see the unrest move across Tristan's face.

"We....uh........we got a hold of each other," Shane answered awkwardly.

"I'm a bit surprised to see him," Tristan said honestly as he motioned towards Jeremy, who still had the towel pushed up against nose, his eyes never leaving Shane's.

"I wondered if he'd come back."

Lena and Zoey moved cautiously into view at the kitchen entry way, "Is everything alright?" Lena asked, her eyes resting fearfully on Jeremy. As if he picked up on their apprehension, Jeremy removed the towel momentarily from his bleeding nose and looked directly at Lena.

"Look, I apologize for my behavior from before......." he said sympathetically, "I don't expect that everyone just get over it and move on like nothing happened…. but not one of you in this room has reason to fear me."

Shane's eyes traveled over the family in the doorway. He understood their skepticism and apprehension. "When we get lined out here, let's all sit down and talk."

"I just wanted to come and tell you good-bye," Lena answered softly, "I have to catch a plane in three hours back to Minnesota."

Feeling instant sadness with her statement, I walked towards her, "You're leaving already?" I asked, a bit broken hearted as I stared into the pale blue eyes.

She nodded sadly and wrapped her arms around me.

"Can't you just stay a while longer?"

"I wish that I could," she answered, her voice full of emotion, "But I want to get back."

Zoey stood quietly in the doorway, her eyes taking in the tearful good-bye, and she understood all too well how Lena's departure could be so upsetting. Her sister had been the substitution for her mother since she was three years old and had taken care of her in every aspect that a mother could. She would feel the loss more than anyone else, but she wouldn't allow the evidence of it to show. Casting her eyes to the floor, she shoved her hands in her pockets.

Breaking our embrace, I moved away. Lena's empty arms were quickly filled by Shane who hugged her briefly and then held her out at arm's length.

"You can always come back here," he said sincerely, "There will always be room for you…and your mate if you so decide."

Slightly embarrassed by Shane's show of affection, Lena blushed, "I appreciate that Shane. One never knows what the future holds, do we?"

Shane shook his head. "No, no we don't."

Jeremy had gotten up from his chair and moved closer, intent on saying his good-bye as well. Taking note of Tristan's quick side step from his path, he didn't make comment but continued until he was face to face with Lena. Her eyes only met his for a split second before she looked away and in that short time he could easily read her fearful hesitation. Reaching down, he grasped her hand lightly in his, which she tentatively allowed.

"I'm sorry Lena," he said, "I hope that one day you can forgive the monster that I am."

Her eyes immediately shot back to his face.

"I don't think that you're a monster Jeremy," she said softly. "Every one of us has the potential to be violent….but that doesn't make any of us monsters."

She clasped his hand with both of hers, smiled and for the first time, held his gaze. In that small moment of compassion that she showed to him, as he stared into the pale blue eyes, Jeremy realized that the sound of her voice and the depth of her eyes leant a powerful fuel to his memory.

Little Fork……..Minnesota…he had been there when he was seventeen…there had been a woman with long blonde hair, pale blue eyes……the name, what was her name??? Finding that he had held her hand for far too long and she had grown uncomfortable, he backed away with his disturbing thoughts.

"Have a safe trip Lena," he said before he retreated back to his chair, lost within the whirlwind of a memory that he now struggled to recall in detail.

"When you get back from taking Lena to the airport, why don't you and Zoey come back by," Shane asked, "I think we all need to sit down and work through some things."

Tristan nodded, "Will do."

Together, the three siblings left and I followed them to the cavernous wide hole that used to have a door, and watched them vanish down the driveway. I already missed her.

Shane came up behind me and placed his arms around my waist. "You okay?"

"Yeah," I answered, "It was just nice having a female friend around."

Chapter 41

The spring gave way to dryer weather and the house that Shane had promised began to take shape. He spared no expense and between he, Jeremy, Tristan and the construction crew, the house was near completion by mid August.

At night it stood silhouetted against the starlit sky, a dark looming form that drew the attention of passerby's as if it were a silent, but somehow beckoning beacon. The stone exterior was composed of a variety of earth colored rock browns, tans and grays that reflected natural beauty and finished with logs, inside and out.

It reminded me of beautiful lodge and I found myself excitedly waiting for the day that we moved in for good. The only question that remained now was what to do with the existing cabin, and my parent's lake house; both too good to be left sitting empty.

Jeremy's initial sketched plans were followed closely, leaving rooms that were spacious and equivalent to small living quarters, each equipped with its own bathroom. Shane and I would share a room, Jeremy, Tristan and Zoey would each have their own on the same level, which left several empty. There were areas for entertaining or lounging along with a spacious, well equipped kitchen and a dining room that appeared to have the capability to seat an army. It was a house that I could get lost in….if I hadn't had a hand in creating it.

Michael and Jeanette had returned as they had pledged, and Shane fulfilled his promise which took place without incident, thanks to Jeremy. Since it was all in the exchange of blood, we subdued Shane's wolf and Jeremy used a knife to make the wounds in the flesh of both the wolf and Michael. When the blood flowed freely, it wasn't difficult to transfer it from one to the other. Although not completed in the strict traditional manner of pack law, this was Shane's pack and he made the laws; or so he told me.

Zoey came around over the course of a few months and I wondered if I had become an acceptable substitute for Lena. Regardless, we became close and I found that I appreciated the extra help with choosing color schemes and decorating for the new house. Jeremy's interest in her was unnerving at times but not in a stalker, perverted kind of way. He was watchful yet wary at the same time and I wondered what was happening within the hidden workings of his brain. Things were so hectic with the house that we rarely had a moment to explore it. Shane had openly discussed his plans for Zoey and in the fall, with Tristan's approval, he would be sending her to school in Chicago.

It was strangely surreal how the pieces of the puzzle that was my life had seemed to fall smoothly into place. A year before, I had no family. With the chance encounter of the black wolf, my life was now filled with people that I felt strongly loyal to, and people that I loved. I often wondered what my life would be like if I hadn't met the beast…where would I be now? Shane had been my saving grace, and with him had come a responsibility not only to him, but to the others that were now a part of my life. Embracing it, I moved anxiously forward, ready to start the next chapter of my life.

Moving day came and we spent an entire day afternoon gathering up my belongings from my parent's cabin. After a couple of days of getting those things situated, we went to Tristan's and helped him and Zoey load their own items. Shane and Jeremy brought their things over in small spurts; some clothes here, towels there….when they had a need for something they disappeared to Shane's cabin to retrieve it.

Packing in some of Tristan and Zoey's boxes, I placed them in their chosen rooms with the assumption that they would unpack them in their own time. Zoey had demanded a pale purple room with black curtains and matching black furniture and oddly, Shane had accommodated, readily giving her what she asked for without hesitation. Tristan had given me the freedom to do whatever I wanted to his room and I had picked neutral, masculine colors that I hoped would satisfy him.

Jeremy hauled several boxes up to Zoey's room and numerous more to Tristan's. On one of his various trips, one particular box slipped from his grip on his way up the stairs, spilling its contents across the newly carpeted floor. Thankful that the items inside had a soft landing and didn't break, he begin picking them up and placing them back in the box. There were several pictures and he glanced over them as he carefully set them back inside the box until he got to one particular photograph and then he stopped.

It was a family portrait of a couple and three children, all fair-haired and with light complexions. The man was stall and sturdy, a strong set in his jaw and incriminating dark eyes. The children were unmistakably Tristan, Lena and Zoey; their chubby familiar faces obvious even to him. As his eyes swept over the woman in the photograph, he recognized her instantly.

Dawn.

Jeremy dropped the picture to the soft pad of the carpet and stared down at it. Vague recollections surged forward and all of the familiarity that he previously recognized began to fill in the missing cracks of his memory.

Little Fork, Minnesota.

He had been seventeen years old at the time he had gone there; young, rebellious and wild. In an attempt to seek out the missing parts of his life, his journey had led him to the small town on the trail of his father which seemed to elude him at every turn. Always a few days ahead of Jeremy's inquiries, he would disappear like a phantom in the mist, leaving him to sink even further into hopelessness. Dawn had come into his life then, at his worse moment when he was ready to give up.

She was working at a bar called *The Hideaway* when he met her. Knowing he was underage but sensing their "similarities", she had served him the drinks he asked for, beneath an attentive eye. As closing time came around and he was nearly passed out on the bar, Dawn had helped him to her car and took him home with her. She managed to help him inside and sit him down at the table.

"I'm making some coffee," Dawn said, "You're going to drink some of it, understand?"

The entire room was a blurry memory, but Jeremy shook his head. "Okay," he mumbled. He could hear her moving busily around the small kitchen and then she disappeared for a few moments. Upon returning, he could smell freshly laundered clothes and knew that she had changed from the cigarette smoke tainted outfit of earlier; the lingering evidence of her job.

The next thing he remembered was the full cup of coffee sat down in front of him.

"Drink some of this," Dawn insisted.

Jeremy did as she told him, bringing the steaming liquid to his lips. Being greatly under the influence of alcohol, he drank deeply and the burning coffee scalded his mouth and throat.

"Damn!" He scowled, slamming the cup back down on the table and spilling part of its contents.

"Hey, "she said softly, "Take it easy….small sips." She retrieved a dish towel and wiped up the spill.

Again, he did as she demanded and when half of the cup was emptied, he felt a bit more alert. Leaning back in the kitchen chair, he looked at her inquisitively, "Why'd you bring me here?"

A light, easy smile graced her attractive face, "I couldn't leave you at the bar," she answered, "What's your name?"

"Jeremy."

"Dawn," she said kindly, in a soft spoken voice.

"You seem lost Jeremy."

Jeremy's eyes wandered over the woman in the chair beside him and his young body responded as her pale blue eyes awaited his answer. Blonde hair framed her lovely face and although significantly older than he was, she was beautiful in a wise, worldly- educated way.

"I've been looking for my father," he responded.

"Your father?" She asked softly, "When is the last time you saw him?"

Jeremy shrugged, "I've never met him."

Dawn raised a delicate eyebrow in question, "What makes you think you'll find him here?"

"I may never find him," he admitted, "But I need to know where I came from."

Dawn smiled then, a kind-hearted, gentle knowing smile.

"You come from here," she said as she patted her chest where underneath her hand, Jeremy could hear the isolated beating of her heart. "It doesn't matter who your father is ….it's who *you* are that matters most,"she paused, "Knowing who he is won't change who you are to become."

Jeremy didn't know what to say but instead let the meaning of her words sink in. Her hand moved across the table and came to rest on his reassuringly and during that fleeting moment when their eyes locked, a mutual understanding passed between them.

Jeremy had spent the night wrapped within the comforting security of her arms and the rest was history.

Holy Mother, Jeremy thought to himself as the fragments began to assemble together. Dawn was Lena and Tristan's mother….and Zoey's. He remembered that Lena had told him once that Zoey had a different father although she carried the Taylor name. His mind drifted back to the response of his body when he touched her…..his blood reacting to his blood, the attitude, her emotionless expression…… *Oh shit.* He quickly did the math in his head.

"You alright?" Shane's voice cut in, startling him as he passed by and sat another box down in Tristan's room. When he turned back, Jeremy still stood silently looking at the frame in his hand, his face pale.

"Hey, you alright?" He asked again.

Jeremy raised his eyes slowly to him then, the shock evident as he shook his head slowly. "I'm not sure," he pushed the picture toward Shane who took it and looked down at it.

"Nice family," he paused, "What am I looking at here, Jeremy?"

"Tristan's family," he answered.

Shane was confused; he already knew it was Tristan's family.

"Okay," he said as he peered at him with puzzlement, "I know that….what about it?"

"The mother……her name is Dawn," Jeremy muttered.

The impatience was apparent in Shane's voice, "You need to get to the point here Jer," Shane said, "I don't know where you're going with this."

"I think that Zoey may belong to me."

Shane's eyes narrowed, "Belong to you? Like your……..child?"

"I knew her mother…………well," he answered, "Lena said that she has a different Dad."

"So you automatically think it's you?" Shane asked, "Geez…..Lena is twenty-five…that would make her mother like…………."

"Forty-two," Jeremy answered before Shane could figure it out in his head, "I was seventeen."

Their conversation came to an abrupt halt as Tristan came up the steps behind them.

"Hey, what's taking you two so long? There are plenty of boxes left on the truck," he chuckled.

Shaking off his thoughts, Jeremy smiled uneasily, "Yeah, yeah, on my way," he hurried away down the steps.

Tristan's eyes moved to the picture frame in Shane's hand and he looked up at him questioningly.

"Oh, sorry, this fell out of the box," Shane said.

Tristan nodded and took it from Shane's outstretched hand.

"Nice looking family," Shane said, "If you don't mind me saying, you've never really mentioned your parents."

Tristan looked uncomfortable. "Our mother fell ill when Zoey was two. She died a year later," he paused, "Our father raised her until she was about twelve and then disappeared. Lena and I think that he went away to die….he was heartbroken when mom passed."

"I'm sorry Tristan, I had no idea."

"I know," Tristan replied, "It's painful for us to talk about…..so we just don't."

Shane nodded in understanding, "What about Zoey's Dad? Lena told Jeremy that she has a different father. Where is he?"

Jeremy shrugged, "We don't know. Mom didn't make it a secret that she wanted another child. Dad couldn't give that to her so she went elsewhere," he quickly added, "That was acceptable in our pack if one of the pair couldn't reproduce."

"I think its common all across the board," Shane answered, "I'm not sure how I would feel about it personally."

"Dad was always partial to Zoey. Especially after mom passed……I think he felt he was closest to mom through her since she was the youngest……crazy, huh?"

Shane shook his head, "Not at all."

Making my last trip up the steps to Zoey's room, I found Tristan and Shane having a serious conversation in the hallway. It stopped as their eyes fell on me and until I made my way past them. Wondering what was going on, I sent a message to Shane.

You two are so serious, what's happening?

I put the box in Zoey's room and sat down on her bed, exhausted. Jeremy had followed me up the stairs and came into the room, placing another box down next to the pile.

Everything is fine, Shane's reply came clearly.

"I'm glad we don't have to unpack this stuff," I said jokingly.

"Yeah, no kidding. For a kid she has a lot of crap." Jeremy answered, glancing around the purple room, "So, you guys sleeping here tonight?"

I nodded, "Yep. You?"

Jeremy nodded in return, "Sure am," he paused, "How about we cook up a meal tonight? We haven't all sat down as a family and eaten here yet."

"That sounds good. What are you cooking?" I joked and he quirked an eyebrow in my direction.

"I'll help," he grinned and together we descended the steps and crossed the living room to the kitchen. Still overwhelmed by the huge space that the kitchen offered, I found myself excited by the idea of actually getting to use it. Together, Jeremy and I decided on dinner and began to prepare for it.

      All joined together at the large heavy oak table, Shane beamed as his eyes drifted over his family. He was proud at what they had accomplished in the short time he had been in the area. Elisa sat to his immediate left and Jeremy was to his right while Zoey and Tristan both sat on Elisa's side of the table. The food was spread out before them and they ate hungrily after their full day of packing and unpacking everyone's belongings. He was happier now than he ever remembered being; he had finally found where he belonged.

      Hearing Jeremy's sigh, he turned to his friend. With the prior knowledge of what was getting ready happen, he braced himself.

      Jeremy cleared his throat and stood up, "I'd like to say a couple of things." The family's eyes turned in his direction. "I just want to say……..I hope that we can all live in this house and not kill each other," he paused, chuckling lightly, "and I'm happy to call each and every one of you family."

      His eyes fell on Zoey who watched him intently as she chewed.

      "Some of us are acquired family…….while some of us are blood." He looked at me briefly before returning his gaze to the young girl and sighed deeply. "There is no way to put this delicately, and we all know that I'm far from that….So, I'm just going to say it and let the consequences fall where may."

      Inquisitive eyes now waited anxiously for his announcement. "Zoey, I'm your father."

      Shane watched as first Tristan and Zoey exchanged confused looks before both stared back at Jeremy. Elisa's mouth hung slightly ajar, her eyes wide with surprise as she gaped at Jeremy and then to him.

      You knew, her words came plainly to his mind. He nodded in response. The room remained silent but Shane could feel the tension closing in. Tristan was the first to speak, his voice was surprisingly low and calm and not at all what Shane had expected.

      "How do you know?" He asked.

      "When I was seventeen, I went to Little Fork," Jeremy began. "I met a woman who was bartending at a place called *The Hideaway*…..her name was Dawn," he paused before looking directly at Tristan, "Was that your mother's name?"

"Yes. Her name was Dawn," Tristan replied skeptically, "But just because you had a fling with a woman named Dawn doesn't mean it was our mother."

"She's the woman in your family portrait Tristan. And it wasn't like that......" Jeremy defended harshly, "She wasn't a woman to have "a fling" with….she was beautiful and kind," he paused, "And she saved a desperate kid from spending the rest of his life in search of something that really didn't matter."

"I think he may be right," Zoey spoke for the first time, "I think he may be telling the truth."

"Why? Why do you think that?" Tristan demanded, his agitation turned on his sister.

"The couple of times that we've touched, I've felt something……strange," she answered.

"I felt it too," Jeremy added, "But I didn't know what it was……..until this fell into my lap."

"Why didn't you ever mention it?" Tristan asked, his eyes still held on his sibling.

"I didn't think it meant anything……but now, I guess it actually did." She was unexpectedly calm and emotionless as she picked up her fork, "Well, that's that."

She took another bite of her dinner.

Surprised by this new turn of events, I sat there gawking back and forth with the conversation and now, Zoey's reaction was anything but the one I would have expected. She was aloof; indifferent. Tristan glared across the table at Jeremy who continued to stand, staring back across the table at Zoey.

"Maybe we should all talk about this?" Shane's voice broke the silence.

Zoey looked up to meet his inquiring gaze and shrugged, "What's to talk about?"

"How do you feel about this?" He asked.

"Nobody kept it a secret that Richard wasn't my real father," she said, "He's the only Dad that I have ever known and he was a damn good one."

Her suddenly accusing gaze settled on Jeremy, "Just because I have your blood and your genes, it won't ever make you my Dad…..my father maybe, but not my Dad."

Good, she was finally allowing some emotion to leak through, Shane thought. Tristan somewhat relaxed in his chair apparently convinced that Zoey would handle this on her own.

"I don't expect it to," Jeremy said before she continued.

"And I hope that you don't have the false notion that you will now wield some kind of power over me."

"I have no such notion," Jeremy said, his expression was one of surprise at her directness.

Pretentiously she added, "So you and I understand one another, right?"

Shane tried to muffle a chuckle with the back of his hand. He couldn't believe that he hadn't seen the similarities between the two of them before. This was going to prove to be quite interesting………..

Strangely and unexpectedly, Jeremy replied in a calm manner, "Yes, I think we do understand one another." With that, he sat back down and picked up his fork and continued eating.

I stared at each one of them. Even Tristan had continued eating and I was still shocked over the latest news. Glancing back at Shane, he was smiling at me.

"So….no one wants to talk about this at all?" He asked again.

"Nope," Jeremy answered.

"No," Tristan said.

"You're asking this, *again*?" Zoey said smartly.

Shane cocked an eyebrow in her direction, "I don't care how you speak to your father...but I still demand your respect," he chuckled but remained stern.

"Sorry," she mumbled apologetically.

Chapter 42

August came and we said our good-byes as Shane headed to Chicago with Zoey. After her first change, he had spent hours and days with her, coaching her, instructing her and running with her. I saw a glimpse of his fatherly potential during that time and I couldn't help smiling with the knowledge that one day, he would apply it to our own children.

The school that she would attend was one especially for our kind. That facility would teach her everything that she needed in order to survive in a world where we were not readily accepted, or recognized. She would be taught respect, discipline and how to survive without the support and structure of a pack. When she was finished there, she would leave as a self sufficient, well rounded individual.

From the window of our bedroom, I watched with complete wonder and curiosity as the white limousine crept slowly up the driveway toward Edgewoods. *Who could this be?*

Jeremy stood at the corner of the detached garage, shirtless and sweaty from working on the landscaping and like me; he observed the vehicle's advance with intrigue. It came to a rolling stop in front of the house and I saw him stride hesitantly but curiosity towards it. The driver, complete in a black suit stepped out and tipped his hat in Jeremy's direction.

Opening the door for his passenger, the gentleman extended a gloved hand and withdrew it confidently fastened on the well manicured fingers of a woman. Pulling her from the car, her classily tailored outfit with matching hat and shoes was the first thing that I noticed. Jeremy stepped forward then, a brilliant smile on his face as he embraced the woman and I detected a hint of silver hair beneath the edge of her hat as she lifted her head in an accepting embrace.

"Mother," Jeremy said as he welcomed her with open arms.

"Jeremy, my boy," she said affectionately, and without hesitation enclosed his sweaty, dirt covered body in her responsive grasp.

"It's good to see you," Jeremy said, "Did Shane know you were coming?"

She pulled back from him and looked at him with kind eyes.

"No," she said, "I took it upon myself to make this little trip. I hope that I am not intruding."

"Never," Jeremy answered, smiling broadly but still with surprise, "But we could have been better prepared if we would have known."

"Prepared for what, my dear? I don't require special accommodations." Her eyes left his face and traveled over the house, falling upon the window where I stood looking down and then back to Jeremy's face, "Can't a mother come to see her boys?"

Jeremy grinned, "Of course. Let me show you inside and then I'll find Shane." He extended his hand and she placed hers within his.

Turning momentarily, she spoke to her driver.

"Charles, would you mind bringing my things inside?"

"Yes ma'am," Charles replied and moved toward the back of the limo.

Shane's mother? This was definitely an unexpected surprise!! He had spoken of her upon occasion and I thought that I would get to meet her one day.... I just hadn't expected her to show up on our doorstep! Running into the bathroom, I ran my fingers through my hair in an attempt to quickly smooth it and then evaluated my clothes. We had all been working outside and I was dressed in shorts and a simple, light t-shirt. If she could stand Jeremy's sweaty appearance, surely she wouldn't be offended by mine!

I crept downstairs slowly, hearing Jeremy's voice and the returning reply in the woman's melodic tones, I waited for my entrance. When there was a slight lull, I came down the steps into their view. Her eyes fell upon me and something unreadable passed across her face as her blue eyes assessed me, and then she smiled sweetly.

"Mother, this is Elisa," Jeremy said, "Elisa, this is Shane's mother, Carol."

Coming to stand beside Jeremy, I extended my hand politely towards her. She accepted it graciously and smiled back, the same dazzling white smile that she had passed down to her son.

"Elisa," she said softly, "So very nice to meet you," she paused, "And how do you fit into this picture, dear?"

"She's Shane's mate, Mother," Jeremy answered before I could speak. I shot a questionable glance toward him before returning my eyes to Carol. She was still smiling pleasantly but I thought I could see a odd flicker within the blue intensity of her eyes.

"Well," Carol replied in a slightly surprised tone, "My son isn't very forthcoming with important information, I see."

"Mother?" Shane's voiced boomed as he came in the back door of the house, Tristan on his heels.

Carol turned toward the sound of his voice and opened her arms to him, "My son," she said.

Shane looked at her strangely before a smile lit his features and he moved to embrace her. "What are you doing here?" He asked as he relinquished his hold and backed away.

"Apparently I would be waiting for years for you to make your way to Boston so I decided that if I wanted to see my son, I would have to come find him myself," Carol answered smugly.

"I wish you would have called," Shane said.

Charles came in the front door carrying Carol's luggage and sat it down, awaiting her next request for his services. Shane's eyes moved from him back to his mother inquiringly, "Are you planning on staying then?"

"It appears that you have the extra room," she said as she gazed around the interior of the house, "Unless that is a problem, dear."

Shane shook his head, "No, no. It isn't a problem." He turned toward the driver, "I'll show you where to put her things, Charles."

"Thank you Sir," he replied respectfully and followed Shane from the room.

Carol's attention then came back to Jeremy, and Tristan standing a few feet behind, "And who is this handsome young man?"

Tristan blushed and stepped forward, "Tristan, ma'am," he said.

"Tristan," she said pleasurably, "I'm Carol, Shane's mother." She reached her hand towards him which he accepted timidly.

"Very nice to meet you ma'am."

"Mrs. Mathews," I said, "Can I offer you something to drink?"

Blue eyes came back me. "That would be wonderful. It was a very long drive….but please, call me Carol."

I smiled and nodded. As we walked toward the kitchen, Shane and Charles met us in the entranceway of the kitchen.

"Charles, we have plenty of room if you'd like to bring your things inside," Shane said.

"Thank you Sir," Charles replied, "If you don't mind, it would be appreciated."

Shane stared at the driver. He was an older gentleman with kind, deep gray eyes and fading brown hair. "Please Charles, call me Shane."

"Yes Sir," Charles said and turned on his heel to retrieve his items out of the limo. Shane grinned at the man's retreating back and then followed the group into the kitchen. Elisa had poured a glass of lemon tea and was handing it to his mother. Jeremy and Tristan stood at the sink washing their hands and he saw his mother's scrutinizing gaze on their turned backs.

"Jeremy, dear," Carol said considerately, "The kitchen is not the proper place to be half dressed."

He turned, his face slightly red and nodded, "Yes ma'am." Immediately, he left the kitchen and I heard his footsteps as he crossed the living room and started up the steps.

Dear Lord, I thought to myself. Although kind and polite, Carol was obviously a force to be reckoned with and one who demanded a certain sense of respect from her sons. I had never seen Jeremy so passive and willing to please, and his odd behavior stunned me.

Meeting Shane's eyes, he looked at me skeptically as if he had read my mind and shrugged.

"I see you've already met Elisa," Shane directed toward Carol.

Sipping the tea delicately, she carefully sat the glass down on the countertop. "Yes Shane. She is quite charming." She smiled in my direction and glanced at me momentarily, "A beautiful girl."

She seemed to speak as though I wasn't standing right beside her. Shane moved to wrap his arm around my waist and leaning down, kissed me on the cheek.

"Yes, she is beautiful...and wonderful."

Carol smiled at her son. "You have built quite a home here," she said, "What are your plans?"

"I'm sure you've had a long trip, Mother," Shane intervened, "Why don't I show you to your room and you can get settled and rest before dinner. We can talk more then."

For a moment I could see that Carol wasn't pleased with her questions being swept to the wayside but she smiled and nodded.

"That's a fantastic idea," she paused, "Please, show me to my room." She pushed her hand toward Shane who took it in his own. Turning, he led her down the hallway away from the kitchen.

Once they were gone, I couldn't help but to comment.

"Wow," I said softly, "She is a very commanding woman." I looked over at Tristan who nodded solemnly but didn't say a word.

Jeremy came back into the kitchen wearing a clean blue t-shirt and had washed away the dirt from his face and arms. His eyes met mine and then he glanced away quickly as if he understood my confusion about his conduct. I couldn't help but stare at him and he grew impatient beneath my gaze.

"What?" He finally snapped.

Shaking my head I spoke, "I've just never known you to be so…….accommodating."

"This is the only time that you will," he answered, picking up a glass and filling it with tea, "Don't get any ideas."

What in the world did this woman have over these two? Yes, I agreed that one needed to be respectful of their parents but I found that I was strangely uncomfortable with the power she seemed to have over them. Secretly I hoped that she wouldn't try her motherly wiles on me….

"So, why are you really here, Mother?"Shane asked as he held the door open for Carol to enter her room. He followed her inside and shut the door as she turned and smiled.

"Why would you think that I was here for any other reason but to see my son? Do you not want me here?" She placed a gentle hand upon his arm, her voice slightly hurt.

"Of course I want you here," Shane answered, "I'm just a little surprised that you were able to find me."

Carol grinned sheepishly, "Son," she said, "You know that it doesn't matter where you go……I will always be able to find you." She embraced him then, and he returned her affectionate gesture.

"I've missed you."

"I've missed you too, Mother."

"Why haven't you called me to tell me about Elisa?" She asked as she dropped her arms from his shoulders.

Shane shrugged, "We've been busy here, as you can tell….and there's quite a story to go along with it."

"I'd like to hear it."

"You will," Shane paused, "How long are you planning on staying?"

"Until I've worn out my welcome and you tell me to go," Carol joked.

Shane smirked, "We'll talk more at dinner," he said and turned toward the door, leaving his mother alone in her room.

With Tristan and Jeremy's help, we prepared a meal fit for *Mother*. Maybe it was just me, but I felt a bizarre sense of discomfort in her presence even though she was nothing but polite to me. Possibly spurred by her obvious power over the two men and my inability to understand the controlling aspect of it, I had difficulty not trying to find some underlying reason for her unannounced visit. I was suspicious; very suspicious.

I couldn't talk to Shane or Jeremy about it and Tristan remained neutral and wouldn't be swayed by my doubtfulness. He was loyal to Shane and I accepted that I would continue to suffer through these distrustful feelings on my own.

During dinner, Shane explained to his mother how he had come to this point in his life, starting when he left Canada. He beamed when he told her about meeting me and I watched as she listened with an expressionless countenance. Jeremy joined in the conversation as it progressed to the time span that he had come to live with Shane and then found Tristan and his family. Shane told her about Zoey and how he had sent her to Chicago to attend the same school that he had gone to. Carol nodded periodically as she digested the information.

"I'm happier than I have ever been," Shane told her, "I couldn't imagine being anywhere other than right here." He smiled across the table at me and I returned it with a smile of my own.

"You've had quite a busy year, son," Carol replied, "I'm glad to see you happy."

Having been quiet for most of dinner, Tristan piped in. "Shane is an honorable leader," he said. "I couldn't be more pleased with him choosing me to be part of his pack."

Almost shyly, Shane smiled and nodded in Tristan's direction. "Thank you Tristan. I appreciate that...But I hope that you feel that I'm more than your leader."

Carol appeared annoyed and gazed over at Shane. "Son," she started, "As standing Alpha you have a responsibility to your pack. It is not about being on friendly terms with your subordinates."

Tristan stared at her for a brief moment before he turned his eyes from her cold gaze. The infamous nerve began to tick in the side of Shane's jaw and I waited for his rebuttal.

"With respect, Mother, I intend to build a solid foundation with all of my pack members."

Good, I thought to myself, he finally put her in her place.

Carol acknowledged his explanation with a quick nod and a raised eyebrow then stood abruptly, "If you'll excuse me."

She turned smoothly on her heel and made her way back through the hallway to her room leaving the rest of us in uncomfortable silence. Charles's eyes followed her as she exited the dining room, but he remained seated and continued with his meal.

Shane was agitated and we all could feel it. Jeremy glanced across the table towards me and our eyes locked.

That didn't go well, his voice came to me.

I nodded in agreement.

We finished dinner in stillness except for the sound of our silverware on the plates. With dinner out of the way, I began to clear the dishes and Charles came to my side for assistance.

"Charles, please, go and relax. You've had a long drive here and I'm sure you're tired," I said.

He looked at me strangely, "I will help with these, miss."

"I insist......Please," I reiterated and hesitantly he nodded, and took his leave.

Although everyone else had left the kitchen, Tristan stayed behind and helped me gather up the dirty dishes, scraping them and putting them in the dishwasher. I had a strange feeling that he was hanging back for a reason.

"I didn't want to say it," he said quietly, as he sidled up next to me where I was loading the dishwasher, "but I think you're right about her."

I glanced toward him anxiously, "Lets clean this up and take a walk," I said in a whisper, "We can talk outside."

He nodded and we finished in silence.

Chapter 43

Shane rapped lightly on Carol's closed door and waited for her to grant him entry. Hearing her voice, he opened the door and stepped inside. She regarded him with a cool fixed gaze as he walked toward where she sat on the edge of the bed.

"Mother, we need to talk," he said as he moved passed her to the window that overlooked the field on the wood line side of the house. He cocked his head inquisitively as he saw Elisa and Tristan cross the edge of the yard together and as his eyes followed them, he tried to dismiss the nagging feeling that something was askew. He turned back toward his mother.

"What is it that you want to talk about Shane? Your insolence?" She asked, "Is that what we shall talk about?" She stood up from her seat on the bed, her posture rigid.

Shane sighed heavily, "It may be difficult for you to understand," he said, "But this pack is my family. I have a deep respect and love for each one of them and I will not treat them as anything less than myself."

She was silent for a few moments as her blue eyes searched the similar colored depths of his. "You will never succeed with this small minded mentality," she replied, "Yes, you may remain Alpha of this," she waved her hand, indicating the house and its inhabitants, "But nothing more."

"I am happy with *this*," Shane extended both of his hands in a sweeping circle, "I want nothing else." The nerved ticked meticulously in his jaw.

Carol shook her head in disappointment, "You could be so much more, son."

Frustrated, Shane ran his hands through his thick, black hair. "Look," he snapped, "I'm glad that you're here but I suggest we talk no more of this....it will only ruin our time together."

Her reply was quick and it confounded Shane with its easy simplicity. "Agreed," she said plainly.

He looked up at her, astonished.

"Don't be so surprised, dear. I know when to accept defeat," she smiled.

Tristan and I walked side by side across the edge of the yard toward the garage, his voice low as he spoke, "There's something about her Elisa...I can't put my finger on it."

"I know," I said softly in return, "I thought that I was the only one to see it."

He shook his head. "No...you aren't. I just didn't want to rock the boat with her being Shane's mom and all."

Jeremy's voice startled us both as he stepped out from the garage bay, "So what's going on with you two?"

Feeling like a kid caught with my hand in the cookie jar, I couldn't think of a quick believable lie to cover the truth. I glanced over at Tristan, whose pale blue eyes watched for my lead.

"We....uh.........were talking about Zoey. She called earlier, you know?"

Jeremy's eyes narrowed as he tried to gauge my story, "You're lying," he said as he cocked his head to one side and grinned wickedly, "I can smell it."

"We're talking about Mother," Tristan answered, "Elisa and I aren't convinced that she's here for strictly the pleasure of visiting her son."

Crap! I thought to myself, now we were in for it....so much for Tristan being my new confidante.

"Shouldn't this be something that you two should be speaking to Shane about, not discussing amongst yourselves?" he asked smartly, his gray eyes boring into mine with intent and his eyebrow cocked as he waited for my reply.

"Of course," Tristan answered for me, "But she's his mother and we think that he's a little too close to be unbiased."

Jeremy turned his eyes on Tristan, "You said yourself that Shane is an honorable leader," he paused, "I believe those were your exact words....weren't they? Did you start to doubt his ability in the time since dinner?"

"Come on Jeremy, don't be an asshole," I said, "Just for argument's sake, how do *you* feel about her visit?"

His eyes studied me warily as if allowing himself enough time to come up with an answer that would satisfy our suspicions. "Talk to Shane," he finally said and turned back to the garage and disappeared inside.

I looked at Tristan who stared back. "Now what?" He asked.

"I don't know. Maybe I'm wrong....maybe we should just wait to see what happens," I answered.

Tristan shrugged, "Maybe."

Shane told me about the conversation that had occurred between them but a week passed by without any other occurrence. Carol's demeanor was friendly and light-hearted and I began to think that I had been unjustifiably suspicious. Her controlling, condescending attitude had vanished and had never returned after Shane had told her how he felt. Perhaps it was the concern of a mother for the well-being of her only son that had brought her to Edgewoods.

I found her to be quite interesting after we warmed up to one another and I thoroughly enjoyed the memories that she shared of Shane's childhood, and his father. Early on the following Sunday morning at breakfast, as we were all seated around the dining table, she told us she would be leaving that afternoon after she finished packing. Even I was a little sad at hearing she was planning to leave so quickly.

Gathered in the foyer as Charles carried her suitcases to the limo, we said our good-byes. She hugged each one of us warmly before indicating that she would like to talk with Shane alone. Jeremy, Tristan and I left the room, allowing them a moment of privacy in which to say their farewells. I saw Charles come back inside and shut the door behind him. It was his nervous glance in our direction that raised the hair on the back of my neck followed by a sudden feeling of doubt and returning suspicion.

Carol smiled up at her son after severing their private, parting embrace. His deep blue eyes looked down, meeting her own.

"I love you mother," he said, his deep voice emotional. Reaching upward, she placed a hand on each side of his face, the slight stubble poking into her palms.

"My beautiful, beautiful boy," she said, "I love you too." She pushed herself up onto her tiptoes and placed a kiss upon his lips...a kiss that he would never remember.

Shane placed his arms around his mother's frame and hugged her tightly. The week had started out rough but had taken a turn for the better once he made her understand that this was where he belonged. Never satisfied with what he would acquire, she had always pushed him to be better, to strive for more. Convincing her that he now had what he had longed for had been easier than he imagined it would be. She had accepted it gracefully and he was thankful that he would no longer have to defend his actions to her. As her lips settled lightly on his, he had only a fleeting thought that something wasn't right…….

"Mother!" Jeremy yelled as he rushed into the room with Tristan and I close behind. Charles stepped out to stop us, a pistol gripped in his right hand. Feeling confused and shocked, I felt lost to whatever was happening.

"Mr. Carrington, please don't make me have to kill you," he said calmly.

Past Jeremy's shoulder I could see Shane and his mother embraced and her face pressed against his in what appeared to be a kiss. It was an unsettling and unnatural gesture between a mother and a son………..

"Mother!" Jeremy bellowed again, "Mother, stop!!" He pushed forward, only to be halted again by Charles' firm pleas.

"Please, Sir," he said forcefully, "There's nothing you can do."

Not understanding what was happening but realizing the urgency in Jeremy's voice I immediately felt panic.

"Jeremy, what is happening?" I shrieked.

"Mother!!" Jeremy yelled again as he fell to his knees, his voice pleading.

The crushing alarm squeezed my lungs, restricting my breath as I watched Jeremy's face fall with helplessness. What was happening? Carol had stepped away from Shane and he stood there silently, his arms limp at his sides.

"How could you?" Jeremy screamed toward her back, "How could you do this to your son!"

She turned then, and came towards him, her face calm, reserved. Charles stood quietly in the corner of the room, the gun still held stiffly in his fingers.

"Jeremy," she said softly, her hand moving to caress his hair, "I had to." He shook his head and shrank from her touch, causing her hand to fall away.

"Why? Why would you?" He implored, his voice breaking as he spoke. The tears welled up in his eyes threatening to spill onto his cheeks.

"What is happening?!" I demanded to know as I searched their faces for answers. Beyond confusion, I could grasp that something horrible had happened, but I didn't understand.....I didn't have the knowledge or experience to comprehend the significance of the strange kiss that I had witnessed.

"She fogged him," Jeremy said softly as he turned his eyes toward me apologetically. The pain that I saw reflected within the gray depths, along with his words brought back the memory of the rogue and Andrea. It screamed loudly from my memory into my present conscience.

Shane had fogged Andrea to make her forget; to make her forget what she had seen. *His mother's gift,* he had told me. I began to tremble uncontrollably and although Tristan was even more confused than I was, he stepped forward and placed his hand reassuringly on my shoulder. *What did this mean? What did this mean?*

Carol turned back toward Shane who still stood quietly, his face blank, his eyes empty. "Go and pack your things, son."

His body immediately took action and as he came toward where I stood, staring past me like I didn't exist, like I wasn't even there.

"Shane?" I said as made his way past without hesitation. Reaching out, I grabbed a hold of his arm, "Shane?" I sputtered.

Turning towards me, his brow furrowed, I shuddered as I looked into his vacant blue stare into the void. Memories of me, of our life together, had been wiped away and there was nothing left that existed or was strong enough to spark any significance in his memory.

Relinquishing my hold on his arm, he continued up the stairs to our room and I watched as his broad back disappeared. Helplessly I looked at Jeremy who met my gaze with his own defeated stare. For a brief moment I stared at Carol and I felt my wolf push upward with every bit of strength and rage that she possessed. Lurching forward I was thrown quickly to the floor, Charles stood over me, his face impossible to read.

"I don't want to kill you Miss Elisa," he said sternly, "But I will."

I scrambled away then and ran to the top of the stairs and into our bedroom where Shane was removing his clothes from the closet, folding them neatly and tucking them into a suitcase. Tristan followed behind me but remained outside the door.

Standing in that room as he silently packed to leave me, my heart exploded into a million tiny pieces and with the detonation the tears came in sobbing waves. "Shane, don't leave," I begged as he continued to move around the room quietly.

As if my tears unnerved him, he came to stand before me, cocking his head slightly to the side. He peered down and smiled, "Don't cry," he said, "Nothing is as bad as it seems at the time." His fingers gently stroked my face before he walked away, "I have to go. We've been here too long and we have to get home."

"This is your home…..our home," I attempted to get the words out through my tears. "Shane," I said, "Please….look at me," When he turned, I spoke again, "Do you know who I am?"

He chuckled then, a strange sound to my ears, "Yes, of course I know who you are."

Confused, I continued to question him, "Who….who am I?"

"Why all the strange questions Elisa?" he asked, his eyebrows knitting together, "Are you alright?"

I felt a slow spread of relief wash across me at the mention of my name and I took a step toward him. "Tell me, tell me what I am to you," I pleaded for an answer but I was also afraid of the one he might give. I grasped his hand in mine.

An odd look crossed his face, "What is this?" he said, slightly disturbed as he pulled his hand from my fingers, "What are you doing?"

My eyes scanned his for any hint of the man that I might recognize.

"This is awkward…." He said.

"Tell me why it's uncomfortable," I said, hurt by his withdrawal from my touch.

His eyes pierced into mine, "We barely know each other Elisa."

His words crushed me and my body gave in to the stinging slap as I slumped to the floor. Vaguely, I saw Tristan out of the corner of my eye coming towards me, his hand outstretched. Shane threw an unresponsive glance in his direction before continuing with his task and while Tristan helped me to my trembling legs and toward the door, I couldn't bring myself to turn and look back. I was a stranger in his eyes; in his vacant, empty eyes.

Thankful for Tristan's strength, I allowed my body to wilt against him. With his strong support, we stood outside the bedroom, leaning against the wall as we waited for Shane to finish packing.

"I'm so sorry," he struggled to speak, "I don't even know what to say." I looked into his sad, pale blue eyes and nodded; it was the only response that I could muster.

Shane finally came out of the bedroom carrying two suitcases and looked at us curiously before mounting the steps and descending toward the foyer. Hesitantly, we followed him.

Jeremy slowly heaved himself to his feet while Charles still stood silently nearby, assessing his every move. Carol stood before him, her face a solemn mask. "I'm sorry it had to be this way, Jeremy."

He glowered toward her, his voice angry, "I don't understand...why?"

An uncertain smile slightly curled her lips upward. "Shane is destined for great things.....greater things than these."

"Who are you to choose for him?" Jeremy demanded, no longer feeling respectful, "He was happy here, he told you that himself."

"He has been happy before and he will be happy again Jeremy, as will you and Elisa. You will move on with your lives and the pain will ease over time," she replied.

"Elisa loved him, Mother. And he loved her.......I believe that he loved her with every part of himself," Jeremy's voice faltered with emotion, "You've stolen that from him," he paused, "One day, when he remembers.....and he will, how will you explain what you took from him?"

Carol stepped toward him and she placed her hand upon his shoulder. "He will understand that I did what any mother would do for their son."

Jeremy slowly shook his head, "He won't ever understand this."

Carol sighed deeply and abruptly redirected the subject, "I need to tell you a few things before we leave here."

Jeremy scowled at her.

"This house has been fully paid for and a substantial sum has been placed in an account under your name at a nearby bank," she said, "You can find the specifics in the dresser drawer in my room," she paused, "Your daughter will continue her education in Chicago and her tuition will be paid until she has completed."

"Why do you care about any of us?" Jeremy snapped. "Just take your son and go. We will survive without your help," his eyes flared angrily.

A note of sadness in her voice, Carol answered, "Shane had intentions." The tone of her voice wavered slightly with emotion. "I know that taking him away is painful enough for all of you. I won't add to that by taking away the financial aspect of his presence."

Jeremy looked up as we made our way down the steps and I saw his searching eyes sweep over Shane's face before they moved to me. Tristan remained close behind, his hand supportively on my arm.

"Say your good-byes Shane. We need to go," Carol said softly and allowed her gaze to drift across our faces before turning toward the door. Charles opened it, took the suitcases from Shane's hands and followed her outside before closing it behind them.

Turning first to Jeremy, Shane smiled, "Brother."

I saw the turmoil in Jeremy's face, the sheen of tears in his cloudy gray eyes as Shane embraced him. Clasping his arms tightly around Shane's frame, the first tear was freed and slid down Jeremy's face. My own tears threatened to overwhelm me at his rare show of emotion and my heart began to splinter and break for the second time that day.

"I'm going to miss you, man," Jeremy managed to stutter. Shane chuckled before pulling away.

"Don't be so dramatic," he laughed, "We'll be together again...we always take up where we leave off," through blurry vision, Jeremy nodded.

Shane moved to me then and looking down into my eyes, he smiled. "You'll be alright," he said, "It's all new and confusing to you right now, but just hang in there," he grinned and motioned toward Jeremy with a wave of his hand, "He'll take care of you."

It took every bit of strength that I could drag from way down deep inside not to wrap my arms around him at that moment and plead with him to stay. I sent a silent communication, over and over in my mind.

Remember, Shane....remember. The tears began to cascade down my cheeks, but he moved on down the line in front of Tristan. He stuck his hand outwards.

Tristan slowly accepted it and nodded, his eyes locked on Shane's.

"Tristan," he said warmly.

"You'll be missed, Sir," Tristan replied respectfully.

Beneath the hot August sun, the three of us stood in unspoken silence on the immense, empty wide porch of Edgewoods. Watching tearfully as the limousine disappeared down the driveway, we were each lost in our own soundless despair. With the retreating automobile, my entire life vanished before my eyes; memories scattered like the particles of dust drifting from beneath the rotating tires as it receded from view. Dispersing the bruised and battered pieces of my broken heart into scattered remoteness, I watched helplessly as the world that had been my life crumbled into a million pieces.

Still in shock and still disbelieving that he had so simply and effortlessly walked away, I expected any minute to see his tall frame striding down the driveway towards us, that radiantly beautiful smile etched into the perfectly handsome face. He would convince me that it had been a horrible dream because I knew he would never leave me.

Any minute...

Chapter 44

Sick for days, Jeremy and Tristan waited on me tirelessly even though we were all exhausted both physically and mentally. It had been a month since Shane's departure and I had succumbed to my depression, remaining behind the closed door of our room, curled up in the bed that we had shared. Sometimes, I found that if I took a deep breath with my face pushed into his pillow, I could still smell his lingering scent there and a fresh batch of tears would ensue; the sobs violently racking my body.

The concern was deeply engraved in Jeremy's face when he came into the bedroom one morning and sat down on the edge of the bed. Sighing heavily, he spoke, "It's time you get up, Elisa."

I opened my eyes and looked at him but didn't have the energy or the care to argue and then closed them again.

"Come on," he said and grabbed the covers, flinging them back from my body, "Get up."

I still didn't move, not caring what he did or said.

"You need to eat...and you need a shower," he said, grasping me by the arm and hoisting me to a sitting position. He raised his eyebrows, "Yep, you *do* need a shower."

"Please leave me alone," I said hoarsely.

"Nope," he answered, "I've left you alone for long enough. We all have to start living again….even you."

"But I don't want to live anymore," I said softly, the tears streaking down my face. He stroked my hair gently and looked into my eyes.

"I know," he said sympathetically, "But you have to get up now….Shane couldn't live with himself if he knew he caused this." He motioned toward her, "We aren't giving up, and you've got to fight for him."

"He doesn't remember!" I blurted out. "How do I fight for that?"

"We have to find something that will make him remember….and then we'll find him," he replied calmly, "But….….I've put a towel out on the bathroom countertop for you, and some clean clothes. Come on," he pulled me from the bed to my feet and urged me toward the attached bathroom. "I'll leave you alone now, but I'll be back in a few minutes to check on you."

Nodding as Jeremy closed the bathroom door behind him, I slowly began removing my well worn and wrinkled pajamas. Jeremy had been unmistakably correct in the fact that I needed a shower but as I moved about, the familiar nausea hit me again and I moved hastily to the commode. With nothing in my stomach, I heaved until the spasms finally quieted. Jeremy was right, I did need to eat.

Standing beneath the stream of hot water, I felt a pang of hunger for the first time in days. My head beneath the pounding droplets, I thought that I heard the faint sound of the bathroom door open and then close again but I dismissed it as I continued my shower.

Perhaps Jeremy was just checking to see if I had in fact carried on with his suggestion. Opening the shower door, I peeked out to be sure that I was alone before stepping out. When retrieving the towel that Jeremy had placed, neatly folded, on the vanity, the small box fell onto the floor. Bending over to recover it, I looked at it slightly baffled... a pregnancy test.

Still staring down at the box, I heard his light rap on the bathroom door. "You alright?" his voice was slightly muffled. Wrapped in the towel, I grasped the doorknob and yanked opened the door, holding the box up in my hand.

"What is this?" I inquired.

He smiled sheepishly, "You've been sick for a while……mostly in the mornings. Tristan and I think that you should do it, just to be sure."

"Really? You think that I might be pregnant?" I replied, feeling a bit mortified that he and Tristan had discussed these things amongst themselves.

"Is it a possibility?" Jeremy asked, "You would know better than anyone."

Vaguely I recalled running out of pills….. But I had gotten more as soon as I was able and resumed the normal schedule. "I don't think so," I responded, but with enough uncertainty in my voice that he quickly picked up on it.

He nodded slowly, a perceptive smirk on his face, "Just do it, would you?"

"Uh…… alright."

With Elisa disappearing behind the closing bathroom door, Jeremy held his breath as he made his way back downstairs. Tristan was sitting at the dining room table consuming a plateful of pancakes that he had made for breakfast. He looked up as Jeremy entered.

"Well?" He inquired, the syrup drizzling down his chin.

Jeremy shrugged, "We'll see I guess." Sitting down, he picked up his coffee cup, "At least she's up."

Tristan nodded, "That's an accomplishment in itself."

Sitting in silence, Tristan finished his breakfast while Jeremy continued sipping his coffee but they were both anxious as they awaited for the sound of Elisa's footsteps on the stairs. Not disappointed for much longer, they looked at each other nervously when they heard them.

How could this be? I asked myself over and over again as I looked down at the double lines on the pregnancy test and panic welled up inside of me. I read the instructions once more, and then yet again; searching for some instantly recognizable error that I had made. I found nothing, no mistakes, no wrong order to the steps that I had taken to arrive at these present circumstances. I dressed in a daze and then combed my hair with an unsteady hand before making my way down the stairs and across the foyer, through the living room and finally into the dining room.

Jeremy and Tristan both looked up at me, the anxiousness carved into their waiting faces. I met the eyes of each one; the stone gray of Jeremy's and then the faded blue of Tristan's. Their inquisitive expressions lingered on my face as they held their breaths.

I nodded.

A wide grin spread slowly across Jeremy's features, "Our ace in the hole," he said.

Made in the USA
Charleston, SC
31 May 2014